WHEN FIREWEED BLOOMS

BOOK ONE - THE LYNX CREEK CHRONICLES

KIM SMART

This book is dedicated to all who are on the quest to find themselves, and to the special people who have invited healing in my own journey. Healing does not have to happen only in the dark. Lighten up.

PROLOGUE
2020

Alaska was no longer a naïve young woman's dream of adventure, with endless daylight and passionate trysts in nature where tree roots meet river bends, and baby bear frolic unfettered in the meadow. It was home; the place that nurtured, whipped, taunted, renamed and rewarded her. Alaska was where a young green Jesse arrived and grew into Aurora, with ditch witch and shovel, grit, and unbending single-mindedness. Aurora and Alaska share secrets buried in the tundra and shadows of the rugged white-capped granite mountains; secrets shuttered in everlasting winter left by ancient glaciers that first greeted her at her new home, the only home to ever resonate with her soul.

Alaska's seasons foretell Aurora's. Mania and adrenaline fueled the summers of younger days. Now, as she inches closer to seventy, the peaceful joy of tending the garden while fresh salmon cooks on an open fire warms her heart and replaces the mania and drinking of home brew with friends. The once forlorn midnight-black days of winter now bring solitude and respite from the busyness of life. She forces arthritic hands into motion to knit a sweater for the newest babe to arrive in Lynx Creek. Morning Sudoku and solitaire keep her brain nimble.

Because her body isn't so nimble, a loaded shotgun hangs near the cabin door.

As the sun set on summer and fireweed blooms at the top, Aurora knows the enchantress will cover herself in a blanket and rejuvenate over the winter to restore blossoms in the spring. A nagging knowing, like so many she has had before, leaves Aurora wondering. Will she see another exit from winter to view those blossoms? She is tired, satiated, and at peace.

UNINVITED NEW BEGINNING

1982
Minneapolis, MN

JESSE CRAWLED into the chair behind the desk, dug her toes into the cheap, faded carpet, and calmly watched as broken fibers danced in the late afternoon sunlight. Tim promised they would lay wood flooring when they bought the house five years earlier. "Soon," he would say. "Soon we will do it."

"Jackrabbit, where are you?" Tim's pet name for Jesse never made sense to her, and she hated it, but not as much as she hated Tim at this moment. She would like to spit the vile taste of his name into a spittoon, but remained composed.

"I'm in the den," Jesse hollered back, knowing he would soon appear in the doorway, and just like that, fall apart.

"Hi, honey. What do you think about…" There it was. His mouth hung open as his eyes moved over boxes, dustless spaces on bookshelves where books used to live, and naked walls where pictures once hung. "Jackrabbit, what's going on? Are we painting?"

She let him stew. Ten seconds. Twenty. "Oh, my God, you're pregnant! We need a nursery!"

Tim, grinning wide but making no eye contact, approached to embrace her.

"Back down! There's no baby coming here," she spat out. "You and your little secretary, Jennifer, can work that one out, but not in my house."

Jesse took a deep breath and willed herself to serenity. Tim stood in stunned silence.

"Look around. You see what's not on the shelves anymore? Your crap! I've done you the courtesy of packing every shred of your stuff. Now get it the hell out of here. I'm lighting the fireplace in five minutes. If there are any photos you want, you best grab them now. You have a half-hour to haul your shit out." Jesse squared her shoulders, fighting against the pain and hurt, adjusting stoically to the balance of loss and change, knowing if she caved to his exquisite button-pushing abilities, she would lose momentum.

"Jesse, let's talk about this. I think you have this all wrong. There's…"

"If you dare say there's nothing going on, I will shoot you on the spot and make it look like self-defense." Jesse reached down and picked up the cherry-red kitchen egg timer she found in a forgotten corner of a kitchen shelf. "I'm setting this for thirty minutes."

"Really, Jesse! Don't you think you're being a bit dramatic? I don't know what you think you know…"

"Well, let me show you what I know." Jesse reached for the stack of 8x10 glossies piled on the desk. Her photography hobby and Nancy Drew skills had come in handy over the past few weeks.

Tim glanced at the top photo of he and Jennifer in a cozy embrace, then dropped his hands to his sides. His chin quivered slightly before he looked at Jesse. Sniffing in the tears escaping through his nose, Tim swallowed back his shame while his arrogance propped his ego. "She means noth…"

"You're down to twenty-seven minutes. Whatever you want needs to be in the driveway or in your pickup truck. Heck, I'll even let you put it in the camper if you promise to get it out of here by the end of the day tomorrow." She paused for effect. "But then, why would a promise you make mean anything? I mean, seriously. Jennifer? But it's worse than that. I have it on good authority that she's not the first. There's Cheri and Vi, Marti, Kimmee, and Colleen. Those are the women I know of so far. You have, in the ten years we've been a couple, never been faithful."

"I don't know where you're getting your information from, but…"

Jesse walked to the fireplace and, despite the stifling hot, dense air of August, lit a long match. She smiled as she held the flame to the edge of one photo, then another. She called back to Tim. "Stop while you're ahead. Just stop! Twenty-three minutes and the clock is ticking. Move on."

Propping her feet up on the desk, Jesse reached for a *Mother Earth News* magazine from a dusty pile under the desk. Holding on to the magazine, and the hope it represented, calmed the agitation within. She absent-mindedly leafed through the pages, making herself unavailable to Tim's panic. Jesse wasn't sure when she fell in love with the homesteading articles and lifestyle how-to's of the magazine, but for most of the last decade, she eagerly awaited each monthly edition. She fancied herself a bit of a renaissance woman, with a garden, herbal tinctures, dreams of a self-sustaining hand-built home, and harvesting as much of her own food as she could. A life away from consumerism. Close to the land. A dream Tim gave lip service to, but never embraced the way Jesse did.

"Jesse, honey, don't go and do anything rash. I want to work through this, with a therapist if we need to. You mean the world to me." To Jesse, this sounded like more of the same, "soon, baby, soon." But soon never came.

"Save it, Tim. I have always had two rules, and you knew them from the day we met. I don't share bodily fluids with third parties outside a monogamous relationship and…"

Tim knew the rules well, and he knew he had broken them. He finished her sentence. "Never lie to you because the truth will always come to you."

"Yeah, like all those extra shifts in the emergency room, your refusal to have a joint bank account…"

Tim hung his head, stacked one box on another, and took them to his truck. He knew Jesse was powerfully intuitive. He had tried every way possible to be the perfect husband at home, knowing what he was doing away from home would break her heart. After putting all the boxes in his truck, he grabbed his bicycle, two suitcases full of clothes, a handmade fly rod Jesse gave him three Christmases before, and a never-used down sleeping bag.

Jesse held a large manila envelope out as Tim prepared to take his last load to the truck. "I attached a proposal for the division of our stuff to the Dissolution paperwork. If you don't like it, give me a counterproposal. Otherwise, I will file it next Friday."

She had already spoken to a realtor about marketing the house immediately to capture the young families looking for a good school district. Jesse was prepared to move into an apartment or a friend's home temporarily if Tim chose to buy her out. No way did she want to live here. There were too many memories and poisonous suspicions about who else may have been in their home, their bed, drinking coffee from their coffeemaker. No, Jesse needed a clean break.

Tim quietly took the envelope and quickly left, knowing no argument would persuade Jesse once she set her mind on a path of action. Jesse sat numbly in the stillness, with so many opposing emotions brewing within.

IT WAS the first Friday in August. As the evening cooled, Jesse opened the fridge, grabbed a bottle of wine, calamari, salad, and tiramisu that she had picked up at her favorite Italian restaurant. She headed to the back deck, steps she and Tim had traveled thousands of times, and fell into the chair. Jesse surveyed the yard where she and Tim used to talk about their future family, where the swing set and wooden playhouse would go. Turning slightly in the wicker chair, she put her nose in the air to catch the scent of English lavender carried on the breeze. She felt surprisingly at peace given the events of the day.

Jesse poured a glass of wine and unashamedly toasted herself. In a quiet but confident voice, she told no one in particular and the Universe at large, "A chapter closed with a sour ending brings sweet reward to the next."

———

"I CAN'T LIVE in that house," Tim confessed to the realtor when they met to sign papers. He wanted out of their home as much as Jesse did. He said that just being in it brought him sorrow, but he visited the property one last time, while Jesse was still living there, after their dissolution was final.

"YOUR HONOR, IT WAS AN HONEST MISTAKE," Tim pleaded. "I didn't realize that the agreement meant that boat and that motor." Unable to accept blame, ever, Tim was struggling to accept his failure as a husband, but promise as a long-term lover to Jennifer despite the infidelity that cost his marriage.

"Well, Mr. Martin, did you have more than one boat and motor at the time of the dissolution?" The judge had thoroughly reviewed the documents and knew the answer.

"No, your honor, we did not."

"Mr. Martin, you're not a stupid man. I can see that you're educated and have a profession in the healing arts. I find it mystifying that you would bring an argument before this court that holds no water. Pun intended. I am ordering you to return the boat and motor to your former wife. You have forty-eight hours in which to accomplish this. If it doesn't happen, I am ordering you to make it right with the former Mrs. Martin, and with the court for wasting my time."

"Your honor, I can't return the boat."

"Please explain yourself, Mr. Martin."

"I am no longer in possession of the boat and motor." Tim looked away from the judge but could not look Jesse in the eye. He had used the stolen property to win favor with Jennifer's family without a thought about how Jesse would feel.

"How is it that you no longer have the boat and motor, Mr. Martin?"

"I sold it."

"Did you sell it for market value?"

"Actually, I bartered it for something."

"Mr. Martin. You have made quite a mess of things here. I am ordering you to pay the cost of replacing the boat and motor to the former Mrs. Martin within thirty days. I have researched the figures submitted by the complainant and concur with her valuation of the stolen property. In addition to the $6,380 replacement cost, I'm adding ten percent for the inconvenience to the complainant who took today off from work to address this situation. Is that clear?"

"Yes, your honor. I understand. It was a mistake."

"I suspect, Mr. Martin, that it was one of many mistakes in your dealings with the former Mrs. Martin. Let's not continue down that path."

"Yes, your honor."

Jesse avoided eye contact with Tim as they left court, feeling somewhat smug for having watched him squirm in front of the judge. The judge's tongue-lashing nearly erased the violated feeling she had that day, shortly before she moved out of the house, when she found the gate to the side yard ajar and the boat missing. Just being near him caused other feelings to stir. As much as she knew they had to end their marriage, at times she painfully longed for the physical intimacy they had shared. It was easy, playful, and gratifying; yet he poisoned that sacred space.

———

Jesse walked the perimeter of the house on her last day there, before the new owners took possession. She slowed as she came to the former home of the boat, feeling a tug in her gut, the sort that comes with betrayal and leaves an ache that hardens over time. She still felt violated by the intrusion and theft of something that was hers by decree and an object she valued, but she was ready to move toward fresh adventures.

"Listen, Jesse, I'm not going to ask you for a lease, and you don't even have to pay re…"

"Of course, I do. I mean, I appreciate you wanting to help me out, but I lost my marriage, not my job. I'm still pushing papers down at the state office and bringing home a paycheck. I'll be fine."

"I know you will be, and you're doing so much better than I was when Max split."

"It's quite a different story though, isn't it? You have Chelsea to care for. Where is that bundle of sweetness, anyway?" Bea's husband walked out on them two years prior, just before Chelsea's first birthday, and other than calling into court for the dissolution hearing, he hadn't been heard from since. "I will pay you $300 a month. You use it for you guys or save it for Chelsea's college, and I will babysit so you can get back out into the world." Jesse knew she was a temporary renter, although she didn't know exactly what she would do next. Meanwhile, she could help Bea and Chelsea and save herself some money.

Jesse hooked the grocery bags over her wrists, tucked her chin under the zipper of her jacket, and charged against the blustery mid-December storm. Inside the dark basement apartment, she turned the heat up, popped the top on the first beer of the weekend, and checked the message on her answering machine.

"Hey Jesse, Craig here. We've got whiteout conditions here. Going to have to cancel our skiing for tomorrow. We'll catch up soon and reschedule. Stay warm." She picked through the pile of mail that had accumulated over the past two weeks, tossing junk mail into the round file and stacking unopened bills on the kitchen table, ready to be taken care of on Sunday night before the new workweek started. Two magazines rested in the pile: *Prevention* and *Mother Earth News*. She read the headlines on the cover of the health magazine first, before turning to her favorite.

Jesse turned to the back page of *Mother Earth News* and started reading. Even as a young child she colored the back pages of coloring books first, before looking at the beginning of the book.

There, inside the back cover of the magazine, was a full-page ad from the Bureau of Land Management (BLM). She read and re-read the fine print. Under the Homesteading Act, they were offering small homestead parcels in Alaska's interior. Applicants could claim five-acre parcels for $2.50 per acre, if they surveyed and marked the perimeter and lived on the land for most of three years.

After taking in a long draw of beer, Jesse re-read the ad again. She closed her eyes and created a vision of herself standing amongst the trees. Sun filtered through the leaves to bathe her peaceful upturned face. As she opened her eyes, her mind was reeling with possibilities and logistics. For $12.50, less than the price of a tank of gas, she could own a slice of heaven. That was the simple part. She had to get there, learn to live remotely, build a cabin, provide her own food, and earn an income for tools and supplies. She quickly leafed through the rest of the magazine, searching for clues about how to accomplish all this. There were a few, but there was no blueprint for newbies wanting to establish a homesteading life in Alaska.

Cryptic notes captured her racing thoughts. She carefully rewrote them, organizing the details into categories, separating them into elements of her basic needs: food, land and shelter, health, safety, money, transportation, and clothing. On another page, she sketched a timeline of activities that, if she were to pursue this dream, would have to be accomplished to build this now-imaginary homestead. Jesse jotted down the phone number for the BLM office referenced in the ad and drafted a list of questions.

The leading question turned her stomach a bit. "Is this opportunity open to single women?" She hated to have to consider it, but she did not want to invest in a dream only to be denied by some nerdy, pencil-pushing, soul-sucking, rule-following bureaucrat who would deny and then serve platitudes up on a silver platter. She wanted this opportunity more than anything she ever wanted - except maybe that BB gun she asked Santa for when she was seven.

Jesse flexed her bicep and folded her hand over its curve. A former starting member of her high school basketball team, she was blessed with a strong, svelte body, but needed more strength and stamina to chop wood, fell trees, haul water and other strenuous activities, sometimes in severe weather. To bolster strength and endurance, Jesse wrote herself a training plan. She jotted down the names of buddies who were gym rats. It would be uncomfortable for her, but she would enlist them for support through inspiration, information, and maybe some training dates. A rough timeline gave her four months to get ready, launch this plan, and hit the road north to Alaska next spring. In her mind, she was already packed - the VW Jetta replaced with a Ford pickup towing a trailer, with an "Alaska or Bust" sign in the back window and a cassette player blaring classic-rock music. The thought of it brought a smile to her heart. "If this works," she thought, "what a dang great big life change in just one year. All for the better."

THE SNOW FELL and wind blew the following day, but Jesse hunkered down in the library, pouring over all the materials she could find on the how-to's of homesteading, adding to the lists. In her mind, she explored conversations she would eventually have to have with her parents and friends. She ran through scenarios of breaking the news to Tim, but ultimately decided he was not entitled to know and did not deserve an opportunity to suck her dreams away again. As the librarian locked the door behind her, she walked to a snow-covered car carrying all the books that the librarian let her borrow. She strode with assurance, head looking to the moonlight, believing that, somehow, this adventure would work out and she would find her bliss at the end of the rainbow, deep in the wild land known as Alaska.

2

___

STARTING LINE

May 1983
  Milepost 1221, the Alaska/Canada Border

JESSE NOTICED the discomfort of a stomach churning with excitement, hunger infused with an undercurrent of anxiety. She squinted and shielded her eyes from the rising sun blazing through the truck's marred windshield, while her free hand groped for sunglasses in the sunny blindness. Glasses on, she stepped out of the truck, refreshed after a long sleep on a gravel pull-off hidden from the highway by heavy brush. She stretched her legs while tromping down tall roadside grasses. Driving the last few miles to the border crossing separating Yukon Territory, Canada, and Alaska was a new level of thrill. Jesse nervously bit her lip while waiting for her turn for the border patrol officer to approach the dust-coated pickup, thinking of the contraband in the truck.

TEARFUL GOODBYES, meticulous packing, double-checking checklists, studying maps, and gut-wrenching guilt for leaving family, filled her last days in Minnesota. As she sat in the border crossing line, Jesse reflected on the painful conversation she had with her parents months earlier. She had watched as her mother paled, heart dropping into her stomach, at the thought of her oldest daughter going so far away and into the wilds. Jesse saw her mother's hands tremble before she grabbed the kitchen table, willing the waves of panic to stop. Belinda pleaded with Jesse not to make the road trip, let alone venture solo into the wilderness.

"Jesse, you can't do that! You're talking about giving yourself a death sentence. I can't let you go. Clarence, tell her she can't go; she always listens to you."

"Belinda, honey, I can't steal the girl's dream." He turned to his daughter with excitement in his eyes, but composure held tightly within his clasped hands. "Jesse, tell us more about this. I'm sure, knowing you, there is a plan and all kinds of preparations going on. How did you get this idea?"

Jesse told them about the BLM information and the homestead prove-up process. She meticulously described a plan to move to Alaska in details she knew would never actually materialize, but hoping the more she talked the easier it would be for them, especially her mother. Jesse spoke of her plan to build strength and stamina, which already showed gains through physical training. She shared her research and the things she was gathering to take with her, plans to dispose of the remaining belongings she didn't need, and the status of her finances that were multiplying through a frugal and focused spending plan.

"You two always told us kids we could do anything in this world, and we should follow our dreams."

"Yes, we did, but..." Belinda's sorrowful pleas initially tugged at Jesse's heart and gave her pause; but when they lasted for weeks on end, Jesse met the whining with silence. There was nothing more she could tell her mom that would calm the fear monster she harbored. Mother's concern and misplaced anxiety made Jesse more determined to be successful, so she could report ecstasy and safety to her parents and invite them to visit. This was a dance she had done with her mother since she first learned to ride a bike and planned a solo road trip to her grandparents' home thirteen blocks away, to go to church with them. She waited five years for that trip - left down Holly Lane, turning right on Jessup Drive, then right on Kelley Court, into the third driveway on the left, house 487.

Jesse felt like a celebrity the day of her departure, with friends escorting her out of town - honking their horns and waving wildly until they pulled off the freeway after several miles and faded in the rearview mirror. She promised them all regular reports and photos. They promised to visit. Her parents didn't join the parade or make such promises. Their response saddened, but did not surprise, Jesse. They would come around when she succeeded.

The Milepost was Jesse's travel bible, guiding her along the Alcan Highway, marking the journey by mileposts, starting in Dawson Creek, British Columbia. The guidebook was a gift from two friends, a married couple she won in the divorce. Rusty and Donna were well-traveled explorers who hoped to visit Alaska one day, and the three of them studied the guidebook for hours over home-cooked Friday night dinners and many Sunday mornings at their favorite donut joint.

"You know we would come with you in a heartbeat if we didn't have family obligations here." Rusty studied his copy of the book as much as Jesse studied hers, and always offered new ideas when they got together.

"I know, and I would love it, but I understand. One day, I bet you'll be up there with me. I just hope you don't miss the land grab opportunity."

"Yeah, we probably will, but it'll still be great to know someone who did it."

Gas stations, rest stops, hotels, motels, and restaurants were all noted in the book. Jesse tracked the mileposts carefully, so the pickup didn't run out of gas. Still, she carried two full gas cans for good measure. The guidebook was spot on most of the time and was a great reference, helping to navigate road construction and find safe spots for car camping and cool things to see along the way. Gasoline stops were up to 250 miles apart, so she followed the book like a recipe for her favorite chocolate chip cookies - the same cookies Mom sent along for the road trip, along with cans of tuna, two home-canned chickens and an assortment of crackers to provide sustenance on the road.

"Hello ma'am. Where are you headed to?" The thirty-something, uniformed border patrol started the interrogation; blue eyes framed in dark lashes peered at her under the bill of his government-issue cap.

"I'm going to Anchorage." Jesse wasn't ready to share her homesteading dreams with this handsome stranger, who undoubtedly had already heard every version of Alaska dream tales.

"Are you visiting or moving in?"

"I'm permanently relocating."

"Well, welcome to Alaska!"

The border patrolman inquired about cargo and contraband. Jesse had spent hundreds of hours researching every aspect of her new life, including the border crossing. She read horror stories of people declaring guns, knives, bear spray, and other personal protection, just to have their vehicles unloaded, searched, and left for the owner to repack. When Dad built the trailer, a homemade box with a topper painted to match the pickup, they created a secret hiding hole for the .375 Holland and Holland rifle that came highly recommended in several gun magazine articles and by gun dealers. She also had a small collection of knives. The last thing she wanted was to be stranded in the parking lot of the border crossing, just inches from stepping into her dreams, repacking the truck and trailer that took two days to carefully puzzle together.

Jesse casually handed the officer her driver's license. She had rehearsed answers to questions about her financial viability, marital status, insurance coverage and health record, but the officer asked none of that.

"Ma'am, everything appears to be in order. You can be on your way, and good luck." Jesse took her driver's license back, and without pausing to put it in her wallet, gripped the steering wheel and resolutely drove away. Within minutes, she crossed into Alaska. Tears of joy slid down her cheeks, gathering up four days of salt and grime and carrying it to the edge of her mouth. She cast it away with the back of her hand and tightened the grip on the steering wheel.

"You've done a fine job getting me this far, Clarence Jr." Jesse patted the dash of the new-used, two-toned blue Ford truck. "Just another 400 miles to go."

Jesse's father, a backyard mechanic, was her most ardent, yet often quiet, cheerleader. After high-school basketball games, he always waited for her outside the car, giving a congratulatory handshake or comforting hug. He was less silent about her current endeavor, often running interference with her mother, who just could not wrap her head around Jesse's "foolishness."

"Clarence, tell her what we saw on TV the other night." Belinda insisted that Jesse come to dinner at least once a week in the months before her departure, an invitation that Jesse didn't consider rejecting. "You know I wouldn't mention it if I didn't think it was important."

"Belinda, honey, you promised you would stay calm tonight. Remember what the doctor said about your blood pressure?" Clarence turned to Jesse and gave her a one-sided wink and grin.

"Blood pressure, Mom? What's going on?" Jesse steered the conversation to more neutral ground, at least for her.

After dinner that night, and several others, Clarence and Jesse hung out in the garage while he thoroughly inspected her pickup, outfitted it with new tires, fluids, windshield wipers and a stereo. "You've got to be able to play good road music to keep you company on the drive."

CLARENCE WOULD LOVE to be on this adventure with his daughter. Jesse felt that in some ways, a part of him was. He painstakingly rehabbed the trailer that he picked up at a junkyard. There may have been more Bondo holding the trailer together than actual metal, but so far (knock on wood) nothing had come apart or fallen out.

Jesse promised to send photos and document each leg of this big, beautiful adventure. With that promise in mind, she pulled to the side of the road to photograph wild horses, black bears, Wood bison, Stone's sheep, mountain goats, and Woodland caribou. While still in the Yukon Territory, an unfamiliar dark blur caught her eye. Quickly pulling to the side of the road, she rolled down the passenger window, picked up the instamatic camera and looked through the viewfinder. She couldn't move fast enough to get a picture before the creature disappeared into the woods beyond the roadway. It was massive! It looked like a giant cow on a horse's long legs.

Goosebumps crawled across her skin while camping on the edge of a lake in British Columbia, as the eerie serenade of loons ushered her into sleep. The hungry howls of wolves off in the distance interrupted that sleep, and an undercurrent of fear kept her from finding slumber again. The excitement of being so close to nature stirred her adrenaline and nudged her back into the driver's seat.

Another night, she stopped early to set up a tent and cook a warm meal. It felt great to stretch her legs in ways not possible when she slept in the pickup cab. At five-feet nine-inches, she wasn't a giant, but she was leggy. The next morning, she woke to hear the gentle stirring of leaves and small twigs snapping. Millimeter by millimeter, she slid the zipper of the tent window down to see what was visiting her camp. A smile rose from her heart and spread across her face at the sight of a doe with a young fawn passing nearby. They stopped to sniff around before sauntering off.

Beauty beyond measure filled the journey, but some parts were not as much fun as others. The Alcan Highway was fraught with potholes and road construction, slowing and stopping travel while large equipment crept at a snail's pace, packing the earth for eventual tarring. Twice Jesse stuttered to a stop and had to change flat tires, and there were now more than a dozen chips in the front windshield. But none of these things stole a moment of her joy.

Jesse had a pristine driving record, and except for twice when she was a child and her mother backed into parked cars, she had never been in an accident. When she passed two wrecks that appeared to be single-vehicle accidents caused by wind or loss of control, a sickly tension spread through her, as if she could feel the fear and pain of the vehicles' occupants. In one, camper components and personal belongings littered the roadside, with a wrecked pickup lying in the ditch. In the second wreck, two horses, one with a bloodied foreleg, grazed in the ditch beside their overturned horse trailer. Emergency vehicles had responded to both wrecks; Jesse rubbernecked with the rest of the passersby, but did not have to stop to render aid. She felt helpless to do anything, anyway.

Immense beauty surrounded the Alcan, a gift of distraction from the sometimes crater-ridden road. A new vista emerged with every turn. Lush valleys followed rugged mountains. Rolling hills and flat plains were thick with vegetation. Fields of flowers lay at the base of foothills, and lakes of every size glistened under the sun over the vast lands. Scores of bald eagles soared overhead, and Jesse questioned the endangered nature of the scavengers.

May days are long in the north. The closer she got to her destination, the longer the days were and the more driving she packed in. Daylight lasted for sixteen hours, which made for long driving times. Keenly aware of the long days of driving, she set a schedule and forced herself to stop along the way, to take a break and take in the sights. As anxious as she was to arrive in Anchorage, she also wanted to be safe and to savor the journey.

Not far out of Tok, on the Glenn Highway headed to Anchorage, Jesse pulled off at a spot where anglers gathered on the packed-dirt shore of a large lake. She watched for a while as small boats came and went. Jesse loved to fish, a passion she shared with her father.

"What are you catching?" she called out to a dark-haired young man.

He held up his stringer with a wide grin that reflected everything magical about that moment. "Grayling and rainbows. Taking breakfast home to the family."

"Thanks, man. Have a great day. Hope the family enjoys the catch."

What a life! He gets up early, takes in the solitude of an early morning boat ride, experiences the thrill of a fish on the end of the line, and feeds his family. She hoped fishing would be near her homestead. Jesse watched a while longer, while stuffing a peanut butter sandwich in her mouth and washing it down with stale water from a plastic gallon jug.

She checked *The Milepost* and her watch as she started the last leg of the journey into Anchorage, knowing that anticipation could make these last few hours the longest. The eye candy landscape drew her in as she rolled down the Glenn Highway.

Jesse's foot lifted from the accelerator, and she coasted to the side of the road. Mesmerized by the view of the brilliant blue sky dotted with silver-white clouds gracing the mountaintops, she leaped out of the pickup and walked across the highway. Standing in the grandeur of nature, the surrounding raw beauty paralyzed her. She felt weightless, her body unhinged from the heaviness on earth; the edges of herself merged with the trees, mountains, wildflowers, waterfalls, and creatures in hiding.

Bliss invaded her. All doubt and fear dissipated. As she embraced all that surrounded her, she formed a pact. From this day forward, she would observe every aspect of nature, breathe it in, and seek to understand and respect it. In return, she would gain wisdom to call upon for survival.

Several minutes later, Jesse returned to the road with eyes wide open to the surrounding life. Her spiritual orgasm spanned ten miles as she continued up the road. She took in the mountains, lush trees, a shimmering glacier, a rustic lodge in a pristine setting, and a deep, dense tree-lined ravine on the verge of turning to fall colors.

"Quaint community, home to accomplished artisans and award-winning authors, this small but lively community invites you to stop in and say hello." Jesse remembered the line from an article she read at the library. Excited to experience the small town of Sutton, nestled in the shadow of the mountains, she pushed against the pain of a full bladder and sunburned eyes. Stopping at the first place that would have a cold beverage and maybe some food, she flew from her truck. Weathered boards of the wooden sidewalk creaked as she made her way into the dark interior of the dusty joint. A jukebox in the corner blared a country song that Jesse faintly recognized.

"Hey there! We'll be with you in just a minute. If you see a place you like, just grab it." A skinny waitress in tight jeans, with thick auburn hair piled on top of her head, greeted Jesse on the way to deliver burgers to a table across the room.

As her eyes adjusted to the dark, she saw about a half-dozen occupied tables in the pub, and as many taken bar stools. There was a small group of bikers to go with the hogs sitting in the dust and gravel parking lot. Two families with children were grabbing from an enormous basket of fries in the center of their tables. Clearly tourists, Jesse thought. Pushing her way through swinging doors, reminiscent of an old western movie, Jesse found the old door with "Gals" scrawled in chipped white paint.

Relieved, refreshed, and ready to eat, she scanned the room. The bar crowd looked like a bunch of regulars, some gesturing and talking, others staring down at their plate or looking for the waitress. Jesse spotted an empty stool and joined them. In an act reminiscent of the Three Stooges, three of the men lifted their beer bottles in her direction as she sat down. She didn't care about the days' worth of road grime on her, or the crazy hair tamed by a bandana. She felt right at home.

"Hey there." She nodded to the fellas. "What's good here?"

The man closest, wearing denim overalls and a sleeveless t-shirt, was about fifty. He patted his round belly. "I never found nuthin here I didn't like." He chuckled. "The burgers are good this time of day. Slim's back there for another hour or so. He puts a fine do on 'em."

Jesse wasn't exactly sure what the stranger meant, but she ordered a burger and a draft beer and enjoyed every ounce of both. Because her mother reminded her a gazillion times about the starving children in China, or maybe it was Africa, she spread napkins out on the counter like they were precious linens and dumped the large basket of fries on top, good for snacking on the way to Anchorage.

. . .

THE ROAD GREW BUSIER as she passed through the farms and fields of Palmer and the hay flats of the Matanuska Valley. She crossed over the Matanuska River and pulled off the highway near the native village of Eklutna. Curious about the spirit houses marking the graves in the cemetery and eager to take pictures to send home, she strolled through the sacred place quietly and stiffly, like she did when she visited the grave of her great-aunt Lottie, who she remembered at ninety-six was very bossy.

The stop didn't disappoint. Brightly colored micro houses, cabins, and log caches dotted the well-kept cemetery. Family of the deceased erected the structures to house the spirit of their loved one until it could make the final journey to the High Country. Based on her research and placards posted onsite, Jesse understood the cemetery micro-city was a unique blend of Athabaskan traditional beliefs melded with Russian Orthodox tenets that forbade the traditional practice of cremation. When she studied *The Milepost,* Jesse realized she had a lot to learn about the cultures that settled this vast sacred land she intended to call home. She made a mental note to find the library in Anchorage and to ask them if there was a remote borrowing program.

AFTER THE SOMBER VISIT, she continued on the Glenn Highway and toward Anchorage, down Eagle River hill, across the river, then up the steep southern hill and toward the approach to Fort Richardson. She wondered how her four-wheel-drive pickup would handle the steep Eagle River hill in icy winter months, if she ever drove to town. She reached into *The Milepost* and pulled out a handwritten page with directions. A friend of a friend had graciously offered her home to Jesse for a few days while she gathered supplies in Anchorage.

Soon she was on the Muldoon exit ramp, slowly rolling past the street signs until she found Old Muldoon Road. After turning, she quickly found the address written on the paper and pulled into a long driveway lined with carefully laid river-rock walls. She would soon see the matching mammoth fireplace in the living room of the red house and learn that it was a raised ranch with a walk-in basement built in 1952 that survived the devastating earthquake of 1964.

It was early evening, but the sun showed no signs of fading.

3

ALWAYS LEARNING

June 1984
    Anchorage

JESSE GRIPPED THE STEERING WHEEL, tense from navigating the city traffic. Tires crunching against the gravel driveway signaled the homeowner of her arriving guest. Charlene was a forty-something divorcee who worked for the state's fish and game department. Lucas, a handsome chocolate lab, wagged his tail so excitedly that his hind end rocked like a metronome.

"Hey there, Jesse. So happy you made it! Welcome to Alaska." Charlene gripped Jesse's aching hand and shook it vigorously.

"Thank you, Charlene, I'm…"

"Please, call me Charlie."

"Charlie. I'm really glad to be here and so grateful to you for letting me stay."

Charlie raised her left arm and swatted at the air as if to wave away Jesse's thanks. "Ah, think nothing of it. It's what we do here. Most of us up here don't have family. We left them all behind in the lower 48 for one reason or another."

"Lower 48?"

"Yeah, that's what we call the contiguous States. You'll see. Life is different up here and everyone from JC Penney to the post office treats us different. Kinda like the sunshine tax in California, there's like an Alaska tax that gets added to everything, if you can even get what you ordered from outside. Anyway, like I was saying, up here, our friends and neighbors become our family and you can count on them to help you out. I know I got a giant heap of helping hand when I got here about fifteen years ago, so I try to give back every chance I get."

"Well, I'm planning to be here just a couple of days. Hopefully, I won't get in your hair."

"Listen, Jesse. It will take whatever it takes to get ready. There's really no rush. And if I can help you out in any way, I sure will. I've got friends and co-workers who've been all over this state and have done lots of crazy things. We've got your back. Now, you got anything in that truck that needs to come into the house? If not, bring yourself in; take a shower if you want. I've got some moose stew in the crock pot and a cold beer in the fridge."

Smiling, she grabbed her backpack from the truck and followed her new friend into the house. Jesse had one clean change of clothes left and looked forward to a nice hot shower.

JESSE'S LISTS documented the plans for her time in Anchorage. Those plans vanished in the long hours of daylight, listening to stories, browsing pawn shops and hardware stores, and chasing the urban Alaska trail. Her one-week visit grew to three. She drew lines through her supply list and rewrote it, noting the recommendations of seasoned Sourdoughs who knew more about remote living in Alaska than any book could tell her.

"I know them gun dealers in Minnesota probably told you to buy that rifle, but I gotta tell ya, you can do better." Charlie's friend Red, a former Denali park ranger, stopped in one day to look over Jesse's gear. "Tell ya what, if you've got a couple hundred bucks to spare, let's go down to my buddy's pawn shop and I'll talk him into a good price on an older, but much more useful one. You can keep this as a spare and make your own comparisons."

"Sure, I'm good with that. I can shoot okay, but I'm no aficionado with guns and ammo." Jesse eagerly accepted her role as a sponge; taking in all the information she could from those who knew far more than she about thriving in this immense, intense place. Finding it hard to sleep with the long hours of daylight, she spent hours adding notes in her notebooks and adjusting supply lists.

Charlie drove Jesse up the highway to Bonnie Lake for grayling fishing early one morning. She watched Jesse fish, noting the knots and tackle she used. Jesse showed good fishing skills, but she needed to learn some tricks about making do when one couldn't hit up the store for new line and lures. Charlie asked Jesse to stay a few extra days in Anchorage so they could fish for salmon. She showed Jesse some survival skills and tricks, learned from experienced Alaskans she met at work and in the field. They caught and canned sixty-four pints of salmon for Jesse to take with her. "You're going to be happy you have this come the middle of winter. One a day will get you through two months. You'll be so sick of salmon you'll want to choke me, but your belly will be quiet so you can sleep, and your skin will be smooth."

Jesse added the crates of canned salmon to the stockpile of pilot bread, peanut butter, dried beans, and rice.

"It ain't like parts down south that are so hot you couldn't keep this on the shelf. Where you're going, you'll have to worry more about food inside your cabin freezing in the winter. Best not to stack it on the outside walls if you've got a choice," Charlie advised.

Before moving to Anchorage, Charlie lived in a cabin in

Talkeetna, a quaint town about 120 miles north of Anchorage, with her boyfriend, Ned. "My life then was without all the niceties I've got now, but at least I could get to a store if I wanted or, if neither of us wanted to cook, we could go to a restaurant if we had the money. You're going off-grid. There won't be any grocery store to run to or pizza to pick up."

It was a reality Jesse had contemplated. She knew she could overcome reliance on the conveniences of urban living. One afternoon, after thinking about what she might miss, Jesse went to the store and bought a few things that were, in the grand scheme of things, extravagances, but she would enjoy them come Thanksgiving and Christmas. Pumpkin pie filling, canned cranberry jelly, chicken chow mein, canned sweet potato and marshmallows went into a small box marked with a big smiley face, a turkey, and a Christmas tree.

Jesse pulled out her calendar and with a thick red marker, drew a box around June 28th, the day she left Anchorage to continue the big adventure. Charlie handed Jesse a care package as she put her clean laundry tied in a plastic bag into the cab of the pickup. Inside the box, Charlie packed doughnuts, coffee, bug dope, a knit cap and fingerless gloves. "Now remember," she cautioned with a half-smile, "If you encounter a black bear, make yourself big. If it's a grizzly, play dead."

Jesse nodded with uncertainty. "That's not at all reassuring. I'm counting on my new rifle to help me out."

"Please yourself. You'll be better off not to get in a brawl with one. You'd better be a great shot." Charlie kicked at the gravel in the driveway, trying to think of something more positive to send Jesse off with. "All kidding aside, if you get in a jam, reach out. If I can't help you, I probably know someone who can."

"Thanks, Charlie, for all you've done. I hope not to be crawling back to your doorstep too soon. When I come back to town next spring, it'll be my turn to buy the pizza." Jesse liked this new friend and already knew she would like the opportunity to spend more time adventuring with Charlie.

"Fair enough. I look forward to it." Charlie pulled Jesse in for a warm embrace. "Stay safe, cheechako."

———

With confidence and excitement, feeling like her dream to become an Alaskan was more possible than ever, Jesse headed the pickup and trailer up the Parks highway. The land she sought was in the shadows of the Alaska Range with its mammoth trio of mountains: Denali, Foraker, and Hunter. She wanted to believe there would be no mistaking the land she hoped to homestead when she drew near. The truth was, it was only a speck in a vast wilderness.

Lost in thought as she gawked at the breathtaking scenery, conversations with experienced hunter-gatherer friends of Charlie ran through her head. "You don't want to drive over the tundra in the summer." Art, a short, stout man with a shiny bald head, flannel shirt worn year-round tucked into faded blue jeans and strapped in place with two-inch wide highway-cone orange suspenders, stroked his long salt-and-pepper beard and spoke in a soft-spoken, shy manner. A trapper from Big Lake, Art was a man of few words, but he felt compelled to share his wisdom. He pulled a crooked finger from his beard and tapped the air in her direction. "That's a nice truck ya got there. Would be a shame if you lost 'er in the mud. This ain't no Minnesota mud, girlie. This is a cross between Florida swamp and quicksand."

Art warned that it would be a one-way trip, if she made it at all. She would have to stop and clear some trail, cut down black spruce, willow, devil's club, and birch to forge her own road deep into the land turned muddy by melting snows and rain. "You'll bury that truck under all that weight, and that would be a damn shame."

"Iffin it were me, and I gots me a station wagon, ya see…"
A thick finger with decades old grime rimming the nail pointed
to a well-worn station wagon in the driveway. "I'd be parkin' it
at the Talkeetna airstrip and have a tail dragger take me in.
Once ya get the lay of the land, up from the air, you can see if
there's a road or a animal trail ya could folla."

"Better yet is to go in the winter on a snow machine or an
Arctic Cat and folla them frozen rivers up to yer place."

Jesse had heard part of Art's story from Charlie. It was a
gruesome tale of a drunken father and a timid mother living
off the land. His father survived WWII physically, but part of
him never returned from the war. Art was ten when his father
stumbled into their home in a small town north of Seattle and
announced to his wife and their two sons that he was leaving
on a fishing boat headed for Bristol Bay, Alaska.

"This is it! My pot at the end of the rainbow is in shight!"
Herman was a big man whose emotions swung violently. He
could go weeks without drinking, but then the irritability and
isolation started. Ultimately, there was a big blowup between
he and his wife, and he would leave in a rage, sometimes
staying gone for days.

"We're going to start a new life in Alashka. Doris, honey,
this is what you'rve been prayin" for. We will have money to
buy ourselves a lil place with an indoor privy and a full-size
shtove. No more waitress jobs for you, sweetness. You can shtay
home and raise our boys. And boys, there'll be rifles and fishin'
poles in your future. It's time you learn the art of feedin' yer
family." And Art never forgot the time his dad dragged a
bloody deer into the camper to butcher on the mini table that
converted into the boys' bed. The family spent all night
butchering. The boys dumped bowl after bowl of bloody rinse
water in the trees at the edge of the property they squatted on,
hopefully far enough away to keep the wolves from the camper.
They had no freezer. The next day the boys begged, borrowed
and stole all the canning jars they could find while Doris

managed a fire in the fire pit and canned most of that deer in a pressure cooker. When Herman fell asleep late on the second day, Doris bagged a quarter of the deer and told the boys to go find some dogs to give it to. She would never get it all canned before it spoiled, and Herman would never know the difference.

Charlie told the stories like Jesse imagined Art would, in his matter-of-fact, quiet way, void of emotion. From the stories she heard, Jesse surmised Art was the real deal. He had lived a homesteader's life. His father fished that entire first season and made enough money to bring the family to Dillingham. Instead of buying Doris's dream house, he bought a wall tent and a wood stove to heat and cook on. "Look honey, I bought you a cushioned seat for the honey hole." Doris looked at him and nodded. Her dreams of indoor plumbing shattered like sheaths of ice that formed overnight on their water bucket when she plunged the dipper early in the morning.

Herman spent the next thirty years chasing shiny things. He mined for gold, fished, trapped, crabbed, harvested and sold firewood, grew sizeable gardens and supplied the family's meat. He taught Art and his brother to hunt and fish, and his drinking days vanished over time. The boys didn't go to school after eighth grade, and only sporadically before that. Their school was the vast wilderness of Alaska, and they learned more about the intricacies of man living with nature than any school could teach.

Art, like his father, had many jobs, but the one he went back to most often was as a hunting guide. He read animal signs in the wild like a predator. His downfall was patience. He didn't have any. The outfitters tried to pair him only with experienced hunters because they knew he was intolerant with anyone who failed to handle their rifle safely, and he did not hide his anger.

———

JESSE SPENT hours weighing her options based on Art's cautions. She trusted his experience and wisdom, but was so far into her plan that she could not fathom waiting until winter to start her adventure. She wanted to acclimate, warming up to the season changes gradually. And so, armed with all Art taught her, Jesse had said her goodbyes. She stopped at a Fred Meyers store to load up on fresh fruits and vegetables. Giddy with excitement, she greeted everyone in the store with a smile. After topping off the gas tank, she started up the two-lane Parks Highway to her new life. The eighty-mile trip took over four hours because of road construction. She did not mind the delays and, when waiting for the pilot car to return to guide the northbound cars, she chatted through her open windows with the road construction crew and other drivers. She knew it was tourist season, but she was still surprised at the out-of-state plates on nearly every other vehicle. Campers and RVs as large as houses turned off their engines and sat, waiting for the pilot car.

"How's it going today? You talked to any fishermen? How's the catch?" There was talk of fishing and camping, visiting Mt. McKinley, and some folks were just heading home to Fairbanks. Jesse studied the scenery of dense old-growth forest in the area and the growing size of the mountain range in the foreground marked the miles. The lush agricultural land of the Matanuska Valley gave way to the less populated communities that dotted the highway. She noted places of interest to visit on her return trip to Anchorage - Palmer, Big Lake and Nancy Lake.

The mile markers passed like pages, turning in a book until finally Jesse turned off the Parks toward Talkeetna. The roadside was overgrown. She searched for signs to the airstrip, where a pilot named James was to meet her about noon. She had been excited to hit the road this morning, so was plenty early for the meeting, despite the delays on the road. The beauty of the mountain range sucked her in with its grand splendor rising through the clear blue sky to meet the sun. The grandeur of mountains to the left distracted her until she sensed something in the road. By the time she saw the moose, the coarse hairs on his rump were passing through her driver's headlight beam. Panicking, she swerved to the right, the trailer jerking behind; her heart raced and her hands, wet with sweat, slid on the steering wheel.

Jesse felt the breeze passing through the open windows and smelled the dank, dusty fur of the giant animal. Gripping the wheel, she brought the pickup to a jarring stop and released the breath that filled her lungs. She glanced into the side mirror, hoping no one saw the near miss. She wasn't so fortunate.

"Hey ma'am, I'm Lucky. Just wanted to see if you're okay. That was quite a maneuver you did there, trying to miss Bullwinkle." The lanky thirty-something hunk with a ginger beard and stocking cap smiled as he walked up to the truck.

"You're lucky? Good Lord, I think I'm the lucky one."

"No, sorry. My name is Lucky. That old bull's a regular around here. I've said for years now we need to build him a crosswalk. So, are you okay?"

"Shoot, yeah. He took me by surprise, that's for sure. I'm glad I only have a few more miles to go. My load's probably shifted quite a bit."

"You headed to the airport?"

"That's right. How d'you know?"

"That's a familiar load you got there. You heading out to a cabin site?"

"I'm flying out to stake a homestead."

"Is that right?" He smiled at the pretty lady, an unlikely homesteader, although she looked like she could probably hike a mile or ten. Lucky had dreams of his own to get some land and build his dog sled team up. He couldn't afford to be too far off the road, though. He ran a summer fishing service and needed to be in town a lot.

"I'm heading up Lynx Creek way. You know it?"

"Sure, I've been by there. I've volunteered out on the Iditarod a couple of times as a handler. Learning the ropes, so to speak. There's a rest stop about ten miles up Lynx Creek from where it meets the Hostage."

"The Hostage?"

"Yeah. That's another big creek flowing out of the Yentna River. Beautiful country up there. From the looks of it, you're planning to stay awhile."

"Long enough to build a cabin and establish my rights to the land. A little late to plant a garden, but I'll forage and put up what I can."

"Well, I won't keep ya. When you get back this way, look me up."

"Do you have a business card or something?"

"No need for that in these parts. Just ask for ginger Lucky."

"Will do. Hey, thanks for stopping to check on me."

"Well, it's what we do around here. Besides, it's been nice chatting with ya. All the best to you, uh, ma'am."

"Thanks, Lucky."

As she drove off, Lucky reached under his cap and scratched at his forehead, a habit he traded for cussing when he got frustrated. He forgot to ask her name.

4

A LUCKY BREAK

Summer Solstice 1984
  Talkeetna

"THIS PLACE IS CRAZY BUSY!" A wide-eyed Jesse reached the lone assistant at the Talkeetna airport office after standing in line for nearly a half-hour, listening to travelers talking over their plans, comparing packing lists and pointing to routes on the aerial maps lining the walls.

"Sorry, hun. Alice is out to lunch, and it's our busy season. I'm Linda. Do you have a reservation?"

"I'm Jesse. I have a noon reservation, but I don't have any papers or anything, I just cal..."

"You're fine, Jesse. Let me..." Linda looked over the reservation book, double-checking the hand-written entries. "We're taking you into Lynx Creek landing, is that right?"

"Yes, ma'am. I'm looking to homestead up there."

Linda had heard this story from excited outsiders before. Overcoming the urge to roll her eyes, she nodded to Jesse, turned, and motioned for someone in the back room to join her. "Hey, James. Your noon ride is here." Turning back to

35

Jesse, Linda continued. "This is James. He'll be your pilot today—our finest! You guys head outside to get your stuff loaded, then come back and settle up with me. Alice should be back by then, so the line will be shorter."

She waved them off and turned to the next customer.

JESSE SIZED up the pilot in a quick glance and handshake. James was about Jesse's size, with a couple inches on her in height. She guessed he was in his mid-thirties. The lines on his face ran deep, perhaps carved by the sun during long hours of flying in the endless Alaska summers. Bright white teeth shone against his tanned face. She led him to her truck and trailer and pointed to the burgeoning load. "Here's my stuff."

James paged through papers on a clipboard and looked over Jesse's load. "There seems to be a mistake. I have here a single flight into Lynx Creek. That's fine. There's a landing strip in the area. But if you're taking all that stuff there on your truck and on the trailer, there's no way I can do that in one trip."

He paused and pointed toward an airplane. "That bird over there, that orange 180, it's going to take I'd say three, maybe four, trips to get it all there. Of course, this is our busy time with all the tourists and whatnot. Let's go back into the office and see if Linda can help us sort this out real quick."

Jesse hesitated briefly. Taking the setback in stride, she followed James into the handcrafted log house serving as the office. She studied the logs and reached out to touch the smooth, bark-free surface, feeling closer to nature the further from Anchorage she got.

James led Jesse behind the desk, next to Linda, to get her undivided attention. "We've got a big haul situation here, Linda."

Jesse explained. "I've got a load of stuff to get out there to help me get set up before winter. I guess I didn't explain very well when I made my reservation."

Linda checked the reservation book, then glanced out the dusty window toward Jesse's load. "Yeah, I see. I am the one that took your call and scheduled you. I guess I figured you were doing what most do and just go out with gas and a chainsaw and a few rations to mark your boundary line and fell some trees to dry for next year. I didn't realize you were going out to stay indefinitely. My mistake. I should have asked more questions."

"Well, I should have given more information," Jesse admitted innocently. "I wasn't even thinking about how much would fit on the plane. I hear lots of people take their load in during the winter when the river's frozen, too. That makes sense. But I'm ready to get my shelter built before snowfall. I've got a bunch of the materials there to shelter for this first winter and then will build something more permanent come next year when the logs are felled and peeled."

"Sure, sure. I gotcha. Ya know, James, we got those folks going up there fishing over the next couple of weeks. What do you say after we do the drop off with enough to get Miss Jesse through a few days, then we take the rest of Miss Jesse's stuff up there during our pickups upriver in the next few days? It's not going to all be there tomorrow, but we'll get it there soon as we can."

James nodded. "Sure, sure, that will work. Now Jesse, what are you going to do with your truck and trailer?"

"I've got it covered," Linda answered firmly and pointed out the window. "She's going to park in the south lot there. Jesse, you were thinking you would probably not need it until breakup, right?"

Jesse furrowed her brows in confusion. Linda smiled. "Sorry, I forgot. You're new to the state. Breakup is sometime in spring or early summer, when the snow and ice melt."

"Ah, that's right. I'm planning to go in for supplies before breakup. I'll need a flight back here and will take my truck and trailer then."

"I see. Well, we can't schedule that now, obviously, but you can hop on the Trapline and we'll get it scheduled when the time comes." Linda made a note in her schedule book and smiled reassuringly at Jesse, who gazed back with a blank stare.

"I guess I'm a bit confused. How does the trapline get me scheduled?"

Linda laughed. James looked down and shuffled his feet, trying his hardest not to shake his head at this crazy young woman thinking she was going to live in the woods for nearly a year with no experience in Alaska's wilderness.

"The Trapline. It's a radio messaging thing, like playing telephone with tin cans. You can radio in a message to the office, and they will relay it on air. We listen pretty faithfully to get our messages for pickups like this."

"Okay!" Jesse's voice was more self-assured than she felt. "I guess I have a lot to learn. James, I'm sure you've got a full schedule of flights."

James and Linda looked at Jesse, both holding their breath with the same thought in mind: *There is no way this gal's going to propose a flight change, is there?*

"This isn't going as smoothly as I envisioned," Jesse explained quickly. "I don't want to hold you up and keep you from your next flight. Obviously, I have some rearranging and planning to do to get my essentials loaded on the plane. Is there any way…"

"Oh, my! Let me just look at the schedule here…" Linda shuffled papers, greeted some other guests who arrived for their flight, and looked quizzically at James before turning back to Jesse. "Tell you what. If it's ok with you, James, let's move Miss Jesse to the first morning flight tomorrow and that'll give her plenty of time to divvy up her stuff and make some piles for, what do you say, three trips total?"

James looked through his notebook while Jesse silently

crossed her fingers and held her breath. She wanted to start this trip on the right foot, and this wasn't it. She needed to get more information on the Trapline and prioritize her deliveries.

Finally, he spoke. "Well, I guess. And Linda, I will take those next loads for half price."

"Hey, I'm happy to pay you." Jesse calculated in her head the added trips and deducted it from her bank balance. The new rifle, supplies and now extra air transport added up, but she was still flush. She felt uneasy about accepting such kindness while trying to develop a relationship with this vital link. "I'm just so sorry I wasn't more prepared."

FOR THE NEXT SEVERAL HOURS, Jesse labored over the sorting of supplies and prioritizing material drops to the Lynx Creek landing strip. On the way home for the night, Linda waved her over. "Hey Jesse, take some time and have a bit of fun tonight before you head into the bush. You'll be glad you did. Go down to the Talkeetna Bar. That's where the locals hang out. They'll share their wisdom and warnings with you. Just take the road there, around the curve to the left toward downtown, and you'll see it on the left down there. It's a big white two-story house-looking place. You can't miss it. Someone will be on stage belting out their original tunes."

"Thanks, Linda. I'm about done here and I'm starving. I'll head over there as soon as I wrap this up. Thanks for your help today."

"You bet. I'm rooting for you to make it out there." She punched Jesse lightly on the arm. "Us women have to support each other. Most of the guys don't think a woman can do what you're about to do. Just saying."

"Thanks for that heads-up. I'll share my story with discretion."

"See, I knew you were a wise woman!"

Linda waved as she drove away in a white Suburban

covered in dried mud and dust. Shiny sports cars with meticulous hand wash and wax jobs were not the norm here, and Jesse found it refreshing. There was no social competition, just living.

A CUTE YOUNG barmaid tossed a cocktail napkin on the bar in front of Jesse. "What can I get ya?"

"Do you have a food menu?"

"Sure do."

In a matter of seconds, a menu and a glass of water appeared beside the napkin. It didn't take long for Jesse to decide. It had been a long day and she was hungry and thirsty!

"I'll have your summer ale on tap, please, and this Denali Park burger, rare."

"Great choices. I'm Stephanie. Let me know if you need anything."

"Jesse here and actually, I need a lot!" she chuckled. "But right now, if there's anyone in here that I could talk to about the Trapline message service, that would be great."

"Of course! Sure! Let's see, old Jay Kemp is over there. I'll have him stop by and chat with you. Interesting man. Real educated, but likes to be away from people most of the time. He'll help you out."

"Thanks Stephanie, I really appreciate it."

JESSE HAD HALF her dinner eaten before she noticed the spicy hot sauce and ordered a second beer. She was just finishing the burger and second beer when a tall, rail-thin man with kind eyes and a weathered face slid onto the bar seat next to her. He held out his hand. "I'm Jay Kemp. I hear you have some questions for me?"

Jesse eagerly returned the handshake, wiped her mouth with the back of her hand, and shared a heart-melting smile.

Her tanned face, framed with sun-bleached hair, glowed with enthusiasm for life. "Oh, Mr. Kemp. Thank you so much for taking the time to talk with me!"

"Jay. Please call me Jay." The corners of his mouth turned upward slightly as he locked eyes with this blue-eyed beauty less than half his age. People around here thought him a loner, but he was just selective in the company he kept. When asked to speak with Jesse, he gave the beautiful athletic-looking young woman one glance and became intrigued to see what she was up to.

"Jay. Thank you." Jesse reached out and patted his hand on the bar. "I'm starting a whole new life up here and learning a lot about what it takes to live remotely. I understand there is a radio program where people call messages in – the something Trapline?"

"Oh yes, Trapline Chatter. It's a real thing and has saved many a life over the last two decades. So, tell me a bit more about where you'll be and what you might need. Are you on a short run into the woods or setting up shop somewhere?"

"I'm setting up a homestead on Lynx Creek."

"Ah, one of those free land programs, is it?"

"Yes, that's right."

"I was glad to see them open up some more of those lots. That's what brought me up here in the late 60s. I ultimately got distracted in the city for a bit and didn't get the land staked, but I made it up to Trapper's Creek and have a cabin out there. A couple times a month I come in here, just because I get tired of my own cooking." He paused for a sip of his beer.

"Enough about me. It sounds like you're going to be staying, so what you need to know is it's KABN radio station. You can find it on AM radio. I think it's about 1170 on the dial. On FM, that's where I pick it up, it's 100.3."

Jesse grabbed a notebook from her backpack and jotted down the information.

"So, you'll need a good transistor radio and plenty of batteries. Do you have that?"

"Well, I think the radio is fine and I have a case of batteries. I guess I'll see how long they last me."

"That's right. You'll be fine. Remember to take the batteries out of the radio when you're not using it. They will last much longer that way. Where you're going, you'll see folks pretty regular in the summertime and can get messages transferred and supplies sent out, at least monthly, if you need. When you'll need it is after fishing and fall hunting is over. So with the Trapline Chatter, you dial in at 9:30 in the evening during the summer and 7:00 pm in the winter. I'm not sure exactly when it changes, but if you listen along on the radio, they'll let you know. If you're having a problem getting reception, and this is important, be sure you take some wire or a coat hanger out with you. Then, you can run the wire out as high as you can get it. Sometimes out there in the shadow of the mountains where the clouds like to hang, it may be spotty."

Jesse added wire to her list of things to get in yet another supply run before she loaded the plane early in the morning. If she didn't find it in time, she figured she could ask the pilot in the morning if there was anything around the airport she could grab. She suspected there would be.

"So, if you need to get a message out to someone who listens to the radio, say, someone in Trapper's Creek, then you send it out with someone passing through the area. If you don't mind, I'll write the phone number for the station here for you." Jay reached for her notebook and took a pen from his shirt pocket. "Give this number to your friends and family. They can call the station and leave a message for you."

"Oh, wow! Now I understand how this works. This is really helpful information. I will find a phone and call my parents before I head out in the morning. They are, actually, my mom is a real skeptic of all this. She thinks I'll be back in Minnesota before snow flies."

"Yeah, funny how that happens. I'm not going to lie to you. This is a tough gig. But you've always got folks around who can help, and they will. Besides, if you're not out of there in two months, you'll be trapped for the winter anyway, unless you've got a track vehicle or snow machine."

"That's the one thing I wasn't able to button up before leaving. I had a lead on a snow machine in Anchorage but could never connect with the seller."

"Yeah, that happens. Tell you what, I can get you a machine and find a way to get it to you. I assume you don't want something brand spanking new, but something with a good maintenance record. Am I right?"

"That would be perfect. I have $1500 set aside for a good used one."

"That should be plenty to get you a decent old one. You should know that we call them iron dogs around these parts. They are used for sled dog training sometimes. In fact, you are likely to see some of that come winter. Some teams will be practicing long runs out that way, and of course, the Iditarod runs not far from the area you're talking about. The Iditarod crew uses the Lynx Creek airstrip heavily to stage equipment and supplies for the race."

"No kidding! I'll have to figure out a way to know what's coming and going out there."

"Ha! That'll be no problem. When you get out there, Sadie Nelson will find you in her own time. If I could give you one piece of advice, it would be to befriend Sadie and never piss her off. That would be your biggest downfall."

Jesse considered his caution. "She sounds like a force to be reckoned with." She thought of her childhood neighbor, Joanie Wren, who was always complaining about Jesse climbing her trees.

"Oh, she is, but she's as elusive as my would-be wife. Sadie has lived in the interior for many decades. She and her late husband Joe ran a trapline out there and were well known for their hides. Sadie, and the kids when they were still living there, brain tanned the hides, working that leather until it was soft as butter. Joe had an uncanny knack for catching the most beautiful specimen. I know there's lots of people who hate the killing of animals, but it's what they did, and they did it well. Joe's been gone about a dozen years now. Sadie refuses to leave. She feels her spirit is married to the trees, rivers, and all the animals in the area. She is very protective and winces at the development that happens."

"She sounds like a fascinating woman."

"She is indeed. I have had the pleasure of knowing her for most of my years here, and fortunately I have stayed on her good side. She still runs a trapline herself. She's a great mentor, but works in her own ways and on her own time. Respect her and she will do the same."

"I will, Jay. I promise." Jesse looked forward to meeting this legend.

"Keep your place tidy or she will scold you. Keep it uncluttered and as pristine as possible. If you pass her smell test, she'll help you immeasurably. I better go now." Jay laughed. "I don't see so well when driving in the dark."

"Oh, I'm sorry. I didn't mean to keep you." Jesse turned her wrist to check her watch. It was dark inside the bar and her back was to the door, so she didn't realize the light was streaming in through the doorway when patrons came and went.

Jay put his strong, worn hand on her shoulder. "I'm kidding ya, hun. Sun will barely go down tonight, and my place is about forty minutes from here. I'll be fine and intend to stay that way for a long time. Tell ya what. I'm going to leave a little package for you over at the ice cream shop over there. They'll be open until midnight, milking the tourists for their money. Good ice cream, but I'm disgusted with their crazy prices. Tell them you're a local and they might give you a discount.

Anyway, don't forget to grab the package. Gabby should be working tonight. Tell her Jay sent you."

"I will. Thank you so much for everything, Jay. Can I at least buy your beer?"

"Well, now there's a story for another day. At this establishment, my third one's on the house and that was my third. Thank you, though. I look forward to getting an update from you one day and I'll get you that snow machine. Listen to your radio."

He threw his left hand in the air and gestured a farewell as he turned and walked away, his long legs carrying him swiftly out the door and down the street.

5

WET AND WILD

July 1984
Lynx Creek

IRRITATED, sore, and still exhausted, Jesse woke early, once again to the strumming of raindrops falling on the tent overhead, then trickling down the steep walls to join their sisters and brothers in the growing puddles that threatened to dampen her bedroll. She looked at the days crossed off on the calendar and checked her food cache checklist to see what she had left. Fourteen days after arriving at Lynx Creek airport with a first load of supplies, her food stash, minimized for the maiden voyage, was fading. The second and third planeloads had not yet arrived. She was hungry from hoarding her food as the days without replenishment passed. Inclement weather prevented two planned trips and "competing trips" bumped the other two. Willing herself not to fall into despair, she mentally listed her accomplishments on the homestead. *Tent, lean-to, and food cache in place—check. Rough staking of property corners —check. Long, wet walks along the creek—check. Sky gazing between raindrops—check. Hours listening to the drone of rain where there should be airplane engines…* Jesse jumped at the sound of twigs breaking, then lay frozen, listening for approaching threats. A raven cawed loudly overhead, as if announcing its next meal.

Jesse thought back to the five trips from the airstrip which she had made over the first three days, pushing the cartloads of supplies from the first planeload, stowed in the brush north of the airstrip until she could return to retrieve them. It was hard, exhausting work, but training had prepared her for it. She thought back to that first night, which seemed like months ago, when she cleared a small area of tree roots and set up the one-person tent. Determined to keep her precious supplies dry, with dark clouds collecting overhead, she had draped a tarp over a rope suspended between two black spruce trees to create a dry area. The next morning, she had risen lazily and moved the bedding to the center of the tent to prevent wicking of the moisture through the tent wall. She breathed in deeply, enjoying the earthy perfume as the rain released scents of desiccated leaves and rich soil. She moved quietly, as a guest in a monastery, drinking in the beauty of the mountains, sensing the snap of branches as unseen animals moved through the area, and listening to the creek lap the rocks and roll in the near distance.

Surveying the property, Jesse analyzed the landscape for her future home. She quickly found no fewer than ten areas that could work. Forming a window frame with her fingers at the end of outstretched arms, she imagined the view from a cabin. She searched for areas where trees could be harvested without marring the pristine appearance of the property. She walked the twenty minutes to Lynx Creek and watched it for the telltale rolls of salmon in water. Disappointed, she realized that fishing was not yet an option, as she was not equipped to eat or preserve the catch. Thinking about the canned salmon she and Charlie had prepared, she doubted she could keep it from freezing unless stored in her tent, which she didn't want to do because of animals. Her gut churned as she thought about the options, ultimately deciding she would ask James if there was a way to store it in Talkeetna for now, since she wasn't equipped to keep it. She hoped he would not have it loaded on the next flight in. Large trees in this area were sparse, compared to the old-growth forests in other parts of the state; a realization that Jesse was coming to terms with as she looked for potential logs for her eventual home. From her research, she knew that black spruce grew in clumps, each one crowding out the others, so the tree girth was narrow, but she had still hoped to find some with a larger diameter. Paper birch and small willows stood on the higher slopes, and cottonwood grew large, up to three feet in diameter, on the stream bars where she could not harvest them. She would need to fell more trees than she expected to get adequate timber to build her home. The question nagged at her. *How many mistakes will I make before I throw in the towel?*

Jesse had strung wire through a tree and attached it to her radio so she could listen to the Trapline Chatter for updates. Banjos, fiddles, and vocalists framed sets of about ten announcements. The sound quality was that of a low-cost vintage radio with loose tin cans installed for extra distortion. Each evening Jesse sat on her sleeping bag in the middle of the tent, with an extra layer of mosquito netting hung over the screen of the open flap. She looked forward to this radio show evening ritual. The announcers and guests were the only human voices she heard, besides her own mumbling of the few songs she knew, while moving about the wild property she hoped to tame slightly. Finally, in a string of messages sandwiched between Hobo Jim singing about maple syrup and flapjacks and an Athabascan fiddler named Bill playing something that sounded like a mix of Cajun and Appalachian fiddle, Jesse heard the announcer's gravelly voice on the crackly radio. "And to Miss Jesse from Minnesota from Talkeetna Air, the weather looks great, and we'll be dropping some fishermen off at 0700 tomorrow. Grab your pushcart and meet us."

Buoyed by the promise that the next load of supplies would land, Jesse felt the tension in her shoulders ease some. The landing strip was a two-hour hike from the property that she believed matched the BLM map as her designated homestead site. Two hours, unless she was pulling the long-handled, big-wheeled cart carrying supplies. Then it took longer.

Relieved by the thought of seeing a human and getting more supplies, Jesse settled in for the night, tucking her belongings into the center of the tent under the tarp, serenaded by raindrops. Her spirits lifted when she woke at five, with the morning sun already shining brightly in a cloudless sky and no scent of impending rain.

The plane was due to drop off a fishing guide and patrons at Lynx Creek at 7:00. She could dally no longer. Jesse picked up the cart handles and pushed it along the barely visible path, created by her prior trips across the tundra. Bent blades of grass and thick underbrush of unripe blueberry bushes padded the trail. High bush cranberries, mountain ash, Devil's club and fireweed created obstacles around which an excited Jesse steered the cart.

With the rain orchestra now quiet, Jesse noticed the birds moving around, leaves dropping to the forest floor, and the distant purr of the rolling creek. Before reaching the airstrip, the rough engine sounds of a Cessna, like a lawnmower trying to cut through the thick underbrush of the tundra, broke through the sounds of the forest. Squinting into the sun, she spotted the plane gliding across the ice-blue sky. As she watched, the plane changed directions. Her stomach lurched as the tail-end faded away.

Jesse stood on the dirt airstrip, scanning the sky. Seeing nothing and hearing nothing, she pulled the cart toward an abandoned outbuilding. Only one corner of the old building's porch had not yet collapsed completely onto the ground beneath it. Fireweed stood proudly in the cracks between the weathered planks. Jesse crouched and gently placed one buttock on the corner, testing its strength. Once assured it would hold her, she pivoted to rest all her weight on the precarious perch.

As she took in the surrounding vastness, Jesse felt small, inconsequential, and alone. She longed for human contact. It was not yet normal for her to enjoy as much time alone as this new life delivered. If the pilot didn't land today, she wondered how long it would be before she heard another's voice, and how long it would be until she found a way to compensate. Singing and reading out loud to an audience of one would not sustain her. Thoughts of Tim intruded into her determined efforts to stay positive. *He would laugh at me now if he only knew.* She wondered if she should have told him about her plans, said goodbye, forgiven his infidelity, felt his embrace once more. *If he let himself, he would love it here.*

A rumble in the air interrupted her thoughts as the plane came back into view. Jesse instinctively drew in a deep breath of the clean air, held it for a moment, and exhaled a silent prayer of thanks as she stood, ready to greet.

James hopped down from the pilot's seat of the Cessna; a broad smile grew across his face when he saw her. He called out, "Hey, Jesse!" before turning to help a female passenger out of the plane.

"Nice to see you, James!" Jesse raised her hand in a wave of acknowledgement as she approached the plane. His toothy smile took her off-guard. He was over-the-top friendly. She decided it must have been for show for the sake of his passengers.

James introduced Jesse to his clients, a couple from Montana, out for a day of coho salmon fishing, they explained. He then disappeared into thick brush on the north end of the airstrip. A short time later, he returned, driving a four-wheeler with extra-large mud tires and a shiny exhaust pipe extending upward to the sky.

"Now, do you two have all your gear and a map?"

Jesse found it odd that the two fisher-people had such little baggage. They each carried a metal tube about four feet long and wore a small backpack. That was it.

"Yes!" the couple responded excitedly in unison. They mounted the four-wheeler in tandem, with Rachel, the wife, on the rear portion of the seating holding both metal tubes. James pointed to a faint opening in the brush, the entry to their adventure for the day.

"See you at eight on Friday evening." Charles gave James a thumbs up and they disappeared down the trail.

"Wow, they wasted no time getting out of here. Where was that four-wheeler and why didn't someone tell me it was here?"

James laughed. "Well, now you've met the Andersons. They are big money ranch folks from Montana who originally sprung from Texas oil money. That four-wheeler, that's theirs. We have a locked storage hut and keep it in there for them. They come up about four times a year."

"Huh. I guess I need to put one of those four-wheelers on my list of future purchases. So, they come up just to fish?" In Jesse's inner circle, there were no wealthy people. The vast majority earned an average wage, or less, as they pursued lives of joy rather than ego-centric power jobs.

"Just between us…" James started.

"What do you mean 'just between us'? I haven't seen another living soul since you dropped me off a week ago!" Jesse laughed, although she felt her pulse rise like she had come within millimeters of touching a hot burner. "Sorry, I've just felt a little stir crazy not hearing a voice other than my own."

"Well, you will get used to that, or you won't. There are a lot of things you are going to experience out here on your own that you couldn't possibly prepare for. It's like wandering in the desert. You'll make your way, build a lot of faith in whatever you believe in, and in the end, you will be rewarded or you will leave. The reward depends entirely on your outlook."

Jesse stared at this man. She didn't expect him to share

anything more than the flight schedule. Now, he seemed like a real person - someone she could be friends with.

"Anyway, like I was saying, the Andersons have a 300-acre parcel a way in. They are just about ready to launch a big lodge building project, but they won't want to advertise it broadly because they fear vandalism and they don't want free-for-all competition to move in and cheapen the area. They are looking to build something exclusive and upscale for their wealthy friends and clients."

"That's interesting. How far away is this property?"

"Around here we measure most often by time rather than miles. It will take them about an hour on the four-wheeler. In the winter, it goes faster. They can travel on the frozen streams between here and there. They would like to use a boat to go in there, and that will take some dredging to widen a part of the river. It's all in their plans."

"I can't imagine what it will cost for them to build all the way out here. Heck, I know what it cost just to get my piddly pile of stuff out here."

"It's all a write-off for them at this point. They aren't looking to make money, just to have a good time. They fell in love with this place about ten years ago and have come every year since. Sometimes they bring their family or friends and hire a guide to go in and set up a bunch of tents, generators, party lights, a temporary kitchen, the whole nine yards. They spare no expense. This time around they had a drop of supplies earlier, before you came up. They will be tenting."

"Why haven't they built a cabin?"

"I'm not sure. I think they would feel like they were settling if they didn't build their dream place." James started pulling Jesse's supplies from the plane. "Sorry I got here a little late today. We give the Andersons a little leeway in their arrival time since they have been longstanding customers. Then, we saw a grizzly with triplets along the north fork a way, so we went up to take a closer look."

"I saw you veer off and figured it must have been something like that since there was no weather in the area."

James reached into the cockpit and pulled out a stuffed backpack. "Well, how about an early lunch on me since I have thrown off your schedule for the day?"

"How nice is that? I would love it, not to eat alone!" Jesse looked around for a place to set up their lunch.

"There's a sandbar down on the river that's got a nice log for lunch. If you don't mind wading the shallows, we can go there." It was a treat for Jesse to have someone around and especially nice that it was James, since he was so familiar with the area.

AFTER THEY SETTLED on the sun-bleached, fallen cottonwood tree, James opened his backpack, and one-by-one took out an assortment of food. "Do you always carry this much food with you?"

"No, only when I'm hoping to meet up with a beautiful woman on a remote sandbar."

Jesse shifted uneasily on the log. James sensed her discomfort immediately. "Sorry, that was pretty corny. I usually do have ample supply, just in case I get delayed. I knew I was coming out here today and, because I hauled it all, I know you have a lot of canned salmon, so I brought something a bit different. Have you eaten bear?"

"No, I can't say that I have, and about that salmon…"

"Well, I didn't bring any bear. I actually don't prefer it. It's a bit too gamey tasting for me." As he spoke, he pulled out two foil rounds. "Instead, I have two big juicy buffalo burgers." He held one out to Jesse. "Gosh, I didn't even think. Maybe you don't eat meat."

"Are you kidding me?!" Jesse grabbed it hungrily. "I'm salivating at the sight of it and I'm sure when I unwrap it, I am going to have an orgasm from the smell. This is the best thing ever!"

James laughed. "Well, that sounds interesting, but seeing as how this is our first date, I don't think I'm ready to watch that."

The ice was broken and the uncomfortableness of their first 'date' dissipated.

They chuckled as James poured soda from a cold thermos into two cups retrieved from his pack. "I didn't bring French fries. I thought they would get soggy before we could eat them. I have some chips, though. I hope that's okay."

"Okay? I may just follow you back to town like a lost puppy."

"Well, that is the hazard of visits like this. How has it been for you out here?"

"It's been… well, honestly, it's been lonely."

"Second to fast food, that's the number one reason I hear for people asking to hitch a ride back to civilization."

Jesse raised her eyebrows and nodded. The order was reversed for her, but given enough time, she may miss the food more than people.

"You know, there are folks around here. And you will see more in the winter."

"You and your passengers are the first I've seen since I arrived. Where are there other people?"

"Well, old Mrs. Nelson is about two miles from here upriver. She'll sniff you out when she's ready. Don't go chasing after her. There are also about a half-dozen trappers who will just appear come winter. You'll see the occasional angler, like the Andersons, come through. But mostly, you'll be alone, unless the government's program to lure people up here with free land really works."

"You sound like you have your doubts."

"I do. Over the past five years or so we've flown folks like yourself up, although they're usually not singles, and if single, definitely not women. They come up once, stay a few days, and never return to build their place. I think it's three years you have to live here, right?"

"I think technically, it's 'most of' three years, but yeah, that's right."

"Well, some of those folks still have some time to get their butts up here and start living. So many started clearing their boundary line and never returned for that mandatory living part."

"I hope some more come. It's such a beautiful place to be."

"You may find, after being up here alone for a time, that it's just fine not to have someone trampling about in your space. Time will tell, I guess."

"That's right." Jesse wiped her mouth one last time with the paper towel James provided. "Meanwhile, I think getting into a better routine will help me adjust. I've just sort of been stumbling through my days, looking over the land and wondering where to start. If I could decide where to build, that would be great. It would help me define which trees to clear and dry for building next year."

"I don't mean to be forward here, but if you want, I could come early next Friday and walk the property with you. I've seen a lot of cabins built out here and kind of have a feel for the geography."

"If it's not an imposition, I would really appreciate that. Input is always a great thing when making such big decisions. Meanwhile, I'll get myself set up."

James had repacked his backpack and stood, reaching his hands up to stretch. He paused and looked at Jesse, a deep crease forming between his brows. "What are you living in until you get your cabin built? I know we hauled up a barrel wood stove, but what are you putting it in?"

"Great question. That big black tote you unloaded there. That's my wall tent." Jesse pointed to the tote.

"Ah, I see. Are you using harvested poles, then? I didn't see a bag of poles."

"That's right. I picked it up at Tent and Tarp. They walked me through setting it up there outside their shop. They gave me the pole measurements and, fortunately, I brought the chainsaw and gas out on my first load, so I've already got the poles downed and ready. I have the ground where it's going mostly cleared, but the roots are so shallow here. I have some more smoothing to do to get the roots out of the way."

"That's how it is on the tundra. The frost is too high for too long for the roots to grow deep, so they just spread out under the surface." James picked up some rocks and casually tossed them into the current. "Say, have you thought about laying some logs down on the ground and overlaying them with plywood for a floor? That would give you a more even surface."

"No, I really hadn't. Is that a thing people do?"

"Anything goes out here, Jesse. You just have to do what works for you. If you're interested, I'll round up some plywood and bring it out with me."

"That would be simply amazing. I can write you a check…"

James held his hand up. "Listen, I'm guessing this won't be the only thing you need, so how about we just start a tab and when you're back in town, we can settle up? Okay?"

Jesse smiled, looked to the rocks, rounded from the repeated river-water massage, and shook her head. "You're going to go broke if you do that for all your passengers."

"Well, I don't. You're a special case, so let's just shake on it and get 'er done."

He took Jesse's hand and shook it heartily. They had an agreement, and the canned salmon struggle was long forgotten.

6

CARVING A NEW LIFE

1984

Homestead

JESSE SAW James as a stable friend, with a spark, much like her best friend from high school, Craig. Years later she had discovered that Craig was crazy about her, but long-since gave up after no reciprocated flirting from her. Occasionally, when Jesse allowed herself to dream of alternate realities, she wondered what Craig was like now, and what their life would be like if she allowed herself to be open to love at that young age. And she wondered what held her back from acting on that spark when she felt it way back when. She wanted to know what changed from that time and when she fell crazy in love with Tim. Ultimately, she decided it was not completely understandable, but there were elements of personality - good and bad, maturity, time and place.

James followed through with his promise to help, asking for nothing in return. After a half-day of identifying, then eliminating building spots for one reason or another, they decided on a cabin location that was unlikely to flood if the river or creek overflowed, had a magnificent view of the mountains and maximized the sunlight. James made her test the radio signal in the area. Satisfied that it was strong enough, they staked an area by 20 feet by 20 feet. Jesse thanked him with words of gratitude and lunch. Days later he returned with a friend, Tommy, who helped set up the floor for the wall tent. Her tent would be two feet above the ground, leaving less snow for her to shovel to get in and out of the front door. They slept out under the stars on the platform that would hold her temporary home, suspended off the earthen floor.

"Now that was a nice lay," Tommy exclaimed when they awakened with the sunrise to the sound of birds flitting about.

"Excuse me?" Jesse caught Tommy off-guard.

"Oh, god, I didn't mean…"

"Jesse, did I tell you about my friend Tommy? His toes are tattered from sticking his feet in his mouth so often. I assure you he didn't mean anything by…"

"I get it!" Jesse laughed. "I was just teasing. But hey Tommy, if you want to make it up to me, can you help me haul that stuff over here and we can set up the wall tent?"

Tommy was a quiet, unpretentious man who knew his way around tools. With a thick, muscular body, plaid shirt, jeans and hiking boots, he looked like a true outdoorsman. There was no electricity, so any saw cut was made by hand and there were no air hammers. Tommy and James worked quietly in unison. Jesse fetched and helped where she could, but tried her best to play a support role and not get in the way. When they were done, Jesse stood back to look over the fruits of their efforts. "You guys have just changed my world. How can I ever repay you?"

"Well, sometime when we're back here on our snow-go's we'll stop in for a warm meal. How's that?"

Silently, she hoped that the three of them would be friends for a long time.

SNOW COVERED the ground and stuck by the end of October. The place where Jesse got water from Lynx Creek was frozen solid, while large chunks of ice floated on the mighty Yentna River.

Exhausted from a day of chopping firewood, Jesse was sleeping soundly early one morning, when on the fringes of awareness, she sensed something and woke with a start. It was dark and cold in her tent home. She reached down into the sleeping bag with her left hand, feeling around for the flashlight, while her right hand snaked down the side of the cot and wrapped around the handle of the rifle. Jesse paused, listening for the noise that had startled her out of a sound sleep. She heard it again. Something was brushing up against the west wall of the tent, opposite where she lay.

Jesse's mind raced through its panic checklist. All food was put in the cache high in a tree at least fifty feet from where she slept. There were no remnants of a fire in the outdoor pit. She had cooked only water on the wood stove. No bear should lurk around without the scent of food, and she wasn't on her period, which could attract a grizzly. Frozen, she lay a moment longer, listening through the pounding of her heart in her ears.

A deep female voice came through the wall tent. The syllables were slurred to Jesse's ears. She couldn't make out what was being said.

"Do'eent'aa?"

Jesse crawled out of the bedding and, with rifle in hand, silently tiptoed to the door and inched the zipper open. Only when she held the door flap open did she turn the flashlight on and shine it into the darkness.

"Jesus!" Jesse jumped as the light met the face of an old woman with dark skin, gray hair, and deep wrinkles across a round face. Her head, held atop a bent neck, reached as tall as Jesse's breastbone.

"No. Not Jesus. I'm Sadie. Sadie Nelson."

"Oh my God, you scared me!" Jesse took a deep breath to calm her pounding heart and quietly dropped the rifle. "Mrs. Nelson, hi, I'm Jesse. Won't you come in? I'll put some wood on the stove."

"No, don't do that. I've got skins on and I'll get too warm. Please, you're living out here in my country. Call me Sadie. Mrs. Nelson is for the tourists that come poking their noses around."

Jesse looked Sadie over. She could see fur sticking out from the bottom of her velvet jacket.

"Okay, but won't you come in? You can have a seat there on my cot." Jesse folded her sleeping bag to the top of the cot, clearing a space for her guest to rest.

"What are you doing here so early this morning? It's still dark."

"Good time… to set… traps." Sadie spoke in short bursts.

"You trap?" Jesse didn't hide her great surprise.

"What, you think I'm too old, too weak? I've been trapping for forty years by myself, and twenty before that when Mr. Nelson was still living."

"Oh, no. I didn't mean that at all. It's just that you're the first trapper I've met up here. I guess I really just don't know much about it, like I didn't think you'd be working in the dark. That seems dangerous."

"You're so cheechako. It's dark all winter. If we didn't work our traps in the dark, we would never work." A wide, partially toothless smile lit her face. Suddenly conscious of her missing teeth, Sadie put a hand over her mouth.

Jesse let the reality of Sadie's statement sink in. The growing darkness crept into her consciousness daily. She slept longer, worked outside for shorter periods, and was often asleep before Trapline Chatter came on the radio.

"Sadie, I've been here for three months. Why is this the first time I've seen you?"

"Oh, I knew you were here, but I got some new great-grandbabies in Fairbanks, so my boy, he came to get me when the last salmon run was about finished. Then, he caught a moose, so I stayed longer to help them put it up. I've been back only a week. A squirrel got in my cabin, so I had to clean it up. This is my first day working, and you need to learn to trap if you're going to be out here, so I came to get you. Get dressed. We've got work to do."

Jesse smiled at the powerhouse sitting on her cot. Sadie was short and old, but she looked strong. Her kuspuk fit snuggly over her body, making her look quite plump. With the furs sticking out the bottom, Jesse couldn't really tell how much of the roundness was Sadie and how much was fabric and fur.

Jesse had already slid insulated Carhartt work pants over her silk long johns. She grabbed her parka and put it on over a thermal shirt.

"You got some good gloves? Fingers and toes are the most important to keep warm out on the trapline. You lose those, you're no good."

Opening a trunk at the end of the cot, she pulled out a pair of down mittens that extended up her forearm.

Sadie shook her head. "Oh, not good. Those get wet and freeze your fingers. You have fur gloves?"

"No, I don't have fur gloves."

"We better go trapping and get some fur for your gloves. Hurry up. Put your boots on. You have good boots?"

Jesse looked in the bin. She had three pairs of boots. She pulled out the tall, lace-up Sorels and held them up for Sadie to see.

"Yes, those are good boots. Until the big snow comes. You got mukluks?"

"No, I don't have mukluks." Jesse reached back into the bin and pulled out the bulbous white rubber monstrosities she'd never had on her feet. James had brought them on one of his trips to drop off hunters. He said it was a gift she would really thank him for come spring.

Sadie laughed. "Those bunny boots look funny, but they will keep your feet very warm. Someday we will make you mukluks. They're more pretty for a woman."

"I have some food with my gear outside. You eat muktuk, right?"

"Muk-what?" Jesse asked, confused again. "I've never heard of that."

"It's raw whale blubber."

Jesse's eyes grew enormous and her jaw clenched shut. "No, I don't know that I can eat that. I'm not a big fan of raw fish."

"Actually, it's more like steak than fish, but I'm just kidding. I don't have any. I've got some moose jerky. But I have a pot of stew on the stove over to my place. When we're done setting traps, we can go over there. You do want to know where I live, right?"

"Yes, I do. I knew you lived near and that one day I would meet you, but…"

"Did they tell you not to come looking for me? Jeez, those guys are so overprotective. Was that James?" Sadie didn't pause for a response. "He's a good guy. Been my friend since he was just a little tyke."

"Sounds like you wouldn't have been there, anyway."

"That's right, but now that it's the first of November, I'm here and we're trapping."

"But Sadie, it's not the first of November. That's next week."

"Says you. I'm saying it's the first of November and the regulations say I can put my traps out. Are you with me, or not?"

"Yes, yes, I'm with you." Jesse followed Sadie out of the tent, then went back in to grab a flashlight.

"You won't need that tonight. The aurora's going to be

huge and there's a bright moon. You'll find your way back home, no problem."

"How far is it?"

"Oh, about an hour's walk. Come on. Stop talking. We've got work to do." Sadie picked up a bundle of traps and threw them over her shoulder. She motioned to another pile of traps laid out on top of a burlap bag. "Just do what I do and learn today."

Jesse did as she was told and followed Sadie's movements as they set conibear and foothold traps. She had no idea what each was for and had never handled them. Sadie was masterful. She slowly and deliberately made each movement so that Jesse could follow along. Together, they set twenty traps over a three-mile stretch. Mid-afternoon came quickly, and the sun was descending.

Jesse had held her own against the cold temperatures until then. With the sun going down, she felt a chill creep into her boots and up the hem of her jacket. They had been walking in snow, with outside temperatures in the teens. Between settings, they gnawed on dried smoked salmon and moose jerky. Hydration came in the form of snow held in their mouths until melted.

When the trap supplies were exhausted, Sadie turned to Jesse and nodded. "You did good. Now, let's eat."

She turned to the north and walked into the trees, navigating around willow thickets. Jesse stayed close. She had no clue where she was in relation to her own cabin.

Within twenty minutes, with dusk looming and shadows creeping in, Jesse spotted a wisp of smoke escaping from a chimney. They were marching in that direction.

A hundred yards from the cabin, there were telltale signs of a homestead amongst the trees - saw cuts on fallen trees, buckets hanging from branches, discarded plywood and metal pieces scattered about. Rusted traps and rotting ropes hung from 12-inch nails driven into the trees long ago. The nails hung higher than Sadie could reach.

Finally, they reached the cabin. Sadie opened the door, expecting Jesse to follow her into the tiny cabin. "Welcome to the Nelsons. This has been our home since the twenties. In 1928, we got the roof on the place."

"That can't be, Sadie. That's nearly sixty years ago."

"Yeah, so?"

"Sadie, did you come here with Mr. Nelson or were you born here?"

Sadie's laugh escaped before she could cover her mouth. "Silly girl. How old do you think I am?"

"I would have guessed sixty." The sharp knife of nature's forces had carved deeply into Sadie's face, but her stamina and strength were that of a much younger woman.

"I'm seventy-six. I came here as a young bride. Mr. Nelson and I. John. We ran away from the Jesse Lee orphanage in Seward. We didn't really plan to be husband and wife, but we knew we wanted to be on an adventure together. I'm not proud of how we got here, jumping on the train, lying to get a ride with crews working on the road, mail wagon, and railway. Heck, even this land we poached."

Jesse looked at Sadie, unsure of what she meant. "Back then, you could stake a claim, just by possession. After we ran away from Jesse Lee - not an easy thing to do because we both had brothers and sisters there - we worked whatever odd jobs we could. We lied about our ages and lived with whoever would take us in for the first couple of years after we left. John was a bit of a hothead. He had a really hard life early on and didn't like to be around people, so eventually, we got some supplies together and made our way out here. We've been here ever since. Well, I have. He passed away about fifteen years ago."

"I'm sorry."

"For what? That he passed? Don't be. He's with Jesus, and

that's just fine. Maybe Jesus can tame him some. John died at the hospital in Fairbanks. They say he had cancer in his stomach. He just stopped eating and wouldn't get out of bed. Our youngest son, Fred, came out to check on us and John had already been in bed for a month, just drinking a little broth I gave him on a spoon. He was skin and bones when he got to the hospital."

Sadie motioned to a chair at the table. "There, sit."

Jesse had become accustomed to following directions throughout the day. So she sat there and surveyed the one-room cabin. She guessed it was about 14 by 16 feet. It was a low cabin with the ceiling only about two inches above Jesse's head. The walls were built of horizontal peeled logs that were shaved flat on three sides. Some logs looked newer than others and were probably replaced over time. The roof had enough of a pitch that snow build-up was less likely to become a hazard. There was a broad overhang around the house, and on the front, the roof gable extended out to cover about a six-foot porch.

An antique black cast-iron bed frame with polished ornate gold scrolls stood in one corner. Sitting atop the antique wooden bedside table was a tattered bible and a Coleman battery-operated lamp. The wood stove, a homemade wooden kitchen table with one chair, a rocking chair and miscellaneous shelves hanging on the wall, filled the center of the home. Handcrafted metal hooks hanging by the door held Sadie's sparse collection of clothes. Family photos were scattered about. For a home that was used for nearly sixty years, there were few belongings in it. The usual junk drawer, purposeless trinkets, dusty book piles, and fancy home decor had no place here. It was as stark and utilitarian as Jesse had ever seen, and Jesse knew her mother would recoil in disgust.

"Can I get you something to sit on?" Jesse stood to look for a stool or something.

"Never mind. I've got my bench." Sadie walked to the wall

behind the table, unclipped a latch and a bench folded down, suspended above the floor.

"That's cool." Jesse wondered what other hidden treasures added to the functionality of the tiny place.

"We raised three children in this home. We made every inch count. Here's some stew for you. It will warm you up." Sadie no longer felt the chill from working outside. Through the years, her weather sense became finely tuned. She knew how to dress, when to eat and drink, and how to maximize the waning sunlight in the winter to stay comfortable while working in the elements.

Jesse had a million questions about their day of trapping, but knew she needed to wait for Sadie to initiate that conversation. She never did. They ate their stew in silence, then Sadie nodded off. Jesse sat and waited, uncertain whether she should just sneak out and let Sadie rest there on the plywood bench or wait for her new mentor to awaken and speak.

Finally, after nearly an hour, Sadie opened her eyes and announced it was time for Jesse to go home. "You go get some rest now. Meet me at the open field where we set traps this morning. You remember the one?"

"Yes, I think so. There's an old barrel there next to a cottonwood tree in the center?"

"That's it. Be there just before sunrise." Sadie handed Jesse her jacket and opened the door. The sky was ablaze with rolling color, illuminated by a bright full moon.

"See, I told you Aurora would be big tonight. Some say those are our whale and seal and deer spirits playing. I think it's the angels dancing for us in their finest dresses. See, there's purple and green and pink and blue. Tonight, they will use their torches to guide you home. Do you know how to get there?"

Jesse looked north to the horizon and pointed toward the

mountain range, barely visible on the horizon. "I know I need to head toward Foraker Mountain."

"Yeah. When you get past that first group of willows there, you will see my tracks from this morning. I left a trail for you. You'll see. Go rest. Tomorrow we will study."

With that, Sadie closed the door.

———

JESSE BARELY SLEPT. She had a strong work ethic and didn't want to be late to meet up with Sadie. Jesse did not know how long it would take her to get to the meeting spot or exactly when sunrise would be. She didn't want to go too early and risk getting cold from standing around, but she couldn't keep Sadie waiting, either.

After tossing and turning for a few hours, Jesse sat up and made some rough calculations in her head. She guessed sunrise would be at about 8:30. The meeting place was probably forty minutes away, and she needed about fifteen minutes to get ready. She reached into a metal container under her cot and pulled out an alarm clock and battery, inserted the battery and set it for seven o'clock.

The piercing beep of the alarm woke her from a deep, dreamy sleep. She lost the details of the dream to the irritability that came with the sound of the alarm. The air was cooler today than Jesse remembered it being the day before. She added an extra shirt and pulled a balaclava over her head. Jesse was parched from the salty foods and low hydration the day before. She pulled out the butane camp stove and quickly heated enough snow for a cup of lukewarm tea before hitting the trail. Not knowing what was in store for this day, she grabbed a piece of pilot bread and a handful of peanuts from her stash, pocketed a flashlight and stacked some wood inside the tent, available to light the stove quickly when she got home later.

The walk across the tundra was noticeably different this morning. Even in the pre-dawn light, she felt more sure-footed and aware of her place amongst the paper birch, willows, and black spruce, and that felt good. She easily navigated to the meeting place, a place that just a few short weeks earlier was rich with ripe blueberries, some of which were dried and jarred in Jesse's cache. The sun was barely reaching through the frosted branches with a few dried leaves awaiting their shed when Sadie appeared at the far end of the open field. She walked in about a hundred feet, then stopped, silently waiting for Jesse to meet her.

"Do'eent'aa?" Sadie called out as Jesse approached.

"Good morning, Sadie."

"Do'eent'aa?" Sadie said, more emphatically this time.

"Sadie, what are you saying to me?"

"That is our Athabascan greeting. I'm saying hello and asking you how you are."

"Oh. I'm pretty good, thank you."

"Why only pretty good? It's a beautiful day in God's country. The sun is shining, the air is clear, the animals are happy and you're not dead."

Jesse chuckled. "You're right. I'm great, and how are you?"

"Yes, great, too. Today, you will set more traps. I hope you watched good yesterday and saw how I chose my places and baited the traps."

"Sadie, I don't even know what animals you're trapping."

"Ey, ey, ey. Poor city girl." Sadie put the two burlap bags down on the snow and bent to open them. She pulled a trap from the first bag. "This one is called a conibear trap. If you were an animal, you would want this one. You won't know what hit you because it kills you right now."

"So, what animals does that one work for?"

"What do you think? This part traps the body of the animal, so it's got to fit in there."

"So, would guess out here it would be for things like beavers and mink."

"Yes, if we put them in the right places. I've caught wolverine, small coyote and lynx over the years, but I've lost traps to the bigger animals that got in them and didn't get killed."

"So when we set them, we need them to be hidden where those animals wouldn't go. Is that right?"

"Yes, and for the furry animals, we will use some scent or some bait. You saw me squeeze some juice on some traps yesterday or leave a bundle of meat."

"I did see that."

"Okay, so then this trap…" Sadie picked up a different one. "This is a leg trap. This catches the animal's leg, but the animal doesn't die."

"Oh, Sadie, that's awful! So the animal is alive, but can't get away?"

"That's the trapper's way, and it's why, once we set these traps, we have to check them at least every two days, and we shoot the animal to release its spirit back into the spirit world."

"So, what do you catch in these?"

"Think about the animals that are out here. What do you think would get in a trap like that?"

"Hmmm, there are those little weasel creatures I've seen along the river."

"That's the marten, and it is one of the most common animals we find in our leg traps. What else do you think?"

"Probably the lynx and coyote, maybe?"

"Good. Yes, that's right. We might also see red squirrel, muskrat, wolverine, and Arctic fox. They are not as plentiful, but the bigger animals bring better money."

By MID-DAY they had covered four miles of tundra in the opposite direction of the day before, setting thirty additional traps. Jesse struggled initially to identify the perfect spot, get the trap set and apply the right bait, but by the end of the day, she had a good sense of the process that Sadie followed.

"So now what?" The burlap bags were empty. The bait was dispersed, and the women were tracking south to the open field they started in.

"Now we wait. In two days, we will walk the entire line and check the traps. You don't have anything better to do, do you?" Sadie looked at the young woman and remembered herself in her youth. She was small but mighty and filled with attitude. She was hardened to the world and hell bent on surviving and providing for her family. John was her perfect partner. They never did actually marry, but she used his last name for as long as they were together and beyond.

"Have you ever been in danger while on the trapline, Sadie?"

"So many times."

"Can you tell me about one?" Jesse could imagine all kinds of difficulties, but she wanted to hear from Sadie what it was like in her real world.

Slowly weaving through the stands of spruce and willow thickets, the two made their way back to the open field as Sadie told a harrowing tale.

"In our early days out here, we were greedy, John and I. We wanted to get as many pelts as we could and make a name for ourselves at the fur rendezvous. It was actually the ice carnival then in Anchorage. We tried every kind of trapping there was and didn't know very much about the land then. About ten miles from here, there's a bog. Water gets trapped in there some years, although I haven't seen that for a few years now. Anyway, it was freezing out, probably about fifteen below. John and I had a small dog team we took out with us to pull the sled with the animals we trapped. We were going to Drummer Creek to check some traps." Sadie stopped for a minute and tugged at her kuspuk. Jesse knew she was buying a moment to catch her breath.

After a brief rest, they started walking again, and Sadie continued. "It was one of those mornings where the snow crystallized overnight, and every time we took a step there was a crunch in the snow. We passed some willows and stepped into drifted snow on the bog. Our dogs refused to go any further, so we tied them down. Snow drifts were eight or ten feet deep. Snow blew over the trail we normally used, and we were breaking a new trail when suddenly, John disappeared. He fell into a water hole under a deep drift and the snow caved in on him. Snowshoes weighed him down, and he couldn't climb out of the hole. I ran back to the sled and grabbed a piece of chain we had on the sled. When I returned, I could see John clawing at the snow around the hole, but he couldn't find anything to grab onto. I had to throw the chain to him, but it was heavy enough that it would have hurt him if it hit him, so I had to be careful. Finally, I was able to get the chain to him and pull him out without falling in myself. I half dragged him while he tried to walk to the sled, and the dogs carried him home. His clothes were frozen by the time we got there. Thank God we had coals in the stove, and I could get the cabin warmed really fast."

Jesse wanted to pull the frail older woman into her arms and protect her from all the elements. "That sounds really scary, Sadie."

"You know the worst part?"

"What was that?"

"I was four months pregnant with our first baby. It really made us stop and think about better ways to do our trapping. We were very careful after that, but still things happened."

They had reached the open field where they would part for the night.

"I'm so glad it didn't end badly, Sadie. That's quite a story."

"Oh, yeah. It's one the grandchildren like to hear about,

and now the great-grands too. In two days, if you want to learn more about the trapping ways, meet me here an hour after sunrise. If you're not here, I'll go on without you."

"I'll see you then, Sadie. Goodbye.

Sadie turned to walk another half hour to her house. She didn't look back. She didn't say goodbye; just settled into her plodding pace and anchored her sight on home. Jesse stood in the middle of the field for a long time, watching for the aurora borealis to appear. When it did, she let the colorful lights illuminate the way home in the darkness.

7

PREPARING FOR CHRISTMAS

1984

Lynx Creek

JESSE ALTERNATED red and green markers to cross off December days on her calendar. With the vast whiteness of winter closing in, her world had grown smaller. Only the sky brought brilliant color, with its bold blue on many days, brilliant sun some days, and dancing lights of the aurora on special occasions. The Christmas season arrived quietly, without commercial fanfare, forced smiles at parties, and media mania about watching your weight while eating fancy finger food at cocktail parties. There were no stores filled with plastic baubles, glitter, and gaudy garland to decorate trees sacrificed for the season or assembled in factories in far-away lands. Jesse found Christmas joy in a small collection of spruce cones stolen from snow-adorned trees, and a spruce bough shaped into a wreath hanging outside on a tent pole, with a bow fashioned from candy bar foil wrappers.

Sadie invited Jesse to spend time with her often. Jesse was always grateful for the warm cabin and interesting stories Sadie shared; reminiscent of times she made pies and cinnamon rolls in the kitchen with her grandmother. With meticulous detail, Sadie helped Jesse tan a hare hide for each of her parents, and agreed to mail them from Fairbanks when she went to spend the holiday with her family.

"They are going to think this is the weirdest thing ever." Jesse smiled as she set the hides on Sadie's table with a pile of papers folded on top, all tied with a piece of thick, brown carpet thread that Sadie gave her.

"Is that so? They have something against hides or hare?" Sadie patted the pile on the table and smiled at her young friend.

"No. They're just more… well, less nature-lovers than I am."

"They will just be so happy to hear from you and know that you are well. I know if I got such a gift, I would sit for hours and pet the pelt in my lap. I bet you they do the same."

"You could be right, Sadie. You generally are. Are you sure Fred doesn't mind mailing this for me? I put some money under the letters there for him, along with the address." Jesse loved the wise woman that held nothing back, not her love and care, her wisdom, her self-deprecating stories or her joyful laugh.

"Of course, it's no problem. Remember, he grew up out here. He knows what it means to help your neighbor out here." Sadie relaxed into the back of her chair with a plastic tote open at her feet, filled with gifts for family. "You see this one? This is a topsy-turvy doll for the youngest granddaughter."

Sadie picked a doll out of the tote and held it up for Jesse to see. "You see here, she has a little girl's face with long braids, bright kuspuk and a fur ruff around her face? When I turn her over, she's a grandmother with gray hair and a boring old-lady kuspuk."

"That's amazing, Sadie! She will love it. You are so incredibly talented. I'm in awe."

"Well, it's not that big of a thing. I will show you one day how to do it." Sadie pulled some more gifts from the tote and shared them with Jesse. There were pairs of mittens, yo-yo's, a couple of fur hats and several little mukluk and mitten Christmas tree ornaments made of felt, stuffed and trimmed with fur. "Here, I'm going to put these in your parents' box. Do you think they will like them?"

Sadie held out ornaments for Jesse to see - a pair of green mittens and red mukluks. A tear rolled down Jesse's cheek. She looked down, wiped it away with the back of her hand, and looked up at Sadie. "They would love those. Are you sure you have enough?"

"I'm sure." Sadie reached out and patted Jesse's hand. "I'm sorry to be leaving you at Christmas, but you can stay here at my place all you want. I mean that. I'll be back on the first of January. The kids don't have to work that day, so they always bring me back then. I'll have loads of leftovers and cookies and candy to share. We can have a late celebration." Jesse adored Sadie and thought it cute the way she referred to her grown children as kids.

"Thank you, Sadie. That sounds nice. I hope you enjoy the time with your family." Afraid she would be convinced to go into Fairbanks when Sadie's son, Fred, arrived, Jesse went back to her place. "I'm sorry I don't have a present for you, Sadie. I would give you something, if only I could think of something special enough for you."

"Just you being here is present enough, Jesse. It's been good for my spirit to be with you and teach you. You are the breath of fresh air this old lady needed." Sadie reached up to Jesse, grabbed her shoulders and pulled her close for a warm grandmother hug.

Jesse melted into Sadie, like a baby into the bosom of its mother. She loved this woman and felt a kinship like she had never before known.

. . .

Jesse napped off and on when she returned to her tent. Feeling the blues crowding in around the edges, she forced herself to get out of bed late in the afternoon. She gathered up the box stored away in a bear-proof container when she first moved to the property, smiling at the Christmas tree she had drawn on the outside. She felt like a kid in a candy store with this stash of special things for the season. She nudged it into her backpack and strapped on her snowshoes.

Guided in the darkness by her headlamp, Jesse found joy in the flotation of the snowshoes over the deep blanket of snow as she made her way back to Sadie's. The cabin was cool, but the coals were easily rekindled. Soon a warm blaze burned, with water heated for tea sweetened with Sadie's fireweed honey. She forced herself to sit in silence, images of past Sunday school pageants reeling through her head. She imagined her parents going to church services and gathering with family. Jesse enjoyed a long time of reflection before tearing into the Christmas box. She reached over to the radio and turned it on. Sadie had left the batteries in for Jesse, knowing she would tune in. It was too early for the Chatter, but some lively bluegrass came across the air pretty clearly.

By the time the Trapline Chatter started, Jesse had eaten a bowl of beef stew and finished two chocolate bars and three airplane-sized bottles of whiskey. She was fortunate to hear the message sent to her over the radio.

"And this message goes out to Jesse out in Lynx Creek from James. 'I have some mail for you. I'll be flying out tomorrow around noon. Meet me at the airstrip.' That's for you, Jesse, and if we don't talk to you again, have yourself a very Merry Christmas out there in lonely Lynx Creek from all of us here at Trapline Chatter."

Jesse tottered to the wood stove and stoked it for the night. She climbed into Sadie's bed and hugged a pillow close, feeling decades of love that rested in the pores of the wood and fused with the dust on the shelves. Amidst a swirl of bliss and melancholy, she passed out.

It was cold in the cabin when she finally woke. As she hopped out of Sadie's bed to build up the fire, goose bumps covered the sparse bare flesh. Her head pounded. She checked her watch. It was near ten o'clock; she had slept twelve hours! That was something she could not remember doing, ever. Jesse grabbed a piece of pilot bread to settle the gnawing ache in her stomach where the alcohol had rested before being absorbed during the night. She shook her head, trying to remember why she thought drinking all that whiskey was a good idea. Then she remembered the Trapline Chatter message.

"Oh, Jackrabbit, you've done it now," she scolded herself. She needed to get dressed fast in order to meet James at the airstrip on time. A distant smile crossed her lips as she remembered bittersweet moments from the past. A quick glance at the calendar resting on Sadie's bedside table told her it was December 17. Eight days until Christmas and ten days to the next full moon. She looked forward to both.

8

EARLY CHRISTMAS VISITOR

Mid December 1984
Lynx Creek airstrip

CRISP SNOW CRACKED beneath snowshoes as Jesse raced to the airstrip. She didn't expect a lot of mail, so she didn't trail the sled. Instead, she had dumped the contents of her backpack on Sadie's bed and worn the empty pack to meet James.

As she moved down the iced creek, Jesse thought about the day she arrived in June, six months earlier. The rivers and creeks were flowing, trees were leafed out and grasses were tall. Just out of Talkeetna, from the air, she saw scores of fishermen and boats on the rivers. She imagined the view from the air would be quite different today. If she were overhead now, she might see a snow-go, or a dog team out training, and possibly moose who would be more visible against the snow without the camouflage of summer foliage.

Jesse heard the plane before she saw it. The sound was not a smooth hum like that of a jet. It was more of a lazy, rugged growl that echoed in the vast valley between snow-covered mountains. She watched as James skillfully landed the ski plane and slid to a gentle stop. He beamed that bright smile as he stepped out of the cockpit.

"Well, hello Minnesota! It's great to see you looking so healthy out here." James meant it. Trips like this weren't always met with youth and health. He had picked up many a train wreck after hiking accidents, boating mishaps, and exposure.

"Hi, yourself!" Jesse returned the smile and lifted her gloved hand in a wave. "Nice to see you, too!"

She was relieved, and if she was honest, excited to see James. He was a good guy. Jesse looked down shyly, realizing what a mess she must be. Since the creek froze, the only baths were spit-baths or the occasional steam in Sadie's maqivik. Her hair was always braided, except for the shampoo time she incorporated into the steam. She looked forward to taking a steam alone with Sadie gone. Maybe even two. Usually they steamed naked together, to make the best use of the hot steam house instead of heating it separately twice, which would be an unforgivable use of hard-earned firewood.

Jesse looked up at the sky. "Looks like a beautiful day for a bird's-eye view."

"Oh, indeed it is! I love my job, but on days like this it hardly feels like a job. Not a single bit of wind or drop of precip. Heavenly, really."

They stood quietly for a moment, savoring the beauty surrounding them.

Several moments passed before James broke the silence. "Where's your sled? You're going to need more than that backpack for all the stuff I have for you."

Jesse looked at him with eyebrows drawn in, straining to understand how he could have much stuff for her.

"Sorry, I should have warned you. The folks around Talkeetna are givers. They donate food and gifts, then pack up care packages and send one out whenever we make a run. You got two of them because they have so many. And there must be some people in Minnesota who love you. You've got a few boxes and an impressive collection of envelopes, which I can only assume are Christmas cards."

"You've got to be kidding me! And all I sent was one measly package."

James laughed. "I'm sure whoever gets that will be happy to hear from you and share all your news."

"Yeah, but they are going to find the gifts to be bizarre."

"Did you send them moose nugget jewelry?" James and Jesse both laughed.

"Nothing quite that bad. I never got the appeal of shellacked moose poop hanging from one's ears or around the neck. I saw those in Anchorage at the store and I'm sure I rolled my eyes loudly." They laughed again.

"It's amazing how many are sold as souvenirs." James shook his head before continuing. "So, since you brought it up, what did you send?"

"Rabbit furs. They were the first that Sadie taught me to do. My parents love the outdoors, don't get me wrong, but they are not the hardcore survivalist type."

"I'm sure they will love them. Just knowing you thought of them and are doing well out here will please them and ease their minds."

James was on the ground now, facing Jesse. She gave him a quick, awkward hug. "Tell you what," he said. "I've got a toboggan over in the storage shed. I'll help you haul these things to your cab. . ."

"Oh, I couldn't ask you to do that!"

"You didn't. I don't have another flight until noon tomorrow, and it's a short one, so I've got time."

"Oh, James, that's so nice of you."

"Eh, it gives me a chance to stretch my legs and look over the place. Just hang out here and I'll be back in a few," he called out as he walked away.

James returned within five minutes, hauling a toboggan with wooden sides to hold cargo.

"Here we go. Let me just climb in and get those packages and hand them to you."

"Ok." Jesse was still shocked by the need for more than a backpack to get her windfall home.

One after another, James handed the boxes out of the plane. There were two styrofoam coolers (the gift boxes from the good people of Talkeetna), a bundle of mail wrapped in a plastic bag and four boxes varying in size from a box that checkbooks come in, to an apple crate. Then, there was a gift-wrapped box that obviously had not come through the mail. It even had a Christmas bow on it.

"I'll carry this one," James announced as he tucked the package under his arm. He pulled a red and white stocking cap out of his pocket, placed it on his head, and grabbed the towrope for the toboggan. "Merry Christmas, Jesse! Your Santa has arrived."

"You really do have the best job! Let's go see what's in these boxes."

"Lead the way."

"I'm actually staying at Sadie's, so let's just take everything there."

When the hard freeze had started last fall, Sadie generously offered to store Jesse's canned foods in her cabin to prevent the food from spoiling during the freeze-thaw cycle. That's another reason Jesse wanted to be at the cabin - to keep the temperature above freezing to protect their food.

While they walked, James told stories of trips he had flown since they last chatted. There were many fishing trips, a couple flights deep into the Brooks Range with hunting parties, and some cabin and lodge building supply runs. Contracted supply and guest runs that kept him busy during the summer and fall, had slowed down. He spoke of the trips to and from the Denali base camp.

"I'd love to get you over there to see the base camp. It's tucked in the north face of Mount Hunter. We'll drop off climbers and gear and return in about a month to pick them up. It's like an assembly line with a long string of people, some who trained together, and others total strangers who may not even speak the same language."

James's winter schedule included flying itinerant teachers out to the bush where they met with students, dropped off supplies and assessed their school performance.

"When you love being outdoors, like I do, there's never a boring day, that's for sure."

"Do you spend time with family for Christmas?" Jesse's longing for family and holiday traditions had intensified more each day as Christmas approached, and she wondered if that feeling would ease as she spent more time away.

"It's only my dad left, and I have one brother. I always reserve at least a week in the summertime when they come up from Oregon and fish, or just hang out. There have been a couple of years when my dad wasn't well enough to fish, so we were more low-key. He's doing well this winter, so we're hopeful we will get another big trip in next summer." James switched towing hands. "How about you? Do you think your parents will come visit?"

"Oh, they had better! My dad would be here in a heartbeat. It's my mom that struggles. She has a lot of anxiety, and she hates to fly. Being away from home is difficult for her. She's really lived quite a sheltered life, but I'm hoping she gets lonely enough for me and curious enough about my lifestyle that she decides to fly up."

"Do you have any siblings?"

"Yeah, I do. We're not terribly close, but they're welcome to come visit anytime and I've told them that. My sister is married to a military man. They are currently stationed in Hawaii, and she has no interest in leaving that to visit Alaska. Besides, they have young kids and are pretty busy. My brother is unlikely to spend the money to make the trip. He's pretty content in his corner of the world in Florida. Come to think of it - I've never visited him, either. I've never been invited."

"All families are unique, aren't they?"

"They sure are!"

The two tromped in silence the rest of the way to Sadie's cabin. Pale gray smoke rose from the chimney and faded into the random clouds overhead.

"Another beautiful day in paradise," Jesse said, barely above a whisper. This saying escaped her mouth often, as if it had become a mantra inseparable from her breath. It was an affirmation of all the beauty found in the enormity and minute intricacies around her. A wondrous co-existence in nature born of a boundless wisdom that surpassed human creativity.

"I'm going to grab some wood and bring it in. Do you have time to join me for a bite to eat, or do you need to get back to town?"

"I've got plenty of time. Thought maybe you wouldn't mind having some company for a while… maybe while you open your presents? At least the one there with the wrapping paper and bow?"

"I would love some company! I'll haul those boxes in, in just a sec. First, I want to get some more wood inside to thaw out."

"How about I take the boxes inside? Okay if I throw a log on the stove?"

"Yes, of course. There's plenty in the wood box inside."

Jesse didn't know why, but she needed a minute alone. Maybe it was all the time she spent in solitude since moving to the homestead, or maybe it was the season. There was plenty of wood gathered, but she used it as an excuse to soothe her overstimulated feelings and worried that James would see through that lame excuse to delay entering the cabin. She filled her arms with logs and split sections to use on the fire later. She glanced at the wood she had already hauled to the maqivik for an eventual steam bath. How she cherished that time of cleansing!

The stream of smoke from the chimney was thickening when Jesse got back to the cabin. Inside, James was heating water in the kettle.

"I hope you don't mind that I made tea without you. I know Sadie makes a great rosehip tea blend."

"Oh, please, help yourself. Thanks for bringing the packages in. I still can't believe there are so many. I feel like a spoiled child."

"I'm sure you've been a good girl this year and deserve all that you get." James threw a smile across the room, trying to get Jesse to lighten up a bit. "I bet if you open the coolers there, you'll find fudge from Jamie Cooley. She makes the best fudge. I heard this year she's packing rocky road into the boxes."

"Oh, if only it came with a glass of fresh milk! Canned and powdered is something I'm getting used to, but definitely not my favorite."

"Well, just maybe you'll find something like that in there. I'm not sure, but I know they have packed frozen half-gallons before, for that very reason."

Jesse opened the first cooler. The donors and volunteers had packed it to the brim with all kinds of wonderful things, including a frozen turkey breast, a pound of bacon, homemade cookies, breads, cheeses, sweets and a small bottle of Carolans Irish Cream. She unpacked a can of frozen orange juice and a Christmas tin filled with different kinds of fudge. There were two oranges and two apples, individually wrapped and lying on top, along with several handwritten Christmas notes in a clear plastic bag. The fruit was not frozen.

"This is just amazing! I feel so spoiled." Jesse held out the fudge tin. "Here, join me."

"Sure, but first I want to see if you find that milk. If not, you might have to use the Carolans."

Jesse stepped from the table into the galley area that served as Sadie's kitchen. She grabbed a plate and a knife, opened the giant can of peanut butter on the shelf and threw a big spoonful on the plate. She returned to the table, where James sat looking over the groceries Jesse had unpacked. Within minutes, she sliced the apples and put out peanut butter for dipping them in.

"This is one of my all-time favorite snacks. These apples are amazing!" Jesse was eating two slices to each of James's one.

"It's probably been a while since you had fresh fruit, huh?"

"Well, Sadie's son and grandsons brought some out, a couple apples and some oranges, around Halloween, but I think they were pretty old when he bought them because they were not nearly as fresh and juicy as these. Let's see what's in that other cooler."

Jesse spotted the milk right off. "We've struck gold! Here it is. A half-gallon of full fat milk! I'm going to set this by the stove and see if I can get it to melt some."

She grabbed a stool and set it near the stove, with the milk carton on top of it. "I feel like a spoiled kid in a candy store wanting immediate gratification."

She unpacked the rest of the second cooler and discovered a small, canned ham, three little cans of pineapple juice, a can of pineapple rings, a bag of peanuts, a quart of yogurt, a small frozen beef roast, six potatoes, two onions, four carrots and a carton of eggs.

"This is really amazing. I need to write these guys a thank you note. Do you have time for me to do that now, or do you need to go?"

"Actually, Jesse, I'm enjoying this. I feel like I'm watching a kid's first Christmas." James looked over at the recliner in the corner, opposite the only bed in the room. "I'm not trying to be forward, but if it's alright with you, I'd like to just hang out here, which means I'll need to spend the night. It'll be dark soon and there are no lights at the airstrip."

In her enthusiasm, Jesse hadn't even considered the logistics that James had to manage. "Of course, I would love the company. And there is so much good stuff here to share! I could go back to my tent and you could have the bed here, if that would be better."

"Heck no. I've slept on many a cot, floor and chair across this state. I just don't want you to feel uncomfortable."

"Well, I might snore, but other than that, I'm good." Jesse wanted James's friendship and who wouldn't like an adult sleepover when you have been isolated from anyone near your age? She did not allow herself to feel any physical stirrings, just a desire to connect with another person who understood, probably better than she, what her life was like. There was nothing wrong with James. He was great - attractive, interesting, accomplished, loved the outdoors... She just didn't acknowledge any feelings of chemistry between them, and if he did, he was too much of a gentleman to let on.

"It's early enough that I could make us up a roast for dinner. What do you think? I've got moose, or moose. Unless you would rather have a bird or some fish. Honestly. I would love to dig into that turkey breast there, but it will never thaw in time."

"I'm good with..."

"Oh, wait! I almost forgot the ham! You will eat ham, won't you?"

"You bet I will. Are you sure you don't want to save it, though?"

"Oh, man. I'm sure! I'll even share my potatoes with you." Jesse started rooting through the boxes, making piles of things to use for dinner, and a pile to put outside to stay cold until she took it to her cache, probably the next day.

"So, if you're not flying today, does that mean you can join me for a drink? I know it's early, but I'm considering this an official holiday."

"Sure, I'll join you for one. That Carolans is pretty sweet. Do you have anything to cut it with?"

"It's really sweet, and with all this fudge waiting to be eaten, I'm not sure I can hack it right now." Jesse walked over and swirled the milk thawing by the stove. "Still pretty frozen."

She continued toward the pile of stuff on the bed that she had dumped from her backpack earlier. She picked up a partially drunk fifth of vodka. "I was thinking of having a shot of vodka with some of that juice. How would that be for you?"

"Now you're talking." James walked to the galley and found two tin cups. He brought them back to the table and set them in front of Jesse, who was shaking a can of pineapple juice.

"Pineapple okay for you, or do you want me to thaw out the orange juice?"

James laughed. "I'm really low maintenance. The pineapple sounds good to me."

Jesse poured them each a drink and made a plate of sliced cheese with some saltines from a tin on Sadie's shelf. "Call Sadie's son, Fred, when you get back to town and have him bring some saltines when he brings Sadie back, will ya? She loves them with her stew, and I'm afraid I might eat them all."

"Will do." James picked up his cup. "I'd like to toast you, Minnesota. I remember the day you waltzed into the Talkeetna airport."

Jesse laughed. "Stumbled in, you mean. I nearly hit a moose on my way."

"Well, I didn't want to mention that, but you can be sure Lucky told that story for weeks downtown. He always painted you in a good light. Anyway, back to my toast. You, uh, stumbled into the airport, the shine of the city barely washed out of your clothes and look at you now. Right at home amongst the wild things out here in the middle of nowhere, but only a quick plane ride to everywhere. Cheers to you, Minnesota!"

Jesse reached out and clanked her tin cup against James's. "And cheers to an early Christmas with a new friend. I truly have the best life!"

Jesse took a drink, set the cup down, and poured a little more vodka in. She did the same for James. They chuckled. "Let's make this a proper party."

9

CHRISTMAS GIFTS

December 1984
    Cozy cabin

"I THINK you might want to save those presents from home for the real Christmas, but how about opening that other one there?"

"Tell me, James. Is this from you?"

"It is, and it isn't. I was doing a little shopping the other day and ran into old Jay. He asked if I had seen you and I told him I was getting ready to come on out and deliver your mail and stuff. He went around that store, picked up a couple things, then went out to his truck and brought something else in and asked that I bring it to you. So, here in this box, you have the Jay and James royal package."

"Really?! You guys are so nice, and I have nothing to give in return."

"Nobody expects you to give us anything. It's not every Christmas that we get a sweet, capable cheechako to root for out here. Consider us your mascots."

Jesse looked over the package, turning it in her hands. It

was about the size of a breadbox, wrapped in Christmas paper with a white background and a small, traditional poinsettia design. A large red ribbon crossed from side to side and a big red bow rested on top.

Jesse set it on the table and rotated the box, admiring the wrapping some more. She was struggling to find the words to describe how she felt, in her borrowed home, with her new friend, sharing the wealth of gifts from strangers, a million miles from what she had known as normal every Christmas before. "I never imagined I would have a real Christmas present to open this year. It's so nice. I hate to break the seal on the paper."

"Rip it off and throw it on the fire," James ordered. "I would normally recycle a brown paper bag, but the store was offering free wrapping, so you have one of a couple hundred gifts in the area wrapped in that paper."

"Well, if you put it like that," Jesse retorted, "let's see what's inside."

Jesse carefully broke the seal on the tape, unwrapped the package and gently lifted the lid off the box. Inside was an assortment of things she never knew she would appreciate so much. Sitting on top was a small bottle of what looked like perfume. She pulled it out and held it up with a puzzled look on her face. Perfume would be impractical for someone living Jesse's lifestyle.

James shrugged his shoulders and smiled sheepishly. "Yeah, well, the clerk said this was a very popular gift this year, and when I told her it was going to a fly-in location, she told me it was an essential oil made by someone in the bush who harvested wildflowers and plants and infused them in the oil, then bottled and labeled it. To me, it smells like spring, and she said it had some lavender in it, so it was good for skin issues."

Jesse screwed the lid off and held the bottle to her nose. With eyes closed, she drew in a deep breath. "This is amazing! Thank you. And thanks to the pushy clerk. Good call."

Next, she pulled out a box of chocolate-covered cherries. "Here's a Christmas staple where I come from."

Jesse opened the box and shared a cherry with James before pulling out a gift wrapped in gold foil paper with a white bow. She gently set it on the table. "Oh wow!"

"That's a present from Jay."

"Saving that for last." Jesse plunged her hands back into the box. They landed on a piece of metal that looked like a cross between a food grater and a miniature rake. Holding it up with a quizzical look, she asked, "Hey, what's this?"

"I guess that means you don't already have one. I was a little worried that you might."

"Nope. I've never even seen one of these. Let me guess. It's for picking up moose poop to make jewelry?" They laughed.

"No, it's for picking berries. It will be great out here when the blueberries ripen. Even with this, you'll never be able to pick all that grows on your property alone in a good year."

"So cool! I look forward to putting it to good use. This year I hand-picked as many as I could, but even I have my limits." Jesse held up her hands and looked them over. "I'm surprised the purple stains are gone. They seemed to last forever." She reached across the table and gently set her hand on James's. "You are so thoughtful."

James blushed and pressed his hips from side to side, wiggling on his chair. "I haven't actually used one, but I've seen them at the lodges I go to, and the women there swear by them."

Jesse pulled her hand away. "There is a blueberry pie in your future, James."

"Oh, I look forward to that!"

Jesse continued to pull gifts out of the box and studied each one. There were three notebooks and a package of colored pens - for keeping a journal or a log, James said. There were two decks of Alaska playing cards, a ceramic mug with a funny saying on it, and lining the bottom of the box were two books:

So Long, and Thanks for All the Fish and *The Unbearable Lightness of Being*.

As she leafed through the pages, Jesse exclaimed, "This is some serious reading!"

"These are popular books right now. Several of my friends recommended them. I thought you might want some brain stimulation out here where you don't get to talk to people much. Except Miss Sadie."

"Thank you! I've already read all the books I brought out. I look forward to tearing into these."

"And you know, they have a dual purpose. Lots of people recycle their books into toilet paper. You can't imagine how many novels are in outhouse holes." They laughed again. "The first time I saw a paperback sitting on the throne in an outhouse, I couldn't figure it out. It's really not a great reading place. Then I learned the truth. Folks sure are resourceful."

"I can't keep track of all the things I've learned from Sadie, and I had studied at the library for months before coming here."

James laughed and raised his eyebrows as he took a drink. "I know what you mean. Books can only tell you so much. Homesteading in Alaska is not the same as homesteading in the Ozarks or Montana, even. The edge is a little sharper and the land more remote and inaccessible here."

Jesse nodded as she organized the new loot and read the back covers of the new books, momentarily lost in thoughts of Christmas moments from years past. A different time, a different place, yet some of the same enduring feelings.

"I think I'll go out and chop a little wood for Sadie. I'm not very good at just sitting around." James got up and put his jacket on, leaving Jesse to her thoughts.

"Oh, sure. I'm going to get these potatoes cooking and get the ham ready to warm up. I'll be out to help stack in a bit."

Jesse labored over the proper placement of the ham in the Dutch oven. The pot had three legs so it would not be resting directly on the wood stove, but she still hesitated to put the pineapple rings on the bottom of the pot, fearing the natural sugars would burn too easily. Instead, she poured pineapple juice in the bottom of the pot, added a few slices of onion, and set the ham on top. She covered the pot, threw another log on the fire and adjusted the vent before going outside to stack wood.

Jesse and James worked side by side until after dark, chopping and stacking wood. They had a natural rhythm together in their movements. "So, have you always wanted to be a pilot in Alaska?"

Stacking a stick of split wood on the pile, James paused, looking off into the distant sky as he recalled his early days. "I had a longing to explore this state from a young age. It was a little later that I became a pilot. Somehow, along life's journey, I met a guy we called Rage. Rage was one of a kind."

"Oh, yeah? How so?" Jesse set her axe down, then brushed wood splinters from her shirt.

James dropped the axe into his target, the center of the next cut of log, splitting it perfectly in two. "He was the kind of fella that shifted into the wind when he was hiking or climbing, adding resistance against his stride. Rage marched on, plowing new trails through the deepest snows, suspending puffs of snow with each step. Once, I asked him why he worked so hard against the elements, instead of working with them."

"Did he have an answer for you?" Jesse was curious why someone would work harder than they already had to out here.

"He sure did, and it was filled with backwoods wisdom and decades of experience. He said it was the best way he knew of to prepare himself for the unspeakable tragedies that inevitably happen in life."

"I guess that makes a lot of sense, but it seems a bit extreme. Certainly not my motto—smarter, not harder. How did he get his name, Rage?" Jesse thought it sounded like a tragic nickname with a loaded story, much like her high school classmate, Jamie Held, who accidentally shot his father in a hunting accident and was forever after known as Trigger.

James finished his swing before explaining. "Actually, his Dutch parents gave it to him. Apparently, it's a family name. It didn't fit his personality at all. He was one of the most humble, honest, hard-working men I ever met. He was like a surrogate father to me, but the big C took him down. The man never had a single accident in his forty years of flying up here."

"He sounds like an amazing man, and you, a lucky one to work with him." Jesse recognized the look of someone lost in thought. She put her axe down and walked to the cabin, leaving James with his memories.

Jesse moved in and out of the cabin, nursing the ham, so it was perfectly warm and juicy when they were ready for dinner. The potatoes were deeply browned on the outside. Inside, they were cooked perfectly, with a rustic smoky flavor. As Jesse set the table, James pulled a bottle of wine from his backpack. Jesse gave him a look out of the corner of her eye, suspicious of his obvious pre-planning for this sleepover.

"Don't look at me like that. I always carry one of these in my overnight pack, just in case. When I'm in town, it's common courtesy for me to take a bottle of wine when I go to dinner at friends' homes. Why should it be any different out here?"

"True," Jesse conceded. "I appreciate it. I haven't had wine since before I came out here."

"Wine, except at the lodges, seems to be a special occasion beverage out here. Except for those folks who make their own. You may discover ways to make it yourself or start brewing your own beer. Lots of folks do that."

James found their tin cups and filled each with wine. "So,

how has the time been for you with Sadie? She's quite a woman."

Jesse recounted stories of learning about traps, tracks and scat. "She has a deep respect for nature and the animals. She prays over each animal harvested and is always teaching me something… about animal behavior, the weather, the sky. Sadie is a walking encyclopedia of how to live with nature. I'm grateful she befriended me."

"She doesn't like everyone. She obviously likes you, or she wouldn't be teaching you these things."

"Well, here it is - our pre-Christmas Christmas dinner." Jesse set the pot and potatoes on the table. She avoided making extra side dishes, hoping instead that they would eat up much of the ham. If there were leftovers, she would put them in lentil soup, like her grandfather had taught her to make.

"It smells fabulous. I can't wait to dig in. Do you mind if I say grace?" James looked at Jesse for approval.

"Of course not. Thank you." Jesse put her hands in James's outstretched hands while he gave thanks for the meal, the friendship, the beauty and bounty of the land they both enjoyed.

"That was nice. Thanks. And here's a toast to the baby Jesus, unexpected gifts, friendship, and my first wood-fired Christmas dinner attempt."

"It looks like a great success to me." James was sincere. There wasn't anything about Jesse that didn't impress him.

Dinner was indeed a success, and there were plenty of Christmas treats to enjoy for dessert. Neither tired of listening to or telling stories and both enjoyed the well-wishes news from the interior on Trapline Chatter. Jesse's ears perked up and it surprised her to hear her name during the show.

The night was clear, and the radio had new batteries, so there was no interference. "And to Jesse of Lynx Creek, I hope you're keeping warm in the cabin. No sense roughing it if you don't have to. And a big Christmas hello to your visitor there. Hi James. Love, Sadie."

Jesse's eyes grew wide, and she threw her hands up in the air. "How did she?"

"I told you that Sadie is quite a lady." James smiled. "She knows everything that goes on out here. We could speculate all night about how she knew I was out here visiting, but it doesn't really matter. Just know - she knows all."

"Noted. I guess it's a good thing she likes you, or she may have given me a piece of her mind."

"Now that's true enough."

Jesse leaned back in the old wooden chair with a belly full of great food, an empty glass with a wine bottle in front of her, and a heart swollen with the joy of time spent with a new friend celebrating the holy Christmas.

"You know, you never opened that present from Jay. I think you set it up on the shelf there when you were cleaning up."

"Oh, wow. You're right! Let me do that now." Jesse tried to reach the package from her seat, but her stretch was not quite long enough. Lazily, she pushed herself up from the chair. "You need anything while I'm up?"

"If that kettle on the stove still has some water, I'm thinking of having a cup of tea with a splash of that milk you got thawed out. I don't think we drank it all with our fudge dessert, did we?"

"That's a great idea. No, we didn't drink all that yummy milk and I'm not sure why! There's plenty left."

Jesse poured hot water into their tin cups and fished tea bags out of Sadie's stash. She got the milk from the cooler and was just about to sit.

"Don't forget the present!"

"Oh! Thanks!" She laughed. "Like they say, I'd lose my head if it wasn't attached."

"Yeah, I doubt that. I think you've pretty much got yourself together. It might be you are drunk on good food and wine. That'll make you for…"

"I'm not drunk. See - I can walk a straight line, Officer Fancy Pants." Jesse demonstrated her heel to toe skills across the cabin floor.

"Yes'm you sure can. I take it back."

Again, Jesse forgot to grab the present and remembered it just as she was sitting. James roared with laughter. "What's your excuse this time?"

"I was just enjoying myself. It's been a long time since I've had so many laughs." She finally set Jay's wrapped package on the table.

"Do you know what's in here?"

"I sure do. I saw it before they wrapped it."

"I can't believe Jay would send a present out for me. You know, I only met him that once and already he's sending me gifts and doing me favors."

"Folks in Alaska can be like that. We have to have each other's backs, you know. The other thing you should know, and it might not be true for you or me, but it's true for many people. They come up here to escape situations and people. A lot of folks want to be as far away from their family as possible, and then, when they get here, they make a new family of their own choosing."

"Is that so? I did not know that." Jesse puckered her lips, pushing the bottom lip forward, like she did when thinking hard about something.

"Most don't know that when they first get here, but as you meet people, you'll hear all kinds of stories."

"I got the feeling that Jay had a story. He's so smart and so kind. I can't imagine what it would be, but it seemed like there was something there."

"Well, if there is, and you're probably right, I have no clue what it is. He really keeps to himself. In fact, it really surprised me to hear he offered to help you find a snow-go."

"Really? I'm going to call you Gossip Gert! How do you know he's doing that?"

"I guess people think it's my business to know everything. I don't know. But I think he has a lead on a good rig for you."

"That's great to hear." Jesse picked up the gift and shook it. She heard a small rattling from inside the box. "Sounds like a baby rattler in here."

"That would be a novel idea, since there are no snakes in Alaska. The ground is too cold for them."

"You are just filled with helpful facts, aren't you? I guess I better open it up and find out." Jesse unwrapped the package and found a beautiful hand-carved ivory cribbage board inside.

"This is amazing!" She ran her fingertips across the scrimshaw and felt the counting holes. "And I love cribbage! I used to play with my dad."

"He told me some about it, if you want to know more."

"Of course I do! Give me the scoop."

James picked up the board. "This is a walrus tusk. The scrimshaw, that's the carving, is a dog team, sled and musher."

He turned the board over and opened the hatch. "See, even the pegs are ivory."

He held them up for Jesse to inspect. "Jay bought this from the artist at a craft fair in Fairbanks. It was the end of the fair and the man was sitting at the table in his booth when Jay started talking to him. He learned about the man's family."

James pointed out the name carved under the image of the musher. "See, here, this is his signature. His name is Fred Kokeok, and he lives in a small village up north called Shishmaref. If you get a map, you can find it on the Chuckchi Sea near Nome. They are kind of famous for their carvers. Anyway, Jay was talking to this Fred, who told him he had sold everything but this one piece. He carves all year and does just the one fair. Everything else goes to art galleries in Anchorage. He held this piece back from the gallery, hoping to use it as an eye-catcher for his table at the fair. I guess it worked if it was the only thing he had left. Fred told Jay he was married to a white woman. She came to the village to be a teacher years ago. But in the last year, the doctors diagnosed her with cancer and they were having a tough go of it financially. They have two kids outside in college and really wanted to fly them home for Christmas as they weren't too sure how much more time his wife had. Jay just knew he had to help the guy out, so he bought this piece. Jay doesn't play cribbage, so he was just waiting for the right opportunity to pass it on, and here you are. He even threw in a little primer on cribbage that he got from someone else in the area, just in case you didn't know how to play."

Jesse put her head in her hands, and soon her palms were wet with tears. She shook her head, then lifted her eyes to meet James. "I am so honored to have such an incredible gift with such a moving story. Christmas on Christmas on Christmas. Please tell him how I cherish the gift, will you?"

"Of course I will, and you can tell him when you eventually see him with your snow-go."

"I sure will."

Suddenly Jesse was exhausted. The day had been filled with emotion, work, socialization and all the good feelings. "I'm sorry, James, but I'm beat. I'm going to put some wood on and hit the hay. Do you need anything before I do?"

"No, I'm good. I'll just do a walk around outside and brush my teeth. I'll turn this light out when I'm done."

"If you want to read or something, that light will not bother me."

Jesse tidied the table, poured out a little warm water, and quickly washed her face and brushed her teeth. She fell into Sadie's bed, wrapped in the blessed feeling of this Christmas experience in her new life.

10

—————

JOY AT CHRISTMAS

Christmas 1984
    Homestead

IT WAS dark when Jesse stirred in bed to the smell of fresh brewed coffee. James wore a headlamp, the light on low as he moved about the cabin.

"Oh, good morning, I think." Jesse stretched her fully clothed body under the covers of Sadie's bed. Deep winter was not the time to sleep alone in anything less than full coverage and expect to get a good night's sleep.

"Sorry if I woke you." James spoke quietly and sweetly, without looking directly at Jesse and shining the headlamp on her face.

"Oh, no. It's all good. I smell coffee and it smells wonderful." Jesse sat on the edge of the bed, taking inventory of her body and remnants from their Christmas celebration.

"I think it will be. I have an electric pot at my house, but I seem to remember how to make camp coffee."

"So, how was that chair for you? I've nodded off in it a time or two myself."

"Yeah. It was fine. I've definitely had worse beds. By about four, I had no choice but to get up and stoke the fire. I think you're a bit more used to the frosty nights than I am. I run a Toyo oil stove at my place as backup to the wood burner. If I don't wake up for wood, I don't freeze."

"Sounds like quite a luxury."

"It's a necessity for me, since I'm gone from home so much and don't want everything in the place to freeze while I'm away."

"Yep, I get it. If you'll excuse me, the outhouse is calling." Jesse threw on her parka and boots and rushed out the door.

By the time she returned, James had a cup of coffee poured for each of them and was whitening his with milk.

"I hope you don't mind."

"Of course not. Throw a shot of that into mine too, if you will. I like to put maple syrup in mine. Would you like a pour?"

"Sounds good. Thanks."

"I think I was dreaming about fried potatoes and onion with fresh eggs during the night. I can taste them. If I cook some up, will you join me?"

"Sounds like a real treat. Could I interest you in a game of cribbage while the potatoes cook?"

"If you play, of course! You didn't let on that you knew how to play." The thought of playing a game of cribbage again animated Jesse.

"Yeah, there really wasn't a good opening for that last night. Anyway, I do and I enjoy it. I've got a running game going with a couple of buddies. We only get together a couple times a year, but there's always a game to get back into."

"Sounds like Dad and me. I'm sure he still has that little spiral notebook sitting by his chair with our game notes in it."

Jesse hummed as she chopped food and tossed it into the fry pan with melted butter. Until James brought the food boxes, she hadn't realized just how much she missed some of the usual staples. She made mental notes for future shopping trips and for storage plans in her cabin.

By the time the duo finished breakfast and several games of cribbage, it was light enough to walk to the airstrip.

"You don't have to walk me to the plane. I'm okay to get back on my own."

"Are you kidding?! It's the least I can do after all you've done for me."

James chuckled. "Well, it doesn't seem like I did anything but bum a sleep and eat your food."

Jesse reached out and gave him a playful shove. "Is that what this was? You were just couch surfing?"

"No, that was not my intent, but you pulled out the groceries and the booze and I couldn't pull myself away."

They laughed as they headed out. James carried the empty sled, and Jesse trailed close behind. "To be honest, James, you really brought a ray of sunshine and I thank you for that. It was so nice to hang out and, my goodness, all the great food you brought! This, my first Christmas on the homestead, will be one to remember. And, I'd have to check the score, but I think I'm ahead in the great cribbage game of the century."

"The game's not over yet. Don't count your pegs before they're played!"

Jesse drew a deep breath in, then held her hand over her nose to melt the ice crystals that were forming there. The sky grew in colorful beauty as they watched the sun breach the horizon and fan out in rays of promise on the tilted earth, which hid light for long hours each day.

"So, what will you do today? Catch up on your soap operas? Hang some laundry out to dry? Check some traps?"

"Oh, nothing so boring. The television is on the fritz, the washing machine is down, and Sadie and I pulled all the traps so I get a vacation, too. I think I will sit around and eat bon-bons all day. Maybe call the masseur to rub my feet later and the house staff will have my bath drawn and bed turned down in the evening." Jesse giggled, a light airy sound she hadn't heard from herself in a long time. Almost flirty, but not quite. "Jealous?"

"Oh, I do like bon-bons!"

"How about you, James? What does your day bring?" Jesse knew he had a flight planned today. She also knew he wasn't dating anyone and had a lot of friends, but she wasn't really sure what his days were like.

"I have this trip to fly, then I'll be home doing some of the same things you'll be doing. Except I will also have to do paperwork for my business, call my family because we stay in close touch, and finish up my Christmas cards."

Silence fell as they walked the last couple hundred yards to the airstrip. As they approached, birds hopped in the trees, sending fresh snow falling from the branches. James threw his gear into the plane, and then started the generator that would warm it up again after sitting for hours in the sub-zero temperature. Jesse helped him remove the thermal blankets that cocooned parts of the plane, and stood with him as heaters warmed the cockpit and engine. James explained the things he did to make sure the plane was air-ready this time of year, and the dangers in the ever-changing sky.

"I've lost a couple of pilot friends who got caught in bad weather, and they were experienced and reputable pilots, so I'm careful. The last thing I will do is radio the Talkeetna airport and get the latest weather report. Only when I get a satisfactory report, will I fly. That's why I always carry survival gear. I can build a shelter in the ice and snow and survive weeks if I need to."

"I hope it never comes to that."

"Me, too, Jesse. Some may think I'm too safe and they are inconvenienced if I'm delayed, but we are all still alive to complain about it."

"I like your attitude. It'll keep you alive. James - it was great to spend time with you. Don't be a stranger. Please stop by anytime."

"Thanks, Jesse. I enjoyed the time, too. Keep me posted on when you want to make a trip to town. I can always deadhead you between runs."

"I appreciate that. There's something about staying through breakup that I need to do this first year. It's some sort of mind bending I have to do to prove I can handle this lifestyle long term."

"I get it. By the way, for what it's worth, I think you're doing great. You don't even seem to have cabin fever. You're strong in mind, body, and spirit."

"Why thank you, sir! That's a compliment coming from you."

"I'm not so special, but I've seen a few things in my flying days, and you are nothing like some of the train wrecks I've seen. Anyway, you have a lot to look forward to in the coming months. We didn't even get to talk about your building plans."

"Ah, yeah, we didn't. If you get some time as the days get longer, stop by for a visit and we can talk about it. I look forward to that."

"I'll do that, yeah, for sure."

James drew her in for a hug, his arms barely reaching around the puffy parka. "Merry Christmas Jesse."

Soon James was in the air, heading to land further north. Jesse waved one last farewell and spoke into the empty cold air, "Merry Christmas my friend."

BEFORE SHE CAME to live on the land, Jesse heard about the desolation of the frozen winters in Alaska's interior. Long dark days, chilly nights, dangerous wild animals, and the absence of conveniences were the negative things she had heard or read about. Her experience did not follow those warnings. Living on the land that first winter, she found it to be far more alive as she paid attention to the minutia. The silence of the vast expanse was deafening some days as she quietly explored the frozen winter, finally alone for several days in her own new space. She listened to the sounds of the birds and the tiny critters that scampered about. She snuck through the brush to watch the animals at work. Watching them without the threat of trapping them was a relief. Spruce hen and ptarmigan surprised Jesse when they stirred within arm's reach. Sometimes she was close enough to see the thick, winter-white feathers covering the feet of the ptarmigan. The absence of mosquitoes was a bonus. The power of the stiff wind took her breath away on those days it visited. When she tried to make a quick trip to the outhouse without properly bundling up in gloves, hat, boots and coat, she suffered the freezing temperatures.

Jesse planned her days around Trapline Chatter, looking forward to the broadcast every evening in the last days leading to Christmas. The well wishes, Christmas stories, and seasonal songs highlighted her evenings. She made daily treks to her homestead, kept the fire built up there and chopped wood, while keeping the fire going and wood supply up at Sadie's as well. There was plenty of time for self-reflection. Using one of the new notebooks, she started an almanac of sorts. Daily, she made notes on the weather, hours of daylight, and animal sightings. Some days she added reflections, if she was so moved.

"December 23, 1984. Sunrise, 10:59 a.m. Sunset 2:41 p.m. 0 degrees at 6:00 a.m. 16 degrees at 2:00 p.m. Heatwave! Decided not to sauna today. Will wait for a colder day to really get the benefit. So grateful to use Sadie's cabin. Looking forward to having my own. We have passed winter solstice (Dec. 21) and now the days are gaining daylight - noticeably.

Took a long walk along the Skwentna River today - heard ice cracking and saw beaver tracks. Going to bed early with a good new book."

On Christmas Eve, Jesse read the Christmas story in Sadie's well-used Bible, which sat on the bedside table. She doodled with her new colored pens and listened to the radio all day. There were many Trapline Chatter messages, including three for her. Her family usually feasted on chili and oyster stew with a wide variety of Christmas cookies and candy after attending the church candlelight service. Jesse was content to be listening to the radio by candlelight, eating split pea and ham soup with a simple baking powder biscuit cooked up on the wood stove, and munching on goodies for dessert.

Jesse chose one of the remaining boxes to open in the evening, another family tradition. It was from her sister and family in Hawaii. Her sister had written a five-page letter, sharing all the news of the family, school activities for the kids, details of life in Hawaii and all the things they would talk about if they were together for the holiday. Jesse took her time reading it, imagining they were having an actual conversation. She read parts out loud to break the silence.

Inside the package were two paperbacks: *Clan of the Cave Bear* and *The Valley of Horses*. Jesse had not read either of them and thought they looked interesting. Typically, she was not a big reader; but she found more time to read now that her commute to work was feet rather than miles, and she spent no time shopping. There were chocolate-covered macadamia nuts, two pounds of ground coffee, pictures of the family, chocolate ornament-shaped candy wrapped in foil, two pairs of wool socks and two pairs of sock liners and a bottle of lotion with a little note taped to it. Jesse read the note aloud and smiled. "Everyone needs a little pampering, even if you can't soak in the tub first." At the bottom of the box was a three-inch stuffed koala. According to her sister's letter, it was from her youngest niece's personal collection "to keep Auntie company."

Jesse put all the gifts back in the box and pulled the box in close to her chest. She closed her eyes and silently gave thanks for her caring family. She prayed for their health and happiness.

JESSE STAYED in bed on Christmas morning, reading with a flashlight. She got up only to keep the stove fueled. It was after ten when she finally got out of bed for the day. She opened the door to find three new inches of fluffy snow and a brilliant sun illuminating the quiet, white world. Jesse promised herself to do no work all day, to keep the cabin extra toasty, and nap if she wanted to. She opened the last of the gifts in shifts during the day. The first she opened in the late morning as she sipped coffee. It was from her brother. She was shocked. Unless they were together, which happened only every few years, she didn't get a gift or even a card from him. This year he sent both. There was no long recitation of the year's happenings, only a "Hope you're doing well up there" and "Mom and Dad really miss you" written on the Hallmark card. In the box, she found a new cassette player, several cassettes, including one with a large #1 written on it, and a jumbo collection of batteries.

"Interesting," Jesse thought as she put fresh batteries into the gadget, stuck the #1 cassette in and pressed play. Her brother's voice boomed through the speakers. He explained his thinking behind this gift. It was two-fold: to document a verbal journal, and to record messages, stories, life, to share with their parents who miss her. She listened to her brother's message three times before setting the recorder down and making a list of things to tell her parents about, but had not yet put in a letter. By the time she finished recording that first message, Jesse had filled two full tapes. She placed them in a large envelope, conveniently provided by her brother, and addressed it to her parents. She would ask Sadie's son to take it to town and mail it for her.

Jesse's father and mother each packed a gift for her, and they were as divergent as their personalities. It was mid-afternoon, and the sun had fallen behind the earth's edge when she opened the gift from her mother. It was filled with softness. There were two long-sleeved silk undershirts and matching long underwear. There were marshmallow Santas, photos of her parents, a high-loft lap quilt, fluffy slippers, two rolls of toilet paper, some newsstand magazines, and a book by Louise Hay: You Can Heal Your Life. Jesse wondered if Mom thought her life was broken. To the contrary, Jesse felt she was just now finding herself, her life. They threw miscellaneous candies in for good measure, and packing material. In a long letter, her mother shared stories of childhood Christmas pageants, favorite decorations and family get-togethers. She also shared her annual garden plans for the coming growing season.

Jesse ate dinner, cleaned up the dish, updated the entries in her daily log, stoked the fire, and poured herself a drink before she sat down to open her father's gift. She knew it would be unique and special. She shared a special bond with her father, who admired her strong-willed force and love for nature. His gift didn't disappoint. She started with the letter. He shared household, church and national political news, updated her on two childhood friends he had recently seen, and then he painstakingly detailed each gift he had packed. There was a spud, a tool for removing bark from logs. His research showed she might go through several of these, of different sizes and shapes, before she had all the logs ready for her cabin. She had peeled some logs in the late fall, but stopped when snow fell. It was a tedious job that required muscle and just the right touch to slide the peeler between the bark and the wood of the log.

Jesse's father explained his search for the perfect do-it-yourself cabin-building book. "In our local bookstores, all such books had details that are not relevant to your project. They illustrated wiring diagrams and indoor plumbing. In the end, I chose two books, and between them I expect you will find useful details to help you have a solid roof over your head by the end of summer."

Jesse spent hours looking through the two books, delaying the rest of the unwrapping for the following day. She drifted off to sleep with a mind racing with ideas for her cabin and a content soul. She was truly happy.

11

WINTER FUN

Early 1985

Sadie's place

JAY KEMP FOLLOWED through on his promise to bring Jesse an iron dog. He rode out with Sadie's son Fred and his wife, who drove Jesse's machine. The night before they arrived, Jesse got word through Trapline Chatter. "And a message goes out to Jesse from Jay. I will deliver your iron dog tomorrow. Stay with Sadie and we will find you."

It was early January and there was nearly four feet of snow piled on the ground. Jesse was gaining confidence in her snowshoes, but knew she could explore further with a snow-go.

"QUIET. HEAR THEM COMING?" Sadie pushed the fur ruff of her kuspuk hood back.

"What?" Jesse looked bewildered.

"Shhhhh! You'll see them coming down the creek soon. Look." Sadie nodded toward a bend in the creek where it reached out to connect with the mighty river. Small clouds of airborne snow lifted as the snow-gos powered toward them.

"Sadie, look! We have company."

Jesse unstrapped her snowshoes, leaned them against a tree, and walked onto the frozen creek to greet the travelers. As soon as he dismounted, she ran to Jay and threw her arms around him. "Oh, Jay, it's so great to see you! And before any more time passes, thank you for the incredible Christmas present."

Jay wasn't accustomed to such closeness, especially with a female. He had been alone in the woods for a long time. But Jesse was young enough to be his daughter, so he warmed into the embrace and gave her a smile. "It's great to be here, and you are welcome. I hear you're on a winning streak." Jay winked.

He turned to Sadie and gave a wave with a giant furry mitten. "Good to see you, Sadie."

Sadie smiled and nodded. She liked that Jay Kemp. He was a smart, solid man who never overstayed his welcome.

Fred introduced his wife, Debbie, to Jesse. "Thank you, Debbie, for bringing my snow-go out. I'm sorry you had to leave your kids and grandkids for the day."

"Oh, don't be sorry. I'm a third-grade teacher. A break from the kids is welcome, even a break from my own!" Debbie was a pale, petite, and pretty woman. Physically, she was the exact opposite of Fred, a tan, burly Alaska Native. Yet their similarities were striking. They were both quick to smile and listened intently in conversation. Their input was informative or positive, not judgmental or adversarial. Sadie had told Jesse how much she liked her daughter-in-law, and she always asked about her whenever Fred came to visit.

The group enjoyed a hot meal, and then loaded furs onto the sleds behind two snow-gos for the guests to take back to town. Jay guided Jesse through the maintenance details of her new snow-go. While Fred and Debbie chatted with Sadie, Jay surprised Jesse with a load of provisions. Carrying a five-gallon jug of gas, she led Jay along the trail to her homestead. He carried a plastic tote with undisclosed items.

Jay, not usually one to talk much, talked the entire trek. He shared the story of an encounter with a grizzly many years before, near to where they walked. "It was a case of bad timing. I was on an early October expedition with some friends who were taking photos of moose for an article for one of those sportsmen's magazines. The salmon had already spawned and died off. The bears were getting ready for hibernation, but had not quite gotten there yet. As our party of four walked through the brush, we fell into silence, each thinking about our own thing, I guess. We were walking sort of spread out, and somehow, we got between a momma bear and her cub without realizing it. It was a stupid fluke thing to happen."

"It seems you broke all the wilderness bear safety rules there."

"It's true. Numbskulls, all of us. When we finally realized what was happening, we started making noise and backing up so the momma and her cub could reunite, but momma threatened a couple of us pretty good. She stood up on her hind legs and clawed at the air toward two of the hikers. Once the cub was within her reach, she tapped its backside and they went running off across the brush. We got some excellent pictures with beautiful fall colors, and the encounter made it into their story."

As Jesse's homestead came into sight, Jay paused and surveyed the area. "You found quite a place for yourself here."

He scanned her cache, wall tent, woodpile, and the lean-tos built out of small logs between two trees to shelter some of her gear and firewood.

"Thanks, Jay." Jesse looked over her homestead's meager beginnings. "I have to admit, I'm looking forward to getting a more substantial roof over my head before next winter.

There've been a few nights I've bunked with Sadie to keep the deep freeze from taking me over."

"Yeah, I get that. Old man winter is one of our fiercest competitors in this world. Well, alongside fire, I guess," Jay agreed. After a knowing pause, he continued. "I see you. You're strong and it looks like you're taking each day as it comes and doing your best. You couldn't do any better than to make friends with Sadie. She'll see you through. It's hard to say how many more years we'll have her looking after these parts. Enjoy it while you can."

"She has been a godsend, that's for sure. Now, what's in that tote? Should it stay outside or go in?"

"Some of both. Here, let me just help you unload it."

Jay brushed off the wood splitting stump to balance the plastic container on. He opened the lid and reached in, pulling out two cans. "Here, this is a real treat, and Sadie will probably want to be invited. This is canned bacon. Most people don't know about it, but it's fantastic cooked over a campfire. You probably want to put that in the cache for now. There are a few other food things here, too, that you want to stash."

He unpacked a box of MoonPies, two cans of beef stew, some jarred moose jerky from his pantry, a notebook and pen, a small collection of batteries, and finally, a bottle of Irish whiskey.

"Oh wow, Jay, what a treat! This will be so good in a cup of hot coffee." Jesse took the bottle and set it in the snow. She flashed a huge smile at Jay. "Maybe even tonight. Thank you."

"You're welcome. It's the little things sometimes that get us through. I've been living alone with the wild things for enough years now that I appreciate very few niceties. In the beginning, I loved every little special thing that came my way. Like a mini bottle of champagne that a couple passing through on snow-gos left one New Year's Day."

. . .

F RED AND D EBBIE were bundling up when Jesse and Jay returned to Sadie's cabin. Fred stoked the fire with hot coals, fresh kindling was stacked, and the few dishes the group used to eat stew were cleaned and placed back on the open shelves in the makeshift kitchen. Jesse spied some new provisions, including a bag of Sadie's favorite hard ginger candies. Sadie's grin was filled with joy from having family around.

"Well, you kids need to hit the trail before it gets too dark. Thanks again for coming out and taking the furs to town. Tell the babies that Grandmother and Auntie Jesse love them." Sadie winked at Jesse, then hugged Fred and kissed Debbie on her winter-pink cheek. She shook Jay's mittened hand and wished them all a safe trip.

Jesse shared hugs with each of the visitors and thanked them for making the trip. "I hope you will bring the kids out one of these days. I would love to meet them."

Fred and Debbie agreed, and the three mounted their machines and drove away.

12

SKIS, SNOW-GOS AND NEIGHBORS

January 1985
Frozen wall tent

THE SOUND of a snow-go slowly advancing up the trail startled Jesse as she awoke, chilled, and needing to stoke the fire. She was curious who would visit when the puttering machine stopped at her tent. The snow crunched underfoot as a visitor approached with a headlamp shining along the trail.

"Good morning sleepyhead!" Sadie announced, as Jesse stepped out to greet her. "It's time to take a trip."

Jesse rubbed her eyes and combed her fingers through her hair to tame it into a ponytail. "Sadie, it's too early for trapping. Where are we going?"

"Well, I've got something to show you." Sadie's eyes glistened, and her round face wore a mischievous grin that foretold a childlike excitement. "You heard about the Iditaski on the radio, didn't ya? If we hurry, we can see some skiers come into the lodge."

"Okay, I'm game. How far is this place we are going?"

"It'll take us about an hour and a half to get there. Get

your headlamp and bring some cash. You might find something to buy."

Sadie waved Jesse back into the tent to get ready, then sauntered back to her snow-go. Jesse contemplated what she could purchase out in the middle of nowhere.

Jesse stepped out into the dark night, the snow crust crunching and giving way with each step. She turned her headlamp off momentarily to absorb the night sky with pale blue-green northern lights streaking upwards toward the heavens, dotted with brilliant stars and a planet or two. Someone on Trapline Chatter said Venus was so bright they could see their own shadow on the way to the outhouse the night before. Jesse wasn't certain, but thought she could see it, too.

Slowly, the pair traveled the frozen Lynx Creek down to the Yentna River, then onto the Skwentna River. Sadie traveled slowly in the dark, guided by the light from her snow-go. Jesse followed behind, keeping enough distance between them to respond if Sadie stopped suddenly or ran into trouble. As they approached the Yentna, Sadie pointed off to the south, down the dark path of the river. Jesse saw some tiny lights bouncing above the river. She pulled up alongside Sadie and shouted, "Are those skiers coming up the river?"

Sadie nodded and opened the throttle on her snow-go to pull in front of Jesse, increasing the pace slightly. The thought of the skiers moved Jesse. She was awed by their feat of covering over 200 miles on skis in the frozen, dark wilds of Alaska. It's one thing to ski groomed trails at the ski slopes and in the city parks in Minnesota, but this - this takes a whole new level of athleticism and guts.

Jesse and Sadie arrived in time to greet the first skiers reaching Skwentna, the turnaround stop, before they headed back to Knik Lake, which was the start and finish of the race. The skiers were greeted with cheers, hot coffee or chocolate thrust into their hands, and an invitation to warm up by the wood stove in a family cabin that served as the event headquarters.

Jesse flew off her snow-go, almost before she turned the key off! There were nearly two dozen people, counting the children big enough to stand on their own, already gathered near the cabin. A couple of spectators were holding signs welcoming the racers. One young boy proudly held up a sign made from a reused cardboard box with child-like uneven letters reading, 'your my hero dad.' Seeing Sadie, he handed the sign to a beautiful young woman standing nearby and ran to her.

"Clayton boy, how are you?" Sadie leaned down to hold the boy in his bulky winter garb in a warm embrace.

"I'm great Miss Sadie. I'm waiting for my dad to ski in. He wasn't the first one, but he will be here soon."

"Sure he will, Clayton. While you're waiting for him, I have a surprise for you." Sadie took off a fur-lined glove, reached into the pocket of the vest she wore under her fur-trimmed kuspuk, and handed the boy something.

"A Yupik yo-yo!" Clayton reached in and hugged Sadie again. "Thank you, grandmother."

"Show me how you can do it, boy."

Sadie nodded to the boy's mother, a beautiful woman with creamy-pink skin, sky-blue eyes, and long thick dark braids trailing from under a wool hat, who now carried her son's sign. "Hello Helen. Congratulations on your sweet baby there. What is her name?"

Jesse noticed a small fur hat peeking out from the top of Helen's zippered kuspuk.

"Hey Sadie. This is our baby, Abby."

"She's a beauty, just like her momma." Sadie lifted the fur hat away from the baby's face to get a closer look at the sleeping beauty. "And that Clayton… that boy has really grown since I saw him at fish camp last summer."

Jesse looked at the boy, trying to put two fur balls, each suspended on opposite ends of a thin leather strap, into an orbit. Sadie noticed the boy practicing, too. "He'll get the hang of it. What have you heard about Jacob? How's the trail going for him?"

"I haven't gotten an update, but I'm sure he's fine. He didn't have any high hopes of winning this thing; he just wanted the challenge of skiing over 200 miles. Crazy husband!" Helen and Sadie chuckled.

"Oh, Helen, I want you to meet my new friend and neighbor. This is Jesse. She's putting up a homestead not so far from me."

"Hey Jesse. Nice to meet you. You have a fella in this race, too?"

Jesse laughed. "I don't have a fella in or out of this race."

"You're kidding! You're homesteading up there by yourself? You've got guts."

"Some may say I have guts, but no brains. But the good Lord blessed me when I met Sadie. This woman here has been an angel to teach me so much this winter and have my back."

"She is something! I live up in Petersville. We're about forty miles north of here. Only a couple dozen of us live there, now that the Schultz family moved into Fairbanks. Four families got together to come down yesterday. Our friends, the Franz's, have an old cabin behind their home and they let us bunk there. It's crowded, but we are having a good time."

"Are you trappers, too?" Jesse loved hearing from the people of the interior. Their backgrounds and lifestyles were so diverse, and occasions like this when they came together were rare.

"My husband does a little, but he's a commercial fisherman. He's away a lot during fishing season. That's when I go to fish camp on the Big Su. A bunch of us set up camp, catch our limit, and do it over and over, as long as the fish run lasts. We get tired, or have to go have a baby, like I did this summer. Sadie kept little Clay there until his dad came to get him after I had baby, here."

Three skiers glided up the frozen riverbed, each wearing a harness around their waist, pulling a sled behind them. There were two tall men and a petite woman, pressing against their poles as their skis rode across the icy ridges carved into the lake by wind.

"Mommy, Mommy! Here comes Daddy!" Clayton tugged at his mother's hem.

Helen looked again at the approaching skiers. None of them were her husband. "Not yet, honey. It won't be too long, though."

Helen was confident that her husband was safe on the ice. He was stubborn enough to outpace any threat that came his way.

A small crowd gathered around Sadie as she greeted long-time friends and handed out handcrafted dolls and yo-yos to the children. Jesse's heart burned a bit deeper as she witnessed the love between Sadie and her community. After meeting several people, Jesse backed out of the crowd and turned to the skiers warming in the cabin.

"Hi there, I'm Jesse. I am so in awe of you skiers! What an amazing adventure."

The petite skier unclamped her skis, and stood them in the snow outside the cabin. She looked at Jesse, studying her face briefly.

"You a reporter?"

"Oh, no ma'am I'm not. Sorry. I'm a new homesteader down at Lynx Creek."

"Well then, thank you. I'm in awe of you, too. I've spent a lot of time in the Alaska wilderness, chasing my adrenaline around like mercury beads on the chem lab floor. But I've never braved full-time living out here. I'm Caroline. I work in the valley in a women's clinic."

"It's a pleasure to meet you. Can I ask you a couple of questions?"

"Sure, sure. Let me just get inside and get something warm in my belly."

"Of course. I'm so sorry. Can I help you with anything?"

"No, I'm good. I'll fill a water bottle or three before I leave, but for now I have everything I need."

They joined the other skiers inside the cabin, where they were warming by the fire with mugs of coffee and bowls of chili. Jesse overheard the tall man saying to the hosts, "it was about ten or fifteen miles back we saw a group of about thirty moose. They're looking healthy."

"Hey Caroline! You're looking great out there!"

"Thanks, Mike. Everything is going smoothly." Caroline waved off one of the race coordinators who rode parts of the trail on a snow-go to check on the skiers and look for overflow on the rivers.

"He's a pain in my ass with all his rules, but the trail has been incredible." She took a sip of her black coffee. "I hate this stuff. The only time I drink it is when I'm outdoors. I'm a tea drinker usually."

Jesse appreciated the direct manner of this tiny but mighty woman.

"So, what about your questions."

"Oh, yes, thanks. Your sled..."

"My pulk. It's a pulk."

"What do you carry in your pulk? It seems like it would just slow you down."

"Yeah, you know what I said about the rules. There are certain things you are required to carry with you and it's enough that we need folks to get it all here and back home again. Most of the stuff will never be touched, but it's for our safety. We have to have the usual stuff you need for a long ski, and then we have to carry survival gear for minus 20-degree nights and blizzards. We have to have food and drink, flares, headlamps, and a first aid kit. Listen, if I expected a blizzard, I would never have left home. I'm not going to sleep on the trail.

I may ski while asleep, but I will not force myself to spend the night on the frozen ground."

"I guess it makes some sense why they want you to…"

"Hey Doc, could you come take a look at this fella's feet? He's got some nasty blisters."

Caroline shouted over her shoulder. "Sure Ed. Let me just finish up my grub here."

"Doc?"

"Well, I'm a nurse practitioner. I work with pregnant women mostly, but I've addressed a blister or two in my day."

Caroline scraped the spoon against the bottom of her bowl and handed it off to the hostess. "Thanks, Annie. Another splendid meal. It hit the spot. Was that your moose?"

"Yeah, we saved some up for you today."

"Well, I sure thank you. Sounds like Ed's got something for me to see over in the other room." Caroline grabbed Annie's upper arm. "I sure hope you're taking good care of yourself, hun. You're looking good. A little tired, but good."

"Yes, I'm good. Ed's keeping a close eye on me so I don't overdo it."

"That's great. He's a keeper." Caroline turned to Jesse. "I might need an assistant. Come along, we'll see what we've got."

Jesse obliged, taking the mug of hot coffee Annie gently held out for her.

Just out of earshot, Caroline explained Annie was diagnosed with breast cancer two years ago and since then, she had undergone surgery and chemotherapy. It was touch and go for a while, but she seemed pretty good. "She's had a hard life following Ed around. He's not a bad guy; he just never put her first. She handled the kids, five of them, while he was away working for long periods of time. Living out here for the past ten or fifteen years meant she had to work hard to keep them warm and fed. That moose in the stew - she shot that and put it up."

A sixty-something man was sitting atop a pile of quilts on Annie and Ed's homemade log bed. "Hey there. I'm Caroline. Sounds like you've got yourself some blisters, eh?"

The skier had arrived at the rest-stop and shortly after, Caroline and Ed took him into the back of the cabin when Ed saw the skier hobbling in wool socks with ski boots in hand.

"Yeah, I should have changed my socks out a while ago, but I'm a little hard-headed. The name is Bill, Bill Chesson from Seward."

Caroline examined Bill's bare feet. "Yup, looks like you had some wet socks on for too long. Jesse, head out to my pulk and grab the blue box in the green backpack. That's my first aid kit. I think I can help you out, Bill, but you're going to need a different pair of boots. Did you bring along a spare?"

"No ma'am, I didn't."

"Well, when I get you bandaged up here, you're going to need another half-size to put your foot in." She turned to where Ed was standing watch. "Ed, do you think you can scrounge something up? Maybe one of your boys left behind an old pair?"

"I'll see what Jacob or Josh might have back there in the shed. They didn't take their ski stuff to college. We might be in luck."

"Mighty obliged to you." Bill nodded as Ed left to search.

Jesse returned quickly with the first aid kit. "There are a couple more skiers coming up the path now. The crowd is really cheering them on."

"As a competitor, it's so much fun to hear the cheers. On this trail, sometimes it's one or two people standing along the frozen shore or even just a sign left on a tree wishing us luck. It's not like the Boston marathon, where people line the streets. I'm so grateful for each person and each gesture. It keeps the spirits up. There was even a couple camped with a fire burning and some warm soup and tea in the middle of the night."

"Bless their souls," said Bill. "That's about when I should

have paused and changed my socks, but I just didn't want to stop and risk getting cold. I grabbed a half-cup of coffee from them and kept going."

"I hear ya, Bill. That cold could set deep in the bones if you let it. Now, let's get these feet cleaned up."

Caroline used an alcohol wipe to clean the blister on the outside of each small toe, then cleaned a safety pin before opening up the blisters to drain. "Now, I know they say to never pop a blister. But these are obviously going to pop with the friction they'll be getting, so I'm going to get the job done and put some ointment on them."

Jesse watched in awe as the confident woman, generous with her time and talent, finished doctoring Bill's feet with large bandages over the blistered areas and wrapped duct tape around the bandages. She cut moleskin doughnuts to cushion the blisters from the inside of the boots.

"Ha! duct tape. I've used it for a lot of things on the homestead, but never thought to use it for blisters." Caroline's ingenuity was impressive.

"I carry a roll with me everywhere. I've seen it used for some pretty bizarre things, that's for sure." Caroline examined her tape job, nodding her apparent satisfaction.

Ed returned holding two pairs of boots. "Well Bill, you're in luck. I've got a ten and a half and an eleven for you to try here. They're nothing fancy and have lots of miles on them, but they should give you some more room. I've got some socks you should try, too. I use a liner and a merino wool sock to keep my feet dry."

"This is embarrassing. I can't believe I'm so ill prepared. You know, I ski all the time around my place down south."

"Yeah, I get it, but I bet you take breaks between long hauls. That's the difference out here. We just keep on going. You've got to, because if you don't, the elements will eventually get you."

Caroline packed up her first aid kit and watched Bill out of the corner of her eye while he put his socks and a pair of the boots on and stood up. She was concerned that he may be weak and too tired to continue.

"I feel like a new man. Thank you so much, Caroline. I'll get my information to you so you can send me a bill."

"That's not the way we do things on the trail. You might need to have my back one day." She was satisfied that after a warm drink and some chili, he would be ready to hit the trail. "I hope I get to see you at the end of this thing and see how you're doing."

"Sounds great. Thanks, again."

Bill followed Ed out to the wood stove to get something to eat and drink. Spectators and neighbors brought pies and cookies and sandwiches.

"It's turning into quite a party here. I'm going to get myself bundled up and hit the trail. Some of these women have been my patients over the years. It's fun to see them and their kiddos, but I'm afraid if I don't get a move on, I'm going to end up wasting too much time standing around. I want this thing done and over with. As much as I enjoy it, I'll be glad when it's behind me." Caroline took Jesse's bare hand in hers and gave it a hearty shake. For a small woman, Jesse could tell she had a lot of power. "I appreciate your help today and it was a real pleasure meeting you. Say, if you ever get to Wasilla, look me up."

"I would love that. Thank you!"

As they headed out, Caroline nodded to Sadie, who was still greeting friends and playing with the children. "And you look after Sadie. She's a good friend and…" Caroline lowered her voice and drew closer to Jesse. "I shouldn't say this, because she's a patient. But she's no spring chicken anymore and, well, it's about time she heads to Fairbanks with the kids. And if you dare tell her I said so, I'll deny it."

Jesse laughed. She understood how Sadie would be offended by the suggestion that she should no longer be on her own. "Yes. She's been really good for me this winter and I'm hoping I have been good for her. Her son keeps a close eye on her, but I've often wondered what I would do if she fell ill or got hurt. I have the radio. Guess I would just call for help."

"Yes, that's right. That's how it's done out here, and I'm sure you know about Trapline Chatter. Using that program has been a lifesaver many times over the years." Caroline attached her pulk and grabbed her ski poles. "Okay, Jesse, I'm outta here."

In a flash, Caroline was headed back toward home, leaning into her ski poles as she moved through the cheering crowd. Jesse heard a woman standing beside her speak. "That's my doctor. Best friend a girl could ever have."

———

JESSE FELL INTO BED EXHAUSTED, alive, and grateful. Snow was melting in the steamer pot on top of the stoked stove. A celebratory nip of Jay's Irish whiskey warmed her throat. Jesse looked around the tent, stopping to gaze at the friends and family smiling at her through photos strung like a clothesline draped into a headboard. She tipped the bottle of Irish whiskey toward the photos. "Here's to you, my old friends, and my new ones."

She swallowed hard and felt the whiskey warm her throat as she tipped her head back. It was only seven in the evening, but the day had been a full one. After the early morning ride, the long day filled with adrenaline and meeting new people and the return ride, Jesse had spent time with Sadie as her cabin warmed up and she told stories about the families of Skwentna and Petersville. Both were happily exhausted. They had agreed there would be no early morning rendezvous. They would sleep until they were slept out and meet in the afternoon for some leftover chili.

13

HEARTS AND DOGS

February 1985
Lynx Creek trapline

TRAPPING, surviving, and getting to know new surroundings consumed most of Jesse's days. On non-trapping days, she lounged under the covers and read a book or wrote in a notebook, crawling out into the cold only to feed the wood stove or run to the outhouse. Jesse marked each day off on a calendar, a ritual she clung to mark time and keep her tied to the outside world.

February 14 arrived. Valentine's day. It had never been her favorite day, but this year it was an invitation to reflect on her married and post-married life. As a way to orient herself and stay out of negative thinking, she made a list of the good things about each. The list of good for today (post-married life) was three times as long as the list of married life, with the benefit of hindsight and all she had proven to herself since that dark day when the suspicions of Tim's affair were confirmed.

The Trapline Chatter show was especially entertaining that night, with shout-outs to lovers and crushes across the frozen rivers and snow-covered land. The show went on and on, with over 150 messages. Jesse stayed awake for about half of them before drifting off. There were poems that started out with "roses are red" and quickly deteriorated to frostbitten toes being blue or similar lines, and often ended with a confectionary sentiment about the loved one. The announcer explained that the Valentine's Day show had a tradition of starting with a message from the show's early days in the late 60s. A trapper was sending a message to his beloved wife in Fairbanks from his trapline somewhere north of the town. He told of the beauty of the aurora at night, which paled in comparison to his beloved's beauty. He promised to return with furs and food as soon as he could, assured her that he was taking the greatest of care, and this year he would have enough money to buy those silk panties she wanted. The wife also sent a message, letting the husband know her belly was swelling with their child; she hoped he would return in time for the birth. And he could forget the silk panties; she wanted wool long johns.

Reflecting on this exchange, Jesse imagined what life was like when Sadie first moved to the area. Jesse wasn't certain she could have done it alone and briefly lamented the fact that she didn't have a willing partner earlier in her life.

Inside the wall tent one late February evening, Jesse kept warm with the small wood stove and sat, bundled up in a sleeping bag atop the cot, with a pile of blankets covering the bottom part. Despite all, her socked feet felt cold every morning, regardless of her efforts. She hadn't felt much like cooking, so she was chewing on a protein bar and drinking tea when, amidst the Trapline Chatter messages, the announcers started talking about the upcoming Iditarod dog sled race. Jesse drew a big dogface on the calendar square for March 2, the start of the race, and made a mental note to get a new calendar when she went to town. This calendar, with exotic flower pictures from places she never intended to visit, was just not appropriate anymore. A calendar with pictures of Alaska would be more fitting, especially for her new cabin, with what she imagined would be its smooth log walls.

Jesse listened intently as the radio hosts talked about the last great race, its history, and symbolism for Alaska. They shared details on the sixty-three mushers registered to run dogs and interviewed some of them. It was there that Jesse imagined what three weeks or so would be like out on the trail. She heard things like, "ice fields that went on for miles" and "waking up in the snow realizing you fell off the sled and the dogs went on ahead of you." Jesse could not imagine the panic she would feel in that situation. Just visualizing such a terrifying encounter, she held her breath while her heart pounded in her ears. She listened through stories of nearly catastrophic moose encounters, falling through thin ice and dog fights. More often though, she heard mushers and race volunteers talk about the bond between dog and man, the unified survival instinct they forge which carries them forward across 1,100 frozen miles to Nome. The $50,000 cash prize was inspiration for the mushers, but the dogs did it for the love of the mushers.

JESSE NOTICED MORE airplane activity overhead while checking traps later that week. "They're flying musher bags in to Skwentna. Each musher has to send ahead their food and stuff to different checkpoints."

"Will you be going to Skwentna, Sadie?"

"Wouldn't miss it. Been going every year they had the race. I used to volunteer, but a couple of years of that was enough for me. Let those young whippersnappers do the legwork. The nice thing about the checkpoint is it's a daytime stop. We can go in daylight hours, see a little bit, then come back. I like to see my friends, but it's too busy for me. All those dogs yapping and people clapping. There'll be lots of picture-taking and story writing by people who fly in from all over the world to report on the race."

"It all sounds fascinating to me. Such fanfare and an incredible feat! I can't imagine subjecting myself and a team of dogs to the rigor of the race."

Sadie looked out across the open field of snow and ice, her gaze extending far beyond in all directions. "John loved his dogs. They were working animals, not pets. That was hard for the kids and I to understand, but we followed the rules. Of course, there would always be one dog that would never make it on the team, so it became a housedog. Our favorite was Puddles, Puds for short. Oh, Puds was a smart, smart dog, but she wouldn't follow the rest of the team. She had a mind to do her own thing. There was never a greater bear scout, and she protected the kids many times from wandering toward bear."

"What happened to her?" Jesse hesitated to ask, but she had a feeling Sadie wanted to talk about it.

"Oh, we'll never know. Puds just didn't come back one summer day. She liked to hunt hare, so we thought she wandered away and got lost chasing them, but she never came back to show us her catch so proudly, like she had always done before. She just vanished. We told the kids God called her to heaven and she rode away on angel wings."

"That's beautiful. She sounds like a wonderful friend to the family."

"She was. She really was."

Jesse sensed Sadie's tenderness. They stood together silently for a few minutes. The circle of life surrounded them. Jesse knew, as she was sure Sadie did, that Puddles likely fell prey to another animal and... the circle of life continued. They saw it every day. They trapped, ate the meat and tanned the hides. Clumps of hare fur, left behind in the brush near their trails, were the telltale sign that a wolverine, wolf, owl, or other creature had a meal or morsel. To some, it would be gruesome. To Jesse, it was the unrefined intelligence of nature.

———

JESSE TRACKED the trapping activities in her notebook, tallying the various types of catch and the prices they got from auction. Sadie sold nearly $10,000 worth of furs to traders and artisans. They caught and processed over 200 martens. Sadie and Jesse brought in lynx, fox, beaver, wolverine, and wolves. They caught many red squirrels, most of which they used as bait for the larger furbearers. Sadie's son, Fred, drove his snow-go in several times over the winter to check on Sadie and haul her pelts and some of the meat to town. Sadie was happy with the season's take and Jesse's enthusiasm for trapping. Jesse was an excellent student. She was attuned to nature. She had mixed feelings about trapping the beautiful animals but recognized the opportunity to learn a skill that may one day keep her alive in the wilds.

Jesse noticed a tightness in her chest and gasped to catch her breath some mornings when the cold air felt dense and stifling. But knowing she had committed to walk the trapline with Sadie every two days meant Jesse would deal with it. Had it not been for that commitment, inspired in part by the fear of something happening to her elderly mentor, Jesse could have stayed in her wall tent for days at a time - feeding logs into the stove, lying under blankets in a sleeping bag and giving way to that ledge holding her up from falling into depression. As awful as the ending with Tim was, at times in the dark early morning hours Jesse clutched the sleeping bag, pulling it tight into her and wishing it was familiar skin resting against hers. Some days, the unfamiliarity of this life that she chose overwhelmed her.

———

JESSE FELT sadness and loneliness in the darkness, but in that cold dark heart of night, she also found her soulmate. When she stepped outside to wave at the stars and dance with the northern lights, Jesse came to life. One night the blackness within deepened in the late-night hours. When the magic light show became intensely bright, it stirred something deep within Jesse. She went to the open field, halfway between her house and Sadie's. There, she danced beneath the naturally fluorescent lights gliding in broad, colorful sheets across the sky. She plunged her hands into the air above her head and draped them across the broad shoulders of the light streams. Her cosmic lover. Jesse swayed and twirled as the stars watched and smiled. She chanted as her body moved to the rhythm of the lights and the humming in her head. The enormity of the world, the wildness of the place, and the deafening sound of silence drew together and created a peephole into her soul.

Jesse fell to her knees, folded her hands, and prayed; a position she had not taken in full since she was in Sunday school at her grandparents' tiny Lutheran church in rural Minnesota. "Thank you, God, for all you are and all you have given me. I am truly blessed."

After this precious moment of communion, Jesse walked back to her tent and fell into a deep sleep. Hours later, she jumped from the cot and frantically threw more clothes on. She was late for her meet-up with Sadie.

14

EMERGING FROM WINTER

Spring 1985
 Lynx Creek wilderness

JESSE TOOK in the jagged edges of frigid winter as they gave
way to longer spring days and shorter nights. The brilliance of
the aurora intensified while the viewing window narrowed as
days grew longer. Jesse's distractions moved to the newness that
came with spring. Early plants reached through the remnants
of snow cover; buds emerged on the trees; newly spawned
offspring of the animals, that first laid claim to this part of the
world, bedded in the tall grasses.

Jesse was in awe of the renewal surrounding her. She was
darn proud of herself for surviving this first winter in the cold
interior of the last frontier. Of course, Jesse had Sadie, James,
and a host of passersby to thank for helping her navigate the
lonely, rugged life she chose, away from modern conveniences
and mainstream America. There were days when she felt ice
form inside the pores of her face and the deep pockets in her
lungs. The mental fortitude that developed was invaluable and
necessary for life in this location, her chosen home.

One early spring day, they were to meet up at the south side of the open field. Sadie wanted to continue her tutelage of Jesse and introduce her to "spring shoots, taps, and tips." Jesse raced to the meeting spot but didn't see Sadie. She paused. Panic rose from deep in her gut. She looked around and listened for signs of Sadie.

Jesse had been to this field nearly a hundred times and each time she noticed something new; it was like watching a time-lapse movie in real time. Today, fresh sprouts were springing up on the plants, and the activity of insects and rodents caused branches and unfrozen leaves to quiver. The longer daylight hours brought about change quickly. Standing water gave way to mud and pools of overflow stood atop thinning ice on the creek. From a distance, she heard the roar of the river, swollen with melted ice and snow.

"Aurora! Aurora!" Sadie's familiar voice called from a stand of paper birch trees near Lynx Creek. Jesse turned toward the voice. *Who was Sadie calling for?* Perhaps someone was visiting with a dog named Aurora. She found Sadie standing atop two rusty metal buckets resting on their rims. She was stretched out as far as she could reach, holding a metal cup against a birch tree. "There you are, Aurora!"

Jesse was confused. For the first time in many months together, Sadie didn't seem to recognize her. "Sadie, it's me, Jesse."

"No ma'am. I'm calling you Aurora now."

"Okay, whatever." Jesse muttered to herself, trying not to make too much of the apparent lapse of her dear friend's memory. She looked at Sadie who, standing on the buckets, was now almost eye level with her. "What are you doing?"

"I'm getting birch sap. If you were here on time, instead of dancing under the ocean of stars all night, you would have been here to see me tap it."

"Ah!" Jesse thought, as understanding hit her. "Aurora - as if born again as the goddess of the great northern lights."

"How did you…"

Sadie laughed. "There are no secrets from Sadie here in these parts."

"But…" Sadie held her hand up to stop Jesse.

"So, just like that, you've changed my name?"

"Happens all the time," Sadie stated firmly. "I have more than one name. Kk'odohdaatlno is my Athabascan name, but they changed it at Jesse Lee Home. I was only called Sadie from the time I was thirteen."

Jesse listened with interest as Sadie said her Athabascan name with throaty and windy sounds separating the vowels and consonants. It was unlike anything she had heard before. "Wow, that's a hard name. No wonder they called you Sadie."

Sadie laughed. "Not even my own grandchildren can pronounce it. They have lazy tongues like their white momma. Anyway, I'll call you Aurora. Jesse doesn't suit you. You're too pretty for that boyish name."

Jesse waved her arm as if to spin Sadie's kind words away into the wind. She reached out to the delicate outer wrapper of the birch tree and stroked her hand over it, watching as flakes of thin bark slowly sailed to the ground.

"Here, taste this." Sadie passed the metal cup to Jesse.

It surprised Jesse to see the clear liquid of the birch sap in the cup. She expected it to look like the maple syrup from the Jack and Jill grocery store back home. She brought the cool cup to her lips and sipped the sap. It was sweet, with a slightly earthy edge. "It's not what I expected, but it's good."

"You thought it would be dark and thick, didn't you? To make it into syrup, you have to gather a lot and boil it hard with sugar. Drinking it like this gives you the vitamins without the sugar. Now, let me show you how to tap the tree."

Sadie pulled a knife from a sheath around her pocket. She pointed the knife at a flat, white area on the tree bark and shoved it into the tree in an upward direction, sinking it in about three-quarters of an inch. She then cut a v-notch spout about one-quarter of an inch deep and lifted the flesh of the tree with the knife so the sap could drip from the first cut, across the v-notch and into a metal cup tied to the tree.

Here was another reminder that Sadie was a godsend. There was no way Jesse could learn from a book all the things Sadie has taught her over the past months. "Sadie, I'm so grateful. You have taught me so many things."

"Well, we only just got started. You have much to learn yet and old Sadie isn't going to be around forever, so let's move it. You take those two birches over there and make your own tap. Here, I brought you some tins and some rope to tie them onto the tree."

Jesse reached out and took the things.

"I suppose you need to use my knife, too. Let this be a lesson to you. You need to always have a knife with you."

Jesse dropped her backpack, unzipped it and proudly produced her hunting knife. "This time, I'm prepared, at least with a knife."

"Good girl, Aurora. You are becoming a fine woods-woman."

"Why, thank you Miss Sadie." Jesse smiled and moved to the next birch stand to tap her own trees. She made a mental note to add thin rope and metal cups to her backpack.

Sadie stood close by and quietly critiqued Jesse's moves. Jesse completed her first v-notch then looked to Sadie for approval. This dance of the questioning eye and single, firm head nod had become a reliable way for the teacher to grade the student. When the head nod did not appear, Jesse would mentally review the steps she took and describe for Sadie where she thought she needed to make adjustments. If correct, a minimal head nod would follow.

After Jesse drew the thin nylon ropes around the tree and tied cups in place, Sadie suggested they move toward the creek and gather spruce tips. In silence, they navigated the game trail, camouflaged by new blueberry plants and partially decayed autumn leaves now freed from their snow blanket.

Small creatures raced through tunnels carved in rotted tree roots and moss. One busy shrew paused momentarily. Its beady eyes peered through the shadows. Before it disappeared into the shadows, Jesse locked eyes with it for a nanosecond. She felt a stirring; to be connected with this innocent living thing in the rawness of nature changed her. It opened her to deeper connections all around.

"Sadie, do you think you will ever leave this place?"

"Now, why would you ask that? This is my home. It's what I know. The kids would have me come stay with them, but I will be here as long as I can be."

Sadie was picking the light green spruce tips from the ends of boughs and motioned for Jesse to do the same.

"It's such an amazing place here. At first, it seemed so quiet and peaceful and now, with spring here, it's gotten very busy with all the little creatures stirring."

"In the winter, when the snow-gos and sled dogs come through, it seems like they are intruding on my space. But I sure don't mind it when the babies are born and start filling up my yard. I'll take the animals over people any day."

15

SUPPLY RUN

Late spring 1985

On the road and in the air

Warmer weather slid in as days grew longer. Jesse felt a mania building up within as she emerged from the hibernating energy of winter. The mania wasn't unchecked; it was a feeling of renewal and relief.

She planned a trip away from the homestead to get building supplies, see new friends in Anchorage and Talkeetna, and restock her cache pantry. She scheduled a deadhead trip with James. On the morning of her departure, she walked by Sadie's cabin to check in.

"Hey, Sadie. How are you this morning?"

Sadie was working in the yard, picking up broken branches resting in the mud.

"It's a beautiful day to be alive! Are you excited about your trip to town?"

"I'm looking forward to getting this building project going, so yes, I am. It will be fun to have a change of scenery and see some of those friends I have met since I got to Alaska."

Sadie stooped again to pick up more sticks. She tucked them in open spaces in the woodpile to use as kindling.

"Aurora, I was wondering if you could do me a little favor, or maybe two?"

"Of course! You know I would do anything for you."

"Well, I don't know about that. But I have some skin dolls and masks that I want to go to the native hospital gift shop in Anchorage. My son would do it, but he never goes to Anchorage. I put them together in a tote." Sadie nodded toward her cabin. "It's on the deck up there."

Jesse secured her backpack and grabbed the tote.

"Inside, on top, there's an envelope with a list of things I need from Black Elk Leather and Freddy's, if you don't mind. It should all fit in the tote when you come back."

"Okay. If you think of anything else, radio it in to James. I'll check in with him before I leave Anchorage. I think I'll only be gone a week. Ten days max."

"Well, don't you worry about me. There's lots of spring work to do. By the time you get back, we may start seeing some fiddleheads and fireweed."

Jesse was curious to try Sadie's favorite spring salad, made of fresh young fern fiddleheads and the early red shoots of fireweed. Unfamiliar with fiddleheads, Jesse studied a picture that Sadie had from an old calendar and laughed at furled tips of the ferns that looked like little green caterpillars coiled up. She hoped they didn't taste like caterpillar.

"I'll be sure to have some fresh veggies to go with it when I get back."

Jesse planned to shop for a used four-wheeler or track machine to eventually bring to the property. She had finalized plans, or so she thought, for her log cabin. She listed all the supplies, prioritizing them so she could stage deliveries. A boat was on the list of things to research while she was away.

Jesse found it hard to leave. The air smelled of freshness. The honking of geese signaled an increase in the bird population. She spotted cranes and swans in the swampy areas near the river, and a few yellow-rumped warblers and ruby-crowned kinglets. The juncos and chickadees filled the air with song as they spent more hours hopping through the trees during the warmer, longer days. And it was hard to leave Sadie. Now that she was not bundled in layers of clothing, Jesse saw how petite and frail the older woman was.

The flight to town with James was quick. They took no time for extra sight-seeing. As they approached Talkeetna, it surprised Jesse to see so many vehicles traveling the Parks Highway.

"It's been so long since I saw traffic. I didn't expect there to be so many cars on the road."

"There is a lot of movement with breakup. People checking on their summer property, traveling to Anchorage for supplies and doctor visits and the like," James explained. "Sometimes it feels like there literally are people crawling out of the woods. There are a surprising number of people who live deep in the interior all winter. Sometimes, when they emerge from the winter, I don't recognize them. Not true for you. You still look healthy and strong. Thinner, maybe, but still strong."

Jesse rubbed her hand across her thigh. She noticed her pants were looser than usual. But she thought that was because she didn't do laundry often and wore at least three layers all winter. She felt good and ready to tackle summer projects. Reflecting on the winter brought a smile to her face. She had learned so much from Sadie and got to meet others living similar lifestyles to hers. She almost felt a little cheated by not being totally alone, but was grateful to have had the experience she did.

"I wonder if my truck will start."

"Sure it will. I'm glad you left your keys with us. We started it up every once in a while. Had it running last week, so I'm sure it's all good."

"You guys at Talkeetna airport are the best! Thanks for looking out for me!"

"Well, here we are." James made adjustments to the plane as they descended into the airport. It was mid-afternoon, mid-week, and a busy place. Jesse spotted her truck. Someone had moved it to a parking spot near the office where she had easy access.

"Are you headed to Anchorage right away?"

"Yes, that's the plan. I have a friend who is expecting me tonight. I owe her a pizza. So, after a nice warm shower and change of clothes, I'll make good on that debt if she's up for it. If not, I'll run down to the store and grab something. I'll be headquartered there this week."

Jesse pulled a piece of paper out of her shirt pocket. "Here's the phone number, in case Sadie gets ahold of you. She might think of something she needs from town and radio you."

"Great. Thanks."

"I know I owe you, so tell me the total and I'll bring cash back to you on my way back through, if that's okay with you."

"Sure, that's perfect. We can check in at the office. I've got it all written down there."

———

CHARLIE WAS as happy to Jesse as Jesse was to see her. They swapped stories; Charlie glued to Jesse's tales of her first winter in the interior. Jesse told all about Sadie and their adventures trapping. She told the story of the wolverine they came upon when they were checking traps. It was ready to eat their catch when they came around a bend to check some traps along the creek. Sadie yelled something at it. The wolverine looked at Sadie and then looked down into the snow, as if she had been scolded, with her eyes. When it didn't move, Sadie fired one shot from her shotgun and the wolverine ran off without a second look. She told Charlie of the bear tracks they saw in the early spring that led to a stand of birch trees where twin moose calves lay, dropped in the spring snow by the momma moose. Sadie said that this momma moose had birthed twins every year for the past three years in the same stand of birch trees, but by mid-summer, there was only one calf remaining. Jesse speculated with Sadie that the bear might have gotten the baby.

Charlie shared stories of her winter escapades as well. She cross-country skied in some local races, enjoyed time with friends, taught a wilderness survival class to adults through the community schools and watched a boatload of videos snuggled in at home and drinking beer. Charlie invited a group of friends over to meet Jesse. They sat around the outdoor fire pit, swapping stories of adventures past and future. Jesse invited them all out to fish, dig an outhouse hole, or just to visit. Her quest intrigued several new friends who promised to visit. She learned more about fly-in fishing trips, halibut charters, hooligan runs, and the Mount Marathon race in Seward on July Fourth that a couple was training for. Jesse screwed up her face in sympathy pain as they described their past efforts at winning the three-plus mile race, climbing up 3,000-foot elevation with 30,000 competitors, most of whom were bloodied from tumbling down sliding shale and rock paths.

After going to what seemed like one hundred stores and a dozen pawnshops, Jesse had gathered everything on her lists, and then some. She talked to her family in a series of phone calls and got caught up on everyone's news. She invited each person to visit her, but doubted she would see anyone this year.

"Honey, I would love to come and help you, but I'm not sure I can talk your mom into coming up."

"Well, make it a solo trip then. She can go to Hawaii and

visit the grandkids and you can come up north and peel some logs. It would be great to spend some time together."

"Believe you me, I've contemplated that approach. Let's just see how things unfold, okay?"

"Sure Dad. Just know that I would love to have you join me for at least a little of this grand adventure."

"Noted, dear daughter. I'll keep you posted through the radio program."

———

JESSE MADE an impromptu stop by Caroline's clinic to say hi to the skier, then stayed long enough to have an annual woman's exam. She thought out loud about how difficult it must be for some women to come to town for wellness exams while working so hard to keep their homesteads going. Afterwards, the two went to Caroline's for dinner.

"Follow me," Caroline directed. "We're going to the end of the world, then we'll turn left and go some more."

As Jesse followed Caroline's well-used Subaru wagon, she wondered if she could ever make her way back to the highway. Caroline's home was a converted Quonset building, down a 500-foot winding road off a side road from a main road. A big cedar deck stretched across the front of the home, with cedar siding that set it apart from the metal half-moon shape that cocooned the home as both the roof and the sides. As they drove into the yard, two beautiful dogs greeted them.

"Meet my boys. The handsome malamute is Mal. Creative, huh?"

"Yeah, that's pretty cute," Jesse laughed as she pushed away a yellow lab trying to lick her face. "Who's this shy one?"

"That's Chance, as in not a chance in hell you can control him. He's strong-willed but a happy and friendly dog, as you can see. He's been to doggie bootcamp twice, and this is how he is."

"Twice? That's impressive!"

"He's a blockhead and I love him. He's my hiking partner. Mal is my skijoring buddy. He can pull like a freight train."

"You don't have to keep them tied up?"

"That's one of the benefits of living out here. Besides, I've tried to tie them up. When Mal was about six months old, I had him chained to the clothesline post. He pulled the whole damn thing over. And Chancey can dig and chew his way through anything."

"This is an amazing place you have here. I love the solitude of it."

"Me too. I rented a lot of rooms and shacks before I put enough money together to buy this place. It suits me perfectly. It's a bit of work in the winter when I have to plow the road, but I solved that by getting that old truck over there with the plow on the front. I have a few neighbors around here and we all use it. Usually they plow me out first, so I don't have to do anything but keep it running. It's a win-win."

"I'll say." Jesse admired the wildness that Caroline preserved on her property. Not that much different from her own, except there were more trees, and it was closer to the grocery store.

"Well, come on in and let's see what we can find for dinner. Sorry if the place is a mess. I live alone and kind of like clutter. You'll see."

Caroline opened the unassuming front door, flanked by door-height windows on either side, and Jesse drew in her breath audibly.

"My God, Caroline, this is not what I expected to see when you opened that door. This place is stunning! It's like a mini museum in this pristine setting."

"Thank you. I kind of like it myself. I grew up in California and saw some swanky places that left a mark on me. I particularly like those industrial big city lofts, so I brought a bit of that with me when I designed the interior. It was just an old, abandoned steel hut when I bought the property."

Jesse took in the vast one-room interior. With its curved spine, the Quonset hut was two stories tall at the highest point of the arc, making enough room for a loft that floated over the kitchen. Stairs, dark metal frames with raw plank treads, were open and suspended. The kitchen was cozy and modern, with an eat-in breakfast bar.

"And look at that art! That's just amazing. The colors and the flow of the shapes take me right back to the open skies at the homestead." Jesse looked at an enormous canvas hanging over the front door.

"I call that Northern Lights IV," Caroline explained. "The first three were much smaller, but with this one, I really think I captured it."

"You painted that?" Jesse stared in amazement. "Caroline, you are an incredible woman!"

"Awe, thanks. One of the amazing things about living here in the valley is that there are so many opportunities to learn new crafts. If I'm not taking a class through community schools, or from a patient, I'm in the library or used bookstore looking for a new craft to try or hobby to study. That's how I originally got into skiing. I moved up here after graduating from nursing school, lived in a rented room, and used every penny to pay my graduate school tuition. The prior renter left some old skis and boots behind, so I took them out to Russian Jack Park and tried them out. The boots were too big, but I wore several pairs of socks and found that I really loved it. It was great exercise, let me blow off steam from work and school, and I met some cool people. We ate a lot of three-for-$5.00 cardboard pizzas and drank cheap beer those first few winters. Some of those folks are still my best friends fifteen years later."

"That's fantastic! I've noticed that the friendships that people develop here are different. There seem to be fewer expectations of one another and more generosity of time and attention at just the right moments. Like this. I wasn't even sure you would be working today, but not only was there room on the schedule for an exam, but here I am checking out your amazing place. That just wouldn't happen in most other places I've been."

"That's what pushed me out of California. I did not care for the artificiality and the pressure of society. My parents are still there and finally, I've got the strength to go back and visit. I love seeing my family, but I get overwhelmed by the busyness of it all."

"Do your folks come to visit?"

"Only a couple of times. My dad is a surgeon, and my mom is a psychotherapist, and they love their insulated, busy lives down there with their work and their friends. Being the socialites they are, they think this is all very crude and terribly unrefined. They think their daughter would be better off back in the city."

"I'm sorry you don't have their support."

"It's no biggie. A long time ago I took ownership of being the oddball in the family and I embrace that. I don't try to be off-the-wall with them, but sometimes it's kind of fun to shock them with stories and pictures of my crazy adventures. I'm sure their hearts skipped a beat with some of the stuff I shared, like me dangling off a cliff while rock climbing or off an iceberg while ice climbing. You know, those adrenaline-junkie kind of things we get ourselves into."

"I've done nothing quite that bold, but it sounds intriguing."

"Climbing is my biggest passion. I've got my sights set on summiting some tall places." Caroline paused in reflection. "But that's enough about me. How about a beer?"

"Sure." Jesse sat on a stool at the kitchen island counter and thanked Caroline as she handed her a cool beer.

Caroline turned back to the refrigerator to take inventory.

"I'm not a fancy eater. It's pretty much protein and veggies for me. There's some moose stroganoff I cooked up over the weekend. I thought it was pretty good, and I've got sprouts and cherry tomatoes for a salad. How does that sound?"

"Like heaven. What can I do to help?"

Jesse made the salad with alfalfa sprouts and cherry tomatoes, while Caroline heated stroganoff on the stove.

"Don't tell me you shot the moose to get the meat, too."

"No, I won't tell you that I did. I have before, but not this one. Sometimes I barter with patients who don't have insurance or cash. I get some good stuff. For example, see those beautiful stained-glass lamps on the end tables?"

Jesse looked over at the handsome lamps flanking the mission-style leather and wood sofa with matching end tables. "They are gorgeous. The colors are so complimentary to your artwork."

"Well, that patient is an immensely talented woman in a horribly abusive relationship. I'm her therapist as much as anything. A safe haven for her to retreat to when she breaks away from the husband and their five kids."

"Stories like that make me so sad. I'm not sure I can understand why the women don't leave."

"There are so many reasons and, as easy as it is to sit in judgment of their decision, I try not to and just support them as best I can. Often, it's just providing that judgment-free zone where they can hear themselves think. Some make plans to leave and follow through. Life has beaten down others, like this beautiful woman. Her husband makes sure they have a roof over their heads, and he gives her just enough allowance to make sure they have groceries for all of them, if she's wise about her shopping. Her life now is more stable than her childhood, so she can't imagine leaving. I believe that if her husband ever laid a hand on one of her children, the way he has with her, she wouldn't hesitate to find a way out. She's a very good momma in that way."

"Your job must be heartbreaking in some ways."

"It is, but the good far outweighs the tough parts. What about you? What will you do to make a living on the homestead? Or maybe you don't need to?"

"I've been thinking a lot about that. I came up here with some money, so I'm not yet desperate, which I know is different from many people. But I will need to do some seasonal work, or something I can do from the homestead, eventually. Once I get the cabin built, I will have more time to do some writing. I'm not bad at it and I've got some stories, but that's a hit-and-miss business. So, I was thinking of maybe working summers in the park at Denali, or maybe going into Talkeetna during tourist season. I could sell fireweed ice cream with the best of them."

They laughed.

"Sure, you could do those things. There are also jobs on the oil slope cleaning rooms and cooking, or working for the state doing some of the more remote things like reporting animal and fish counts and such. I'm sure you'll get something figured out when you need to. It would be a shame, though, if you had to leave your homestead in the summer. That's the most glorious time out there. Not that winter is bad, it's just…"

"Harder." Jesse finished Caroline's thought, and while she believed it, she hoped it would get easier.

Jesse, too, felt sure that all would be figured out. With friends like Caroline and the support that appeared so easily in these parts, anything seemed possible.

SWATTING at bugs and covering her eyes with her sunglasses and a shirt, Jesse tried to sleep in her truck at a pullout near Nancy Lake on the way back to Talkeetna. The longer daylight and the plunging temperature when the sun finally went down made it especially hard to sleep. It was cold, but she had endured far worse in the wall tent. She looked forward to a warmer winter in her cabin, even if it wasn't entirely finished. The wood stove she chose for the cabin would allow her to heat and cook, like Sadie did. Compared to the tiny stove in the wall tent, it seemed mammoth. James thought he could bring the stove in on a special trip. If not, she would have to haul it in on a sled during the winter, which would delay moving into the cabin. Somehow, she knew it would all work out as it should.

16

ONCE IN A LIFETIME TRIP

Summer 1985
Lynx Creek Homestead

"THAT'S IT! We get these last sheets of steel on the roof to seal you in and out of the elements." Clarence straddled a log rafter, munching on a candy bar. He had brought a few cases out with him, knowing they would need quick fuel and wouldn't want to take time out for cooking. Besides, he and Jesse often took stolen moments to share a candy bar on fishing trips, road trips, or working together in the garage. "The view is fantastic from up here today. I can see the top of Denali finally."

Clouds had shrouded the grand mountain most of the time.

"I couldn't have done it without you, Dad." Jesse poured cold coffee into a tall mug. The coffee was hours old and set on the ground near the fire pit that now lay dormant for the day. She and her dad were in their second week of cramming all the work they could into the long hours of daylight.

"This has been an adventure of a lifetime for this old Minnesotan! Your mom doesn't know what she missed out on."

"She's just not built the same way we are, Dad. Her fears get in the way. It's amazing that she agreed to spend time in Hawaii this summer."

"The call of the grandchildren is strong. I think she's realizing that these may be her only grandchildren, and if she wants to be part of their lives, she needs to go to them."

Clarence tucked the candy wrapper into his shirt pocket and held his hands out for Jesse to slide a sheet of barn red metal roofing up to him. "I'm going to feel accomplished after we get this all buttoned up. I still can't believe you lived in that wall tent all winter and didn't freeze solid."

"Some days I look back and can't believe I had the guts to do it. Sadie helped me out a lot. She's a wise woman."

"You talked about her when you called last spring. I expected to meet this amazon woman with the brute strength of a man. Instead, she's the most graceful, petite elder. It's been a great joy to get to know her. She sure has stories to tell!"

Before Clarence arrived at the homestead, Jesse entertained several spontaneous building parties. At different times and during various phases of building, friends stopped in and stayed for long weekends to help. Sometimes she had a heads-up on Trapline Chatter and sometimes she didn't, but it was always great to have extra hands to help. Inevitably, they brought some food and drink from town. She felt guilty having people give away their time on the precious summer days, so she always tried to make it a time to build special memories. While there, the guests often took time to fish.

There was always plenty to do when she was alone, too. She felled trees, cleared roots from the building site, peeled bark from the fallen logs, chopped deadfall into firewood for the winter and the cooking firepit, and other building chores.

Jesse felt a cadence taking hold in her life, periods of hard work alternated with long hours lost in the magic of her new home.

Jesse listened faithfully for updates on barge deliveries. Most of the building supplies were being delivered by barge. It took some time, but she found enough open spots on the barge schedule to get both supplies and tools delivered. The barge could not come up the creek but would drop off her load on the riverbank and she would haul it up the creek. James was booked heavily during the fishing season, but he stopped in a couple of times to help.

Jesse was especially grateful for help digging the permanent outhouse hole, as well as the holes for the cabin's floor support pillars, which reached down four feet and up four feet off the ground. Jesse hoped that the long overhangs of the roof and the raised floor would prevent the lower logs from rotting under the wetness of snow.

After visiting Caroline's cabin, Jesse adjusted her plans to include a half-loft, giving more space for storage and guest sleeping. She had to find some taller trees, but could do that and haul them to the building site fairly easily. The footprint of the cabin was quite a bit larger than a standard trapper's cabin. Since she planned to live there year-round most of the time, Jesse wanted adequate space for herself and the dog or dogs she would eventually get. Looking at the 20 by 24 feet of floor, with no interior walls, Jesse felt like she was building a mansion. Finishing the interior would take more time and money than she wanted to leverage right now, but she was confident that over time, she would have a comfortable, if not beautiful, home. Once the roof was installed, the wood stove set in place in the center of the cabin, and the chimney plumbed, the essentials would be done before the next winter snow settled in.

———

"TELL me again about meeting that lady Iditarod winner." Clarence asked as he swept out a corner of the cabin, one of the last chores of the day.

"Actually, I met that woman, Caroline, at the Iditaski race checkpoint about ten miles upriver from here. Sadie and I also went to the Iditarod at the Skwentna checkpoint, but we had a stand-off with a moose on the trail and got there later than we had planned so we missed several of the racers, including the now-famous Libby Riddles, the first woman to win the Iditarod." Jesse paused and stretched her back after hours of picking up building debris from the ground surrounding her new home. "It's a nighttime checkpoint. Sadie worked up there for several years, passing out warm drinks and supporting the dogs and mushers. The mushers rest their dogs on straw spread out on the ice. They check in at the cabin, get something to eat and drink, and if they have a dog that needs care, they can have a vet see it."

Jesse paused again to haul a load of scraps from inside the cabin to the woodpile and continued as she walked back into the cabin. "We finally got there at about midnight, instead of the ten p.m. we were shooting for. You would think we would be exhausted, but there was so much going on. Between the noise from the dogs, the cheering, and all the opportunities to help, it kept us revved up and, we were psyched to be that close to the action. Sadie joined the ladies in the cabin serving food and I helped heat water down on the river. We took a little nap on cots in the cabin after the mushers went through and then came home."

"Well, that Riddles sure made a splash around the world. Can you imagine weathering the storms she did and braving it to be the first to finish? That's a gutsy lady!"

"I hear she's not only an incredible musher, but a really nice person, too. I'm sorry we didn't get to see her, but it was quite an event, anyway."

It was ten in the evening and the sun was setting, an orange glow filling the horizon. After another day of work, father and daughter sat contentedly outside, watching the last embers fade away.

———

"We've done it, Dad. We've built a home!" Jesse stood by the front door on the temporary steps leading up that would eventually be replaced by a large deck. She popped the lid off a beer left behind by the last group of helpers, handed it to her dad and grabbed one for herself.

Clarence leaned in and clanked the neck of his beer bottle against Jesse's. "I'm so proud of you, girl. You have surpassed all I could image you would accomplish out here in a year."

"Yeah? And I feel like I have just begun. I have plenty of future projects in mind, too. I still wish we could figure out a root cellar set-up, but I'm afraid of the mold in the dampness. The outhouse is buttoned up, so that feels good. I will get a shower house and sauna up, probably next year. I'm sure Sadie will let me use hers until then."

"Poor Sadie. I bet she'll miss you visiting so much to get out of the cold tent."

Just then, they heard a rustling along the trail leading toward them. "Poor Sadie, nothing." Walking with a peeled diamond willow walking stick, Sadie came up the trail with a grandson in tow. "This here is Joe. He's come to stay with granny for a couple of days."

Jesse guessed Fred dropped Joe off to help Sadie gather up firewood, as the cold would be upon them soon.

"It's nice to meet you, Joe. I'm glad you could come spend some time with your grandmother." Clarence held his hand out to shake the young man's. He was probably a young teenager, a little taller than his grandmother, with the same dark hair and eyes.

"Nice to meet you, sir. I told Grandmother I wanted to

learn to trap so I can make some money. She said I first had to come out and help get the traps ready for the winter."

"Taking my job, are you?" Jesse joked with the boy.

Joe looked at Jesse, then down at the ground. "Sorry, Jesse, but I need to make some dough. I want a new snow-go this year."

"Hey, man, I'm just joking! I'm glad your grandmother is teaching you about trapping. She is amazing."

Joe looked up at Jesse, relieved and smiling. "It's okay, really?"

"Sure thing!" Jesse looked at Sadie and smiled, then looked toward her cabin with its freshly peeled logs and new metal roof. "As you can see, I've got my hands full with this cabin project here."

"It sure is a fancy cabin, isn't it, Joe?" Sadie drew her lips into a thin line and forced herself not to smile with pride. "My new friend, Aurora there, might just be too good for these parts."

"Sadie, don't be filling his head full of those lies. You know I'm just a cheechako trying my best to live with the elements. Joe, she's just kidding. Your grandmother loves me, too." Jesse grinned at the boy.

"Hey Sadie, can I interest you in a beer? We have a couple hanging around here yet and we had them cooling in the creek earlier. And Joe, I think we have a soda around here, too."

"That would be great. We've been oiling and fixing up traps all day, but had a little time to put together some sandwiches. When Joe came out, he brought me a pantry box full of all kinds of fresh food and we wanted to share with you. He even brought a big bag of that fancy kettle corn from the fair."

"That's so nice! One thing I've learned since coming up to visit Jesse, if you play your cards right out here, you're never going to go hungry." Sadie, and the others who helped, impressed Clarence with the generosity of time, talent, and a variety of food and other gifts. Everyone shared what they had, including Jesse. Nobody was a stranger, and everyone was equally welcome to stop by.

"Has to be that way out here. It's why we don't put locks on our cabins, most of us. Never know when it's life or death for someone to get out of the elements or away from danger. Jesse here. She put a lock on her door, but I'm going to convince her to leave it unlocked when she's away, just in case."

"Maybe. I'll probably lock up my tool shed when I get it built, though."

"That might be. Or, I guess you could just leave your wall tent up with the stove in it. That would help someone out who is in need, too."

"The problem with that is, I don't trust it to last too long. Anyway, it served me well over the last year. I've moved most of the stuff into the house, trying to make it feel a little homey. With all that room now, I don't know what to do with myself."

"Ain't that the truth? You better have an extra bed for old Sadie to come visit. I might be the one getting cold in the winter."

Sadie laughed heartily. She loved having Jesse's company, especially over the past winter. She silently wondered just how many more winters she could withstand the harshness by herself. Every year her trapline got smaller and smaller and last year, with Jesse's help, it was quite productive; but she didn't want to tie Jesse up. Sadie was happy that Joe wanted to learn how to trap and keep the tradition alive, even if only as a hobby and not as a way of life. Sadie's own son learned the lifestyle growing up, but Sadie encouraged him to go to school and raise a family in town.

Sadie's lifestyle was harsh. She loved it, but had grown into it over many decades. The first winters were challenging, like they are for everyone choosing to live in the extreme conditions they faced some years. Coming from the orphanage, where nothing was really hers, to having a life abundant with scenery, nature, food, and for most years, companionship, she wanted for nothing but good health so she could continue to enjoy the solitude. She had a feeling that Jesse was cut from similar cloth. She thrived under the demands of the seasons and survival, and had a naturally creative and curious outlook that would help her continue to thrive.

Jesse and Clarence walked Sadie and Joe part-way down the trail so Clarence could get a little more time in with Sadie, a woman who astounded him with the detailed knowledge she had of the area and the history of Alaska.

Just one more sleep and they would leave the homestead and head for Anchorage. Clarence could fly home from there and Jesse would make one more supply run before winter set in. While they listened to Trapline Chatter one last night together, James confirmed their flight out the next day.

"It's so fun to hear these messages come across the radio. I have a better appreciation for how much it means when we send our greetings in. You know, being so many thousands of miles away, it's easy to let our imaginations get carried away, thinking about all the dangers out here, but I will leave tomorrow with a better understanding and a greater faith that you are well, healthy, and happy, my precious daughter."

Jesse sat next to her dad on the makeshift stoop of her hew home and rested her head on his shoulder. After a long silence, she reached up, kissed him on the cheek, and whispered, "Thanks, Dad, I love you forever."

Clarence sighed. "It's going to be hard to leave this place tomorrow. It's been such an adventure."

"And I am so grateful we had the time together, Dad."

———

In one of her Christmas notebooks, Jesse recorded the names and contact information for all her visitors. There were so many that she was sure she would forget the details if she didn't. Among the visitors was a sweet, enthusiastic young couple, Rona and Dave, who migrated to Homer two summers before. Dave explained that they both worked on fishing boats during tourist season and for the school district during the school year. They wanted to move north to Alaska's interior. "We love Homer, we really do, but it's a bit too civilized for us, even as a small town at the end of the road."

"Everyone works seasonal jobs plus other jobs to make ends meet. It's really a beautiful place, and we see whales, which we won't see around here, but we want freedom to challenge ourselves to really live deep in nature, where we are providing most of what we eat and harvesting from the earth and sky the little we truly need to subsist."

Rona, whose long, thick, blond braids framed a round sun-freckled face, explained that part of her upbringing was spent living in an abandoned train car on the off-roads of Oregon. "My mom was a hippie-wanna-be. She is an accomplished poet and now is an English professor. But fifteen years ago, she was in an anti-establishment phase and took the three of us kids and her then-boyfriend out to a piece of property rented from some old coot she ran into at the bar. Honestly, it was great for us as a family, and it didn't hurt any of us educationally. We hauled a ton of books out there from Goodwill and donations from friends. And every time someone came out to visit, which was at least every month, they would bring booze, pot or other stuff, leftovers from their refrigerators and a box of books."

"That sounds like an amazing chapter in your life, Rona. All kids should be so lucky." Jesse enjoyed this couple and was happy to learn that they had bought a parcel of property about five miles south. She would see them more often when they started building.

"Now that we bought the land, we will spend the winter saving up and getting supplies together to start building, hopefully, in the spring." Dave looked like the Alaska dream catch for any young girl. He had dark wavy hair, bright blue eyes, five-day stubble and arms made of steel.

"I've learned a lot building my place, and I have lots of tools to share, if you need. I would also suggest that you do some pricing. Your most affordable options for getting supplies out here are to get a snow-go, if you don't have one, and sled it out in the winter, along the frozen river, or having it barged up the river and then using a four-wheeler to haul supplies from the river to your building site."

"Thanks for those thoughts, Jesse. I always appreciate talking to someone who has done it and has helpful ideas."

"Oh, happy to share. Do you know about Trapline Chatter?" Jesse wanted to share with this young couple all the things she had learned in the prior year that helped her succeed.

Rona and Dave looked at each other. Dave responded on the couple's behalf. "No, I don't think we have heard of that."

"It's how we stay in touch with the outside world here. It's a nightly radio show that brings messages to and from those of us who live in the interior. I listen every night. If you know you're coming up, give me a holler on the Trapline. I'll gladly meet you and help you haul stuff or whatever, if I'm around. At some point, I'm going to have to get a job, at least a seasonal one, and put some cash in the bank for future expansions and replacements."

"Hey, the boats are always looking for help during tourist season. I'm sure we could get you a spot for next summer if you want to join us. We probably will work through next summer and put the cash in the bank. We will tent so everything we make will be available for our building project. Tips are pretty good for deck hands, especially if the fishing is good, which it has been during our time." Dave's blue eyes danced as he shared his idea.

Jesse agreed to consider it and asked them to keep her in mind if they heard of any openings. She wasn't sure she wanted to leave in the summer, when living was easier on the homestead, but she might consider it for a season.

17

CURIOUS, CLUMSY AND CHARISMATIC

Spring and Summer 1986
  Lynx Creek

JESSE EMERGED from the harsh frozen depths of her second winter in Lynx Creek to the luscious hopefulness of spring. This winter, the first in her cabin, was filled with days of awe and days of awful. Her dear friend Sadie stayed in Fairbanks after Christmas, hoping to return after breakup. She was hospitalized with pneumonia and suffered a slow recovery. Sadie's son visited her cabin every few weeks, and Jesse kept the trapline going. Sadie sent word that it wasn't necessary, but Jesse was already in the routine and looked forward to filling the otherwise quiet and sometimes lonely days with meaningful activity. Besides, she would share the income from the pelts. That was a necessity, as she looked to make additional improvements on her property.

Early in the winter, Jesse followed the radio news of a continuing decline in oil prices, causing many Alaska employers to issue pink slips to Alaskans. As the social and economic forecasts became grimmer, Jesse stopped listening to all but Trapline Chatter. There was a burgeoning interest in living off-grid in remote Alaska as people across the state examined their options. Jesse silently considered the possibility of more settlers in the area, as Alaskans adjusted to hard times.

While checking the river for overflow one early spring day, Jesse encountered three men on snow-gos attempting to navigate the heavy slush of the trail beside the river. They explained they were out looking at a plot of land for sale through the state land office. Jesse spent a little time with them, giving the lay of the land. One man made her feel uneasy. She felt him staring at her, and he took her picture when he thought she wasn't looking. For a stranger, he was a little too friendly.

"Thanks for all the info, Jesse. It was nice talking to you." Bill, a plain-looking thirty-ish man from Kenai, reached out to shake her hand. "I'm thinking this is a little too remote for my fiancé, but it sure is beautiful out here. If it was just me, there would be no question. George here, on the other hand, likes his alone time and may be more interested. We were all hoping we could find a place near one another since we all work the same shift on the slope."

Jesse didn't want creepy George nearby. "Yeah, I know there are a few slope workers who live up Trapper's Creek way, but they are closer to the road than I am out here. Maybe that's a better place to look."

"We've heard that suggestion before, so we'll try to check it out. We may have to wait for breakup now, though. We're kinda pushing it out here today with the warm weather," explained Jonathan, the quieter man with sad eyes.

"Good luck finding what you're looking for. I'm pretty new yet at this lifestyle, but it can be rewarding, in a rugged, symbiotic kind of way. I've certainly learned a lot."

Bill was on his snow-go waiting for his buddies to mount up and ride back to town. "I bet you have! I've spent a lot of time outdoors, year-round, but I've always been able to escape the elements if I needed to. I can only imagine it would test all your senses to stay calm and think through some of the hairy situations that come up."

Jesse was not about to share some of the challenging moments she had during this winter, alone. Most of them involved an overactive imagination, but others were less benign – like the encounter with a hungry wolverine that insisted on picking at her traps.

Jesse set traps in a two-mile radius so she could travel only in daylight and check each trap. One bitter cold day, when the wind died down and the trees stood tall and frozen in time, she was lost in thought, carrying a bag with two martens, both stiff as a board. She rounded the trail to the south when she spotted the wolverine pulling at a trap holding a large beaver with thick dark fur. Jesse pulled out her shotgun, loaded the barrel, and took aim.

Adrenaline coursed through her, making her nauseous. Gripping the gun tightly helped stop the shakes from taking over her hands. She didn't want to shoot the animal, aware that it was just trying to survive. She yelled at it to leave, thinking it would run off into the brush. Instead, the wolverine charged toward her with its jaw wide open, baring a mouthful of long, sharp teeth with long tusk-like canines. Puffs of steam flew from its mouth and nostrils as it grew more and more aggressive and the hairs on its back fluffed up. The terrifying image would be etched in her mind forever. Jesse's aim that day was remarkable, despite the stress. With one shot between the eyes, that wolverine was down.

Jesse tanned the pelt, initially thinking she could have it finished with purple felt to hang in the cabin. But having dead animals hanging around her was not the Feng Shui she was striving for. She lived with wild around her outside; she wanted to have some control over the aesthetics inside her home. The pelt went to auction, and the proceeds would go toward the next phase of her dream life.

As the snow-goers rode off, Jesse looked around and noticed the changes along the river. The amazing vegetation adapted to the long, cold winters and short growing season. The trees had roots that ran shallow and parallel to the surface. Soon, there would be fresh shoots on the spruce, paper birch and willow trees, and sedge stems would rise in their stately triangular shape. Delicate and deceptive devil's club shoots, precursors to the large spiny plants, would fill in along trails. Infusion of spring and summer light would warm and nurture the earth, where muskeg would fill in with moss and berries. The picture would eventually be complete with speckles of wild iris, Sitka roses, poppies, dwarf dogwoods, and brilliant pink wild sweet pea, adding color and texture to the landscape. Alpine forget-me-nots would hug the earth, their delicate petals on hardy plants aptly representing Alaska as the state flower. Jesse hoped to find the darling and delicate pink spring Fairy Slippers and twinflowers this summer. Elusive and ethereal, they reminded her of little pixies.

Jesse kept a close eye on the river as the ice started to break up. Broken ice could jam on the severe curves and sandbars of the river and cause backups, with water overflowing and flooding the banks when the jams released. Her property was far enough away from the river and would not be impacted directly, but trails would become impassable. Lynx Creek was narrower and deeper, so the risk of dangerous flooding was significantly lower; but she kept a close watch there too, since that was an important source of water for her.

Jesse elected not to join Rona and Dave for the tourist-fishing season in Homer. Sadie returned in late May, and Jesse felt compelled to be around to help her. Sadie had Lynx Creek flowing through her veins, and Jesse wanted to help her enjoy every minute possible in her own home. On one of his last winter visits, Sadie's son explained that the family was planning to visit Sadie often during the summer, but they could not be there all the time. Jesse told him she would keep a close eye on Sadie and help in every way she could.

Jesse tapped the birch trees and made syrup for Sadie and herself. She harvested devil's club, fiddlehead, and fireweed shoots to supplement rabbit or fish entrees. Harnessing the lightened mood with the longer daylight, she did spring cleaning inside and outside Sadie's cabin as well as her own. Sadie's wood supply was still healthy, but Jesse topped it off with rounds harvested from deadfall and broken branches for kindling. She swept out the steam house and staged fresh wood in the stove for the next steam.

In early summer, the mosquitoes were terrible. Large and plentiful, the pesky insects infuriated Jesse, buzzing around her head when she tried to sleep. She didn't remember them being so abundant during the first and second summers at the homestead. There had been a heavier snowfall this year, and a wet spring, so the mosquito hatches were more successful… for the mosquitoes!

A few weeks after Sadie returned, the first fireweed blossoms appeared. Sadie and Jesse spent lazy afternoons harvesting the blossoms. They dried some to make a stomach-soothing tea, boiled some for syrup, and treated mosquito bites with crushed blossoms. In a few short weeks, they lined their pantry shelves with jars of the magenta-colored jams and syrup.

The rains came in late July. The Skwentna River swelled and gnawed away the banks with its rapid flow. Jesse and Sadie listened to the radio each evening. It was the highest the Skwentna had reached in over a hundred years. Before it was over, two homes perched on the river's edge slid as the banks beneath them gave way. There was nothing Jesse and Sadie could do to help.

Had they seen this coming, Sadie's family would never have let her return. They could not visit. There was no safe way for anyone to travel. The river swelled to levels unsafe for travel, and the trails were too muddy for four-wheelers. Jesse and Sadie had their hands full, keeping the chill off the cabin. After being ill, Sadie was thinner, and despite their best efforts, could not put much weight back on. Her mood was bright, though. Sadie loved being in her own home.

"I would never complain about being with my family, but there is nothing like being back home where I have so many memories. Part of my soul stays here when I leave and I'm never quite in my skin when I'm away."

"Sadie, it seems like the winters and probably the wood stove smoke are hard on you, though. Do you think you will go back to town this winter, where you can see the doctor if you need to? And have heat without the smoke?"

"Not you too, Aurora," Sadie answered dismally. "That's all my family wants to talk about."

Sadie opened the cabin door to watch the rain. It was a steamy, wet August day, another day of gray sky that faded to a darker gray late in the night. Sadie sat in her chair and watched the rain drip off the overhang, making puddles around the cabin. Her mood brightened. "I just want to live today, okay? This is the day I want to enjoy, rain and all. This is just another season, and I want to enjoy it like all the others."

Jesse wasn't certain if Sadie was talking about the dreary, rainy weather, or Sadie's station in life. It didn't matter. Jesse sat quietly with Sadie until it cooled down in the early evening.

"How about I heat some stew, Sadie? It will be good to have something warm before bed. It feels like this dampness is going to bring cold to us tonight."

"Help yourself, Aurora. I just want to layer up and go to bed. Do you think you could read one of the Psalms to me tonight?"

Since returning, Sadie complained of blurry vision. She often asked Jesse to read to her in the evenings. Sometimes Jesse read from Sadie's well-worn Bible and sometimes it was a classic tale from a tattered leather-bound series that smelled of mildew and dust when Jesse turned the pages. Outside, there appeared to be nothing wrong with Sadie's eyesight. She could still spot an eagle high in a tree a mile away, or a no-see-um cloud hovering on the edge of the trail at dusk.

Jesse was thankful that she stayed on the homestead for the summer instead of working on a fishing boat in Homer. She loved Sadie like a grandmother, a sister, a best friend, and would do anything for her, including reading her to sleep. Most evenings, as Sadie quietly slumbered, Jesse snuck off to her own cabin for the night and returned early in the morning. She often found Sadie still asleep in bed. She had aged ten years in one. Jesse wasn't sure if this decline was because of being sick, normal aging, or having been away from her home for so long over the winter. She watched carefully, and it seemed that Sadie grew stronger as the weeks went on. Despite all, she was still witty, would recall readings from previous nights when she had appeared asleep, and shared related stories from her own life or her application of a passage from the Bible. But she was a long way from being the woman who left last Christmas.

The rains finally subsided in mid-August when they harvested rose hips and berries. They dried and crushed the hips, remnants of the spent Sitka rose blossoms. Sadie had introduced Jesse to rose hips in tea early in their relationship.

"The vitamin C in these is really good for us, and crushing these hips is building my muscles. I can feel it." In prior years, Jesse was not as patient as Sadie in harvesting, drying, and crushing them. This year, however, Jesse sat beside Sadie, making a ritual of crushing while Sadie reminisced. She never tired of Sadie's stories. Each day was a new adventure in Sadie's story land. Sometimes she talked of her childhood before the orphanage. Other days she talked of life in the orphanage, her family and friends there, and the wild abandon carrying her into the depths of the interior of Alaska.

"Sadie, have you ever been outside Alaska?" Jesse caught Sadie pausing between stories.

Sadie puffed out her bony chest and held her chin high. "Why, sure I have! I used to represent Alaskans in Washington, D.C."

"You did?" Jesse had grown accustomed to Sadie's stories and was seldom surprised anymore, but this was a side that she had not expected. "What was that like?"

"It was a different time, that's for sure. It was before John died and my kids were out of the house. I was at the fur auction in 1959. Let's see… I was a youthful fifty-one then. The good old days. Anyway, Governor Egan was just a few months in office and was trying to get a council together to meet with mucky-mucks in D.C. They schooled me in the orphanage, so I spoke English well. It was just a chance meeting, but it turned into about a decade of meetings, reviewing materials, planning speeches, most of which were canceled, and five times I flew to D.C. to present information. Mostly it was to support natives getting land, but it also was important to talk about atomic fallout and damage to flora and fauna, education, health care and more. We even did presentations on native arts and dress. One year, we took a group of dancers who performed traditional dances. They thrilled the audience, but I don't know if it meant the tribes or the state got any more funding. That's really what it ended up being about, and that was one of the last years I went."

"What was it like to be in the middle of politics?"

"Honestly, I hated it. I didn't really care what those people thought of me. At first, I felt important, but mostly, it became a nuisance, especially after John died. It wasn't easy for me to get in and out of here. I had dogs, and I was nervous flying."

"That surprises me, Sadie. You are so fearless out here."

Sadie sat quietly for several minutes. She pointed to a stack of books on the bottom shelf of the one bookcase, but didn't have the strength to pull out the book that she wanted.

"Aurora, will you pull out that world atlas book there?"

Jesse did and, after wiping the soot and dust off the spine on her pants, handed it to her. Sadie leafed through the book and pulled out an old newspaper article, yellowed with age. The black and once-white photo was nearly smudged out. She handed it to Jesse and pointed to herself, the most petite of the dozen people on the page. There she stood in the center, the White House in the background.

"Out here, I know what the risks are. I know how to prepare for them and avoid danger, mostly. Up in that tin box in the sky, I had no control and D.C. seemed so big and busy to me. Besides, I'm not a political animal. I'm native, but I was transplanted from the traditional native culture when my parents died. I used a lot of what I learned growing up to survive out here, but I don't really see that as being exclusively native knowledge. I mean, really, look at all the white folks making a life in rural areas without utilities. I'm not trying to deny my native heritage. I just don't pretend to speak for others the way the politicians wanted me to. I just tried to be real about this lifestyle. There were land grabs, native rights and treaty discussions, and oil rights conversations happening all around me, but I was really just window dressing. It was just too much."

FOR THE FIRST time in about thirty years, fish camp didn't happen because of the flooding. Decades before, Sadie established the fish camp by inviting family and friends to gather in late August along the river's shore. In those three decades Sadie watched the children from the various families grow up and return with their own children to enjoy camping, playing, fishing and putting up the harvest. Knowing that Sadie could not travel to camp this year, friends harvested and prepared salmon for her, and sent it out by plane. Jesse met the plane at the Lynx Creek airstrip and brought several boxes of jarred, canned and bagged salmon back for she and Sadie to share.

Sadie was up and puttering in the yard when Jesse arrived. She walked over, put her thin arms around her waist, and rested her head on Jesse's chest. It seemed that Sadie had lost about three inches from her already short body. "Oh, Aurora! I have the best friends, and you are at the top of the list. This is . . . just the best present ever."

Sadie reached into a plastic baggie and held up a piece of salmon jerky. "This is my candy! This makes me happy!"

18

DARKNESS

Fall and Winter 1986
Homestead

JESSE WAS WAITING in Sadie's yard when Fred and Joe came to get her. It was a sorrowful parting as Sadie left for Fairbanks with her family that late September day, when fall death and decay had already taken hold in the leaves and undergrowth. She promised Jesse to return after Christmas. Exhausted and saddened by her friend's leaving, for the first time on this homestead Alaska adventure, Jesse questioned her emotional ability to live the remote life. She managed being alone. It was drowning in loneliness that she feared.

Rona and Dave put off their move to Lynx Creek for another year. After fishing season closed down, they made only one trip to the property, flying in to the Lynx Creek airstrip and hiking to their property for a week. They staked out the likely home site and felled some trees. The fishing season had not been as lucrative as they needed. The fishing charters canceled about half of the trips because of weather. Jesse was thankful she didn't join them. The time spent with Sadie was precious, given her upcoming absence.

Jesse greeted Rona and Dave with open arms as they stopped in for an overnight visit before flying back to Homer. They planned to work for the school one more year, then hopefully be better positioned to take the full-time remote plunge. It was good to see friends who were excited about moving to their homestead, and Jesse felt she had some pearls of wisdom to share from her own journey.

"We could see how high the creek rose with all the debris pushed up on shore. We're glad we aren't right on the creek after all." Dave was recounting their adventure to their property and what they accomplished while there.

"I think I found a suitable spot for a garden, too. It's out in the open and should get plenty of sun. It's not too far from the house." Rona's eyes were bright with excitement.

"I hope you have better luck with your garden than I have so far. The first year I got here too late to put one in. My second year, I turned some soil and cut out a bunch of tree roots, but only planted a few things. Unfortunately, the animals got to them before I did. My fence was not sturdy enough. So this year I planned to reinforce the fence, but the rain made it impossible to get much done."

"And it sounds like you were spending a lot of time helping Sadie. You were her guardian angel this year." Rona reached out and patted Jesse's hand. She turned away to check on the brewed tea and fried Spam and biscuits she was making for dinner, letting the tears brimming in her eyes settle back in place. Being premenstrual was not helping her to manage the sadness she felt these days.

"Well, it worked out that I could help her spend more time at her home. She loves it out here, and I know her family has commitments in town."

"I hope she has a wonderful winter and can return in the

spring." Dave hoped to hear some of Sadie's stories from the early days.

"You and me both. She's a strong woman in spirit." Jesse paused and took a drink of tea. Desperate to change the subject, she looked at the wind-up clock standing on the shelf by her bed. "It's about time to catch Trapline Chatter. We should make sure your plane is still planning to come tomorrow."

Jesse reached over and switched on the radio. There weren't too many messages this evening - a few people planning hunting trips and making mail runs. The air service from Talkeetna confirmed the Lynx Creek run for the following afternoon.

"I wonder who your pilot will be. I've met five or six of them coming from Talkeetna." Jesse enjoyed meeting each of them, but James was who she most looked forward to catching up with. She hadn't seen him since spring, and that was a brief visit, when he delivered some mail and a couple looking at property a few miles east of Jesse's homestead. There was no time for cribbage during that visit. James dropped her a message on Trapline Chatter several times, just to remind her to reach out if she needed anything. He knew she was helping Sadie out under the strain of the rain and floods. His messages of good will always made her smile.

THE CESSNA TOUCHED down the following afternoon. James emerged from the cockpit, his aviator sunglasses reflecting the bright sun shadowed by his brilliant smile. Jesse greeted him with a big hug.

"James, my friend, it's so good to see you! You got quite a tan over the summer, didn't you?"

"In the past month, since the rains went away, mostly. What a crazy summer we had. Not the most fun one of my career, I can tell you. How about you? You're looking good."

Jesse looked away for a long moment, then back at James. Her smile was half-baked, and the enthusiasm had escaped her eyes. "Yeah, I'm good. Thanks."

James wasn't buying her line. "Is that so? You care to take a ride in with us? They don't have much gear and I've got some down time. How about you come in? We'll catch up and I'll bring you back out tomorrow, if you want."

Jesse was usually anxious in the face of spontaneity, but analyzing the situation, she determined that there was nothing she had to stay for. Her cabin would be fine for a short time, and she could pick up a toothbrush if James didn't have any extras. She shrugged her shoulders and looked at Dave and Rona. "You guys mind if I ride in with you?"

Dave shook his head. "Not one bit. We can spend a few more minutes together. That's great, but I call dibs on the co-pilot's seat. I love the view."

"Fair enough." They loaded up, Jesse taking the seat behind James.

"You all in a hurry, or do you have a few extra minutes?" James was checking dials and getting the plane in position for take-off.

"We've got time. What's up?"

"Just thought maybe you would like to see the flood damage up at Skwentna. I've seen nothing like it on these rivers here ever. I've seen that flooding in other parts of the state, but never around here. Sure did a number on some properties over there."

"I would really appreciate seeing that, James, especially after listening to it on the radio over the summer. Sadie and I really wanted to help, but there was no way we could get there."

"There is nothing you could have done. This was not something a sandbag brigade could have helped. The river was violent with all the water, and taking out anything in its path. You'll see."

James flew over the area along the river outside of Skwentna village and showed them where the banks gave way and rerouted the river. Uprooted trees landed on sandbars and were jammed against the banks. A cabin rested diagonally on a steep bank. The river had scooped the dirt from under it, causing it to collapse in a heap. Another home was lifted off its foundation by the raging waters and carried downstream, where it rested now in piles of rubble.

Jesse shook her head at the sight. "Those poor people! What an awful thing for them."

"Yeah. Thank God nobody was hurt. The family used that first cabin there recreationally, and thankfully the family wasn't there. The other one is a permanent residence, but as soon as they discovered chunks of riverbank falling into the rushing water, the couple got out of there, taking as much as they could and moving it to higher ground. I hear they are planning to rebuild, but will have to start over to get funding for new supplies. I'm not sure what they do for work, but I heard they have some rental properties in Anchorage. Maybe they will have to sell something to get a new start out here. I think one of them is a photographer, and that's why they want to be out here full time."

"I would like to meet those people and help them if they need labor when they rebuild. If you hear anything more, could you pass on the info?" Jesse was serious. That was how this part of the world could survive, by not-so-close neighbors helping each other. She appreciated the help she had received with her building, and was more than willing to offer the same to others.

"Yes, of course."

The group fell silent for the quick trip to Talkeetna, awed by the destructive force of nature felt by seemingly innocent intruders. In less than thirty minutes, they were on the ground and parting ways.

"Until next time, my friends." Jesse pulled Rona and Dave in close for a group hug.

"Until next time," the couple responded in unison.

James looked at Jesse as they walked to the office. "Let me take care of some paperwork here, then we can run down to the Roadhouse and grab a steak and a beer, or maybe a pizza. What are you in the mood for?"

Jesse hadn't given a thought to her appearance. She wasn't planning to come to town. Her hair was several days past its last washing, her muck boots were the gray color of dried mud, and mud rimmed her jeans.

"Do you think I look presentable enough?"

"Are you kidding?" James chuckled. "You'll fit right in. We're a motley crew around here and very accepting, especially of those just like us."

Jesse shrugged and walked into the airport office while James held the door.

"Well, if it isn't Minnesota Jesse! Hi honey, how are you doing?" Linda hopped up from the chair, pulled her reading glasses off and came around the desk to give Jesse a hug. "It's so good to see you again! Looks like you weathered the summer storm okay."

"I did better than some. James showed us some of the wreckage. There but for the grace of God go I."

"Yes, those poor folks. Anyway, it's great to see you. Are you in town for long?"

Jesse looked to James. "Just for the night, unless James is booked tomorrow, then I guess I will stay a little longer. I'm crashing on James's couch, so I don't want to wear out my welcome."

James laughed. "No chance of that. I have two couches. If one gets worn out, you can move to the next one."

Jesse smiled. This was a nice reprieve from the gray, wet summer and the dreariness of Sadie's ill-health.

. . .

"I'm glad you came to town, Jesse. I had a sense you needed a change of scenery." James picked a piece of pizza off the pan in the middle of their table.

"Really? How did you know?"

James shrugged while chewing through a bite of pizza. "I've seen it before, with others. You just don't have the same spark in your eyes you normally have."

Appreciating his honesty, Jesse nodded slightly in agreement. "Honestly, I've been feeling a bit like I might have been overly confident to think I can live like this."

"What part of it do you mean?" James looked over the rim of his glass as he took a drink of soda.

"I think it's being alone, mostly. I'm not scared of the hard work, but I really got spoiled those first two years when Sadie was out there. I've relied on her company and knowledge, and yeah, I guess her caring for me. I doubt I will see her until late spring, if at all. I'm pretty worried about her. And then I think about my own parents. I haven't seen my mom since I moved up in '83. That reminds me, I really want to call them before I head back to the cabin."

"Sure, of course. Feel free to use the phone at my place. But do you think a phone call is going to be enough? Permanent fund dividends will be here soon. It sounds to me like you're lonely. You could use that money to get a ticket and spend the holidays with them."

"I hadn't even thought about that. This will be my first year to get a check. How much do you think it will be?"

"I heard in the neighborhood of $550, but they haven't officially announced it yet. It won't cover a round-trip ticket completely, but it would cover most of one."

Jesse's face brightened a bit with that thought. "You know, you might have a good idea there. I'll at least call around and see what the ticket prices are and when I talk to my folks I'll try to find out where they're planning to be for the holidays. I don't want to suggest I'm coming and get their hopes up just yet."

James looked up and waved as a friend walked into the restaurant. Jesse was reminded that she was on his turf, where his friends and clients were. She was glad they remained platonic friends. It suited them both. Would she ever be ready for more?

"Well, I think that's a good plan, Jesse. And, if you find you need a little more time in town, that's okay. I'll take you back whenever. I may just have to put skis on the plane if the snow gets too deep, but we'll make it work."

JESSE REACHED her mother the next morning.

"Hi, honey. What's wrong?" Her perpetually anxious mother could not fathom why Jesse would call instead of writing.

"Nothing, Mom. I just came to town to get stocked up and take care of some business. How are things there?"

Thirty minutes later, they were caught up, and Jesse learned her parents planned to spend Thanksgiving and Christmas at home. Her mother was busy with church obligations and her dad had to work. Jesse told her mother how much she appreciated the letters, packages, and Trapline Chatter messages.

"Well, you know how much your dad loved his trip up there. He still talks about it every chance he gets, and you, and your house. He is so proud of you, Jesse. I am too, but I sure miss you. After you and Tim split, I knew you wanted a change, but oh my, I didn't see this one coming. You are a brave woman."

"Thanks Mom. I love it. It was a little different this year. I didn't get to spend a typical summer with lots of sun and fishing, but next summer will be better."

"That's right, Jesse. Just have faith."

"Yes. I will."

The call ended, and immediately Jesse knew she needed to visit, for her soul. She wanted to be connected again to family, in a new way, as a maturing woman - a woman who was raised in Minnesota, but was now growing up in Alaska. Jesse burned to have a different relationship with her mother. One where she wasn't always trying to soothe the anxiety her mother wore like a crown of jewels. She wanted what she had with Sadie, with her mom.

———

TIME PASSED, despite the loneliness, as nature continued its unfolding. By the time she was ready to fly to Minnesota, there was plenty of snow to drive her snow-go to the pick-up point arranged with James. That way, she could drive back to the homestead when she returned from vacation.

"Hey, James! Thanks a million for picking me up." Jesse crawled off her snow-go after a nearly three-hour ride. She was a slow, cautious rider. With each trip, her confidence grew, and she could eventually navigate like a pro, she hoped.

"You're welcome, of course," James spoke as he reached out for a quick hug. "I was thinking, when you come back, you could take a route that would go by Jay's place if you wanted to."

"That's a great idea. You can show me on the map when I get back, if you don't mind."

"You're looking more relaxed. You must be excited about this trip."

"Honestly, I am. I know it'll be cold and snowy there too, but it will be great to see my folks. The only thing I'm not looking forward to is the frozen cabin I return to. I'm so glad it's a dry cabin. Winterizing the plumbing would be a whole other complicated thing at a time like this."

James laughed. "You just remember that the next time you

complain about having to go out in the cold to use your outhouse." He held his hand out to take Jesse's backpack to load into the truck.

"Always the wise one. I'll try to remember that."

JESSE TOOK in the view as they drove to James's place. It was dark when they arrived. She planned to stay the night and head to the airport in Fairbanks the next morning with a friend of James's. Her ticket was nearly $1200 round-trip from Fairbanks, and it would take about two and one-half hours to get to the airport from Talkeetna. Her plane didn't leave until the next evening, but her ride wanted to take advantage of the few daylight hours to drive in earlier. She didn't have any gifts for her parents, the only family that would be in Minnesota for Christmas, so she hoped to find something at the airport gift shop.

Prepared for bed and ready to settle in for the night on the couch, Jesse felt relaxed, yet excited about her first trip outside. "I'm really glad you suggested I go see my parents, James. You are such a great friend."

"What I didn't tell you is that I've had my own bouts with cabin fever and doubts," James admitted. "I've made more than one trip to see the family and fortunately, I've found that to be a cure. For me, it's better than a trip to Hawaii, like so many people take."

"Honestly, that sounds great, too. But right now, being with my family is exactly what my heart needs."

19

HAPPIER NEW YEAR

1987

Just beyond the homestead

JESSE FELT HER MOOD LIFT, her spirit lighten, and life seemed brighter, even in the dark of winter. Spending time with family was the infusion she needed. She hadn't realized it on her own; she needed James to recognize cabin fever and prescribe the cure. James explained that it was common for people with cabin fever not to realize they were blue. They were used to showing up and getting through every day. Autopilot kept them suspended in their routine. Jesse promised her parents she would never wait so long to visit again. Regular correspondence and occasional phone calls, while wonderful, did not replace the warmth of a reassuring hug, a caring gaze exuding unconditional love, and the excitement of sharing stories of an uncommon life first-hand.

Jesse noticed the beautiful sounds of her hidden nirvana more than ever now. Refreshed after the visit to Minnesota, she returned to the homestead with higher energy levels and clearer vision. While away, she realized just how jarring the outside world was. Airplanes, buses, pews filled with people, pageants, and shopping exhausted her to the core. Her soul thrived on being disconnected from the masses. Upon returning, she embraced the natural silence of her tiny space in the universe, with its rugged white frosted mountains, sparsely boughed Sitka spruce trees and naked paper birch. The birds sang freely, their songs filling the wide-open spaces while their little bodies hunkered down onto the trees.

Jesse brought home a case of notebooks, journals, unlined sketch pads, and fine-point markers in every color she could find. To keep positive vibes coursing through her, she committed to writing in a journal. The goal was to write something every day, but she refused to denigrate herself if she didn't. Realistically, four or five days a week would meet her needs. Nobody, except herself, was around to critique and criticize, rain on her parade, or exert demands. While she had heard it said many times that each day was an opportunity for a new beginning, here she lived it.

Yet another realization came: although she loved the solitude, she also needed a community, in moderation and on her terms. The blessing of Sadie's mentorship and companionship which she enjoyed those first years on the homestead was wonderful, but it was unfair to rely on that relationship alone. Jesse knew she needed to venture out and get to know others, even if just to get a better lay of the land. Here, it was not like living in the city or even in a rural area on a country road. In interior Alaska, you had to plan a good chunk of time, and prepare for uncertain conditions and trails, in order to meet and spend time with neighbors; and some of those neighbors weren't so eager to get to know you.

One mid-January day, fresh into the new year, Jesse wrote in her journal and studied an updated map of the area, a gift from James, before heading out with a hatchet and pink construction tape to mark some trails leading towards the nearest neighbors to the west. On glorious mornings like this, with crisp fresh snow deeply dusting the well-worn paths, everything seemed new and fresh.

A dot on the map marked a cabin that was built in the fall. Mr. and Mrs. Melcher now lived there year-round. James heard of them from a colleague, but all he knew was that they were in their mid-forties, and they were nice. Jesse estimated the Melcher place would be about ten miles away, heading west and slightly south. She was determined to meet and welcome this new couple to the neighborhood.

On this gorgeous day, she set out to mark a trail toward these new neighbors, and to evaluate how much work it would be to clear the trail so a snow-go or a four-wheeler could make it. The sun rose at 10:26, two minutes earlier than the day before and about an hour after civil twilight started its gradual and glorious illumination of the sky. As the sun crested in golden brilliance over the horizon, three shotgun blasts roared through the natural stillness. Jesse jumped as the shocking sound reverberated in the valley. Rarely was anyone close enough for her to hear his or her shotgun. She recalled a conversation with Linda at the Talkeetna airport on her return from Minnesota - Alaska State Troopers had been out flying in the area because of moose poachers.

The vastness closed in, and a pang of anxiety rose in Jesse's gut. She didn't want any trouble, but was worried trouble may come to her. It was her nature to think the best of people until proven otherwise. So, she speculated that perhaps a family simply needed to eat in these harsh economic times, and were out hunting. Not wanting to radio in a false report, Jesse slowly and quietly leaned toward the shotgun noise and followed it. She crouched slightly toward the ground and, as quietly as she could on snowshoes, cautiously placed one foot in front of the other. The murmur of voices floated through the stillness. It sounded like there were three of them, upstream about 120 yards. And they were loud - almost like a frat party, something Jesse had experienced only once, as once was enough. One voice was female with a loud, shrill laugh. There was something else that sounded a little frat-ish and put Jesse on high alert. They sounded drunk. If they were drinking just after sunrise, she dreaded an encounter.

She squatted behind an uprooted tree, frosted with a thick layer of snow, unstrapped her snowshoes, and gazed over the frosty terrain. In the dead of winter, there wasn't much brush cover between her and the shore of the creek. Jesse was armed, as she was when there was a risk of encountering a predator, but she had no interest in needing a gun to defend herself from a human. She wasn't sure she even could, or would. Her muffled heartbeat filled her ears. What if these were her new neighbors?

"God, I hope not," silently slid through her mind.

Still crouched, Jesse slowly moved toward the ruckus, holding her breath with each step, fearing a twig would snap, scaring up a spruce hen or ptarmigan, calling attention to her presence. Inching closer, she found a ridge of deadfall to scoot behind without being seen, as if the shadows and wind worked in her favor. It took her within fifty feet of the trio. They were taking turns sitting beside and taking pictures of a freshly killed bull moose with a massive rack, which Jesse estimated to be about six feet from tip to tip.

When the group finished taking photos, the two men retrieved hack saws from their snow-gos and removed the rack with the skull plate. Jesse was horrified. It took all the self-discipline she could muster to keep from yelling out the anger and disgust she felt. Looking over their gear, three snow-gos and one sled, she suspected they had no plans to harvest the moose. They were only there to collect the mammoth antlers.

Jesse slid back into the shadows and quietly retreated. As soon as she could stand upright without the possibility of being seen, she strapped her snowshoes back on and ran as fast as her 25-inch shoed feet allowed, all the while listening for movement coming from the area of the fallen moose. The group still had work to do to remove the heavy antlers and load them onto the sled.

The cabin was in sight when she heard the snow-gos start and head off to the north, the same direction their trail entered from. She believed that would take them northeast. She was eager to reach the radio and call in what she saw before they got too far away. The new-to-her radio was rarely used, but she was happy to have it available now, along with the new map from James that helped her describe to the troopers where she saw the kill site.

"I could be wrong, but I don't think they were planning to harvest the meat. I heard the snow-gos leave, and it sounded like they were heading up toward Trapper's Creek, but you know how the sound can echo out here."

Jesse threw radio protocol out the window. She wanted to give them all the information possible, not caring who was listening, even it if was the poachers.

"We understand and thank you for calling. Our troopers have a plane near there. We'll get them mobilized and see what they can find."

"What about that moose? It will be wolf bait if we just leave it there. I'm not real thrilled about that."

"Understood. If they can get to it, they will salvage the meat and donate it to the Pioneer's Home or a shelter if it's fit for human consumption, or to the zoo or mushers, if it's not. We'll try getting back to you on the radio to give you an update. For now, sit tight where you are and stay safe."

Only after the radio call did Jesse notice that her hands were shaking. She was angry and afraid. Stepping outside, she scanned the area for sights or sounds of anything menacing. She searched the sky for signs of a scout plane, knowing she had only moments ago ended the radio call. Once assured that the poachers had not followed her, caught her scent, or overheard the radio call, she stepped back inside and, in a rare move, locked the door. She was satisfied when it was latched, and two guns were loaded and within reach of her chair. Today, that didn't feel like enough. She sat in her favorite chair facing the door, inhaled and exhaled deeply, consciously working to slow her pounding heart and still her shaking hands.

Within thirty minutes, which seemed like hours, a plane flew overhead. It circled the area of the moose kill until it found a place to land on skis. Feeling relieved, Jesse drove her snow-go out to the area and met up with the troopers. She was with them when their counterparts confirmed, by radio, that they had encountered the three poachers and were taking them in for questioning.

"Will they be arrested?" Jesse asked anxiously.

"They very likely will. While I can't say too much about the case, I can tell you we suspect them of causing multiple poaching incidences, property damage and theft from several cabins. All in all, you were very lucky that you didn't run into these folks out on the trail. They seem pretty volatile. And, it sounds like for this one at least, they admitted what was obvious, so there's likely no reason they will ever know you had anything to do with identifying them. Once they lawyer up, that could change, though, of course."

LATER, as she reflected on the day and wrote in her journal, Jesse felt an exhausted letdown. While waiting for the evening radio news and Trapline Chatter, she sipped chamomile tea and studied the fabrics of the lap quilt, warming her body and soul. It was a Christmas gift, made by her mother.

While unwrapping the gift in Minnesota at Christmas time, Jesse's mother had explained how this collection of red, green and tan fabric with black silhouettes of bear, wolves, fish, and moose printed on it, called to her while she was browsing in the quilt shop. As she was working on the quilt, Jesse had called and told them she was coming home for the holidays.

"I was still working on it when you came home. You can't imagine the sneaking around I had to do to get it finished without you seeing it." Jesse's mother sat rigidly upright with head held high and an exaggerated smile on her face. Jesse rose, hugged her mother, and thanked her enthusiastically.

Jesse's cabin was "cabin-ey" only in its structure. She had selected bright colors and flowy designs with more artistic flair. God had painted a perfect nature scene everywhere she went outdoors; she couldn't top that. Wanting to bring a sense of herself into her home, it was not merely an extension of the outdoors but a bright spot, like a fresh flower blooming in the perfect forest. The quilt fit in flawlessly. It brought comfort, solace, and a sense of protection for Jesse and her home.

The radio news hour started. The trooper's report was promising. "Based on information received from an observant citizen, troopers in the Matanuska Valley located and detained three individuals hauling a freshly harvested 72-inch moose bull rack off the interior snow-machine trail system near Trapper's Creek." The reporter continued, "The suspects were taken in for questioning and the remaining carcass was retrieved and is being processed for distribution. The troopers credited the tipster with bringing closure to a months-long investigation of poaching in the interior."

Jesse felt no satisfaction; she had no intention of getting others in trouble. But even in the wilds, there must be some rules, or anarchy would rule. In her mind, freedom was one thing, but forced aggression was quite another.

20

YEAR THREE MID-YEAR SOLSTICE

1987

Front porch

BY SPRING, Jesse had moved past the moose murder and embraced the joyful feelings that come with longer days and warmer nights. She foraged in the spring and would continue to do so throughout the summer. By fall, she would have full pantry shelves with wild blueberry and raspberry jam, fireweed and birch syrup, pickled carrots and beets, and jars of dried rosehips and fireweed blossoms for tea.

Sadie returned in mid-June and stayed until Thanksgiving. She arrived pale and subdued, but being in her element and reconnecting with nature was like medicine. She appreciated family for taking her in when she wasn't feeling well, but Sadie thrived in her own environment, where she could control her schedule, foods, and activity.

"You've missed me, haven't you?" Sadie's playful side emerged shortly after returning.

"Oh, Sadie, let me count the ways!" Jesse smiled back at

her beautiful, witty friend. "I especially missed you when the mud swallowed a four-wheeler trying to get out there by Loon Creek. That was a mess-and-a-half, I'll tell ya."

"Do tell, Aurora. I haven't heard this one yet."

"There's a guy moving in up the creek there, along the Loon as it forks to the right off the Lynx. He was hauling in some building materials over the winter with a snow-go and sled. After it got too slushy, he tried to haul another big load up there with a four-wheeler and sled, but he got bogged down and nearly buried that four-wheeler. I was working in the yard, cutting some firewood and watching the birds, when I heard some noise upstream on the Lynx. You taught me to always be on the lookout for predators, so I am."

"Good girl, Aurora. You're very smart, and you listen well. I hope you had your shotgun handy."

"Yes, well, I did, but I ran into the house for more ammunition, just in case, and my camera. You know, I wasn't sure what I would find. That's about the time the bears come out of migration and start poking around. You know how hungry they are."

"That's right, they come out of their dens pretty worked up."

"I crept along the Lynx until I saw some willows waving along the shore a couple hundred yards up, I guess. I froze, then slowly sunk to the ground. It was pretty sticky the closer I got to the creek, so I stayed back on the outside edge of the brush."

"I bet your ol' heart was just a-beating. I remember that feeling. Now, when it does that, it's just because I'm old." Sadie put her bent fingers over her heart and laughed.

"Oh, Sadie. You'll never be old as long as you keep that laugh and the brightness in your eyes." Jesse had noticed how much more alert Sadie had become since she returned. She didn't stay in bed as long and she had more strength overall.

"My heart was beating loud and strong, and I was afraid

that if it was a bear, it would hear the lub-dub too! But before I saw any bear, or tracks, I saw a tall, good-looking, in a rugged sort of way, man, walking down along the creek trying to follow a map. Well, you know we don't get too many strangers out here, so I'm always a bit cautious."

"All you have to do, honey, is show him your gun first." Sadie held her hands up as if to point a rifle into the distance. "Once he sees that, you'll know if he's trouble or not."

"I would have done that if I didn't sink into the mud and nearly tip over while I was crouching there watching him. I grabbed a bush to steady myself and the man froze. He wasn't armed. He was close enough by then I could see his eyes getting big as saucers."

"You must've scared the heck out of him."

"Yeah, I did. We had a good laugh about it later. Keven is his name. I'm sure he'll stop by here one of these days and you can meet him. Since the creeks have opened, he's canoed down to check in. Anyway, I came out of the bushes with mud up to my knees, but that was nothing compared to him. He was completely covered in mud, including streaks across his face that looked like war paint. When he caught sight of me, he called out, telling me he was looking for a cabin that, according to his map, should have been along Lynx Creek. When I looked at the map, it was actually your cabin that was marked. It must have been an old map, because my place wasn't on it."

"What did he think he was going to do at my cabin?"

"He was hoping to find a come-a-long to get his four-wheeler unstuck. I had a couple from building my cabin, so we gathered chains and shovels and supplies and hiked them back to where he was stuck. That rig was so buried I thought it was a total loss, but he was not about to surrender it to the mud. We worked for hours, first building a walkway across the mud, then unloading the trailer so it wasn't so heavy."

"Was he able to salvage anything?"

"Actually, he was. Like he said, it's just wet dirt and it

would wear off eventually. We worked into the night to get him unstuck. We got some logs under the front tires eventually and then we could pull it out of there. By the time we got done, we were exhausted, covered in mud, hungry, and working in the dark. He came back to my place for the night. Keven was so muddy I made him take his clothes off outside and put some of mine on to come into the house." A wide grin crossed Jesse's face as she described the memory. "It was hysterical seeing his long legs poke out from beneath my sweatpants. My sweatshirt barely covered his stomach, he's so tall."

"That must've been a sight. I knew I was missing all the fun out here. I do hope I get to meet this guy. Sounds like he has some grit."

"I think he does. I don't know him too well, but he comes from Texas. He's worked as a roust-about on the slope, but doesn't want to work full-time. He works seasonally so he can enjoy, as he puts it, 'the beauty that God gave us.' He loves Alaska. He's a sportsman, but only for his use. He's not interested in the trophy kills."

"If this guy comes around, I want to meet him. I think you might be a little sweet on him, do you think, Aurora?"

"No, I wouldn't say that. Not any more than I am with James. It's just nice to meet good, solid people out here. People you can eventually rely on in time of need. Besides, Keven has a girlfriend. He says she's outdoorsy, but he hasn't convinced her to come out here yet. She works in Anchorage. He visits her when he's not on the slope or out here. In fact, he's there now, spending some time with her and getting supplies."

"What's he living in out here?"

"He put up a lean-to while he's working on his cabin. He's not as close to the creek as we are, so he's building on shorter piers—only about a foot off the ground. I'm not sure how that will work for heavy snow, but I wouldn't try to tell him what to do. I have a feeling he might have a short fuse. Anyway, they are coming up next week, on the 21st. You can come over and meet them."

Jesse acted casual about it, but she was planning a big party for summer solstice, with a couple of added surprises. That would be the longest day of the year, and Sadie was in good spirits. Jesse looked forward to surprising Sadie.

"To Jesse from Minnesota. I'll be in at 8 tomorrow with two boats-full of stuff. Have breakfast ready. See you then, signed James. P.S., I will have three passengers." The Trapline Chatter announcer delivered the message, as Jesse listened with anticipation. She was puzzled about who the three passengers were, hoping they were joining the party and not just customers he was bringing out to fish. She was happy to hear that James was boating in rather than flying. That made her job easier. The groceries and supplies would only have to be hauled a short distance to her front door, rather than from the airstrip.

As she sat at the table listening to the radio and checking over a list of preparations for the following day, she remembered the candelabras. When visiting her parents over the holidays, she spotted her grandfather's brass candelabras in their basement storage. For many years, they had decorated holiday tables with festive candles in them.

"Hey Mom!" Jesse called up the stairs.

"Yes, dear."

"Do you use these candelabras of Grandpa's anymore?"

"No. I meant to take them to the church garage sale last summer, but it slipped my mind."

"Do you think I could take them to Alaska with me?"

Jesse's mother climbed down the stairs and watched as Jesse ran her finger across one, clearing the dust away. She thrust her hand on her hip and said, "Now, what on earth do you need those for way out there in the boonies?"

"I've had dreams of throwing special, intimate parties out in the woods with these candelabras on the tables and friends sharing stories and sharing food, family-style. Just because I'm out there doesn't mean I can't have some fun and fellowship. I think it would make celebrations extra-special." This whimsical side of Jesse rarely showed, but she had a rich inner life and frequently came up with ideas that others wouldn't understand.

"Take them if you want. Just remember, your grandfather brought those with him when he moved from the old country. They were his mother's, and it meant so much to him that we used them all those years he was with us. I feel kinda bad that I haven't used them, but I'm happy for you to take them, if you want."

"I want." Jesse picked them up and cradled them like precious babies.

Now, in her cabin, as she prepared to throw her first big party, Jesse dusted the candelabras again and opened the box of candles. One by one, she set the candles of various colors in place. With daylight lasting deep into the night, she wasn't sure if she would even light them. But it thrilled her to have them to make a statement on the table. Now, she just needed to get a long table built outside, so there was room for all the guests.

Jesse walked outside and looked over the pile of logs she had prepared. James was bringing a portable sawmill to hook up to her chainsaw so they could build a table and benches. Satisfied that she had plenty of logs in the right lengths, she walked over to the fire pit ring. During the first summer on the property, she had dug a big hole and lined it with large river rocks. She spent many nights around the fire pit and, the few times she had guests, it was the centerpiece of their communion. She added a few logs to the small stack near the pit, ready to feed the fire the following day. Looking up into the sky, she wished away any clouds that threatened to bring rain to her party. She stocked the outhouse with extra toilet paper, protected inside coffee cans, and added flowers to an empty jelly jar, setting the arrangement next to the coffee cans.

Finally satisfied that she was as ready as she could be, Jesse went to bed. She wakened several times during the night - excited, anxious, and finding it difficult to sleep with so much light coming in the windows. By five a.m., she was up and preparing for the day.

Jesse had purchased a solar oven during her second year at the homestead, ordered from a supplier specializing in supporting the off-grid lifestyle. She had only used it twice. It felt extra-fancy to be baking a cake in it for this special day, and she would add fresh fruit and whipped cream - if James included these from her long list of things to bring. James had become her best pal during the three years on the homestead. Three years! Jesse was giddy thinking about it. Oh, this was going to be the party of the year!

THE SLOW PUTT-PUTT of boat engines brought Jesse to the clearing on the shore of Lynx Creek near her cabin. She had carefully looked over the platform leading up the creek's bank to her vast, un-landscaped yard, and had cleared additional shoreline to accommodate the extra visitors expected to arrive for the day's festivities. This was her first largish gathering. She was equally anxious and excited for the day to begin.

"Ahoy, captain!" Jesse shouted down the modest slope as James guided his boat to shore. The second boat held back, waiting patiently, but Jesse recognized the man with his hand on the motor. "Oh, wow! Is that Jay you have there with you?"

Jesse beamed as Jay waved. "Hey, Jay! Great to see you!"

James smiled. He knew Jesse would be excited to see Jay, who had shown such kindness along her journey.

James parked the boat, jumped out and and gave Jesse a warm hug before turning to his passenger, who was waiting to pass over the wet bags filled with groceries. Bleach-blonde long hair was barely tamed by a baseball cap. "Jesse, this is my friend Shelly. Shelly, this is Jesse."

Jesse walked to the boat to help haul the cargo. Shelly extended a tanned hand, wrist adorned with well-worn bangles. "Jesse, it's so great to meet you. I've heard so much about you, and even though we haven't met, I'd like you to know how much I admire what you're doing out here." She continued without taking a breath. "James talks all the time about how you've built your own place, after living in a wall tent, and you trap and…"

"Nice to meet you too, Shelly. Thanks." Jesse looked sideways at James, smiled and raised her eyebrows. Apparently, James had shared at least some of Jesse's story with Shelly. Jesse was curious about this friend of James and just how she fit into his life.

They unloaded the first boat and guided it down shore to make room for Jay and the others, who would arrive later.

Jay's passenger stepped out of the boat and held his hand out to Jesse. "Hey, I'm Carson, a friend of James and Shelly…" Carson nodded toward Jay, "… and now this great guy here."

"Hello Carson." Jesse felt a flip in her gut. Carson was dreamy. Tall, strong, clean-shaven with tanned cheeks and the telltale raccoon's eyes of someone who wears sunglasses a lot on long Alaska summer days. "It's a pleasure to meet you. Welcome."

Again, Jesse looked at James, this time with a grin and a wink. She appreciated his taste in extra guests.

"And Jay!" Jesse threw her arms around him. "Oh, how good it is to see you again! How did James wrangle you into this project?"

Jay smiled and reciprocated Jesse's firm hug. "He threatened to put an ad in the paper, claiming I was the region's most eligible bachelor."

Jesse laughed. "Well, I can see how that would encourage you. I'm so glad you are here!"

Jesse took the supplies as Jay handed them to her. "Nice. I see you have the portable sawmill. This is going to work great to build us a long table for tonight."

Jesse grabbed a second case of beer from Jay. "You guys are planning to spend the night, right? I don't want any boat captains under the influence tonight."

"Well, we'll catch a few winks before we head out. Some of us have at least a partial day of work tomorrow." James nodded toward Carson. "Carson works with me, flying out to some of the lodges this summer. We hustled to get some extra trips done so we could both come out today."

"Well, I'm one happy homesteader to have you here. Per your request, I have breakfast underway." Jesse had prepared blueberry cornbread, bacon, fried potatoes, and eggs which she now had warming at the fire pit. "The only thing I don't have is a decent place for you to eat. You'll have to perch on the deck or cop-a-squat on a log."

The group headed up to the cabin, each person carrying a load of something. They dropped the cargo and gravitated toward the fire pit.

"That coffee smells terrific."

"Good! There are some clean cups over there on that makeshift table." Jesse pointed to a partial sheet of plywood lying atop an old barrel that she had hauled in from the shoreline of the Yentna River the prior summer. "Some of us might have to use glasses."

Shelly reached into one of the coolers and pulled out fresh cream.

"Is that real cream? You guys know how to make a girl happy." Jesse held out her cup to catch some of the cream as Shelly poured it into her own coffee glass.

"So, what kind of work do you have for us today?" Jay looked around, smiled, and nodded. "Looks like you have this place buttoned up nicely. I've gotta tell you, it's a far-piece nicer than mine."

"You would have to prove that to me, Jay. But I have to admit, I'm pretty proud of myself and grateful for all the friends and family who pitched in to help me bring this dream to reality." Jesse paused and took in the joy of her homestead life, the beauty of the land she called home, and the gifts of friendship she enjoyed.

"As James probably told you, I'm having a triple celebration tonight, and I've invited the people I know in about a ten-mile radius - so not too many, really, but enough to feel like it's a party. Who knows? We may get some fishermen drifting by that decide to join us."

Jesse smiled. It could happen.

"James said you were having a solstice celebration, and I assume that's one thing you are celebrating. What are the other two?" Carson looked over his coffee cup with sparkling dark eyes, watching for Jesse's response. She was an interesting woman. And good-looking, too.

"I don't know if you are familiar with Alaska's Homesteading program, but in order to prove up a homestead, you have to live on your staked homestead for most of three years. I have just reached three years since I set foot on my acreage. Once the paperwork is done, this place is all mine!"

Jay raised his cup. "Cheers to Jesse and all you have accomplished! You are a remarkable young woman."

The group clinked coffee cups and recycled jar-glasses, toasting Jesse for this major accomplishment.

"Awesome! So that's two. What's the third, or is that a surprise?"

"It's a surprise, but for my neighbor Sadie. She's hit a rough patch with her health, although she's doing better now. She'll be eighty in December and she will be with her family in Fairbanks then, so I'm throwing her a half-birthday party. That's why I need a long table and some benches. Normally, I wouldn't care if everyone just sat on coolers and on the ground, but Sadie deserves a sit-down dinner, as it were, out here in the middle of somewhere."

"Then it's a long table and benches you shall have." James knew Sadie, and wouldn't be surprised if she showed up in the middle of the day. "If Sadie comes by today, what should we say?"

"It's fine to tell her we are just getting organized for the solstice party. She's planning to come over for that later. Honestly, I didn't expect so much help today. If any of you want to go fishing, or take a siesta, that's fine with me. I have some cooking to do, but once the table building is done, I'm set to go."

"I, for one, don't mind sitting around and watching these young bucks work," Jay announced. "If it's alright with you, I brought my sketch pad and may just wander around some to see if I'm inspired."

This was the first that Jesse heard of Jay's artistic inclination. Her heart was already soft for Jay, as he had been so kind to her. Knowing now that he had an artistic side too brought an even deeper appreciation for the man to her heart.

"Of course. You just wander wherever you like. Go into the cabin and take a rest or play cards. Hey, I've got this beautiful cribbage board in there, if you want to learn to play." Jesse smiled at Jay, a silent thank-you for the Christmas gift he sent out on her first Christmas at the homestead.

"First, let me make sure these guys know what they're doing, then we'll see." Jay filled his plate with breakfast.

BY MID-DAY, a twelve-foot table was built, the ground leveled, and benches put in place around the table. Eventually, Jesse would put a clear marine finish on the wood to protect it, at least somewhat, from the elements.

Shelly helped Jesse cook and prepare the food. She looked

over the cake as Jesse pulled it from the oven. "I've never used a solar oven before. That is really cool."

"It is really a neat thing to have, and honestly, I don't use it as much as I could."

Shelly was open and chatty. Jesse learned that she worked at Denali National Park seasonally, coming up from Connecticut to work in the summer. This was her ninth year. She had met James during the second summer there. "We had a brief fling at first, but he knew I could never move here permanently, and his heart is in this country. I could never ask him to leave it. So, we vowed to stay friends, probably like you and he are."

Shelly looked at Jesse. She couldn't hide the curiosity from her face. "He's told me he was sweet on you when he met you, but over time, he came to understand that you had some heartbreak and weren't really looking to get into another relationship. He didn't share any details, just that he respected your journey and loved you as a friend."

"A wise friend," Jesse mumbled before turning away to look busy. Wetness grew in her eyes. It was true. She didn't trust anyone to be as close as she had let Tim be. The brokenness was slowly healing, but she had proven that she could survive, not without others but without a mate. Maybe it would change one day, but for today, Jesse was grateful to have such good friends.

Around four, another group of friends arrived. The Melchers, Gary and Carol, joined in the fun. Gary brought home-brewed beer and a guitar. Carol presented Jesse with a plate of brownies. "I'm sorry, they might be dry. We have a propane stove. I don't use it much, really, because it doesn't hold the heat well and so things have to bake longer."

"I'm sure they will be great. I'm going to take them inside, away from the flies and grabby fingers, if you know what I mean." Jesse smiled as she looked over the small work crew. "Can I get you something to drink? I've got beer, sodas, lemonade, tea . . ."

"I would love a soda. It's a luxury we rarely haul out, but a treat when we get it."

"I know exactly what you mean. These guys hauled stuff out for me this morning and I've been delaying my indulgence."

"Hey Jesse, hope you don't mind that I brought my guitar. I kinda like sharing a song around the fire on days like this."

Jesse gave Gary a generous hug. "Of course, it's fine. I blast my radio sometimes, but you know how that is out here. It's certainly no replacement for live music."

"Yeah, yeah, that's right." Gary was a quiet, humble man, and it surprised Jesse to learn that he was an entertainer.

"He likes to bring pleasure through song, to friends and family," Carol explained, flashing a smile toward her husband. "When he was much younger, he tried to raise a few extra bucks playing here and there, but mostly, it's his way of bringing a bright light to other people. It's one thing he did while we courted, and it sealed the deal for me."

Keven and his girlfriend, Lynn, arrived at about six o'clock. They were out canoeing and "strolling through the neighborhood," as Keven liked to say. As a result, they arrived later than planned, but well within the pre-dinner socialization time that Jesse penciled in her plans. Lynn was delightful - happy and bouncy. She obviously adored Keven and seemed to love the area. They pulled out a backpack and quickly assembled a salami, cheese, and cracker plate to share with all.

"It is so incredible out here." Lynn looked with wonder around Lynx Creek and Jesse's cabin. "I feel like I can touch the serenity. I wish I could bottle it up and sell it."

"Hey, that's an idea. Maybe you could work on a perfume

or an essential oil that brings in the colors and scents of the area." Jesse hadn't thought of it before. If Lynn didn't do it, maybe she would experiment with some infusions and oils to see what she could come up with.

Lynn laughed. "If I had an ounce of creativity, I would do just that. I'm more of a human being than a human doing. I do my job, and when it's done, I just do whatever I feel like doing. Often, it's watching clouds, camping, hiking or playing in my garden."

Lynn explained she was a case manager for developmentally challenged adults. She spent her workdays teaching them life skills and enjoying as much of Alaska as they could get paid for in their program. "Sometimes I question the things we do and bill the government for, calling it activity therapy or some such thing, but the clients are happy and living as good a life as they can under the circumstances."

"It sounds like very rewarding work, Lynn. I'm grateful you, and others, have the heart and patience to do it."

Jesse introduced them to the other guests while James took the four-wheeler to Sadie's to escort her to the party.

"It smells amazing here, Jesse!" Rona called from the shore as Jesse rushed to greet the couple pulling their canoe in. "I'm getting hints of brisket and barbecue sauce roasting over perfect coals."

"And a little bit of hops and barley. I think we made it to the right place, honey." Dave put his hand on Rona's shoulder.

"Correct on both accounts. Too bad you can't get a whiff of the brownies and whipped cream cake." Jesse threw her arms around them both. "It is so good to see you two!"

Laughing, Dave pulled his head back from the group in order to be heard. "It's great to see you too, and we are happy to be here."

"I can't believe you are finally out here and getting ready to build. You know I'll be over to help you just as soon as you give me the sign."

Rona stepped back from the group and waved her hands high in the air. "Sign, sign. . . giving you the sign."

The group laughed.

"Great. You'll have to give me all the details. For now, I could use your help. James should be back shortly with Sadie and then I plan to serve dinner. I don't want to keep her waiting too long. She's usually in bed early."

Rona followed Jesse to the kitchen, carrying a hostess gift meant for Jesse. It was a handmade clay pot with a plant growing inside. "Before I forget, this is for you. I made the pot with the third graders I worked with last semester."

"Oh, Rona. Thank you! Is that a pepper plant?"

"Not just any pepper plant. It's a jalapeño plant, so beware."

"How fun!"

James returned with Sadie just as Jesse was placing the food on the table. As Sadie took her place on a bench at the head of the table, everyone fell silent and watched the petite matriarch.

Sadie looked up as she sat and saw everyone watching her. "Aurora, look at what you've done! It's a proper party out here. And just look at all these fine people. Can they all sit, too, or do they need to keep watching the old lady here?"

"You heard the lady. Find a seat!" Jesse ordered. "Rona, would you help me pour the wine? Tonight, for your gustatory delight, we have a variety of things to choose from. There is baked trout, courtesy of Keven, who landed them this afternoon. There is chicken stuffed with garlic, barbecued brisket, a beautiful fresh salad, baked potatoes with all the fixings, garlic bread, pasta salad with olives, artichokes, mozzarella, tomatoes, and salami, and corn on the cob."

The air filled with oohs and ahs. "Welcome to the Lynx

Creek's first annual solstice celebration!" Jesse called out, unable to contain her excitement. "Now, my friend Gary here has offered to bless this meal and be prepared for him to serenade us after dinner, too. Gary…"

"Thank you, Jesse, and thank you for gathering us here together on this special day for Alaskans, where we get to embrace the longest day, and do so among very fine and special people and a glorious bounty. For those who care to join me . . ." Gary reached his hands to his neighbors, and the wave spread throughout the table until all were joined in the circle. "To the great almighty, we give thanks for this day of celebration of light, life, and love - your love, the love of friends, old and new, and for our special friend Jesse who has brought us together to join in celebration. Bless this food for our health and strength. Amen."

"Amen" reverberated around the table.

"Might I just add, thank you to my late grandfather for the beautiful candelabras he brought from his home country of Norway and that my mother forgot to take to the church yard sale and for the gift of this new table and benches, courtesy of James, Jay and crew. I am forever grateful. Now, dig in!"

James raised his wine glass. "And to the cook."

"To the cook!" echoed across the yard.

WITH EVERYONE'S HELP, Jesse put on a solstice party to remember. In true Alaska style, two paddlers pulled their canoe in to see what was going on. Jesse welcomed them with open arms and handed them a paper plate. She was grateful for the small stash James had thrown into the supplies.

For nearly two hours, the group laughed, ate and drank. Occasionally, a story so interesting was being told that the entire group listened in anticipatory silence. There were stories of ocean rescues, friends lost in anomalous ice storms, dog team escapades, and whale hunting. Around this table, there was no effort to tell tall tales over enormous salmon or mammoth-sized moose. Each had seen their share of enormity in Alaska's wilderness. Instead, the tales were of survivors, adventurers, and the harsh reality of an untamed land.

The sun was still bright in the sky at nine o'clock. The table was cleared, and the candelabras lit for whimsy and party atmosphere more than for ambiance. Jesse approached the table with a cake frosted and decorated with fresh fruit. "Today we have a special birthday."

She walked slowly up one side of the table and hesitated near a guest. She looked at Keven. "Perhaps it is yours?"

"No, my birthday comes in October."

She moved and stood behind Jay. "Then it must be yours."

"I was born in February, although I stopped celebrating birthdays some time ago."

Finally, Jesse walked on and stood behind Sadie. "In fact, we are celebrating a half-birthday today. Sadie, we wish you a happy seventy-nine and one-half birthday."

Sadie's eyes grew big with surprise as Jesse started singing and the others joined in. "Happy birthday to you . . ."

The smile on her face showed how tickled she was to be honored.

"My little Aurora. I will remember this day forever, especially when my December birthday rolls around and I will be far away from this magic place. Thank you and thank you for not trying to put all those candles on the cake. We could have a forest fire." The table joined her in laughter.

As Jesse cut the cake, James raced up the shore to his boat and returned with a package of reusable plastic champagne flutes and three bottles of champagne in a bag. "I have one more celebration to announce, as it appears our modest hostess is not sharing. With the pop of this cork, I hereby unofficially declare that our friend Jesse has fulfilled her obligation to become the proud owner of this Lynx Creek homestead."

The cork released loudly as the group cheered. James passed the bottle to Rona, who filled glasses and passed them down the table, as James uncorked a second bottle. When everyone had a glass, James moved to Jesse's side. He put his arm around her shoulder and held his glass high toward the clear blue openness above them. "To Jesse! For all the dreams you have accomplished, for building your homestead, so you can generously share it with us, and for fulfillment of all your dreams in the future. We love you."

Carol pulled out her camera and captured the smiles and raised glasses sparkling against Lynx Creek in full bloom.

Jesse looked to James and mouthed "thank you." The light danced off the puddles dammed in her eyes as she spoke to all. "Thank you all for joining me and for celebrating. You mean the world to me."

As Jesse was tidying up in the kitchen after dessert, Sadie joined her to share thoughts about the guests. She was eager to report on her keen observations. She was happy to meet Keven. "Now, that's a guy you can count on. He has a good heart and strong hands. His know-how will get better with experience out here."

Sadie was a little skeptical of Lynn, doubting she had the gumption to live in the woods where she would have to work hard. "If she ever comes out here, it will be because they're having a baby or she gets fired. Mark my words. She has him in her heart, but not the desire to be isolated and working all the time in the elements." Jesse couldn't disagree.

"And won't they make beautiful children? Especially if the children get his curly hair and long legs and her round face and dark eyes." The couple's collective features were striking, which is something Jesse rarely paid attention to, especially since leaving daily multi-human encounters.

Not long after, James took Sadie home and returned to join in the singing around the campfire and the companionship of sun worshipers enjoying the longest day. Before sunset, the local guests headed out to their respective homes. Jesse gave her bed to Jay for the night while she lay on a cot on the deck. Carson, James, and Shelly unrolled their sleeping bags near the fire.

Sleep followed the sun, so it was a quick night for all. Knowing that the last two boats needed to leave early, Jesse used the camp stove to make coffee and an egg breakfast.

"You threw a great shindig there, Minnesota." Jay sat on the edge of the deck enjoying a hot coffee, steam rolling off the top in the early morning hour.

"Here, here!" Carson called out as he strolled from the shore, a fishing pole in hand. "Have you got another cup of that hot jo?"

"Sure I do. You been fishing already?" Jesse looked on as the handsome bloke approached the deck. "Hey, I'm sorry we didn't get to talk much last night. By the time the neighbors left, I think the wine and champagne took me down."

"Not to worry. We will have another chance, if you don't mind a visitor. This is a great creek. I saw some fish feeding in there, but there was no catching for me this morning. I think a fly rod would be a load of fun with those grayling."

"I think you're right. I have to confess that my fishing here has been more for the meal than for the Zen of it, so I've not yet tested a fly rod. You're welcome to bring one out anytime and give it a whirl." Jesse handed Carson a steaming cup of coffee. "I think I've got a bit of cream left if you want, there, in the cooler."

Jesse went back inside to finish breakfast. When she returned to the porch, James and Shelly were there with sleeping bags bundled and supplies stacked, ready to return to town.

"Good morning, sleepyheads. Just in time for breakfast. Why don't you come in and fill your plates, all of you, and I'll pour some more coffee?"

They ate in silence, tired from the short night's sleep and absorbing the remnants of joy from the night before. Finally, Jay broke the quiet.

"You know, Jesse, I've been an Alaskan for many a year, and it's been a glorious life. But I can see that the life you are making here, all by yourself, is so much richer, more significant, and more enjoyable than my little life."

"Oh, come on, Jay. I heard you telling some juicy adventure stories last night. You've had a great life up here."

"It's true, I have. But I came here with a chip on my shoulder, and I spent many years being bitter and hiding out instead of making a life. There is a big difference, and if I was a different person and could do it over again, I would do more of the kind of living you're doing. You obviously love it here, and still find ways to have meaningful relationships and sprinkle your life with joy."

"Thank you for saying that, Jay." Jesse hesitated momentarily, gathering words to express her innermost feelings. "This is a dream I couldn't bring to life when I tried living the traditional way. I choose to be grateful every day and, believe me, as you know, there are many challenges. But a day out here, with the shotgun loaded while the wolves howl and the wolverine stir, keeping the stove fed an endless supply of logs, and making the freezing cold trip to the outhouse on the coldest day in winter is a thousand time better, for me, than the best day of my marriage or my old job was. I don't regret any of it, because I learned a lot, mostly about myself. Right now, I wouldn't trade this life for anything."

. . .

WITH EVERYONE GONE, the stillness and the sounds of nature again took over Jesse's homestead. Leaving the last of the clean-up for later, Jesse made herself another cup of coffee and sat alone at the amazing new table with her journal, pens and pencils. She was eager to attempt to put on paper the tumult of feelings and emotions that filled her. Such sadness that the party was over! And yet such joy and love for the people who so easily accepted and shared her life, alone in the Alaskan wild. Memories of this would keep her warm and secure through many cold winter nights.

21

WOMEN'S WILDERNESS COMPETITION

Early December 1988
 Talkeetna

"THIS MESSAGE GOES out to Jesse at Lynx Creek, from James. If you're ready for a quick change of scenery, pack a bag and bring your snowshoes for the weekend. I'll pick you up at the airstrip on Friday noon and take you home Sunday after sunrise."

Jesse recognized the voice of announcer Don on the radio. Hearing her name called out always felt a little like the pre-game team introductions when she played high school basketball. Everyone was listening then, but now when she ran to the center of the floor, no one watched!

"I wonder what James has up his sleeve." Jesse spoke to the open air of the warm cabin as she walked toward the door and opened it. It had become common for her to speak to only herself in the solitude of the cabin. The singular response was the stillness of the cold night air and the immense glowing lights overhead that immediately caught her attention. It was time for one last visit to the outhouse before feeding the wood stove and crawling under a pile of blankets and quilts.

While sitting on the ice-cold toilet seat, she thought about a magazine article that she read recently. The author called out the multitude of ways Alaska is God's country. There were many references to earthquakes, which Jesse had felt a couple of times, as well as a reference from the Old Testament about a giant windstorm in the sky, coming from the north and moving across the sky like an immense cloud of brilliant light with a fire at its center. An apropos description, Jesse thought. Yet nothing could quite describe the aurora that lit up the Alaska sky and life during the long nights of winter. Cold walks to the outhouse were bearable, almost pleasurable, in their presence.

Friday arrived quietly. The sun shone brightly, reflecting off the trail to the airstrip like a glistening path of diamonds and sequins leading to the winter home of Oz. At the end of the path, instead of a mythical wizard, Jesse found a real boy, or rather a real man, there to greet her.

"Ok, mystery man. What's this all about?" Jesse smiled as she handed over her backpack and snowshoes for James to stow in the cargo hold.

"Whatever do you mean?" He presented a quizzical face with furrowed brow and no sign of joviality.

"Funny boy! I guess I'll just wait it out. But do you think I will have time to hit the grocery store tomorrow before we come back? I'm craving fresh food."

"Of course we can. And I won't be flying anyone else out, that I know of, so buy as much as you want."

James walked to the passenger side of the plane and opened the door for Jesse. "It was a beautiful flight out today. I thought it might be after the sky show we got last night."

"Wasn't that amazing? The aurora never ceases to amaze me with its brilliance." It was true. Jesse never tired of the

Alaska sky, or any of Alaska - except perhaps the aloneness, sometimes.

They were back at the Talkeetna airport in no time. Jesse was more curious than ever by then. "So, what are we doing?"

"Patience, friend. Let me just check in at the office and then we will be on our way." James tossed her his truck keys. "Here, go get the truck warmed up, if you don't mind."

Jesse caught the keys clumsily in heavy gloved hands, picked up her gear and headed to the truck, the same one he had when she first met him - an old black Ford with a white topper on the bed. She tossed her gear in the back and crawled into the driver's seat to start it and get the heat going. It was a beautiful day with the temperature hovering around zero.

A SHORT TIME LATER, they were parked on the main street in front of the iconic Talkeetna Bar with its two stories towering over the shorter cabins that flanked it. Jesse liked the feel of the place, with its old hard wood, an abandoned upright piano in the back hallway, assortment of novice and professional musicians gracing the stage, and always a friendly face behind the bar. Jesse didn't come to town often, but when she did, she always stopped by.

"Why is it so busy here today?" Jesse asked in surprise. The main street was full of vehicles and one of the side streets was blocked off to cars. Several small groups of people hung around outside the bar.

"I guess you didn't hear. Tomorrow is the Talkeetna Bachelor's Auction. But first..." James put his arm in Jesse's and tugged her gently toward the door. "We're going to sign you up for the Wilderness Woman contest."

Jesse planted her boots firmly against the sidewalk. "Oh, I think not! There will be no contest for this girl."

"Come on! At least come inside and see what it's all about.

It supports a noble cause, it's a lot of fun, and you'll be great at it!"

"Oh really? How many times have you done it to know it's a lot of fun?" Jesse glared at James.

"Well." James laughed. "I haven't done it, but I've watched it, emceed it, and have friends who have done it and I know you're a shoo-in for this kind of fun. Besides, all the proceeds go to the women and children's shelter, and I know you can get behind that."

Jesse did like a good round of fun now and then, and depending on what she had to do, she might be good at it. And he just had to throw in the bit about the charity.

"I will at least go see what it's about," she conceded.

"Great!" James smiled and pointed at the door. "The sign-up is in the bar."

Once inside, James ordered a beer for each of them. It was early for a drink, but James thought it might provide some courage to the reluctant Jesse.

Halfway through the beer, Jesse stood to go to the table with the contest entry information. James stood to join her. She held up her hand to stop him. "Sit yourself back down there. You've done enough. I'll sign up, or I won't, but I'll do it on my own."

Jesse's attempt at delivering a stern admonition was thwarted by the sparkle in her eye and the smile that crept into the corners of her mouth. James grinned and sat back down. "Yes, ma'am!"

"So, what is this thing all about? My friend ambushed me and brought me here to compete, but I don't have a clue what I have to do."

"Hey there, what's your name?"

"If I tell you, are you going to write it down and make me sign something?" Jesse felt like playing up the oppositional charade longer.

"I promise I won't write your name down until you tell me to. I'm Sarena. I'm one of the volunteers at the women and children's shelter, and, well, just about any other charity in town. We're pretty small around here, so we need all hands on deck. Anyway, the challenge, if you choose to accept it, involves a few races, and by the looks of you, you will have no trouble completing them. There's the hauling water race, the fish-catching cluster, the snow obstacle course, cutting and hauling firewood, and my personal favorite, the make your man a sandwich and deliver him a beer."

"Excuse me?"

"Well, you have to have a sense of humor for that one, and it's meant to be a joke. You make up a sandwich and race it, and a beer, back to your guy sitting in a recliner."

"I don't have one of those."

"What? A recliner?"

"No, a guy."

The volunteer let loose a hearty laugh. "Oh, honey, we simply use the bachelors. They will be auctioned off tomorrow evening. Hope you'll join us for that, too."

"I think my friend over there…" Jesse pointed in James's direction, "…is in a lot of trouble. He left out a bunch of details when he flew out to the homestead and picked me up."

"James? I can't imagine! I mean, he's been one of our top bachelors for the past few years."

"Are you serious? I mean, he's a great guy and all, except for his apparent forgetfulness, but years?" Jesse was truly perplexed.

"Couple of things you need to know, I guess. Around here, for the ladies, the odds are good, but the goods are odd, like we say. Lots of guys, but most are quirks, if you know what I mean. All the bachelors are being auctioned, not like a prize pig or a dating game, but for what they bring to the table. James brings a free flight-seeing tour with him to the auction block and that drives up the bids. He's very popular."

"Yeah, and I bet he packs a picnic knapsack, too." Jesse muttered under her breath as she turned toward James, furrowed her brow, and pointed her finger at him sharply. "He's got some 'splainin' to do when I get back to the table."

"So, Miss, what'll it be? I've got a line forming behind you there, and the race starts in about ninety minutes. Are you in, or out?"

"Hey, Sarena..." James called over.

"Hiya, James. Your..."

"My friend Jesse is in," James continued with a smirk. "And I'll pay her entry fee. It's the least I can do since I ambushed her the way I did."

"Just tell me one thing." Jesse was curious now. "What are the snowshoes for?"

"Oh, yeah. We provide the bunny boots for the water race, but for the other races, except the snow-go, of course, you'll be wearing your snowshoes. It keeps the playing field even, they say."

"Good lord, I don't know what I'm getting myself into, but sign me up."

Sarena pointed to the beautiful silver fox fur hat sitting on a mannequin head on the table. "I didn't even get a chance to tell you what you can win. That beautiful fur hat, two Alaska Airlines tickets, and a table in the front row at the Bachelor's Auction tomorrow night."

Jesse completed the paperwork, checked out the competition lining up behind her, and pet the prize hat before heading back to her seat at the bar. James was waiting with a grin that spared no width. She pinned the bib to the front of her shirt - lucky number 13.

"Okay. You got your wish, but you didn't tell me anything about being a highly desirable bachelor!"

"Did she tell you that? Bet she didn't tell you that all but one time my older neighbor Violet won the bid for me, and half the time she didn't even want the plane ride. It's kind of a deal we made a few years ago. I help her out all year on handyman-type projects, and she puts a little of the money that she would usually pay a hired hand to help her into a jar. Then, she brings the jar to the auction and donates it by bidding on me. It works for all of us, actually."

"Now that's downright sweet. You're a good man, James, even if you are a sneak. You're going to have to buy me a shot, or two, one before and one after the race."

"Happy to oblige. Hey Steph!" he called to the bartender. "Bring us a couple shots of Johnny red."

He turned back to Jesse. "You know you're branded now."

"What does that mean?"

"Only single women can enter the race. That bib there, it's a sign to all the bachelors in town. They'll spot you coming a block away and make a play for you."

"Oh, great. This keeps getting better and better. Where's that drink?"

Stephanie waddled over with two shot glasses filled to the brim. "Here you go."

"Stephanie! I hardly recognized you. You look like…"

"Don't say it! I know. A beached whale. I'm only eleven months pregnant, it seems."

"I wasn't going to say that, but it does explain the waddle. Congratulations!"

"Thanks! Sorry I can't chat, it's a busy time around here. Had to call Judy to come in early and help. This extra bump has me working a little slow." Stephanie patted her belly gently. "This weekend is going to be a madhouse. Let's catch up later."

She shuffled off to fill more glasses from the tap while Jesse and James downed their shots.

"I think it's time we get you organized, champ." James

nodded his head toward the door. "I'll show you the lay of the land."

THEY WOVE their way through a couple dozen people to get out of the bar, and then again through a crowd on the street. James greeted nearly every one of the fifty or so people they passed, each one happy to see him again and wishing him well at the auction. A giant bonfire was now burning at the main intersection of the small street, and people were gathering around. Heading past the bonfire toward the banner that hung across the far end of the street, Jesse's eyes met with the glacier-blue eyes of Lucky.

"Well, if it isn't Minnesota Jesse! How the heck are you? You're looking well." Lucky threw his arm around Jesse's shoulders and gave her a tight squeeze. "I see you've got your snowshoes there and a bib. Don't tell me you're joining the race! You're a shoo-in, no pun intended."

"It's great to see you, Lucky!" She pushed her elbow into James's ribs. "This guy here tricked me into entering the race. We're just taking a stroll around town, taking notice of the events and..."

She stopped and nodded toward two women standing about fifty feet away in tank tops and spandex pants. "The competition? Those women over there look serious!"

James and Lucky smiled. "Helen there runs the ice cream shop, and her friend Barb is a schoolteacher. They're in this to meet guys, not to win. They'll be three sheets to the wind by the time the race starts. It's all kicks and giggles to them."

Jesse smiled at Lucky's description. "That'll be me. I mean the kicks and giggles, if I ever decide to do this again. Say Lucky, are you in the auction tonight?"

"I sure am. I'm pulling one of James there's stunts and adding a fishing trip to the package. Maybe I'll get some decent bites. Some years, the winning bidders had some odd ideas of what to do on our date. I sure like helping the shelter out and it's fun being in front of all those women at the auction, but I'm not much interested in cleaning out someone's crawlspace for a date. Who knows? Maybe one day I'll meet someone special amongst all these single women."

He winked at Jesse and smiled. "Well…I'm the scorekeeper for the fishing race, so I guess I'd better go check in and get my instructions. Good luck, number 13! I can't appear biased, but I'll be rooting you on in my head… and when you're wearing the bunny boots and your buckets are full, just shuffle."

"Thanks, Lucky."

Jesse turned to James as Lucky walked away. "I'm not crazy about being in this race, but I sure appreciate the way this town works together and looks after its own."

James squared his shoulders and stood taller, boasting his pride in participation. "It really is a great place in that way. Not everyone is involved in every activity, but most are involved in something. It's part of small-town living, and I like it."

"LADIES AND GENTLEMEN, we are ready for the official start of the Talkeetna Wilderness Women's race." A burly bearded bachelor stood on a makeshift stage in the middle of the street and bellowed into a microphone. "We have twenty-seven wild women in this first race. The top five will move on to the following races. We have single women from all over the world joining us today to snag the top bachelors around."

Whoops and hollers rose from the crowd, now over one hundred people strong. A lean young woman, clad in a fur hat, bunny boots and a fur bikini, stepped forward with a silver platter. The announcer picked up a beer sitting atop the platter and took a long drink.

"Now that's the perfect wilderness woman right there, don't cha think?" The men in the crowd roared while the women, including Jesse, booed.

"The announcer is our postmaster," James explained. "He goes by the name of Wiley Joe, but I have it on good authority that his name is actually Sasha Vargo."

"Seriously folks, all in good fun here," the announcer continued. "We bachelors know who the stronger sex is, and it ain't us. Now, back to the races! This first one is the water run. We will have six heats of this race. Each woman will have two five-gallon buckets. They have to run down the icy street, trade their empty buckets for two new buckets filled with five gallons of water. That's about eighty pounds of water those gals are going to haul back up the street here—without spilling any."

"What the heck, James! Eighty pounds of water?" Jesse was ready to throw in the towel, but truth be known, she hauled at least that much weight with some regularity.

"You'll get through that just fine. I'm more eager to see how you handle that foul-mouthed, snus-spitting, unshaven, unshowered bachelor demanding you serve him a beer and a sandwich."

James folded his arms across his chest, stifling a giggle and avoiding eye contact as Jesse's jaw dropped.

"Dang you! This just keeps getting…"

"Hey folks, look who's here! Last year's winner, Stacy Stone. Heya Stace, won't you come on up and talk to these friendly folks a minute?"

Jesse watched as a pretty, obviously pregnant, thirty-ish woman joined the announcer on the stage.

"Hi everyone!" The crowd roared as the reigning champion Wilderness Woman waved her fur-covered mitten in the air and smiled.

"So, Stacy, tell us. What was it like to be the winner of this crazy competition?"

"It was the greatest accomplishment of my life, besides catching the most incredible bachelor, and…" she rubbed her pregnant belly "…and co-creating this amazing little bachelor or future wilderness woman."

The crowd erupted in whoops and hollers.

"And there's the proud poppa now. Last year's Bachelor Bob! You may all remember him - local schoolteacher, PhD in botany, escaping the rat-race known as Southern California, loves yoga on the deck at sunset and cooking hot cross buns on the wood stove. Did I get that right, former Bachelor Bob?"

A handsomely rugged man with kind eyes, a generous smile and the traditional beard, smiled at Stacy and put his arm around her shoulders as he took the microphone. "Almost, there, Joe. I don't bake hot cross buns or eat them, for that matter. But I sure am the luckiest former bachelor of Talkeetna!"

More cheering erupted from the crowd.

"It sure looks like the two of you are getting along nicely. When is the junior due?"

In unison, the couple leaned into the microphone. "St. Paddy's Day." More cheering rang through the audience.

"Mrs. Bob, I know your husband is a teacher, originally from Los Angeles. Can you please tell us where you hail from and what you do here in Talkeetna?"

"Sure. I am a cartographer, and I work for the Feds drawing maps. I was living in Duluth, Minnesota, when I came up for the race last year."

"Well folks, a lot has changed in the last year for Bob and Stacy here. Please join me in a round of applause for their good fortune on this very day a year ago."

When the raucous applause subsided, Wiley Joe continued. "Now, Wilderness Women, it is time for the first heat of the first race of the second annual Talkeetna Wilderness Woman contest."

As the first group of women lined up at the start, he held up a wooden gun. "When I blast this gun, the race will start. I need a moment of silence to get this party started."

Within seconds, the crowd was completely silent, except for the shrill wailing of an infant in the distance.

"Three, two, one." Wiley Joe held the gun in the air and pulled the trigger. A tethered cork flew out, making a whistling sound and spraying orange powder into the air. Jesse noted the tricky start. She could easily miss it if she wasn't paying close attention.

As the contestants raced, Wiley Joe shared their bios with the audience. Jericha was from Phoenix, Arizona, where she worked as a dental hygienist, ran long foot races in the desert, and won billiard competitions.

Jesse elbowed her friend. "There you go, James. She looks lovely."

"Yes, she does. Let's see how she holds up to these temperatures. I hope she makes it to the end of the race."

"She will. I can feel it in my bones." Jesse shouted words of support to the stranger.

"I gotta tell ya, these women are all working their tails off out there. They look good."

"And did you notice the smiles on most of them? That's what the crowd is here to see. In the end, it doesn't matter who wins. It's all in good fun, like Wiley Joe said."

Jesse continued to cheer for the racers.

JESSE WAS in the third heat. Her stomach rolled like a ship in high seas. "I wish I had waited for that shot."

"Ah, you'll be fine." James patted her shoulder. "Just get out there and have fun. They are."

James nodded toward a contestant who had thrown herself into the lap of the burly bachelor and fed him a bite of the sandwich.

Standing at the starting line, Jesse looked at the contestant to her left who wore a gold superhero cape over a red onesie suit with 'Alaska or Bust' written across the butt flap. Unable to make eye contact with her, she looked to her right and saw a less svelte contestant in a flamingo pink tutu over spandex pants and an oversized sweatshirt. The woman had heavy makeup on, and dark ringlets sprouted from her head. She made eye contact with Jesse.

"Hey, I'm Amy. Can you tell me, please, what the hell I'm doing here?"

"Hi Amy. I'm Jesse." Jesse smiled, hoping to ease Amy's panic and encourage her to respond in kind. "Why, you're looking beautiful and catching you a bachelor."

Amy's shoulders softened, and a radiant smile grew on her face. "Oh, yeah! I needed that reminder! I came on a dare, up from Homer. I had a girlfriend who was coming with me, but she got sick and had to stay home. I'm just a little freaked out."

"Well, Amy, I know what you mean. I got tricked into this whole thing, but my friend over there..." Jesse pointed to James and waved. Amy waved and James waved back at them. "He tells me to just have fun. It's not an actual competition. And just think, if you don't do well in this race, you can be done for the afternoon and still go to the Bachelor's Ball and bid on those boys."

"Hey, thanks! Great advice. Can we catch up for a beer later?"

"You've got it, Amy. I'll be watching for you."

"Ladies, on your mark, get set..." the weakest whistle-pop from the toy gun went off. Jesse watched for the colored powder as the crowd was louder now.

Jesse grabbed the empty buckets and started running to the end of the street to trade them for full ones. She was halfway there before she remembered to paste on a smile and look out at the crowd. It was as if she was watching in slow motion. Fists pumped into the air, women clapped, and children jumped up and down, cheering them on. When she dropped the empty buckets and grabbed the full ones, each filled with forty pounds of water, she was shocked back into the moment. The smile turned into a grimace as she hunched forward and lifted the buckets just enough to clear the icy street. She shuffled as fast as she could back toward the starting line, biting her lips together as if that would keep water from splashing over the bucket's brim. She was the first to deliver her water buckets, now a few cups lighter. Thankfully, it was a warm day, with temps just below freezing. Had it been much colder, the water would have frozen on the ground, creating a hazardous skating rink.

James met Jesse after the race, holding a beer bottle out to her.

"Here ya go. Great race! I'm sure that will put you in the top five and into the next race."

"Eh, I don't know about that. It was interesting, but I won't be surprised if some of these other women put me out of the race." Jesse guzzled half the beer in one gulp, realizing how much effort she'd put into the race.

THEY AMBLED toward the bonfire where a saxophone was playing to the crowd.

"Great run!"

"Good job, Minnesota!"

Random cheers came at her through the crowd.

"See, they all think you did great." James pointed to a large art easel propped up on the side of the street. "We'll check the board over there after a bit and see if you're in the final five."

"So, was it any fun?" James thought he knew what she would say, but wanted to hear it from her, anyway.

"It really was kind of fun, for a girl who's been hiding out in the woods. I thought I would be really nervous, but once the race started, I was fine."

"Glad to hear it. I thought you might get a kick out of it."

The duo chatted with bystanders while waiting for the heat results to be posted. Women in all states of dress threaded through the crowd, to and from the raceway. Nearly an hour later, they watched as a race official posted the heat results.

Jesse walked toward the poster, but James grabbed her shoulder and held her back.

"It's going to be real crowded there soon. Let's just go over by the announcer. He'll be announcing the top five soon, and then the next race will start."

They walked back toward the starting line and as they approached, the announcer named the top five.

"Ladies and gents, the race results are in. Over there, in front of the Forest and Fireweed store, you will find a full list of all the racers and their times. It is my pleasure to announce the top five racers who will advance to the next three events. Those contestants are..."

Jesse grabbed James's arm when she heard her name. She was in second place.

"See, I told you!"

Jesse squeezed his arm, sharing her excitement. "Yes, you did. Now what do I have to do?"

James smiled and nodded toward the announcer.

"Ladies, it is now time to make your man a sandwich and take him a beer. For this race, you need to give us back our bunny boots and strap on your snowshoes. You have fifteen minutes to get ready and stand on the start line. You will each be assigned a bachelor and a number on the start line. See y'all in fifteen."

"Well, I guess I'll go get my snowshoes. Never really thought I would need them today."

"Hope you don't mind. I brought them up from the truck. They're waiting for you behind the bar. Steph's holding them for you."

"Well now, aren't you just the thoughtful one?! Come with me to get them?"

"Of course. I got you into this, I'm going to see you through it."

Sometimes Jesse thought James was flirting with her, but he never really made it obvious. She was just glad he was there.

"We have our five finalists. Each will take a turn from the starting line. Their bachelor will be sitting on his throne, waiting to be served his sandwich and beer." Wiley Joe repeated the bios for each of the five women, then appealed to the crowd, "Won't you please give me a round of applause for these beauties."

When the applause and cheers faded, the announcer started the race for the first contestant. She was Marilyn from Anchorage, a nurse, second runner-up for the past two years, and still searching for Mr. Right. Marilyn was wearing a white fur headband, white shorts, and a camo tank top. She looked like a marathoner to Jesse.

Jesse was third in line for this race. She looked around from the starting line and started giggling at her predicament. The bachelor sitting in the old recliner that served as the throne was one of the grungiest she had ever seen. "On your mark, get set…" Jesse waited for the popgun to fire, but instead heard the discordant sound of bagpipes and the announcer yell "GO" simultaneously. Jesse ran the course length to an official standing at a picnic table in the middle of the street.

"Take the bread. Put the meat, cheese, and mustard on it. Grab a beer and run it down to that grimy bastard sitting in the velvet chair. Toss it in his lap and cross the finish line. And, hey, Lulu's our number one contestant in this event. She follows you. You won't have a better time than her, but she's lousy at the wood chopping." The middle-aged man with a beautiful smile and bald head encouraged her with his look. "If you can chop wood, you're sitting pretty. And I do mean that."

By the time he was done talking, Jesse had the sandwich made. She opened the beer, threw her head back and poured a stream of the amber liquid through her open lips as the crowd cheered her on.

"Chug it! Chug it! Chug it!"

Jesse briefly glanced at the crowd and smiled before racing toward the bachelor, thinking hard about her delivery. Would she hand it to him like a dutiful servant, throw it at him, or dance seductively? Not until she reached the epitome of the burly mountain man in a red and black buffalo plaid wool shirt did she decide. She swiftly shoved the sandwich and beer in his direction and raced across the finish line. She wasn't in this race to make friends and her strategy paid off. She finished a millisecond behind the winner, Lulu.

Two more events followed: ice-fishing and log sawing. The ice-fishing contest involved a fishing pole with a magnet as the hook thrown across the ice toward a wooden 'salmon' with metal for the magnet to attract. She had to catch as many fish as she could in one minute. She landed five fish and tied for first place.

The log-sawing contest required the contestants to saw a tree into five logs, at least one foot long, and stack them in a pile at the opposite end of the racecourse. Again, Jesse came in second place.

"Well folks, let's give these ladies a big round of applause. As you know, no winner will be announced until the Bachelor's Auction tonight. These gals all did a great job and all of them are winners in my books. I hope you all join us tonight and find out who the official winner was. That's at seven in the community center. Bring your checkbooks and your cash ladies, and you can walk out with a bachelor."

22

TALKEETNA BACHELOR'S AUCTION

December 1988
James's place

"Wow, don't you look handsome!" Jesse put her spoon down to admire James as he emerged from behind the partition that separated his bedroom from the rest of the cabin. He wore jeans, a blue, orange and tan dress shirt, and a tan corduroy jacket with leather patches on the elbows. A pair of shiny dress shoes replaced the usual hiking boots.

With a smile, he leaned forward into an exaggerated bow. "Why thank you, miss. You look mighty fine yourself. That denim skirt is great. It was cool of Stephanie to loan it to you."

"Yeah. Thanks for thinking of that. Her sweater shows more cleavage than I am comfortable sharing, but hey, this is a weekend for bending boundaries and trying new things. Besides, how often do I get to attend Talkeetna's greatest show on earth?"

"You laugh now, but I bet you by the end of the night, you're going to be pretty pumped up that I brought you here."

Jesse had mixed feelings about the evening. She couldn't

care less about her standing in the afternoon's events. It was a fun thing to do and once was enough. It would take a special invitation for her to entertain returning next year. Meeting the people of Talkeetna was like going to a large family gathering as a child. There were so many stories. People came from such a variety of backgrounds, but the magic of the place united them as if they were related. She missed family, especially around the holidays.

"Hey, what's going on in that head of yours? Your light dimmed a bit there."

"Oh, sorry. It's nothing. I'm okay." An answer, she realized, that she had overused in this lifetime, and it hadn't served her well. She hesitated before continuing.

"Actually, I was just thinking about my family. Even if you don't have blood relatives here, Talkeetna is like having a family. I don't have that around me, and I kinda miss it."

"I get it. I do. I am fortunate to have developed quite a nice substitute family here in Talkeetna, and in Alaska, really, but it didn't happen overnight. I had to plant some seeds, help some folks out, and let them help me, in order to build bonds. Hey, I'm your surrogate family, okay?"

"Yeah," Jesse nodded in thoughtful agreement. "Sorry James, I didn't mean to discount you. Really, I didn't. You've been a great friend, from that first trip to the homestead. You've saved my bacon several times and I don't know how I could ever repay you."

"I do. Have fun tonight, okay? And whatever happens, I'll get you back to the cabin, alright?"

"Alright."

"And, if you need a safe word, if someone's carrying you off and you need rescuing tonight, just say something about Strawberry Hill, and I'll step in."

Her eyes widened. "You don't think…this isn't going to be dangerous, is it?"

James laughed. Sometimes, maybe even often, Jesse was literal. "Not unless you drink too much. Now let's go."

As they left the cabin, James tucked an envelope under his arm and held the door open. He even opened the pickup door for her once outside!

Jesse stood in awe of the still beauty around her, mixed with the civilization she didn't want to appreciate, but did. "What a beautiful evening. I love the way the lights shimmer and reflect on the snow. I don't get to see much of that at my place."

"It's cool," James agreed. He loved this lifestyle. He enjoyed the gamut of Alaska beauty. "But it's harder to see the northern lights when they're out, and the raw beauty you see is less apparent here. Both are nice, just different in ways many people never come to appreciate."

It was a short drive to the VFW Hall, where the Talkeetna Bachelor's Society hosted the auction. The parking lot was filled with every variety of vehicle around, from snow machines to a retired limousine. Most were smeared with a thick film of road grime.

"Jesse…" James turned to her as he turned the truck off. "Have a great time. Laugh louder and longer than you have since last summer. It may be your last chance for a while."

Jesse knew she came across as serious and thoughtful, but also knew how to have fun, perhaps just in a more subdued manner than some. With a smirk, she saluted James. "You've got it, mister. Loud, long, and fun, that's me…at least for tonight. You, on the other hand - not too much fun for you! I need a lift home tomorrow."

James laughed. "That a girl, and don't worry about me. I'll

be sober all night. I don't want my winning bidder taking advantage of me."

"You're a good guy, James. Don't let anyone ever tell you otherwise."

"Okay!" he nodded flippantly. "Now let's get this party started!"

Jesse knew James was a man of character her father would love. All cleaned up like he was tonight, her mother would, too.

THE SCENE that greeted them as they entered the VFW Hall seemed a cross between a New Year's Eve costume ball and a Sadie Hawkins dance. It was lit for a romantic-esque mood with candles on the tables, silver streamers, and a disco ball. Women were in all manner of dress and makeup, and crossed all age groups. They all shared the same societal infraction—they were single. The bachelors were an interesting lot. As it was close to Christmas, it did not surprise Jesse to see some Santa-looking garments, but she was a little surprised at the various applications of the traditional red and white furry swatches. There were hats, bib overalls with no shirts, and tiny, well maybe not exactly tiny, patches fancied as G-strings, over parts unmentionable. The G-string guy moved with grace and flounce, attracting the attention of similar kinds, but unfortunately not the attention of true bidders. As she came to meet the bachelors throughout the evening, she learned that two of the men were openly gay, but loved the charity and wanted to support the women and children. They felt compelled to take part as part of their personal calling. She commended them and recognized in herself that desire to help those she would likely never know.

A VOICE CALLED out as she walked further into the hall. "Oh, Jesse! There you are!"

Sarena rushed over and slipped her arm through Jesse's. "Let me escort you to your table. There's already a pitcher of beer, or three, poured for you, and if you would rather have a glass of cheap wine, I have that too."

"Sarena! Aren't you darling in your pink tutu and fancy make-up?! What's the deal with the table? Don't you have to pay extra to have your own table?"

"Hun, you're a finalist in the women's competition. You get to sit in the reserved section with some other special guests."

"Well, color me surprised! What an honor."

"Yeah, and here's your 'male' order catalogue." Sarena handed Jesse a brochure. Each page of the brochure had a photo and biography of one of the bachelors on auction, as well as responses to questions.

"Cool. Thanks for this. Do you have any recommendations?"

"For you?" Sarena picked up the beer pitcher and poured Jesse a glass of beer. "Well, I'm no matchmaker, but I'd say number 17 would be a good one for you to consider."

"Thanks for that. I'll study them up and see if I agree."

"Hey, and here's Ms. Birdie and Lulu. You probably remember Lulu from the women's competition."

Jesse reached her hand out to shake Lulu's. "Actually, I wouldn't have recognized you. You look so different in a dress and makeup."

Lulu was a beautiful woman in her late twenties, Jesse guessed. She wore a tight cobalt blue sweater over a short black skirt, and fishnet stockings with hiking boots. Large gold hoop earrings dangled from thick lobes, and the previously plaited auburn hair now flowed across her shoulders and down to the middle of her back.

"Hun, that's the game. Show the bachelors you can work with 'em during the day and play with 'em at night. These fellas are lonely, and they like it when we dress up for them."

Jesse knew what it was like to spend days and weeks with

only herself as company. During busy times, she could wear the same work clothes for days on end, and even though she could smell herself, she didn't care. There were also nights when she put on her one silk nightie, albeit with wool socks and sweater, to remind herself that she was still a woman and occasionally enjoyed cocooning in softness. She nodded in understanding. "I see where you're coming from. Anyway, you look beautiful."

"Thanks. So, what's your story? You look like someone who wouldn't need to go to an auction to find a guy." Lulu poured herself a beer and drank half of it before Jesse could patch together an explanation.

"Well, I don't really have a story, I guess. I have a homestead up on Lynx Creek. My buddy just talked me into doing this thing today and coming here tonight, after he flew me to town."

"Are you kidding me? You mean you weren't training for this? I mean, I spent at least twenty minutes a day trying to up my speed in the water bucket race. You were tough competition."

"Ha! No training here. I didn't even know what the events were until this afternoon. Anyway, I haul a lot of water just to stay alive and I couldn't keep up with you, so your twenty minutes of training paid off." Jesse lifted her glass. "To Lulu and sloshing buckets!"

"Here, here!" Lulu lifted her glass, as did Ms. Birdie.

Jesse turned to face the older woman on her right, dressed in the finery of a woman living in a metropolitan city twenty years prior. "And Ms. Birdie, what is your story?"

Sarena, who stood by while the women became acquainted, interjected. "Ms. Birdie was our top bidder last year, so she gets a seat at the head table with you fine ladies."

"That's right. This year, last year, and nearly every year this auction has existed. I missed out one year, but that's because I was down in Anchorage having my gallbladder out."

"Oh, this sounds like so much more fun than that." Lulu recognized Ms. Birdie from prior years, but never took the time to talk to her.

"Indeed, it is. I don't get out in the winter much anymore, but I love this event. I've been a widow for many years, and really don't fancy having a man around. But it's kind of nice to have a date and reminisce about the old days."

Ms. Birdie gazed at the empty stage with a faraway look in her eyes.

"Do you fancy anyone in the male order catalogue tonight?" Jesse patted the open catalogue on the table in front of her. She had not yet found any merchandise she was interested in, and wondered if she could even muster the desire to play the game.

"Honestly, I haven't looked through them all yet, but those I saw didn't move me so far." Ms. Birdie put her reading glasses on and looked back at the catalogue.

"Ladies, can I fill your glasses?" A bearded bachelor, dressed in leather chaps over an orange speedo bathing suit with a plastic yellow lei entangled in heavy, dark chest hair, approached the table with a fresh pitcher of beer. "Compliments of bachelor number nine here."

The ladies each muttered a thank you as they put their noses into the catalogue to research the particulars of number nine.

"So, number nine, those are some nice chaps. Do you get to ride much around here?" Lulu's question oozed with double entendre as her full, pouty lips formed each word slowly in their bright red, glossy glory.

"Sure do!" number nine retorted. "Polaris, Skidoo, Harley, and an occasional moose." He winked and walked off.

"Lulu, did you see his answer to the question about the perfect date?" Ms. Birdie pointed to print in the brochure beneath. "Says here, he's looking for a gal who can harvest a bear during the day and feels amorous in a teddy at night."

"Amorous? He says amorous?" Jesse frantically looked at the page. "He does, it says 'amorous.' I wonder if someone helped him write this."

Lulu laughed and slapped her palm against the table before reaching for a glass of beer. "Now that's funny!"

She lifted the glass and motioned for her tablemates to do the same. "To Jesse, with a hidden but wonderful sense of humor! May the good and odd one land in her lap tonight!"

"Hey, look, the master of ceremonies is starting." Jesse pointed to a man behind the podium. "And it's the same guy who narrated the races today…Wiley Joe."

"Yeah, he does this every year. He talks like he's a bachelor, but his long-time girlfriend has him on a short leash." Lulu seemed to know the ins and outs of the event like the back of her hand.

"Why am I not surprised?" Jesse took another swallow of beer and looked around the room. She chuckled to herself at the absurdity of her life. She loved living alone in the woods… usually. And she realized how much fun it was to get a little crazy with a bunch of strangers, too.

"LADIES AND BACHELORS. Welcome to the seventh annual Talkeetna Bachelor Ball and Auction." There was a pause while the room erupted in applause. "Tonight, we have a veritable smorgasbord of bachelors from which to choose. Each of them will display their, ahem…talents for you. As they come up on stage, I will share their bio with you, as well as any tidbits I have gathered through my super sleuthing. But first, we have a bit of business to tidy up from the Women's Wilderness races this afternoon."

Applause erupted again, as Wiley Joe paused while the board members of the women's shelter lined the stage, holding the race prizes. Wiley Joe introduced each board member, three women and one man, and described the prizes.

"Now, if I could get the spotlight, please."

A tall, lanky bachelor, dressed in bright orange-slicker bib overalls with a sparsely-haired, muscular chest proudly on display, stepped onto the stage. He carried a large hand-held lantern and placed it on the floor in front of the speaker's podium.

"Hey Andy, they have you on light detail tonight, eh?" The man with the lantern nodded and smiled. "Ladies, this is my good friend, Andy. You'll get all his details later, but I've known this guy for what, twenty-five years?"

Andy nodded again. "He's the real deal. Now, I'm sure you'll ask me why he hasn't already been caught, and there's a sad story around that he may choose to tell you one day, but I can vouch for the fact that he is house-broken."

Andy looked at the ground, his hidden laugh belied by heaving shoulders. "Anyway, you all keep him in mind when you do your bidding. But for now, let's find that head table. Miss Birdie, where are you?"

Jesse's eyes dropped to her lap as her tablemates waved their hands high. "Right here, Wiley Joe."

"Andy, can you please get the spotlight over onto that table in front there?" Andy approached the table and smiled. Unable to avoid the spotlight, Jesse looked up from her lap.

"Ms. Birdie here is our resident historian in Talkeetna. She single-handedly built our community library - except for the actual building. Her late husband, Nels, built that beautiful Scandinavian-style log cabin. Together they made an impressive pair. Tonight, Ms. Birdie has the honor of introducing our three finalists for the Women's Wilderness race. Andy, can you come get the mic for her?"

Andy retrieved the microphone from Wiley Joe and brought it over to the table.

"Thank you for that lovely introduction, Joe. You know, I just love this event. Together, we all do so much good for the people of our community. Sometimes, we just need to lend a helping hand to our fellow humans and help them through the rough times. I remember when the women's shelter was first started and since then, I'm sure we have helped over three hundred women, right here in our own small community and for that, I ask that we all raise our glasses."

The head table clinked their glasses, toasting the charity, as did the rest of the room, now filled with two hundred single women buzzing in anticipation.

"Now, I would like to introduce you to the three finalists from the Women's Wilderness competition from earlier today. First, we have Marilyn. You may recall her as the petite blonde elf on the racecourse. Marilyn took third place in each of the races and third place overall, but she had to race back to Anchorage, where she works the night shift at one of the hospitals. For her efforts today, Marilyn earned a Talkeetna Bachelor's Auction sweatshirt and beer mug. Let's give it up for Marilyn."

With a loud "Woop! Woop!" Ms. Birdie led the room in cheer.

"Now, if you followed the races today, you know that the next two women vied for the top spot, and they raced each other and traded wins in the various events. First, back for her… What is it, Lulu?" Lulu held up three fingers. "Lulu has been in all three of the Women's Wilderness races, and for those of you who were with us last year, you will recognize her as the second-place winner. Stand up Lulu."

As Lulu stood, bachelors peered out from behind the curtains and catcalls rang through the air as the audience laughed.

"Lulu hails from Fairbanks, where she works with the Head Start program as a pre-school teacher. Lulu tells me she is looking for a bachelor that is burly and strong, loves nature, can provide for his family and has a soft heart. Lulu, I have done some shopping for you and suggest you have a look at numbers 8, 17, 23 and 32." The crowd laughed as Miss Birdie held up the Male Order Catalogue.

"Also at the head table tonight is newcomer, Minnesota Jesse." As Jesse stood, another round of cheers, catcalls, and peering bachelors ensued. "Jesse comes to us from her homestead in Lynx Creek by way of bachelor, lucky 13, James, for all you gals looking for the perfect fella. Jesse has worked a variety of odd jobs and lives a subsistence lifestyle out there and does it all alone. Gals, Jesse isn't looking for a guy, or a gal for that matter, but let's cheer her on, hoping she finds a new friend tonight who loves the wilderness as much as she does."

"And now, the moment you've all been waiting to get beyond so you can see those bachelors. The winner of the Third Annual Wilderness Woman's competition, by the narrowest margin in history of the competition, is Lulu of Fairbanks!"

A mad rush of bachelors descended on the head table and carried Lulu away to the stage. She was crowned and photographed with all the bachelors.

"For her efforts, Lulu gets that beautiful silver fox hat handmade by Alice Beaver, and 40,000 Alaska Airlines miles."

"And for Minnesota Jesse, we have 20,000 Alaska Airlines air miles and some sealskin gloves made by Agnes Fox and donated by a generous benefactor. We hope you'll come back and try again next year." A small group of bachelors descended on Jesse and ushered her to the stage for her gifts and more photos.

"Ladies, thank you for supporting the women's shelter. Now let's have some fun!" Ms. Birdie looked around until she spotted Andy. "Andy, get this mic back to Wiley Joe."

"Congratulations to our winners," Wiley Joe bellowed. "And now, ladies, you all get the chance to be winners. In our usual tradition, I will surrender the podium to the lady of the show, the brains behind this night. Give it up for TJ!"

He handed the microphone to a middle-aged woman with a brilliant smile and flaming red hair set off by a black tuxedo. She immediately took command of the stage amongst the rowdy women in the room. "That's right ladies, we are now going to get down to business! All the men are now forbidden to be in the building unless they are on the catwalk. For tonight's auction, we have thirty-two gents eager to earn your donations and show you a good time…"

Jesse's mind wandered as TJ played to the crowd and laid down the rules for the main event. It was surreal to her that she was here, at the VFW in a room full of women, having won second place in a competition she knew nothing about at the start of the day. She was proud to be spreading her wings, trying new things, and meeting new people without the bitterness that used to creep in when she found herself around happy couples. Briefly, she contemplated how to explain this gender-bending night, where the women were fierce competitors in the essential activities of living in the wilds and the guys got cleaned up and strutted their stuff across a colorfully lit stage.

"Ok, friends, here we go! First up, we have a treat for you. Martin Grove is a transplant from Dallas. He came up to work on the pipeline and never looked back. Marty, as we know him, works on the slope two weeks on and two weeks off, which he says is his best asset." Marty, dressed in a shiny navy suit with a white shirt, red tie, and rose in hand, sashayed across the stage and down the catwalk, moving to Abba's Dancing Queen. "Marty's looking for an intelligent woman who won't complain when he goes fishing and hunting on his days off and likes to party hard when he's in town."

Marty turned around, shook his head, and called out. "Check your glasses and read that again, there, TJ."

TJ took off her reading glasses, rubbed them against her

tuxedo, and placed them back on. "Let's see here... Marty's looking for an intelligent woman who won't complain when he goes fishing and hunting on his days off and won't party without him when he's out of town." The crowd, filled with anticipation and alcohol, roared.

Marty raised a thumb up, then held the rose out to the women on either side of the catwalk as he made his way back to the stage.

"Lift your coat tail" a woman in the back row crowed.

Marty turned his head over his shoulder, grinned, raised his suit jacket and bumped his butt from side to side to show off his well-developed glutes. The crows responded with wild cheers and catcalls.

"Okay ladies, you've seen the goods. Marty is a good-looking fella and a hard worker. I'm sure one of you knows what he could do for you. I'm going to start the bidding at $50." Ms. Birdie raised her hand for the first bid. In the end, she was not the prevailing bidder, but Marty earned $240 for the shelter.

THE NEXT BACHELOR, Sean, walked on stage with long dirty blonde hair pulled back into a thick ponytail and long, muscular legs showing beneath his kilt. He had moved to Talkeetna from Scotland nearly a decade prior. Now divorced - through no fault of his own, in his version of the story, Sean carried a picture of himself with his two young children.

"Ladies, what do you think of those cute kids? Does his extra-cute extra cargo appeal to any of you women?"

"Ah, ladies, how can you pass up this hunk of a guy with that sexy accent and beautiful spawn? I've run into Sean and the kids fishing down at the river. Makes for a pretty picture." Bidding for Sean started at $100 and ended at $470.

Jesse leaned into Lulu. "I think that bidder's got a vision for how the night will go. How about you?"

"You know, I always wondered what those women from Anchorage were thinking, coming up here for the auction. It's not like these fellas are going to be driving down to Anchorage to clean out their garage or fix the garbage disposal." The two giggled.

"And our winning bid goes to—"

"I'm Carol." The excited and slightly wobbly bidder, dressed in a sexy black cocktail dress, net stockings, and high heels, yelled from the middle of the room.

"Carol, it is! Hey Sean, I hope the ex has the little ones for the night."

Sean blushed and nodded his head as he waved to the crowd and exited the stage.

"Dang, that's a lot of money. James didn't prepare me for this." In her head, Jesse was calculating the money she may eventually get for the few furs she brought into town and the unspent Permanent Fund Dividend from the state. Maybe she could budget $300 for this tonight. It was for a good cause, and she knew that the money and the good would come back to her somehow.

Ms. Birdie leaned close. "Honey, one benefit of sitting at this table is that I'm here to help. I don't need to be taking a bachelor home. I've got the best handy man and no need for a date. Let me help you out. Just get yourself a good one."

"Oh, I couldn't!"

"Honey, it's not like I'm paying you. It all goes to charity, and I would donate anyway, so never you mind about taking a little help from a new friend."

"Well, thank you Ms. Birdie. Maybe it won't come to that, but I'll keep your generosity in mind if it does."

Lulu found her winning bachelor in number eight.

"We have a special treat for you ladies. Let me just read his bio for you here. Number eight is super great; he loves to hunt and fish. He fled Minnesota to find himself amongst the trees, and the snow, and to chase his wish. In winter he writes his stories and sings of the glories of the man upstairs who has his back. Summer finds him flying in fishermen and homesteaders with their poles and their hopes and their pack." JT paused and looked up from the note card she was reading. "Alright ladies! Here's our poet laureate for tonight, Mr. Casimir Meade, former Minnie-so-tan, now Talkeetna's favorite volunteer fireman when he's in town, and one of those all-around great guys. Come on out Casey, and show these ladies what you've got."

From stage right entered a gorgeous, lanky hunk of a man in a dress shirt, khakis and a leather bomber jacket flung over his shoulder. Women across the room simultaneously inhaled audibly. His curly hair was styled, his teeth were polished white, and he moved with confidence.

Lulu gasped and grabbed Jesse's arm in excitement. "Oh, my goodness! He looks like Kevin Costner in The Untouchables, and he's mine!" Lulu looked at Jesse excitedly.

"Honestly, I don't know what or who that is, but good luck to you. He's beautiful."

Jesse hoped Lulu would have outstanding success but expected there would be a lot of competition.

As expected, the bidding was high for Casey, but Lulu stood her ground firmly and, with a nod from Ms. Birdie, made the final bid of $630. Jesse could only guess that Ms. Birdie had made the same offer to Lulu that she made to Jesse, to sweeten the pot.

With intense excitement in her voice, JT interjected as the applause quieted down. "Well, ladies, we have an unexpected treat for you tonight. We have an extra bachelor joining us at the last minute. Officer Ball, will you please join me on stage?"

The women scanned the room for Officer Ball.

"Ladies, as you know, we have a strict rule here during the Talkeetna Bachelor's Auction. No men are allowed inside the building unless they are being auctioned off. Officer Ball, here, did not follow our rules, and it so happens that Officer Ball is a single thirty-two-year-old man, currently living down the road in Willow. He tells me he is a lifelong Alaskan, loves to play his guitar and sing, visit family in Homer, help his friends design and build their off-grid houses, and fish in his free time. What do you say, ladies? Shall we put Officer Ball on the catwalk?"

The room filled with whistles, applause, and whoops.

"Well, Officer Ball, the ladies have spoken. It's your turn to walk the line. Billy, play his song."

Roxanne by the Police blared over the loudspeaker. The baby-faced officer, with a stocky build and crew cut, hesitantly started down the catwalk. But by the time he reached the end and turned around, he had a pep in his step and a smile for the ladies.

"Okay, ladies, let's start the bidding for Officer Ball off at $75. Who will give me $75?"

A voice rose from the far side of the room. "I'll give you $200 for that hunk of a man."

Jesse looked up and saw Amy, whom she had met at the starting line earlier in the day. Amy was standing on her chair waving money in the air. Still with heavy make-up on, she had exchanged the tutu for a slimming black dress and a flaming red boa. Her wild ringlets were tamed into a stylish hairdo, and with flawless porcelain skin, she looked like she belonged in a magazine ad for Pond's cold cream.

Jesse couldn't help but send out shouts to support her new friend. She stood and clapped. "You go, Amy!"

"You know her?" Lulu looked at Jesse.

"I met her at the starting line today. Pink tutu. Lots of make-up."

A smile grew across Lulu's face, and she stood with Jesse. "Go, Amy, go!"

The Wilderness Women clapped and cheered for Amy. Nobody bid against her.

JT pointed in Amy's direction. "Well, Amy, you've won yourself a State Trooper. You be careful, you hear?"

JAMES BROUGHT in $550 for the auction and his neighbor was not the winning bidder. She bowed out at $450 and three women continued to bid. Melanie from Palmer was the winning bidder, and if Jesse could have picked a perfect woman for James just by looking, Melanie would have been it. She was pretty, appeared friendly, and her petite frame would fit nicely in a plane. Jesse couldn't wait to hear more from James about this temporary master.

FINALLY, with bachelor number 17, Jesse found herself interested enough to bid. And bid she did, with the winning and highest bid of the night - $725. She was ready to stop at $350, but Miss Birdie kept reaching over and raising Jesse's hand. Jonathan was from nearby Trapper's Creek, where he owned an RV park and convenience store just off the highway. He looked less like a businessman than a naturalist. The feature that tipped Jesse over the edge in his favor was the tiny puppy he cradled in his flannel-covered arms. The puppy would be ready for its new home with the winning bidder in ten weeks, but he would hold on to it longer if the new owner needed more time to get ready.

"Oh, Ms. Birdie, I've been wanting a dog to come with me out to the homestead, but do you think a puppy will make it out there?"

"You'll never know until you try, honey. It's going to be a gorgeous chocolate lab when it gets bigger. That dog alone is worth the price of the bid."

. . .

By the time they got through all thirty-two registered bachelors and the state trooper, it was after midnight.

"As is tradition, you can all head over to the Latitude for breakfast. They are expecting you. And as is also tradition, they won't be serving alcohol, so empty your pitchers before you leave. The bachelors will be over in a bit to meet you, and you can make plans for your date. We thank you all for your donations. Together, we have raised over $25,000 for the women's shelter, and that's something we can all be proud of!"

"Let's go to the Latitude, girls." Lulu prompted Jesse and Ms. Birdie to go.

"I'm going to bow out this year, girls. You have a great time. I mean it. I invested in you and now, make me proud! I want to hear all about it next time I see you."

Miss Birdie slowly made her way to the door as Jesse and Lulu, arm-in-arm and prizes in hand, followed the crowd out and down the street to the hotel and restaurant.

"Get ready for more partying. This place will be hopping with people meeting people and waitresses trying to set you up. These are good town folks who want to keep their bachelors happy and sticking around. We can go get a table and the guys will be over after a bit."

23

FEELING LIKE HOME

March 1989
Lynx Creek Homestead

FOR THE FIRST time that she could remember since moving to the homestead, Jesse felt more content than not. She sang and smiled more and the lengthening days, with the promise of eventual spring, brought renewal, excitement, and wonder.

"Rosie! Rosie! Come along now." Jesse turned around on the trail and coaxed the puppy to join her. "That's a good girl. Let's get going. We have things to do."

Jesse imagined her feelings to be that of a new mom. She was proud of her Rosie-girl and how quickly she was learning to navigate the magical place they called home. As she watched, the puppy pushed her nose through the remnants of dirty snow and came nose-to-nose with a vole! Her tail wagged like a helicopter propeller, making her butt look like it should be filmed for the Bandstand countdown dancers. Jesse laughed heartily.

"Enough, Rosie-girl!" Jesse tried to choke down the laughter. 'Let's go fetch some water from the creek. We're going to have to take our Saturday bath tonight, even though it's only Friday. That okay with you?"

On cue, Rosie looked at Jesse and wagged her tail in agreement.

———

JESSE THOUGHT back to that day the month before when Jonathan visited. It was a cold and clear day in February. He drove in on his snow machine, navigating organically marked trails, rivers, and creeks to find her hideaway. His arrival was announced via radio message a week earlier, and Jesse looked forward to it. Their original meeting, at the Latitude after the Talkeetna Bachelor's Auction, was memorable. The self-assured bachelor had joined the table Jesse shared with her new-found friends. He was even more handsome than the stage lights revealed. A couple of years older than she, he was muscular and brimming with vitality. They had talked that night until the early morning hours, with some innuendo and flirt peppered in.

"Hey there!" Jesse waved from her porch as Jonathan guided the skis of his machine in her direction. She knew he couldn't hear her over the machine's noise and his fur-lined hat, but anxiety had kept her in motion all morning and it helped to call out and wave. Jesse tried to reframe the anxious feeling as excitement, but there was a subtle undercurrent of uncertainty about having Jonathan, or any man, in an intimate space in her life. Some of the angst, she knew, was related to infringement on the wildly confident and solitary lifestyle she had built, out of necessity, to prove herself competent in self-sufficiency. But she was also aware of that tiny but tentative scab covering the not-quite-healed wound of Tim's unfaithfulness. In so many ways, she had learned to surrender her ego, but in this one area, she still felt vulnerable.

Jonathan pulled his hat and gloves off and snuggled up to

Jesse in an awkward hug, which kept the jacket on his upper body from barely brushing against hers. He found her lips, shadowed by the ruff on her jacket, and passionately kissed her without pressing his chest against hers. Jesse's heart leaped into her throat and a mini quake shook her insides. She shook off a recurrent but nagging thought that she was just a potential exotic booty call for this self-assured hunk who stood before her in all his glory.

"It's great to see you," she blurted out. "How was the ride?"

"Ah, hun, it's great to see you, too. The ride was good, but…" Jonathan unzipped his jacket and reached in to pull out a curled up furball. "I think this little one needs to stretch her legs a bit."

"Oh, baby girl, come here!" Jesse scooped Rosie up and pulled her in close. Rosie looked up at Jesse with bright puppy eyes and eagerly buried her tongue in the corners of Jesse's upturned mouth.

They planned to spend Friday and Saturday at the cabin, with Jonathan leaving on Sunday. Most of the adult attention would be spent puppy watching and training. Jesse was grateful for the distraction. As much as the thought of Jonathan sparked something in her, she enjoyed being alone most of the time. Jonathan was flirtatious and almost aggressive in his attempts to get Jesse's attention. She felt guardedly excited about his desire for her. However, where he wanted to venture at warp speed, she was ambivalent and raced Rosie out for potty breaks to escape his advances. Eventually, she warmed into his embraces to avoid appearing unwelcoming, or worse, frigid. She did like him and loved having occasional company, but did not feel a longing for attachment, despite his good looks and hunky body.

"I hope you don't mind stew and biscuits. That's a fancy dinner for me." Jesse pulled out a few pantry staples reserved for special occasions, planning to serve a remote cabin-fancy dinner, complete with pickles and olives as appetizers. This time of year, the pantry stock was low and there wasn't much fresh food to be had. She worried she would appear pathetic somehow if she asked him to bring groceries.

"That sounds great to me. I eat most of my meals on the go or out of a can or package at my desk in the office. Lots of trail mix. A home-cooked meal sounds great." Jonathan opened his backpack and pulled a fifth of whiskey out. "Can I pour you a drink?"

"Sure, a short one. There are some jelly jars there on the pantry shelf. Please, help yourself."

Jonathan entertained Rosie while Jesse kept busy at the woodstove.

"I can't believe you cook on the woodstove. Not too many people can master that."

"Well, I don't know about mastery here, but I certainly don't starve. In my first year or two, I ate a lot of burned things. I tried throwing it out for the critters, but even they wouldn't have it."

Jonathan chuckled, then sidled up to Jesse and kissed her on the check. "I'm sure it will be great, but if not, I know a way we can take our mind off our hunger."

Jesse sighed a little and smiled weakly. At that precise moment, she glimpsed Rosie's back legs collapsing into a squat. "Rosie, no!"

"Ah, I've got this. Come on girl, let's get you outside before your mom burns the dinner." Jonathan scooped up the pup and took her out.

Rosie followed Jonathan back in through the door, shaking the snow off as she did. "She sure seems to handle the cold well. You must have taken her out a lot."

"Yeah. I took the pups out with their mom so they could get used to being outside and learn their potty habits from her.

It's worked pretty well, but as you can see, there's room for improvement."

"Well, it won't be long, and she'll have it figured out, I'm sure."

THEY LINGERED OVER DINNER, with great conversation about their families and life prior to Alaska.

"What made you stay in the great North, Jonathan?"

She remembered he said he was from Oregon and he came up with the military, but he never elaborated on why he stayed. In Jesse's world it was getting late, although it was not yet eight o'clock. She kept trying to think of questions to ask, to help her stay in the moment. It was a stretch to stay present with Jonathan and not move into worrying about what he expected from her on this first visit. While she felt viscerally attracted to him with all the stomach flips and gooey feelings, she had years of building up a shield from men after the hurts with Tim. She was finding it hard to let down her guard. Maybe it would be different if she had a friend or someone close to talk about this with; but the only person was James and the thought of processing this with him didn't sit quite right with her.

"You know, my usual response is that I saw an opportunity to build a life here and be an explorer." He paused and gazed at her seriously before continuing. "But I like you, and I think you deserve more of an answer than that."

Jesse slowly reached for his dirty dishes to stack them out of the way while he poured another whiskey for each of them. She wasn't certain why she deserved anything from him. She wasn't anything special, except the new mom to his pup.

"When I enlisted, I was right out of high school. I partied hard that first summer after high school before boot camp and found myself in a bit of trouble. Not with the law, really. That would have been a problem with the service, but there was a girl. Well, two, actually, and it seems, well, like I might have a couple of kids back in Oregon. I don't know for sure, but that's what I've been told."

Jesse sat in silence, thinking of something appropriate to say that wouldn't be as insulting as she wanted it to be.

"I know, before you say anything, it was cowardly of me not to find out the truth and man up. I mean, I could have two incredible kids out there and not know them. It was always my intention to make a bunch of money and get back there and make it right, but the business isn't really what I thought it would be, and I have to put most of what I make back into it just to maintain it. It seems like I'm on the hamster wheel and am never really going to get where I think I need to be to even show up and introduce myself as a dad."

Jesse swallowed hard and looked at her hands as she thought of what to say. While fuming inside, she over-saturated her words with sweetness. "That must be really hard, not knowing, and wanting to do something productive but not being able to."

Bullshit echoed in her head.

"Yes, it is. I'm glad you understand that."

Jesse bit her lip.

"Actually, that's a part of my life that's hard to talk about. I've gotten pictures of the kids that are supposedly mine, and sometimes I just lose it when I look at them. It's just so hard not knowing and not being able to be there."

"How about your family? Are they in touch with them, or do they know more?"

"Well, my dad has been estranged for a long time…"

That explains a lot. Jesse felt so judgmental, but her thoughts came honestly.

"And my mom moved away when I joined the Army. She went to California to be closer to her sister. I'm an only child and with me out of the house, there was no reason for her to hang around there. If she knows anything about those kids, she sure hasn't said anything to me."

Jesse rose and cleared off the table, trying to take her mind off the sad picture Jonathan was trying to paint.

Jonathan grabbed her wrist as she stood up and pulled her towards him. He grabbed her around the waist and forced her into his lap, hugging her. "I just knew you would understand, and it was safe to tell you. Thank you for understanding."

Jesse felt sick to her stomach and stuck. She wasn't one to ignore her instinct. If she told him how she really felt, she wasn't sure she would be safe. She knew her shotgun was loaded, and she could use it if he became violent, but she didn't want to deal with that. Instead, she swallowed hard, smiled, and said a prayer. A triple-combo she had used many times before, in different circumstances, when she questioned her safety.

"Oh, look who's ready to go out again." Jesse pointed to Rosie, who went to sit by the door. "Would you mind taking her out while I see to the dishes? Would you like a cup of coffee?"

"Sure, I'll take her out. Come on, Rosie. No coffee for me, but pour me another whiskey, will ya?"

Jesse was happy to pour him a tall whiskey, hoping it would make him pass out. She flipped on the radio to hear what was left of Trapline Chatter. Maybe she could get him to talk about some of the people on there, if he knew them. She had come to know the people, or of them anyway.

"She's a really good girl." Jonathan nodded toward Rosie when they came back in. "She heard some rustling in the woods and sniffed at the trail in that direction, but came right back when I called her. She's going to do good out here."

Well. She's going to do well, you mean. "That's great." Jesse handed Jonathan his whiskey while she made herself an instant coffee. "I like to listen to Trapline Chatter in the evening, like most people on the road system watch the news or tv in the evening. I feel more connected with the world when I do."

"Yeah, I get it." Jonathan took possession of the recliner and patted his lap for Rosie to join him.

He really is a lost soul. Jesse turned her attention to the radio. "Hey, sounds like Talkeetna is getting slammed with weather on Sunday."

"Oh yeah? That's not good." Jonathan mindlessly patted Rosie, who rested comfortably on his lap, as he took a long swallow from his jelly jar.

A quiet, sullen vibe settled in the cabin, and Jesse was relieved, but on guard. She divided her attention between Trapline Chatter and Jonathan's activity in the recliner. His jelly jar was over half empty and his eyes closed. She waited a while longer before rescuing Rosie and taking her out for a last pee before bedtime. Jesse spent the night listening for Jonathan's stirring, hopeful that he would have to beat the bad weather coming and leave early.

LONG BEFORE SUNRISE, Jesse made baking powder biscuits and opened the special jar of dried beef to make gravy. Breakfast would be more akin to shit-on-a-shingle than biscuits and gravy, but she was hoping it would be a warm send-off to a man she was having difficulty respecting.

It was after eight before Jonathan woke for the day. Breakfast was ready and Rosie had been out to pee three times.

"Well, good morning, sleepyhead!" Jesse tried to sound cheery and light. She did not want to poke the bear or leave a bad impression.

"Good morning. Sorry, I guess I was more tired than I knew. I've been busy working on the RV park. Late nights, you know."

"Yeah, I'm sure there's lots to do there to get ready for the season. I have some warm breakfast here, if you want, before you hit the trail."

"What day is it? I thought I had until Sunday to enjoy your sweet company."

"Yes, that was the plan, but remember, last night, we talked about the storm coming? You decided it was best if you try to beat it."

Jonathan rubbed his head. "Ah, yeah, I remember. Thanks. I should have breakfast and take off. Hey Jesse, you've been great. Thanks for listening to my sob story. I just knew, somehow, that you would understand."

"Sure. Happy to be a sounding board. Sounds like you have good intentions. I hope it's not much longer before you get back there to meet them."

"Yeah. Thanks." Jonathan surveyed the room. "I'll just take Rosie out before breakfast."

When Jonathan returned from the potty break with Rosie, Jesse had his breakfast and a big mug of steaming coffee on the table. "You've been a great host. It's a beautiful place you've made here. I'd like to come back and visit when there aren't any storms looming. And of course, you are invited to come visit me anytime. Guests will start arriving at the RV park in May, when the road opens for RVs, and it will be October before I close for the season."

"Hey, thanks. Let's keep it open and communicate on Trapline Chatter. Thank you again for bringing Rosie out. She's going to have a great home here, and I couldn't be happier."

They exchanged small talk of things to be done at the RV park and Jesse's spring shopping trip to fill the pantry. They drained a pot of coffee while lingering over breakfast, waiting for daylight to break so Jonathan could start his trip home.

Jonathan moved in to give Jesse a hug and a kiss, but Jesse turned her face slightly to avoid his booze, coffee, and breakfast breath. Undeterred, he tightened the hug a bit. "It was really great hanging here with you, even if it was a quick visit. I would like to do it again, and maybe next time I could join you in that comfy bed of yours."

"Hey, yeah. Let's see what happens. We'll stay in touch. You get home safely and let me know on Chatter that you made it."

"Sure, will do." Jonathan reached down to rub his hand back and forth across Rosie's back. "You be a good pup, ya hear?"

Jesse waved as Jonathan sped down the trail to the creek. He would follow the creek several miles before turning on a well-used trail to the next leg of his 30-mile or so journey home. Rosie sat shivering on the deck. Her presence warmed Jesse's heart. "Well Rosie, it's just you and me now… let's keep it that way. Come on in."

24

NEIGHBORLY

April 1989
Nolan Lake

THE LAST WEEKS of winter were brutal. The snow grew heavy with moisture. It accumulated to thigh-deep piles and clung to Jesse as she worked throughout the days to keep the porch and outhouse path cleared. It became a study to know how much of the white carpet to leave on the trail to avoid icy patches as the temperatures fluctuated and snow gave way to slush and then crystalized again. Jesse recalled one occasion when the snow came in droves, with the wind pushing it into crusty piles; suffering from cabin fever, she had felt too blue to get out and shovel it often enough.

"I'm embarrassed to tell you this," she spoke out loud to Rosie. "But I actually had to crawl out that window over there because I was literally snowed in. I couldn't budge the door open against the heavy snow."

Jesse leaned in and snuggled the growing puppy. "Now that I have you, that will never happen again, I promise."

Jesse was grateful to have Rosie for company on the long

days indoors. She made up games, mostly involving hiding treats in increasingly hard-to-reach places. Rosie was exhausted by the end of the day, which came early given the gloomy skies. There were no visitors after Jonathan left. She used the time wisely to recenter herself, alternating between raging, weeping, and writing, and exhausting herself as well by the end of those days. After clearing her self-pity for being alone, what felt like an unending state that she wanted but didn't, and after chastising herself for having expectations that Jonathan would be the love saint who saw the sun rise and fall in her eyes, she prayed for peace. In that time of silence, Jesse realized she had passed a lot of judgment on Jonathan, without even trying to meet him where he was, emotionally or spiritually. Jesse was probably one of the few people in the world he spilled his secret to.

"Invitation going out to Minnesota Jesse. Some of us are gathering at Nolan Lake for an Easter celebration. Bring your new pup and a sleeping bag. We have a bunk and plenty of moose stew and beer. If you have any extra pilot bread or chocolate, bring it. Rona's got the cravings. Yep, you heard it here first. We're expecting again. Hope to see you there. Come Saturday, April 2 and stay two nights or more if you like. Your pal, Dave."

Jesse was happy that the radio reception was good, despite the weather. The new antennae system was an improvement over the coat hanger and tin foil she used in her early years. Messages like this were important. A gathering sounded just right. She had Rosie, but the weather had taken a toll on her mood. Besides, she really liked Dave and Rona, and they would assemble a colorful group of characters for this celebration. While Jesse loved her big open church and worshiped in the wild regularly, communing with humans rather than birds, berries, and barren branches would do her soul some good.

Jesse pulled the 1988 calendar off the nail in the wall and studied the picture of her old high school. Each month displayed a building from her home community in Minnesota. It was this year's version of one she received annually from her parents for Christmas. She was certain it was supposed to keep her from forgetting them and her roots, as if she ever would. They could never understand why she didn't write or call regularly, even after her dad visited and saw how remote she was.

"Well, Rosie, if the weather is clear in two or three days, we're taking a road trip. You like those, right?" Rosie's front paws reached up to rest on Jesse's thigh as she sat at the kitchen table, and her tail wagged in response to the question. Since arriving, Rosie's legs had grown longer, and she had the sweetest and most curious personality. Despite the cold and stormy weather, she got outside to do her business, and only occasionally caught sight of a squirrel to bark at.

Jesse rooted through the pantry to find pilot bread, chocolate, and anything else that would be a treat to take to a craving, pregnant Rona. She found a half-eaten box of See's turtles and a full box of chocolate-covered cherries, remnants of a Christmas gift, as well as all the fixings to make a big batch of no-bake chocolate cookies. By the end of the day, she had over a hundred cookies made, packaged, and piled together with the other things ready to load on the sled for the trip to Nolan Lake.

RONA AND DAVE were Jesse's nearest neighbors, except for Sadie, who hadn't returned to her cabin for over a year now. As far as Jesse knew, Sadie was still alive in Fairbanks with family - at least she was at Christmastime when James took in a package from Jesse. Nolan Lake was about three miles northeast of their cabin on Lynx Creek. Jesse marveled at the couple, who apparently were now pregnant with their third child in three years! Only once had they spent an extended period away from their cabin, built with the help of Jesse and other friends and family.

In September, a month before their second baby, Paxton, was born, they packed up and went to town. Rona had seen the doctor every month, or two, depending on the trail conditions, and an early ultrasound showed that the baby may have heart problems. They stayed in Anchorage with friends for about two weeks before the baby was born and about a month afterwards, while the doctors repaired a small hole in his heart. Little Paxton was doing great now and other than the scar on his little chest, no one would ever know he had a problem. Jesse whispered a prayer of thanksgiving and health for Rona and Dave with this newest pregnancy.

Early Saturday morning, Jesse was dancing in the kitchen to music blaring from the radio. It was nearly time for her a big shopping run to Sam's Club in Anchorage, so she no longer had to hoard battery life. A rap on the door startled her. She stared at Rosie and asked her, "Who on earth could that be?"

Picking Rosie up, she looked up at her gun in its place over the door and glanced out the window. There were new snow machine tracks, but she could not see the vehicle or its owner.

"This is suspicious," she whispered into Rosie's ear. As she opened the door slowly, James shouted, "What took you so long?"

He let out a roar of laughter at the sight of Rosie in Jesse's arms. "Oh, my! Look at how big that girl is! Can I come in?"

Jesse put Rosie down, grabbed his jacket sleeve, and pulled on it. "Of course! Get in here."

She closed the door quickly behind him. "What brings you out today? I'm getting ready to head on up to Nolan Lake this afternoon."

"Oh, good! I came by to see that you were coming for sure."

"You're going, too? That's so cool. I had no idea." Jesse took James's coat and hung it up while he played with Rosie. "You want to just hang with us for a bit and we can ride up together? Or do you need to go up early?"

"Naw, I'm good. I have some food and drink stuff on my sled, but ya know, it's not even freezing out there anymore. The Chinook blew in and things are warming up."

"Oh, good. I knew it felt warmer in here and I didn't freeze my buns off in the outhouse this morning. I thought maybe it was just me and my wishful thinking. I guess I could have checked the thermometer."

"Ah, it's all good. Rosie's looking great. Has she turned out to be a fine pup for ya?"

"She's the best! I don't know how I lived without her for so long. She's a little work, like all curious puppies are, but it's been really great for me to have something to focus on outside myself. That can get a little boring, ya know."

"Well, I doubt the inner workings of your mind are ever boring," James smiled. "But I understand about being by yourself a bunch. I haven't talked to you since Jonathan came out. By his account, he had a great time."

Jesse choked and nearly spit out a mouthful of tea. "What the heck are you talking about?"

"Well, I bumped into him at the gas station near Houston last week. He said he brought Rosie out and spent the night. Had a great time and thought you were a super cook, to boot."

"Oh James, if only I could tell you the entire story. Suffice it to say that *his* good time was not *my* good time, but I am grateful for Rosie."

"Interesting. I'll take your word for it."

"Good." Jesse sat in contemplative silence for a moment, then drew in a sharp breath. "Oh, no! He will not be at Nola…"

"No. No. He's not part of that crowd at all. I was probably only invited because they wanted me to haul up some stuff for them."

"Oh, I'm sure that's not the only reason you're invited. I haven't met a single soul who doesn't adore you. Speaking of which, how's things with Melanie? She looked like a fiery mistress at the auction. Did you have your date yet?"

James's cheeks flushed, and he looked down. "Boy, we haven't talked in a while, have we? Yeah, okay, I guess the date was okay. We had dinner one night in Wasilla, and she wants me to come to her place in Palmer. I… I haven't done it yet."

"Done it, or done IT? What are you saying, James?"

"No, I mean, I haven't committed to going to her place in Palmer, okay? I mean, I just don't know. I've been a bachelor all my life. I don't really know about this courting stuff, and she seems pretty experienced."

"Yeah, I know what you mean. When you're like us, it's pretty easy to sit back and judge others. After Jonathan left here that weekend, I realized that I probably was being more judgmental than I had a right to be. I may try to look him up when I go to town and take another stab at getting to know him." Jesse paused for a moment, deep in thought. "I'm not telling you what to do, though. You'll have to decide that, but what I'm saying is, sometimes you don't know until you try it."

"I get it," James nodded. "I'll figure it out, but not today. Today, I'm hanging with my pals and getting caught up with all yer neighbors. How long has it been since you all got together?"

"Well, I don't know who all is going to be there, but I saw a bunch during the Iditarod, and some I haven't seen since the annual summer solstice shindig here."

"Oh, yeah! That was another great one. It was super to see the gang again, except Sadie wasn't there. I saw Randy Anderson the other day while picking up a pizza and he had bumped into Fred in Fairbanks. He said she had a good winter. Maybe you'll see her out here for a visit this year."

"That would warm my heart to see her out here, doing what she loves."

"Yeah." James took the cup of coffee Jesse handed him and they sat in silence a few minutes.

"It…"

"Wha…"

They both started talking at the same time and fell into familiar laughter.

"You go," Jesse prompted James.

"Well, I was just going to say how nice it is to see you again. I know it hasn't been what, a month since I brought your mail by, but we didn't really get to talk, and I do worry, no, that's not right. I do think about your wellbeing between visits and pray that you stay well."

"Thanks, James. That means a bunch to me. It's been a fine winter and got even better when Rosie came to live with me. She's going to keep me young, that one."

"Oh, I bet she will. I miss having a pup, but not all my clients want to fly with one, and I'm gone too much to leave one home all day. I hope you don't mind if I just love on yours now and then. She doesn't seem to mind at all."

"She's such a good girl. You'll have to come back when the snow is gone and help her learn to navigate the wild animals. She's so curious and friendly. I'm expecting she'll find herself too close to the wrong new friend one day."

"That's bound to happen. You'll have to learn the art of removing porcupine quills."

"I'm sure. I'm going to have a bite to eat before I take off. Would you join me, and then we can load up to go?"

"Sure thing. I never turn down an offer of food. I'll stage the wood so you can stoke the fire before we go."

. . .

THE RIDE to Nolan Lake was beautiful. The snow was crusted and plentiful along the trail, although it wouldn't be long until it gave way to slush and goop that would prevent snow machines from moving along the paths or breaking new ones, for that matter. Lynx Creek was solidly frozen, as was Nolan Lake when they arrived there. Soon, the tundra would do its spring cleaning and the discarded beaver branches would line the shores, globs of gunk left over from disintegrated plants, and animal waste. But for today, there was vast whiteness beneath a clear blue sky and the world was theirs. They took their time moving up the creek, soaking in the welcoming warmth of the sun and the pristine new snow.

They stopped a couple of times just to take in the view, with Denali reaching into the heavens in the background while the anticipation of spring stirred beneath them with restless hibernating animals and plants preparing to grow. A small herd of moose grabbed at tree branches, their big bulbous noses leading open jaws into the aspen and birch trees to chomp down and break off toothpick sized twigs to feed their enormous bodies. The cows would calf in about six weeks and a new cycle would begin right here. A quick break to watch the moose, and Rosie, turned into thirty minutes as they breathed in the surrounding glory. Jesse and James were amongst the few to witness the miracles all around them.

"That sunlight shining over there..." James pointed toward the nearest mountains to the west. "When the sun is at that height right there and reflecting off the crystals in the snow, it's like a mirror when flying over it. It can be nearly blinding for a split second. The first time it happened to me, years ago, I got so disoriented for a couple of minutes, I thought my eyes would never adjust again."

"How is it now?"

"For one thing, I've gotten better sunglasses. But really, experience has taught me about changing angles and heights ever-so-slightly, and the reflection and view changes significantly."

"James, I think you have a platform for a new self-help book right there."

They laughed.

"Yeah, well, I'm not much of a writer, but I'm happy to give you that vision to use in yours, if you want."

"Thanks. We probably should saddle up and keep going. They're going to wonder if we're coming."

"Sure thing. It's so nice not to have to worry about being in the dark so early. That's another nice gift this time of year."

THE GATHERING WAS A BLAST. Jesse was happy to see Dave and Rona, their daughter Skye, and Paxton.

"Oh, my goodness, I can't believe how much they have grown!" Jesse took Paxton from Dave's arms and flew him around like an airplane, zooming headfirst toward the snow with a quick turn to the sky. He laughed and clapped his hands. She handed him to James, who was just as eager to get some kid-time in, and found Skye playing nearby.

"Has anyone seen Skye? I have a sweet treat she might like, but I can't find her anywhere," Jesse called out to the half-dozen adults standing nearby.

"I haven't seen her anywhere. I think maybe she's gone to bed." Jay held a beer up to salute Jesse and grinned. Gosh, it was great to see him again.

"I here, Annie J. I here. Canny?" Skye stood up from behind a sled piled with wood.

"Oh, my. There you are! Come here and see Auntie J." Jesse was Auntie J. to her siblings' children and spread that moniker to the family of her choosing in Alaska. She loved it that Auntie J. was one of the first names Skye learned.

"Come with me and I'll show you what I've got. Maybe you can take me to your mommy. She might want one, too."

"Paxy too?"

"Well, I'm not sure Paxton can have one, but we'll ask mommy." Jesse took Skye's tiny, gloved hand in her own to be led back to Dave and Rona. She waved to the small gathering building the fire. "I'll be back with treats for you all, too!"

JESSE MADE a couple of trips on the snow machine back to Rona's cabin to gather hot food and drinks and sled them back to the small crowd now gathered around a roaring bonfire. Some brought camping chairs, while others perched on makeshift stools that would eventually be tossed on the fire. After they delivered the warm stew, one friend offered Jesse their chair to enjoy the beautiful evening.

"Have a swig of this. It makes the glow even brighter." Martin, a friend from up by Skwentna, passed Jesse a bottle of Jack Daniels. She took a swig and held it in her mouth, before feeling the burning warmth trickle down her throat.

"Thanks. That's a warm-up for sure."

Around the circle she heard tales of winter trapping, ice fishing, sick relatives, and a vacation in Hawaii. The orange glow from the fire spread across the faces and onto the snow-covered lake and filled her with the warmth that comes from breathing in life with others. Whether or not it was the Jack Daniels, Jesse didn't care.

SEVERAL TIMES DURING THE WEEKEND, Jesse allowed herself respite from the noise of the gathering. She wandered off the lake and into the shrub skirting, even deeper into the old growth forest, to listen for signs of life there. Ravens cawed and rabbits scampered as she approached. Chickadees, the ever-present song masters of the interior, greeted her as she intruded on their quietude. When she returned to the group, she was refreshed and eagerly engaged in storytelling. They filled the two-night celebration with fellowship and raucous laughter, acapella singing, some yodeling and two of the couples did some clogging as the rest of the group kept time by clapping their gloves together or banging spoons on pots.

During the day, they all chopped wood, cleared trails, rode snow machines, ice-fished, or helped Rona in the cabin. Jesse was happy to find herself alone with Rona in the cabin. "How are you feeling, really, Rona? Paxton is so little yet; I can't believe you have the strength to do this again."

"Ah, what would you know? You're just the worrying Auntie." Rona teased. "Actually, I'm feeling great. Dave takes such good care of me and these littles haven't been able to get into too much trouble yet, but with spring and summer coming, there will be plenty of opportunity. I'm afraid I'm going to have to build a taller pen for Paxton outside. He's a far more aggressive climber than his sister was."

"I kinda hate to ask, but have you had an ultrasound with this one yet?"

"It's okay. I'm going in at the end of the month for my first visit. You know how it's been out here, kinda hard to find a decent forecast to travel in. Besides, what Paxton had isn't genetic, so it's really unlikely to happen again."

"That's good. You know, if you ever want me to keep the kids, I'm happy to. Now I have Rosie, and I'm sure they would love playing with her."

"That's a great idea. I'll talk with Dave about it. Of course, we know you're there, but hate to impose."

"Listen Rona, there's no imposition. I mean, what else am I going to be doing?"

"Well, a little birdy told me you had an overnight visitor a few weeks back. I mean, you just never know."

"Really?! No. Just no. I can't imagine that happening again. A birdy, huh?"

"That's what these gatherings are for, to catch up with, gossip, and love on your neighbors."

The two women laughed as they put their jackets, hats, and gloves back on to ride back to the gathering. Today they were serving moose chili, roasted ptarmigan, baked pike, and potatoes. A royal feast in these parts.

At night, Jesse tried to be the last to crawl into a three-tier wooden bunk in the bunkhouse. It was increasingly difficult to sleep around others when she spent most of her time alone. She lay in her sleeping bag, staring up at the wooden slats of the bunk above or the wooden ceiling just inches from her face, thinking about shared evenings of her pre-Alaska life. Flashes of high-fives across enormous platters of pizza and pitchers of beer, and clinks of crystal glasses in intimate, dimmed corners with sparkling winks of shared secrets. Then, there were hugs of encouragement from friends and family, people who didn't really get her but wished her the best all the same. She missed humans, but also needed space to breathe.

Maybe now she had breathed enough to allow another human in. Maybe.

25

SENSITIVE AND SINGLE IN SPRING

May 1989
   Trapper's Creek, Alaska

Spring erupted on the back of the Chinook winds, pushing moisture from the snow into the earth to make giant mud pies, while freshly minted green carpets and iris stalks erupted. Rosie spent the days digging still-frozen sticks from piles and chasing squirrels, brazen in the warm daylight that came earlier and left later each day.

Jesse perched herself on a fallen tree that rested horizontally against its distant neighbor at just the right height to fashion a birch bench. She had come out to use the outhouse and found herself watching the night's ice crystals melting as they met the rising sun. The beauty of the fresh spring morning took her breath away. Rosie was still asleep on their shared bed.

She closed her eyes and felt the warmth of the rising sun on her face. Her thoughts faded into a mystical vision, where she wore a white gown. Birds hopped around beside her while hares and squirrels played at her feet. Jesse felt herself smiling and her heart sung with ethereal music. Much like a fairytale of her childhood, a handsome man, a woodsman in her vision, approached. He raised her hand to his mouth and pressed it against his lips. Jesse felt wetness on the back of her hand and shook it as she opened her eyes. She had left the cabin door open, and Rosie, with tongue hanging out, stood at her side.

"Wow, that was weird! I drifted off, girl, to some strange place of lollipops and daydreams. Let's get you fed, and then I want to take you down to the river. It's time you learn these trails. Besides, the squirrels need a respite from you!"

JAMES FLEW out a few days later and took Jesse and Rosie to town. She borrowed his truck and drove to Anchorage to do some shopping. They stopped to visit Charlie, who talked Jesse into spending the night so they could get caught up. James had expected this; he didn't anticipate her to be back for at least two days and he had other transportation to use. Charlie brought out extra ice packs to put on the fresh produce and things that needed to stay chilled in the coolers in the back of James's truck.

"THIS IS SO KIND OF you, Charlie. Are you sure I can't take you out for dinner or something?" The two sat in Charlie's dusty, cozy living room. She confessed on their first meeting that she had no use for dusting, since it didn't do any good anyway and she was gone too much to care.

"I'm positive. I am around people most days and I just like to hang here in my own space. Besides, I want to get to know Rosie here, and Duke is happy with the company. I bet you don't get many chicken pot pies at your house. How about we have those tonight? I know it's not fancy, but it's a change of pace for you."

"You can't imagine how wonderful that sounds! Chicken is

the one thing I really fill up on when I come off the homestead. It's so hard to keep out there, except canned." Jesse squished her nose up as she shared. "And honestly, I never did acquire a taste for it that way."

"Hey, I get it. That just sounds nasty, with that collagen jelly stuff on it. Nope. Not for me either. How about I put in two for you? I think I'll have two myself, just for good measure." Charlie fished the familiar red boxes out of her freezer and turned the oven on. "Say, I've got some red wine here, or a beer. What's your pleasure?"

"Now you're getting all fancy on me. Wine sounds great." Jesse joined Charlie in the kitchen. "I can pour it. Where are you jelly jars?"

"Oh girl, I have a genuine wine glass for you! No jelly jars required unless you really want one."

"Naw, I was just kidding ya. If I remember right, the wine glasses are in this cupboard." Jesse pulled a glass out for herself. "How about you? Will you be joining me?"

Jesse didn't wait for an answer and pulled out a matching glass.

"You know it. Let's get this party started." Charlie uncorked the bottle and poured them each a generous serving. "Here's to another year of survival in the wilderness!"

"And to my first Alaska friend," Jesse added.

"Awe, now you're getting sappy on me," Charlie responded playfully.

The two spent the evening catching up on the year since they last visited. They both agreed that it had flown by since they last saw each other. Some of the talk was a repeat of shared stories in letters exchanged throughout the year.

"So, I know it's not really proper to ask, but is there a love interest yet? How about the guy whose truck you have? James, right? He's been hanging around a long time now." Charlie leaned forward as she pressed Jesse for information.

"James is a great friend. Really great, but nothing else. I bought a guy at the Bachelor's Auc…"

"Wait, what? You bought a guy? Are you sure you should be saying this out loud?" Charlie scooted to the edge of her chair to get the scoop.

"Chill. It's not like that." Jesse laughed and held her hand up to stop any insinuations Charlie may want to throw her way. "You know, the Talkeetna Bachelor's Auction—the fundraiser?"

Surely, Jesse thought, every woman in Alaska must know about it.

"I'm kidding ya. Of course, I know what you mean, but I'm just surprised, I guess, that you came out of your hidey hole to catch a guy." Charlie leaned back into her chair and waved Jesse on to continue her story.

"With the help of some apparently well-off older woman, I bid on a guy named Jonathan. I really just wanted the puppy that came with the package, but he was quite a hunk, too."

"Yeah? So, what happened?" Charlie got up to pop the pot pies into the preheated oven.

"He brought Rosie out to my place one weekend in February, spent the night in the recliner, I might add, then went back to his place in Trapper Creek."

Jesse shared the details of the visit, that is, the ones that she was willing to share.

"Well, do you think you'll see him again, this Jonathan?" Charlie quizzed in a doubtful tone.

"As a matter of fact, I was thinking I would swing by his place on my way back to Talkeetna. He has an RV park, and it's open for business now, so he should be around."

"Sounds cool. I guess if you don't have any expectations, it should work out just fine."

"Fair point. Since you were so generous to let me stay, I think I might just stay in a while longer tomorrow and go to Michaels to get some art supplies. I've been thinking I might want to write and illustrate a children's book. There's so much cool stuff to share from nature. Anyway, it's just a thought, and this is my best opportunity to pick out some things," Jesse shared pensively. She hadn't said it out loud to anyone, but the thought stuck with her now for some time, and if she was no good at it after trying, nothing lost.

"That sounds super cool. I've got no creative ability, as you can see from my house, but I admire those who do."

"Not sure I do, either, but I'll keep you posted on that." Jesse melted into the chair and watched as Rosie tried repeatedly to get Duke to play tug-of-war with her. Jesse didn't know if she could pull off a children's book, but she knew magical transformations happened in the Bible and in real life for some people, so why not her?!

"Oh, boy. I can't believe I ate them both, and we finished a bottle of wine! That was the best thing you could've offered me, Charlie." Jesse rubbed her belly and smiled mischievously. "Now, let me clean up the dishes."

"Are you sure you can handle it? The creases in those foil pans are pretty difficult to clean," Charlie teased.

"Are you seriou…"

"Absolutely not! You put those foil pans right there in the trash where they belong. Boy, you are easy prey, girl."

"Well, if you knew my mother…"

"Yeah, I've got one like that, too. I'm going to go downstairs and watch a little tv. Come if you like or make yourself at home up here. As always, use the phone to call your folks, or whatever. Mi casa es su casa."

"Thanks again, Charlie. I'm going to take Rosie for a walk, soak in the tub a bit and hit the rack. I'll see you in the morning, right?"

"Yes ma'am, I'll be here with the coffee on. Have a great walk and rest, and I'll see you later." Charlie grabbed a beer and headed down the stairs. As she led Rosie out the front door, Jesse heard Charlie laughing at the television.

THE NEIGHBORHOOD WAS frenetic with kids riding bicycles, people raking their yards, cleaning out and turning the soil in flower and garden beds, and washing cars. By the time they returned to the house, it was nearly ten o'clock on a school night and there were still children playing in the streets, shooting hoops and riding skateboards.

"Rosie, this is what happens in Alaska in the summer. Everyone gets manicky. I'm counting on you to keep me sane, girl. Your bedtime is now, and never later." Jesse admonished, Rosie or herself. She wasn't sure which.

AFTER BREAKFAST WITH CHARLIE, Jesse and Rosie headed out to run more errands, do some paperwork with the state, go to the bank, and turn in observation data for a small project she did over the winter for a conservation group. It wasn't much income, but it didn't require a lot of her time, either. Each day after waking, Jesse thanked God for not having to go to a job filled with paperwork, stale office air, shared coffee pots, and gossip. However, not having a standard job also meant that she wasn't earning a retirement, didn't have health insurance, and didn't have the opportunity to meet friends or a potential mate in a structured environment, and she was ok with that. She had a major medical health insurance policy that didn't cost too much and paid cash for her annual physical and dental exam. Given her lifestyle, she was rabid about caring for her teeth and being safe to prevent injury.

BY LATE AFTERNOON, Jesse and Rosie were gliding along the Parks Highway on their way to Talkeetna. They stopped at

B&J's in Wasilla to pick up a new chain for her chainsaw and some bar oil. She enjoyed going here to see what they had to outfit the homesteader, who they seemed to cater to. She found new heavy-duty rain gear on sale and bought it, the same way she would have bought a new pair of shoes to wear to the office in her past life. They pulled off at Miller's Landing for ice cream, one for each of them.

"Alright now, girl. That's the last stop before we see your momma. Maybe."

Jesse talked herself into stopping by Jonathan's RV Park, since it was just before the turnoff to Talkeetna, anyway. As she got closer to the Petersville Road turnoff, near the RV park, she felt nauseous. She gripped the steering wheel tighter, slowed, and signaled to turn into the drive. Jesse took a deep breath, trying to force any expectations she had to dissipate. She hadn't been in the park before, but easily found the office, where she assumed she could find Jonathan. As she turned to get Rosie's leash, she saw them out of the corner of her eye.

Jesse's heart leaped into her throat and a mini quake shook her insides as she did a double take at the sight of two forms embracing on the steps of the RV park office in nowhere, Alaska. She recalled the quiet, but persistent, thoughts from a handful of months before - that Jonathan saw her as a potential exotic booty call - and she cursed her intuition. The Talkeetna Bachelor's Auction was a great place to get a puppy, but the pup was a ploy to lure slightly intoxicated women looking for a good time, to the confident, hunk of a man that slipped too easily into Jesse's fold in a land known for good odds and odd goods. Damnit! For years after leaving her narcissistic and perpetually unfaithful ex-husband, she refused to allow any man into the sacred intimate space of her mind. She broke that rule with Jonathan; and now saw his true colors, wrapped in the arms of some fly-by-night damsel in a diesel renovated bus on her 50 men in 50 states tour.

Jesse threw the pickup in reverse and threw gravel as she

sped out of the park, cursing herself for stopping. By the time she hit the Talkeetna turn, she was shaking so badly she had to stop. She grabbed Rosie's leash and took a long walk into the woods, away from the highway. After marching off the ego-hurt and betrayal, she reminded herself that they weren't an item. She was just thinking of giving him a chance. She walked back to the pickup, threw the tailgate down, and sat while Rosie nosed rocks around the pullout. Jesse retrieved a chocolate bar and soda from the groceries, both treats she would normally save as a reward after a hard day of work, but emotional eating took over as her mind and heart vied for her attention. Rare for her, but a weakness she was aware of.

Jesse knew she was highly sensitive and easily set off by lights and sounds, tastes, colors, criticism, insincerity, Teflon-people, the condescending spouses of others, and complainers without proposed solutions, and she found it damn hard to live under others' expectations. She reminded herself that adventure may not have been the only reason she sought the solace of life alone in remote Alaska. She just knew - she had a knowing, like she knew she needed to write a children's story. But she was often afraid to put voice to it, because it might be wrong. People she met over the years called her empathic. She didn't know what it meant, so she read up on it, and recognized herself in the words. She felt everyone's everything so strongly, adding to her feelings of overwhelm. Yet she had a vehemently resilient soul.

Jesse realized the burden of being a creative with a pathological self-critical streak, and it was the hardest for her to recognize and manage. Living alone, where no roads pass but the Iditarod, became the opportunity she needed to face her insecurities, day in and day out, and manage those elements of her unique personality she could no longer set aside.

Maybe she wasn't ready for another human in her life after all.

26

SOULFUL WOMEN

Summer 1990
Homestead tundra

THE WOMEN eagerly chatted around the bonfire, getting caught up after months of living in the darkness of winter. Jesse stepped away into the protective shadow of the black spruces to find herself a pocket of private air. She wasn't used to sharing her five-acre homestead in the middle of nowhere with another tame soul, let alone eight. As the sheltered oxygen filled her lungs, she turned back to look upon the unique group of women - sisters that now filled her life. Collectively, each represented a piece of her in their irreverence, kindness, fortitude, boldness, beauty, sorrow, and a touch of magical thinking. Some had become the man they hoped to marry when they set their sights on living in remote Alaska. Others, sometimes sadly so, became the wife their husbands needed to survive the lonely Alaska days and nights. These women were an eclectic ensemble of Lynx Creek dwellers and wannabe homesteaders, some of whom were still married to the mainland with its conveniences.

IT WAS RONA'S IDEA, sometime back in February, to start an annual women's gathering in the spring to honor the renewal that came with the season that was often underappreciated. She was still nursing their youngest, Leah, a beautiful, petite child who looked just like her mother.

"It's just that I know, and you know, living in town, you don't appreciate the magic of it all as much, even when you try. There's nothing like immersing yourself in the experience and getting dirty in it." Leah tugged at Rona's nipple as she looked up at her animated mother. They shared a smile. "See, even Leah thinks it's a great idea."

"She does, does she?" Leah turned to look at Jesse, who looked away so the baby would get back to business. "I don't think it's a bad idea. In fact, it's a good one. But how do we do it out here? It's so messy in the spring."

"Well, let's make it May, then, when we usually are less muddy. The trails are not so muddy, and the earth is alive with budding and crawling things. I've got some great ideas on journaling, and look at you, miss artist..." Rona pointed to the many iterations of watercolor pictures strung around the room —material for Jesse's eventual children's book, she hoped.

"Oh, boy. Now you're pushing it," Jesse groaned. "You know, I don't know how to paint."

Rona put Leah down and stomped across the room, unfastening one of the latest pictures from the drying line strung along the west wall. "Girl, this picture here tells a story in itself. I know you don't think you're any good, but you taught yourself how to do this. That's the kind of fortitude and resilience and dream-chasing these other women need to hear about. You know, Jesse, we're the lucky ones. Yeah, we don't have big bank accounts, at least I don't..."

"Ha! And you think I do?"

"No, I don't know and don't care. That's what I'm saying.

What we have here is a love of a life closer to mother nature, closer to God, closer to each other than what either of us had before we came here. I know I got lost in the shuffle, the coffee shop trips, the cool fashions, the latest self-help books... all the things."

Rona paced, her arms waving through the air trying to get Jesse to see her vision of a sacred women's circle, gathered in the wilds of Alaska letting it all hang out, finding support in friends, old and new, and making lasting memories.

"Yes, there's magic here, but you and I both know that you can't give that to someone, and while I felt it the first moment I stepped off James's plane, not everyone will."

Jesse pulled a jar of smoked salmon sticks and some crackers from the pantry. She grabbed the kettle of hot water off the stove to fill the two cups.

Rona was playing on the bed with Leah and Rosie. "Hey, you got any chocolate in there?"

"You're not!" The tea kettle slammed down on the stove harder than Jesse intended, startling Leah.

"Maybe... but I do just like chocolate, and you always seem to have some."

"I swear you are part rabbit."

"Maybe full rabbit at this rate."

"Well, back to this bright idea you have." Jesse grabbed a notebook from the top of the pile on the end of the table and pulled the repurposed tin can filled with colored pens and pencils to the middle of the table. Purple was her power color. She plucked the darkest purple pencil from the can and started making notes. "Who and how many do you think we should invite?"

"That's the easiest part, I think. Somewhere between eight and twelve would be ideal. This is a group we want to stick together for a long time, so I was thinking of Carol, of course, and Keven's girl Lynn..."

"That's right. She's living out here now, isn't she?"

"She's planning to spend nine months here and the hardest winter months in town, staying with pals and working, at least this year. She'll be back by May for sure."

"Who else were you thinking?"

"Well, that's four. I was wondering if you think your friend Charlie would want to come out."

"That's a great idea. I know she's really busy, but if I get the invite out soon, maybe we can get on her calendar. That's another thing we need to do… pick dates."

Jesse made a new column on her paper and grabbed the calendar off the wall. "But first, let's finish this invite list. I met this awesome woman, Debbie, at the Talkeetna library, and we've exchanged some letters. She's been out once and just fell in love with it out here, but she's terrified of going it alone. Just to have her spend some time with strong women would be great, I think."

"Yep. Add Debbie to the list. I was also thinking of Melanie."

"Who?"

"You know, that woman James is seeing."

"That's right. He brought her to solstice last year. I wasn't sure he was still hanging out with her. I don't know that this is really her thing out here."

"That's my point. I think she should spend some time in the thick of it out here, so she gets a really good dose of what James loves. Sorry, but I just don't think they're a great match."

Jesse looked at her friend quizzically. "And who made you the matchmaker?"

"Nobody. It's probably a bad idea, but I like James a lot, and would hate to see him get in too deep with someone who's not a good fit."

"Okay, okay. You can invite her if you want, but if it weren't for being friends with James, she's not someone I would typically have in my close circle."

"I get it. Let's put her as an alternate. Besides, I haven't talked to him since around Christmas. Maybe they aren't even a thing anymore."

Rona brought Leah back to the table, and they snacked on salmon and the few assorted chocolates left in a box Jesse got from the Talkeetna ladies at Christmastime.

By the end of the discussion on invitees, they had arrived at a list of seven women in addition to themselves and possibly Melanie.

"I think we should call Linda at the Talkeetna airport and see if she's heard of anyone else staking their land out here. I know I was very blessed to have Sadie out here when I got here. What a leg-up it would be for a newcomer to have a ready-made group to fold into."

"True. I thank God for you every day. That's why I think this thing would be just a great opportunity."

———

As Jesse looked onto the group of beautiful, fierce, powerful, creative women, she knew Rona was right. They are needed in this special niche in the world, where they can make others feel safe, and loved, and free from the trappings of their everyday life. Over the five days together, they had heard spontaneous stories of abuse, love, self-hate, betrayal, joy, hope, and gratitude. After years of hoping, praying, and experimenting, Jesse felt like she finally had a community that met her where she was at - strong, single, yet human. Exhausted yet exhilarated, the energy of these few days would carry her through for several months.

27

TRUTH HURTS

October - December 1990
    Peru to Lynx Creek

LYNN ROUNDED the curve twenty feet ahead of Jesse as they climbed the trail from San Pedro de Casta to Marachausi. With each step Jesse felt increasingly heavy with doubt, irritated with the all-women's organized tour intruded on by the married leader's male Peruvian lover, upset by the admonishments Lynn delivered when Jesse distributed inconsequential gifts of crayons and notebooks to the village children, and uncertain about the rebirthing experience ahead of them.

Now on day five of their fourteen-day pilgrimage, Jesse's self-examination of why she agreed to this trip grew in intensity. The only somewhat rational explanation was that she saw something in Lynn which held promise for a friendship that could withstand infrequent visits, necessitated by their separate remote existences, and the thought of exploring a warmer climate to escape the messy Alaska breakup was appealing. Eager to drink in life, Lynn, with a bubbly, outgoing demeanor and constant questions, was the opposite of Jesse.

Just the night before, while Jesse was trying to fall asleep, Lynn babbled on about another camper, at a volume too loud to be contained within the nylon tent walls.

"Jesse, I was talking to Denise, and she told me she's here to heal her pain after her husband ended their nineteen-year marriage and married the associate pastor at their church."

"Shhhhh! Lynn, there is no privacy here. I don't want to talk about this now. Save it for when we're alone!" Jesse rolled over in her sleeping bag and scooched down to cover her head.

"Oh, sorry. She said it to me like it was an okay thing to talk about. I just thought that since your ex-..."

"Don't say another damn word, and I mean it! I'm not here to talk about my ex, his affairs, or anything. You can talk about you to those other ladies..." Jesse whispered forcefully, each word ground out through a clenched jaw. "But don't you mention one damned thing about me, or my life, or why I'm here. In fact, Lynn, I don't know why the hell I am here, except I thought you were cool. But now, I'm..."

"Irritated. I know. It's something I get a lot. I just don't know when to turn off."

"This would be a good time to turn off, Lynn."

"I'm sorry, Jesse. I really am. I'll let you sleep now."

Lynn brushed and re-braided her hair, then slunk down deep into her sleeping bag. She listened for a sign that Jesse was asleep. Her closest friend in Lynx Creek, and she'd pissed her off. A tear pooled on her inflated camp pillow as she admonished herself to do better and tone it down.

By morning, Jesse was ready to move on and forget the exchange, but Lynn wanted to process it.

"I'm really sorry for last night. I guess I was just so into this women's communal thing and trying to be one of the gals that

I forgot how much you value your privacy. Please forgive me, Jesse. I would hate for this to come between us."

Jesse pulled Lynn in with a one-armed hug and agreed to let it go.

Encouraged by this, Lynn continued. "I mean, it seemed like a really good reason to do this whole retreat, honestly. I mean, I'm here because, well, I'm trying to decide if I want to stay with Keven or leave Alaska, or…"

"Lynn! Seriously, if you haven't talked to Keven about this, I don't think I want to know. He's crazy about you, and you seem like you're in love with him, and you're living most of the time out at the cabin, and…"

Jesse heard the voice of wise sage Sadie in her head. *She won't make it out here.* She continued speaking in a gentler tone. "You know, let's just drop it. You make whatever you need to make of this pilgrimage. But please, don't share details about my personal life. I'm happy to tell anyone that asks the parts I'm comfortable sharing. And you're right, I will get something out of this. I just don't have an agenda. I hope you find what you need."

As THEY MOVED up the mountain, thoughts of watching melting snow accumulate and mix with the thawing earth dotted with the brilliant green of fresh growth called to Jesse. The group kicked up noxious dust while making their way to the promised land of the stone forest and burial chullpas. There, they would take part in rebirthing exercises to reclaim their feminine power. Jesse hadn't realized she lost her feminine self, but fell into the marketing trap as she read the brochures before sending in the down payment. She allowed herself to entertain doubts, especially since she had not birthed a child.

"Ok ladies, we have reached one of the most profound shamanic experiences of our quest. Our shaman-guide will lead us down into the burial temple, or chullpa, and guide us through a breathing and rebirthing healing. You may find it a little uncomfortable, but I promise you, if you stick with it, you will shed cellular fears that have held you back in life."

As they descended into the dark subterranean cavernous space of the clammy stone burial tomb of the ancients, Jesse's heart paused, sunk to her stomach then into her throat before it beat again. In that moment, she knew she had made a terrible mistake. She steadied herself against the walls of the space, now filled to capacity, closed her eyes, and choked back the bile rising into her throat.

A kind fellow retreater whispered, "Just breathe and go with it."

Jesse struggled to catch her breath as the walls closed in on her. She wanted to climb back to the sunlight, fresh air, and solitude of the stone forest above ground. For the entire ninety minutes inside the burial tomb, Jesse counted her fingers, over and over again. She did not know what the shaman said or what breathwork she was supposed to do. When the group leader announced it was time to ascend the stairs and exit the chullpa, Jesse raced to daylight and ran to open air, gasping as if she had been underwater.

THAT EVENING, the shaman and helpers served a traditional meal and listened to translations of talks given by local villagers. They spoke of how their sacred lands were being desecrated by city-dwellers who came out to party and left litter on the mountain. Later, they lay in silence on their sleeping bags outside the tent, staring up at the sky filled with brilliant stars.

"Jesse, are you awake?" Lynn whispered, breaking the silence.

"I am."

"Um, can I ask you something?"

"Sure, but keep it down, will ya?"

"I'm whispering, Jesse, as soft as I can."

"Dang, everything seems so loud."

"It's weird, isn't it, that thing we did today? I don't know what to think about it, but I feel a bit traumatized."

Jesse propped herself up on an elbow and looked in the general direction of Lynn's voice. "Sucked, big time. What did it do for you?"

"Well, I certainly was not reborn. I mean, I didn't feel anything. It kind of freaked me out the way some people were shaking and wailing. I'm not sure what I expected, but it was weird."

"Can we just not talk about it? I think it's bunk and these people don't know what they're selling."

Jesse had read about rebirthing and how it can be a powerful spiritual experience. That was not what she got. She quietly wondered how much of the $2795 went to this part of the pilgrimage. She wanted a refund.

———

LATER THAT YEAR, Jesse held a solstice-Christmas party. Among the five families invited were Keven and Lynn. When Keven arrived alone, Jesse felt vindicated for the thoughts that she and Sadie shared long ago about the woman's soft side that would keep her from being a full-timer at Lynx Creek.

"Hey Keven. So good to see you." Jesse welcomed him into the cabin, looking behind him for signs of Lynn. "Is Lynn coming?"

"Uh, no. She's in Anchorage."

"Ah, sorry. I thought maybe she would be out for the holidays."

"No. Not this year." Keven looked off toward the mountains, a sense of longing in his far-off gaze. Despite being evasive about Lynn, Keven seemed to enjoy himself at the small gathering.

· · ·

"I HAVE A SMALL GIFT FOR YOU." Jesse emerged from the pantry carrying a stack of presents wrapped in handmade paper, tied with twine, catching in a sprig of spruce in the center. There was a gift for each of the five families. "Before you open it, I want you each to know how important you are in my life. Living out here, where we get to be so close to nature, it's good to know that you good folks are not so far away that I can't call on you to help. And some of you, you know who you are, just happen to show up at just the right time, as if you have a crystal ball and can see my needs."

"Ya mean like when yer snow-go was halfway into Spring Creek with the last breakup?"

"Crawley, I mean, I didn't tell anyone about that, but yes, Crawley and Jane here hauled me out of the creek, back-end first last spring when I was out playing around." Jesse smiled sheepishly. "Thanks, Crawley, for helping me out, and for embarrassing me in front of my friends here. Merry Christmas to you!"

"Heck, Jesse, ain't a single one of us in the room who hasn't done somethin' as dumb, but like ya say, we're all here for each other."

Crawley was a kind man in his mid-forties. The wild suited him well, with his lazy eye and a few missing teeth. Jane, fifteen years his junior, had joined him from Oregon two summers ago. She was a quiet but pleasant girl whose goal in life was to make Crawley happy and to have lots of babies. In a girls chat last summer, she told Jesse that, "The good Lord hasn't seen to it yet that my womb is fruitful, but we pray every evening that if it's His will, we shall be so blessed, and we promise to raise our littles up to know Jesus." Jesse wished Jane well in her endeavor and vowed to include them in her own nightly prayers. Seeing Jane now reminded Jesse of that prayer, which had fallen by the wayside in recent weeks.

283

"Well, anyway, it may seem a little selfish for me to give you this gift, but I think if you look close enough, you will see things you recognize in it. And by all means, if it doesn't suit you, share it with someone who might get a kick out of it."

"Is it okay if the kids open it?" Rona held their gift high overhead to keep the kids from grabbing it, despite their efforts.

"Of course! It's actually for them, anyway."

"Oh, wow! Mommy, look!" Skye had already torn the paper off and was paging through a book. Sky pointed to a picture of a chocolate lab with a paisley bandana. "Look, Rosie!"

"Jesse, you published it! You really did it!" Rona jumped up to hug Jesse. "I'm best friends with a real live author!"

"You remember all those paintings strung up around my house? The publisher actually used them."

"Yeah, I see that. This is amazing."

Each family looked through the pages of their own book, pointing and laughing.

"Check this out, Keven. That looks like the wolverine you were stalking two years ago when you lost your cat."

"Say, Dave, what page it that on?" Keven was as excited about the book as anyone in the room. He quickly flipped to page twelve to see the drawing of a tabby cat that looked like his Sam, high in a spruce tree while a wolverine circled around the bottom of the tree.

Jesse smiled at Keven. "The difference in this story is that Sam gets rescued."

Jane blushed as she held up her book, opened to the title page. "Look guys! Did you see the author signed too? This one is personal to Crawley and me, but Jesse…" Jane gently rested her hand to her womb. "I wonder if you could do us a favor and say it's for our little peanut, too."

Jesse grabbed Jane in a big hug. "Of course, I will! Oh, boy! This is exciting. When might we meet little peanut?"

"I haven't seen the doctor yet, but I'm regular like the Big

Ben and so we're thinking I'm four months now. So towards the end of breakup, we should meet him or her."

Carol lifted her hot chocolate. "A toast to our beautiful and talented friend Jesse and to little peanut."

Following the toast, the guests sang a modified version of *For She's a Jolly Good Fellow* with a mangling of the original words made up in honor of Jesse.

They exchanged more gifts. By agreement of the partygoers, all gifts had to be handmade. Jesse felt that she might have stretched it a bit, since hers came from a publishing company. But she had provided the words and the pictures for the book, and was quite proud of her accomplishment, even if it never sold a single copy.

Jesse held a pint jar under her nose to take in the fresh scent deeply. "Ahh heavenly! Keven, thank you to you and Lynn for this beautiful lotion. It smells like delicate roses."

"It is. Lynn says she isn't crafty, but she sure can make a mean potion. That stuff does wonders even for my hard-working hands. My summer callouses are almost gone already."

"Well, you tell her thanks for me, until I see her myself."

"Sure will."

There were jars of beautifully colored jams and jellies, three-day smoked salmon sliced into perfect little rectangles and jarred, Christmas ornaments, and knitted potholders. Jesse ran her fingers over each one, marveling at the bounty from a group of free spirits finding their way in the backcountry. "You guys are all so crafty and generous. Thank you all so much. Treasures, all of these, and all of you."

"Agreed." Gary smiled out to the group as he pulled his bride, Carol, closer in. "Jesse, we thank you from the bottom of our hearts for pulling us together at this special time of year, a time that can be hard since we're separated from families. But a great time to rejoice in all the good Lord has given us. I am happy to see you all once again and Carol and I thank you for the gifts. Much as I hate to break up this party, we will have to be leaving now while we have about enough light to get back to our place and stoke the fire for another cold night. You all be well and feel free to stop by and see us anytime."

The families shared farewells and thank you's as they bundled up and headed out with their gifts, along with leftovers from the gathering. Rona, Dave, and the kids stayed behind, as they extended the celebration some by spending the night with Jesse.

Keven lingered by the door before leaving. "Say, Jesse, I didn't want to say anything before, but I wonder if you could amend what you wrote in my book, too."

"Oh, Kev, I just assumed that Lynn and you…"

"Oh, yeah, we're together, and we will have our own little peanut, but we call it a jellybean. Could you please add jellybean to your message in the front of the book?"

"Oh, my gosh, yes! You seemed a little distracted, and I was worried that maybe you had split up or something, but then you had the beautiful lotion gifts and I…"

"It's fine. I am distracted. Lynn is in town taking care of her final business before she joins me full-time, and she's having an ultrasound before she leaves town. She may even know if we're having a boy or a girl. I don't really want to know, but she learned to knit so she could make something for the baby, and she wants to know what color yarn to bring out." Keven smiled; the look of love for Lynn and their pregnancy could not be mistaken.

Jesse edited her inscription on Keven and Lynn's book and sent him off with a big hug. She turned to clean up, grateful to see that Rona had already started the job.

"Now doesn't that just take the cake!" Rona remarked as they worked together. She had listened to Jesse rant about the trip, and Lynn when they first returned. "That trip to Peru must have done her some good after all."

"Well, I guess I was wrong in several ways. I'm glad they are happy and clearly, a whole new chapter is opening up for her. This is going to be an exceptional year for the Lynx Creek tribe!"

28

FAREWELLS AND HELLOS

Spring-Fall 1991
  Springtime at Lynx Creek

ALASKA'S SEASONS stand apart from those of the rest of the known world. Springtime starts with break-up in April and May, when daylight extends past bedtime and morning comes in a rush, pushing the stars out of the way. Melting ice and snow baptized the thawing ground that will soon be blessed with sprouts and shoots. Muck boots are essential footwear. Jesse gave up her disdain for muddy clothes long ago, when she realized one couldn't keep up with the laundry using only a washtub and clothesline. That would entail constantly boiling water.

Under marvelous blue skies, Jesse and Rosie hiked for miles up and down the creek, studying the flotsam collecting along the shores while robins and thrushes bounced from branch to branch, gathering supplies. As May matured, green life sprung up around them and visitors passed through on their way to explore the area and visit seasonal cabins. One day, as they were heading back toward the cabin from upstream, a familiar voice greeted them on the trail.

"There are two of my favorite girls. I spotted you along the shore from the air."

"Yeah, I caught your wave." Jesse gave James a big hug. As the plane flew overhead earlier, it had lilted from side to side, James's way of saying hello. "What brings you out this way?"

James held his hand up so Rosie couldn't dot his fresh khakis with muddy paws. He bent down and patted her on the head. "Took a couple folks working for the feds up to Rohn Roadhouse on the Kuskokwim. They'll be up in that area now until September, doing some data collection for one of the federal programs. It was such a nice day, I thought I would come along this way and see what kind of activity there was and what shape the runway was in."

"Glad you stopped. Do you have time to join us for dinner? Rosie and I have been pretty busy watching the birch buds arrive today. Did you ever notice how fast those leaves come on?"

"Well, only every year about this time." James smiled at his friend as he scratched Rosie between her ears. He loved these visits. "One day I'm flying, and the trees are barren and the next day, they're green. I had seen nothing like it before I came out this way."

James adjusted the backpack hanging by one strap over his left shoulder. "I'd love to catch up. I even brought food to share, just in case you were available."

"What a treat! This time of year we're always at the mercy of whatever's in the pantry and maybe a hare snare here and there. Still seems strange to me, this way of life. If my friends back in Minnesota really knew what my days were like, most would lock me up and the other few would beg to join me."

"Ain't that the truth? Yours is a unique life, you know." James kicked at a tree root in the path. "Hey, I saw your book at the new visitor's center up the Parks the other day. I have to say, I felt so proud to see it there. I hope you do a bang-up business with all the tourists this summer."

"Oh, that's sweet. Thank you. It would be kind of fun to know there were kids out there who liked the story."

"And the pictures. I think it's awesome. I hope you do more of them."

"I have some ideas, but if this book tanks, I'm not sure I'll keep trying."

"Seriously? I doubt there are many authors who make it with just one book."

"I never thought of it that way," Jesse mused. "Honestly, I still don't think of myself as an author. It's just something I felt like doing."

"I sincerely hope you feel like doing it again."

They arrived at Jesse's property line in time to see a moose cow and calf walk down the trail. Rosie barked and the calf paused, but the cow just kept walking toward the creek.

"Beautiful," the two said in unison, then smiled. They stood in silence until the animals disappeared.

"Ah… that vision will carry me for many days to come. It never gets old." James looked at his friend. He put his hand on Jesse's lower back. "Shall we?"

They walked in silence up the trail to the cabin, listening to the songbirds busy in the trees.

"I'm eager to see what surprise and delight you brought this time. You always seem to have some tasty treat when you come out this way. One thing I enjoy about break-up…" Jesse turned to James and invited him in by holding the cabin door open. "We get to see our friend more often."

"Nice of you to say, Jesse. I look forward to it, too."

THIS FIRST VISIT of the season extended late into the night as they got caught up on activities of the past few months. While he was outside visiting family, she was busy reading and writing and keeping the winter chill away. James shared calzones from a Talkeetna restaurant; Jesse warmed them on the camping stove. He had a thermos of gourmet coffee and baklava from the same restaurant.

"This is a feast! It sure beats the spam and pilot bread I planned on having."

Jesse was ready for a run to town for supplies. She had delayed the shopping trip this year, waiting to coordinate with the arrival of a new canoe, being towed out by friends, that should arrive any day now. "I'm hoping that Samuel and Grace make it by one day with my canoe. Then, do you suppose I could hitch a ride back with you one of these times that you're out this way? I'm not going to do a big Sam's Club run until fall this year. By then, I might have a better idea if I need new art supplies or not."

"That makes perfect sense. You know I'm happy to give you a lift anytime. I hope you get your canoe soon. That old one of Sadie's you've been using has seen better days, for sure."

"Yeah. So you know, her son sent a message. She can't come out. She's in awful shape and I need to get in to see her soon. That's another reason I need to get to town and drive up to Fairbanks. Sounds like maybe she only has a few weeks left. I sure miss having her around out here, and can only hope that one day, I can be a mentor to another young woman, the way she was to me."

The two sat in silence for a bit, thinking about Sadie's incredible life and the legend she had become to remote homesteaders.

"Now that would be a story to write!" James looked up and pointed a finger at Jesse. "And you're just the right person to write it."

"I appreciate your confidence, but I'm not so sure I could ever capture her larger-than-life story on the page. Believe me, I have thought about it, and even have some ideas for pictures, but I don't know that I could ever do more than a children's book."

"Well, something for you to think about." He smiled. "It's not like you don't have the time."

"You speak truths again. I appreciate the way you poke me with reality when you come out. Now, how about one final game of cribbage before we hit the rack?"

————

"There she is. The legend herself!" Jesse walked into the nursing home where Sadie was spending her last months. The Alaska Pioneers Home in Fairbanks was home to those like Sadie who had built their lives living close to the land and watching as the beloved area evolved from a territory to a state, with all its trappings. Oil revenues made this home possible for such pioneers to live out their final days, if they could prove their longevity in the state. Most had attended Pioneers of Alaska picnics and worked as volunteers to keep the extensive grounds beautiful and the residents cheerful.

Sadie turned her head away from the window, where her fading eyes could barely make out the birch forest surrounding the home. A smile lit her face as she recognized the voice of her friend. She greeted Jesse with in a raspy, whispered voice. "Aurora, my friend!"

Slipping a hand from beneath the covers, she reached out to her friend. "I've been thinking of you." Sadie paused to catch her breath. "Did you catch any wolverines this year? You know they can be so nasty mean, but they make beautiful hats."

"Sadie, it's so good to see you! And yes, I did catch a wolverine this year. He made a mess of my woodpile and had my dog, Rosie, riled up, so I dug out the traps and took care of him. I haven't made the hat yet, but I'm sure it will be beautiful. You taught me so well."

"Yes, I did, and you were an excellent student." Sadie looked at her son and motioned for a drink of water. "You know, Aurora, I hate laying in this bed here. I keep telling my boy to take me to the cabin and let me be, but he thinks this is better for me."

"Your son is right. You've got good people here to take care of you. It's comfortable. You don't have to catch your food or haul water, and your family can visit." Jesse looked to Sadie's son and affirmed his position with a smile.

"Jesse, do you think you could come back later? I had a dreadful night and I'm just so tired today. I want to talk to you when I feel better. It's important."

"Of course, I will." Jesse squeezed Sadie's hand gently, leaned over and kissed her on the forehead. "You rest now, and we'll talk later."

As she stepped toward the door, Sadie called out, "Bring your notebook. I remember the one you had where you took all your notes. You bring one of those and a sharp pencil, will ya?"

"I will, Sadie. I will."

FOR THIRTEEN DAYS, Jesse visited Sadie and listened to her stories, writing notes in a red notebook like the ones she always used in her early days at the homestead. Some days Sadie had energy for hours of talking, and others she became winded after fifteen minutes, needing to rest for a while before sharing more. During the evenings, spent with Sadie's son and his family, she filled in the details he knew. Sadie's other children and grandchildren from outside arrived in the final forty-eight hours, adding more color to the stories.

In the end, Jesse filled three notebooks. She contemplated James's suggestion that Sadie's legacy was to be documented in a book. Jesse still wasn't sure that she was the right person for the job; after all, she had no education in writing or publishing.

But she would at least have the stories documented, so something useful could come of them. Besides, it was a great way to spend meaningful time with her dear friend, who seemed to want to share in her end days.

Early in the morning on the eleventh day, as Jesse lay awake on the couch at the home of Sadie's son, the house phone rang. Jesse knew immediately that Sadie had left them. For confirmation, she glanced over to the son and daughter-in-law standing at the phone. The legendary Sadie had departed for the vast wilderness beyond, a place she spoke of often, where she would reunite with her beloved husband, and they would resume their adventures.

Later that day, Jesse thanked Sadie's son for the days of respite on his couch and the many meals and stories they shared. She offered her condolences, but elected not to stay for the family's mourning and the community's celebration of Sadie's life. She felt the need for solitude. A more intimate celebration would happen back at the trapper's cabin, where the older, wiser woman schooled the naive Jesse in the ways of the wilderness nearly a decade ago.

———

Summer went by quickly, yet had a drag to it following the passing of Sadie. Her family visited the trapper's cabin and took a few personal things as remembrances, but left it mostly intact.

"Jesse, I want you to know that Mom told the family many times she wanted you to use whatever she had out here, including the cabin. Please, feel free to use the cabin and anything there. It would make Mom happy to know that this place that meant so much to she and Dad was still useful."

Jesse turned slightly sliding away, with the back of a hand, the tears forming in the corners of her eyes. "Thank you. Your mom changed my life, and it's just like her to be so generous. I will keep an eye on it, and use it judiciously, I promise."

"Well, she has one more request, and it's kind of your payment, she suggested in jest. She knew about your children's book. She hoped that one day, she could be in one of your stories. I think that's why she spent those last days telling you so much of her, our, family history, most of which I'm sure you'd heard before."

"I didn't realize..." Jesse felt overwhelmed with emotion and love for her mentor. She and James had spoken of the need for someone to document Sadie's incredible journey, but Jesse had no idea that Sadie wanted Jesse to carry her story into the world. "I just didn't know she saw me that way. I mean, we were such pals out here, where we were all about the trees, the weather, survival, and being one with our world. We never talked about my book. I didn't know that she knew."

"Oh, she knew! When it first came out, she heard someone talking about it and recognized your name, although she almost always referred to you as Aurora."

"She talked about me? I mean, I talk about her all the time, and all that she taught me..."

"Of course she did! She saw a lot of her younger self in you and just knew you loved living out here as much as she did. Anyway, when she heard about your book, she insisted I pick one up right away. We read it after dinner night after night, for months it seems, and she studied the pictures. It thrilled her so much to see things that reminded her of all those years living out at Lynx Creek."

Jesse was stunned. It was an honor and a privilege to be trusted to tell Sadie's story, yet she wondered if she could fulfill such an honor. Whatever the case, she was now obligated to try.

———

The annual summer solstice celebration was bittersweet. Twenty-three friends joined Jesse for the largest solstice party yet. The gathering of eclectic friends and their cool contribution of foods, ranging from candy bars and gorp to elaborate layered casseroles, added to the day's festivities. There were several toasts in honor of Sadie, and to Jesse's seventh-year celebration of homesteading.

The group walked the trail to Sadie's cabin and planted wild irises and columbine in one of Sadie's favorite spots to rest and watch the creek flow by. Gary gave a blessing for Sadie's life and those who wanted to shared stories. Jesse could have spoken for hours about all her adventures with Sadie and the stories Sadie shared, except she couldn't; it would have exhausted her emotionally. She was happy to celebrate the small but mighty woman, but a raw ache still bled within Jesse. She had lost her first best friend in Alaska, her mentor, and in the end, the one who trusted Jesse with her life story. It was a burden and a blessing.

James flew in for the celebration and spent the night, as did several others, now a tradition on this longest day of the year. He approached Jesse as she stood pensively by the creek, watching the water move gracefully over the shore's gravel and parting to move around boulders. "Hey, how are you doing?"

"Oh, hey. I'm good. I was just thinking about this water and the powerhouse we knew as Sadie." Jesse unfolded her arms and ran her hands through her hair, feeling the deep warmth from the long day in the sun.

"Want to share?" James found a fallen log to perch on nearby, giving Jesse his full attention.

"If you look out there at the creek, you see those two huge boulders in the middle? The water doesn't fight them to get over the top. It gently rolls around the edges, getting where it's meant to go and softening the edges of the rocks. That was Sadie. Rarely did she go head-on with an issue. Even when she was involved politically, as she described it to me, she approached things from a side angle, bringing a fresh perspective to whatever the issue was. She taught me that about animals, too, and all of this…" Jesse held her hands open to the boreal forest surrounding them. "We spent days chasing the sun coming through the trees when deciding where to put my garden when I first moved here, so we could work with it."

James listened as his friend, who was so alive with her experience of wilderness living and the loss of her mentor, told of the impact Sadie had on her and shared snippets of her wilderness wisdom.

When Jesse took a long pause, James stood, reached out, and put a hand on her wrist. "I think you've already written Sadie's book in your head. The things you just told me, they are beautiful and powerful. You shared stories of a meek young woman who followed her love out here, raised a family, was irreverent when she needed to be, but brought a philosophy of life that took her places while rarely leaving the beautiful life she never took for granted. That's amazing."

Jesse looked into the eyes of her friend and felt his words deeply, breathing in their truth, the truth that she couldn't see for herself. She did have the story. More importantly, she had an ally that believed in her.

Moving slowly towards James, Jesse felt a deep sense of belonging and gratitude for sharing a harsh, heavenly, magical place with wild animals, some of whom came in human form, gifted and generous friends, and contentment. She felt mostly contented. With the passing of Sadie, she came to acknowledge a small tear in her fabric, one she had chosen to ignore, for the most part. More than ever before, she wanted intimacy. A deep emotional connection. Maybe physical, too, but more importantly, she wanted someone she could trust with her deepest thoughts, the feelings that moved her to tears and exhilaration, and the intense dreams that visited her in the long winter nights.

Jesse stood facing her friend. "Did I ever tell you how much I appreciate you?"

"Many times, but it's always nice to hear."

James reached out and enfolded Jesse in his arms. Comforted and content in the embrace, neither moved nor spoke for several minutes. James finally broke the silence. "You are a dear friend, Jesse, to many of us."

"Speaking of which, I probably should get back to my guests."

James followed in silence as they moved away from the solitude of the creek's edge into sounds of laughter filling the spaces between nature's beautiful things near the cabin. His heart was full.

———

Jesse moved through the summer doing the usual gathering for winter, catching and canning fish, watching wild things grow, canoeing to visit neighbors, camping on sandbars, and making mental notes of all the beauty so she could revisit it on a whim in the darkness of the long winter. Not a day went by that she didn't think of Sadie and the book she would write. When the work was done and she couldn't fall asleep under the lingering daylight in the late-night hours, she looked through notebooks of Sadie's stories, made notes, drew sketches, and filled three more notebooks with potential material.

She made several trips to the Skwentna area, visiting friends, and traveled further north up Lynx Creek and up the east fork of the Yentna River in the Alaska Range, to Dall glacier and nearby rarely-wandered lands of Denali National Park, with its sculptured carpet of spiny Devil's club and roses, blueberries and lingonberries, willows and pines. Jesse's animal tracking skills continued to develop. She recognized grizzly and black bear prints, moose and caribou scat, and grinned as she watched red squirrels and fox slink through grasses. On the slow, meandering paddle toward home, after several days of camping out and drinking in the glorious beauty of nature, just when she couldn't imagine anything finer, Jesse looked up to see a golden eagle nest and heard the throaty kraa of a raven matron soaring overhead.

Ravens reminded Jesse of the cycle of life in the interior. She had grown to know and love the mysterious, quirky ravens, and recognized their warning calls when unrest stirred in the forest. The yells of the ravens, as she watched them dance on scavenged, wasted salmon carcasses beached along the riverbanks, were amusing. Hearing a raven rage pierce Jesse's and Rosie's ears, warned of intruders infringing on their personal space and triggered a vigilance in them. Through the years, Jesse came to love the soft sounds of the mating call shortly after the first of the year, when the light lingered and warmed up the midday, sometimes to the single digits below freezing.

The ravens above her canoe now passed sticks between their proud beaks while in flight. Jesse watched from below, contemplating the elegance with which they danced in the sky, gliding towards each other, gracefully passing the stick, then arcing out and back again. With the image seared in her memory, Jesse returned to paddling toward home with a renewed sense of wonder.

———

As SHE PUT summer to bed, harvested her garden vegetables, wild berries, and salmon, Jesse spent the evenings building a list of essentials for a fall grocery run while listening to Trapline Chatter. Any day now, she expected James to fly in with an empty seat to take her back to Talkeetna, where she would borrow his pickup and drive to Anchorage to do some shopping. One mid-September evening, as she sat at the table with the door open to the setting sun and evening sounds of the wilds, the expected message from James came over the radio. "To Minnesota Jesse. I will be by tomorrow, near dinnertime. Meet you at the airstrip. James."

Expecting to fly back to Talkeetna with James, Jesse took a final inventory of the pantry, packed a backpack and studied her list one last time. Before James arrived the following day, Jesse's cabin was spotless, fishing gear stored away, and the laundry washed and hanging to dry. She had seen James very little over the summer. It was his busiest season and Jesse was grateful for each visit they had, although they were more brief than other times during the year. He always had fresh produce or a treat from the bakery for her, and she shared stories of adventures she and Rosie had. And always, the comfortable enjoyable embraces that never seemed to last long enough.

Rosie heard the plane first and ran with excitement up the airstrip and back to where Jesse sat. The puppy impatiently waited for the pilot's door to open, knowing that James always had a treat on hand for her. Jesse hadn't noticed the passenger when James approached to land, so was surprised to hear the passenger's door open as she greeted James with their familiar hug. Looking past James's shoulder, she saw a young woman step from the front of the plane toward them. As the woman drew closer, Jesse pulled away from James. He held her for a moment longer to whisper in her ear. "Be gentle. She's hurting."

Confused and excited, Jesse flashed a look at James, who gave her a knowing smile and nod. "I brought you a gift, Jesse."

The young woman, dressed in oversized jeans and a black leather jacket over a Sturgis Rally tank top, looked up through dark hair that covered much of her face and whispered tentatively, "Hi Auntie J."

Jesse grabbed the girl and pulled her close. Aubrey sank into Jesse's arms and shuddered as she gasped for air between sobs that suddenly burst from depths unseen and never felt.

The embrace lasted for a long time before the girl quieted and spoke. "I was a brilliant student... went to college, scholarships, kept the curfew, went home for Sunday dinners, even so, my life crumbled into a shithole. I'm sorry, Auntie J., I meant to be more than I am."

The words stung as Jesse suddenly realized how the past year had shattered her sweet, innocent, niece to a nearly unrecognizable shard of the once pristine princess, who had been sheltered from the realities of a mother's addictions, a father's infidelities and the cancer diagnosis of a loved grandmother. Jesse tightened the hold on the shadow of her once-vigorous niece, debilitated from months of heavy drinking, drugs, serial abusive boyfriends, and the harsh realities of life. Jesse drew in a deep breath and prayed for forgiveness that she hadn't unwedged herself from her solitude to cushion Aubrey from life's blows.

"I'm glad you're here, little A. So glad."

ACKNOWLEDGMENTS

My first words of gratitude go to my parents, who model adventure and acceptance, and prompt me to dig deeper and explore more of life. To Linda Zeppa of Intuitive Writing / Creativity, thank you for bringing so much more than coaching and editing to our relationship, including your energy and support. Angela Pruden, thank you for your thoughtful proofreading talent and encouragement. Finally, to my children and grandchildren, thanks for sharing your stories, listening to mine, and always being on my side.

ABOUT THE AUTHOR

Kim Smart is a storyteller, nurse, attorney, and student of life. *When Fireweed Blooms* is her seventh published novel and the first in the new series, *The Lynx Creek Chronicles*. Kim's fiction works are inspired by personalities, experiences, and narratives from her life and the lives of friends and family. Kim has been a lifelong writer and today weaves in stories of the characters she meets at home and across the globe. Kim was raised in South Dakota and *grew up* in Alaska where *The Lynx Creek Chronicles*, is set.

You can learn more at www.kimsmartauthor.com or through the social media links below.

ALSO BY KIM SMART

Tangled Ribbons

War and the Holocaust tear three young girls from their youthful innocence.

Catapulted into their new lives, they become extraordinary women of resilience, grit and grace.

An unrelenting pursuit of forgiveness and peace for humanity follows.

The essences of individual humans are substantially more alike than they are different. Gertie Hall lives this truth as she rises from the young child of a Hitler henchman to a world-renown advocate for human rights. Through scientific endeavors, humanitarian efforts and a tireless fight to right the wrongs of her father, she explores her feminine self, intellect, ingenuity, and grit.

A hole remains in her soul where war ripped two childhood friends away, and Gertie's own father was complicit in the disappearance of their families. Tangled Ribbons, scene by scene, captures the life of Gertie, intertwined with the stories of her friends, Sarah and Hannah, who flee fiery Berlin and establish new identities and new lives in faraway places.

Late in their lives, Gertie offers a heart-wrenching plea for amends and enfolds a new generation in their healing.

If you love to read about inner strength, the pursuit of justice, and the power of friendship, you'll love *Tangled Ribbons*.

Get Kim Smart's *Tangled Ribbons* now and experience the journey of healing.

Falling for Home

Jesse loves his hometown girl...

Kerry has dreams beyond Buffalo Ridge...

..can they both have it all?

Jesse loves the ranch life as much as he loves his hometown sweetheart. As they drift apart, he finds himself following a winding path searching for life's meaning.

To find love, he must first find his voice.

Kerry's dreams are larger than Buffalo Ridge. To pursue her dreams, she leaves everything behind. Her pursuit to become a veterinarian consumes her. Opportunity for lasting love disappears. Will she find her way back?

Can two small-town friends find happily-ever-after?

You'll love the dance of life and tug of emotions as Jesse and Kerr test boundaries in this first novel of Kim Smart's Buffalo Ridge Ranch series.

Get this sweet, clean, contemporary romance now.

Two for Love

A handsome widower cowboy, a woman from the city with a son, and the wide open spaces of the colorful Badlands.

Steve Davies lives his life in the shadow of his late wife's dreams. To emerge from his grief, he must take a chance. Hoping to expand the dreams they had together, he starts a dude ranch. In the process, he hires a cook - a city girl who brings along her son.

Bella Giordano needed to find safety for her young son. On a whim, she moves them from Manhattan to the Badlands of South Dakota, hoping the small town life, away from mob threats and smog, will be good for them both.

Will grief dissolve and a new opportunity be enough to build a new family?

The second novel in Kim Smart's Buffalo Ridge Ranch series sets the table for new opportunities and the possibility of love. Will hurts heal and love grow?

Taking Chances

Chance Davies, champion bull rider, goes from being rock star of the rodeo to broken and lost after a final ride turns into a tragic accident. He is forced to return to Buffalo Ridge Ranch for recuperation after many years on the circuit. Through hard work and challenging himself, his body starts to heal. But will he allow his mind and spirit to heal and open up to new opportunities?

Sheltered from love, Pauline Whyte was always a misfit in the small town of Buffalo Ridge where everyone knew her family's business. She escaped the town gossip for a few years by moving away, only to have to return to care for her ailing father. Somehow, in this small town, love finds its way to her. Can she accept it?

To let love in, they must overcome loss and pain. Will her misfit ways fit into his new life for a happily-ever-after?

The third novel in Kim Smart's Buffalo Ridge Ranch series brings a story of overcoming the odds. Is that enough to find true love?

Dressing Up Stella

Stella Davies lived far away from Buffalo Ridge Ranch. Fearing repeat abandonment, she built the life of a cowboy nurturing her herd on the rugged edge of nature in Arizona. But to find happiness, she must face these fears. When she moves to the remote high desert, she is forced to face her fears.

Ranching was in Brandon Cage's blood, but a new career as a lawyer changed his focus. He buried himself in his new profession and totally ignored his heart's desires.

Do they have the gumption to clear the way to give love a chance? Will their love arrive in time to find a life happily-ever-after?

The fourth novel in Kim Smart's Buffalo Ridge Ranch series is about overcoming past hurts and prioritizing love.

Christmas Market Reunion

Brooke Linton, 26, is stuck in a rut, aggressively pursuing professional recognition in corporate Miami with little

time for fun. She tries to convince herself that life is great, so long as she has a good job, family at Christmas and she can sing in the church choir.

A chance meeting with an American in Amsterdam gives Brooke a glimpse into what life could be like outside the office.

After returning from vacation, her professional world falls apart. Through soul searching and discussion with a sister, Brooke grows to see this as an opening to create a life of her dreams. Little did she know how far those dreams would take her.

This sweet, wholesome romance will surprise and delight you with world travel, unexpected encounters, and fairytale weddings. The question remains. Can a chance encounter on foreign soil turn into something more? Get Christmas Market Reunion today and lose yourself in happily ever after.